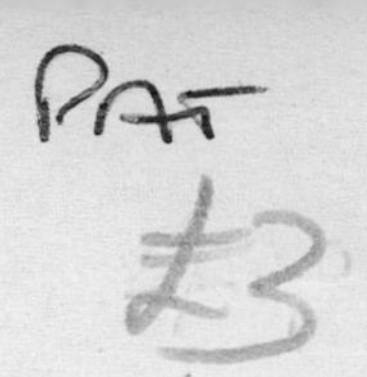

Mary Wesley was born near Windsor in 1912. Her education took her to the London School of Economics and during the War she worked in The War Office. She has also worked part-time in the antique trade. Mary Wesley has lived in London, France, Italy, Germany and several places in the West Country. She now lives 'rather a hermit's existence' in Devon. She has previously written for children and claims that her 'chief claim to fame is arrested development, getting my first novel published at the age of seventy.' This first novel, JUMPING THE QUEUE, is published by Black Swan, as are her later novels, THE CAMOMILE LAWN, THE VACILLATIONS OF POPPY CAREW, NOT THAT SORT OF GIRL, SECOND FIDDLE, A SENSIBLE LIFE and A DUBIOUS LEGACY.

Also by Mary Wesley

JUMPING THE QUEUE
THE CAMOMILE LAWN
THE VACILLATIONS OF POPPY CAREW
NOT THAT SORT OF GIRL
SECOND FIDDLE
A SENSIBLE LIFE
A DUBIOUS LEGACY

and published by Black Swan

HARNESSING PEACOCKS

Mary Wesley

BLACK SWAN

HARNESSING PEACOCKS
A BLACK SWAN BOOK 0 552 99210 0

Originally published in Great Britain by
Macmillan London Limited

PRINTING HISTORY
Macmillan edition published 1985
Black Swan edition published 1986
Black Swan edition reissued 1986
Black Swan edition reprinted 1988 (three times)
Black Swan edition reprinted 1989 (twice)
Black Swan edition reprinted 1990 (three times)
Black Swan edition reprinted 1992 (twice)
Black Swan edition reissued 1993

This book is set in 11/12 pt Plantin

Black Swan Books are published by Transworld Publishers Ltd., 61–63 Uxbridge Road, Ealing, London W5 5SA, in Australia by Transworld Publishers (Australia) Pty. Ltd., 15–25 Helles Avenue, Moorebank, NSW 2170, and in New Zealand by Transworld Publishers (N.Z.) Ltd., 3 William Pickering Drive, Albany, Auckland.

Printed and bound in Great Britain by
Cox & Wyman Ltd., Reading, Berks.

for Toby

Harnessing Peacocks

'Hebe,' the old man called.

'Yes.'

'Take these letters to the post for me.' He had sat in his room writing his letters as if nothing untoward was happening, filling in time usefully while waiting for the arrival of his elder granddaughters and their husbands. With a flip of his hand he indicated the pile of letters. Hebe took them. He did not look up.

'Close the door.'

All her life he had said, 'Close the door,' driven mad by people who left doors open.

Picking up the letters Hebe viewed his profile, the profile worn by various ancestors hanging in the hall, the dining-room and up the stairs. She wondered whether he would be surprised if she said 'I love you, I am sorry for you, I understand how you feel, could you try just once to understand me?' Or, she thought, gripping the letters between nervous fingers, I could just hit him, hit him as hard as I can. She left the room, closing the door. Her grandmother, resting on the sofa in the drawing-room with the door open so that she could see what was going on, heard the door close, did not look up.

Hebe ran down the steps into the garden, turned left across the grass burned khaki by the hot summer, walked away from the pink brick house with its kindly windows to the orchard where she would be out of sight. Here she took off her shoes to walk barefoot, pushed her hair back behind her ears and followed the path which led to the churchyard and beyond the church to the post box set in the wall.

In the churchyard she stopped to watch tortoiseshell

butterflies clustering on moon daisies growing in the uncut grass and sunning themselves on headstones. Some headstones lurched sideways. 'Your parents would turn in their graves,' her grandfather had said several times. He had a habit of repeating himself. Had the people under those stones turned in their graves because they, too, had a troublesome female relation? Troublesome was a mild term compared with whore, liar, disgrace, slut. Hebe stared at the headstones. She felt numb, exhausted by the row which had raged off and on ever since she had come back from the doctor and broken the news which had led to the long interrogation, the painful remarks, the accusations. Hebe wriggled her toes, drew her long hair forward to screen her face. Here in the churchyard, if one sat long enough, it was sometimes possible to see a hedgehog and quite often toads. In her misery Hebe picked off the heads of daisies, stuck them between her toes and viewed the effect. It gave no comfort. Peering through her glasses at an inscription beside her she traced with her finger, 'Died in the course of duty'. The poor sod, she thought, making use of one of her brothers-in-law's expressions. She took the daisies from her toes and laid them on the grave. So much for duty. She heaved herself up and began a circuitous return to the house through the stable yard. From the only occupied loose box her grandfather's brood mare whickered. Hebe went to stroke the soft nose, sniff the animal's sweet breath. She blew into the horse's nostrils. 'How are you, then?' The horse fidgeted, kicking out with a hind leg. In the corner of the box a goat eyed her with its strange split eyes.

'She'll get used to it. Company for her.' The odd job man came up beside her, carrying a pail of fresh water.

'What happened to her foal?'

'It was a little mule. Your grandfather wasn't pleased.'

'How did it happen?'

'Ran off, didn't she, broke through the fence. Met one of them Forest donkeys, I'd say.' He laughed, putting the pail into the corner of the box. The mare laid her ears back. 'Now then,' he said, coming smartly out of the box and bolting the door. 'She'll soon forget.' Hebe watched him walk away, loathing him. 'Here,' she said to the goat, 'post these.' The goat snatched at the letters and started to munch. 'So he murdered your foal,' Hebe said to the horse. 'He's arranging an abortion for me.'

From the drive Hebe heard the sound of cars. Her brothers-in-law would be arriving, Robert, Delian, Marcus, married to her sisters Ann, Beata, Cara, driving their Jaguar, Range Rover (must buy British) and Alfa Romeo (all right to have a foreign car if you worked in Brussels). Hebe left the stable yard and slipped back into the house to position herself in the hall, to listen to her elders' and betters' discussion, a formality to ratify a conclusion already reached. Drawing her skirt about her knees she sat on the stairs. All her relations articulated clearly – it had never been necessary to tell them not to mumble – and since both grandparents were slightly deaf they made a point of speaking up.

They were having a drink. She heard the clink of glasses, shuffle of feet, the chair creak as her grandfather sat. 'Well, then.'

Her grandfather's old dog came in from the porch where he had lain all afternoon, crossed the hall and scratched at the drawing-room door. 'Let the dog in.' The door was opened and the dog went in. Grandfather waited until the door closed and repeated, 'Well, then,' and Robert, married to the eldest granddaughter, started the proceedings.

Firstly the family name must be protected, he observed. He suggested a private clinic. Though expensive, the cost was an investment as the matter would be dealt with immediately, no messing about.

Secondly, though of course of less importance, the sooner they acted the less chance, Robert cleared his throat, of his constituency getting wind or Marcus Bank (boards of directors were conventional people). Hebe heard Delian chip in. 'Shouldn't we consider other ways?' His tenor voice was hesitant. 'This situation does occur in families, in the arts, even in politics.'

'We've been into that, Delian. If we knew the man, if he were, as it were, all right, we could get a settlement. As it is, we haven't a clue. There is no hope of her getting support. Letting the situation go on as it is is simply not on.'

'It's obvious it was some sort of hippy, most probably black.

That is why she will not tell us who the man is.' Hebe had heard variations of this theme for days.

'Most families have skeletons.' Delian tried again. There was a teasing note in his voice. 'I mean look at the Bible, look at poor old Joseph.'

'He knew who it was!' cried Cara, interrupting.

'Delian, keep blasphemy out of this.' Grandfather was crushing. 'Please keep to the point. This is no time for bad taste jokes.'

Suddenly, like a pack of hounds finding a fresh scent, the decibels rose. Ann's voice soared above the others. 'We have to think of our children, Delian. I don't want some funny sort of cousin for mine, I am sure Cara doesn't and your wife Beata is having her first baby at any moment. You must consider her.'

Hebe felt a wild desire to laugh. She took off her spectacles and polished them with the hem of her dress. 'And who,' continued Ann, 'who on earth would want to marry Hebe, if she's burdened with this multicoloured child? We really must think what is best for her. We are not selfish, uncaring people. Let Robert decide what is best for the family, best for Hebe.'

For a few minutes the assembled relatives voiced their views. Hebe heard yelped half-sentences containing the words careless, selfish, liar, not too late, soon be over, forgotten in no time. Then Robert quelled the chorus, shouting them down, using the knack learned to quell hecklers at political meetings. 'Let's stop nattering, shall we? I shall ring Doctor Armitage now. I must get back to London tonight. I am flying to New York tomorrow.' The ration of time he was prepared to give was up. The voices stilled. Hebe heard him use the telephone, make the arrangements. A room in the clinic. Operation in the afternoon. Home next day. Splendid.

Listening to Robert's civilised voice buying freedom from embarrassment, eliminating a social nuisance, she thought, I love those people, they are my family, they are not casting me out, they are just making sure I fit into their scheme of things. A puff of wind blew in through the open door. The sky was lurid, long-hoped-for rain on the way. It was growing dark and chilly. On the other side of the door she heard Robert again.

'That's settled, then. Can you drive her up in the morning, Delian?'

'No problem.'

'Good, good.' Robert's dry hands rustled as he rubbed them together. 'Right then, we should be off. Ready, Ann?'

'Time for one more drink?' Her grandmother's voice.

She is afraid of being left alone with me, thought Hebe, but she has not lifted a finger to help me.

'No, no thank you, we should be on our way.'

Hebe raced up the stairs, forcing leaden legs to work, reached her room above the porch and shut the door. They would not come near her tonight, they thought she would have gone to bed. Shivering with anguish she pulled on a cardigan, changed her shoes, took from the dressing-table drawer her mother's pearls and rings – Ann, Beata and Cara had the best pieces – stuffed them in her bag, counted her money, seventeen pounds, turned off the light, stood listening by the open window. Rain was beginning to tap on the Virginia creeper. Below, the front door opened, light blazed into the drive. Cheerful voices bidding a goodnight chorus. 'Goodbye, then, goodbye.' 'Glad that's settled.' 'Very grateful.' 'Not at all.' 'See you soon.' 'Drive carefully.' 'Lovely night.' 'If you call rain lovely.' 'We need it for the crops.' 'Goodnight, goodnight, God bless.'

She watched Robert and Ann kiss the grandparents, get into the Jaguar, drive away.

Next, Marcus with Cara climbed into the Range Rover, then Delian alone in the Alfa Romeo.

'Give our love to Beata,' they called. Beata, being pregnant, had not attended the conference; she might have been upset; must not risk a miscarriage.

The cars, their headlights probing through the summer rain, streaked down the drive to the main road.

'Time for bed.' Grandfather turned to go in. 'It's been a tiring week.'

Had the nightmare only lasted a *week*?

'That such a thing should happen to us!'

'Good chap, Robert. Head screwed on. He'll go far, mark my words.'

Hebe waited while her grandfather let the dog out for his run, standing in the porch calling to him in tender accents not used for any other creature. The front door slammed. The kitchen door closed on the dog as he went to his basket. Stairs creaked as the old man climbed up to bed, switching off lights as he went. The long-case clock in the hall struck eleven.

'It's late.' Grandfather's bedroom door closed. The house grew quiet. Hebe waited.

She felt infinitely tired, sleep an overwhelming temptation. Would a couple of hours matter? But if she failed to wake? The child in her womb kicked out for a swim. She crept down the stairs, felt among the coats slung across the hall table, found her coat, went into the kitchen. The dog in his basket wagged his tail. She bent to stroke his head, feeling the silky ears. The dog mumbled and chop-chopped his jaws. 'Bye, Smut.'

Out in the rain she hesitated. Above the porch her grandfather threw up the sash window.

'Splendid downpour. Just in time to stop those silly buggers on the Water Board banning the use of garden hoses.'

Her grandmother answered something inaudible.

'Astute fellow, Robert. Settled that hash in no time. Can't think why the little fool couldn't be like her sisters –'

'The poor –'

'Poor nothing. We have cherished a crocodile.'

'My hearing aid is on the blink. I can't hear what –'

'I said we have cherished a crocodile. *Façon de parler*.'

'Crocodiles are wonderful mothers.' Faint hint of discord.

'We are not giving this one the chance of showing how wonderful.' He slammed down the window.

Hebe put on her shoes, pulled up her coat collar, stepped out into the rain. She hoped never to hear those voices again.

1

The young mothers walked abreast, pushing their double buggies. Each buggy held two children. The younger children sucked dummies, the elder sprawled in resignation behind the plastic covers protecting them from the drizzle. The women paused to stare in shop windows, turning to one another to comment on the contents. They filled the width of the pavement. Both were pregnant. People attempting to pass stepped into the gutter or shrank aside in doorways.

Hebe's gorge rose. She felt an almost joyful desire to jostle the young mothers, to shout at them to give way, give them a start, force them to show consideration. That both were heavily pregnant only made Hebe the more furious; she had never, when carrying Silas, taken up so much space; she had never let Silas suck a dummy; come to think of it, Silas had never had a buggy. She had carried him in a sling next her heart.

Cherishing her uncharitable thoughts, Hebe prowled behind the women, disliking their swaying rumps, their mechanically turning heads, their abrupt bursts of inane laughter. As her intolerance grew she felt her face grow hot and her glasses beginning to steam over. She let the women draw ahead, took off her glasses and wiped them, enjoying the slippery feel of glass between finger and thumb.

At the street corner, still talking, the women pushed the buggies off the pavement. An approaching car jammed on squealing brakes, missing the children by inches, nearly giving the driver a coronary.

'Can't you look where you're going?'

'Stupid git nearly killed my Kevin.'

'Look where you're going, look –'

Hebe swung round the corner, grinning with vengeful delight. Carrying her glasses so that she could see as little as possible of the street she deplored, she wondered whether in her absence of patience and lack of charity she had ill-wished the women. She felt a glow of power, both irrational and delightful as, increasing her pace, she set herself to climb the hill.

Without her glasses she could only see a blur of dark brick, each house as awful as its neighbour, purplish brick with light beige brick round the windows, uncompromising, solidly built, hideous.

Starting the climb, stiff for even the young and healthy, paradisical for the free-wheeling bicycles of reckless children, breathing the damp, salt-tinctured air, she became aware of a smell she could not define, coffee, pepper, smoke, with connotations of the panic nightmare which visited her, catching her as it did now, to bring horror so total that she stood holding her glasses, her hand pressed to her chest, then moving to shield her eyes, in an effort to black out the towering buildings rearing up to blot out the sky, bending inwards to stare from sightless unlit windows with the eyes of deep-sea fish. She heard jeers and laughter, the mindless chatter of an unseen crowd surrounding her with frightful cheer, isolating her in a dreadful cocoon so that she sweated and trembled, unable to move, as the voices began their litany.

'Who is the man? It might be anybody. Who is the man? Don't speak to your grandfather like that. A long-haired layabout. Dirty feet. Beards. You are a whore. Your sisters never – Who was the – Guitars – Don't answer in that tone of voice. Earrings, cannabis, heroin. Probably a Communist. Dirty fingernails. Who was the man? Can't speak the Queen's English. Don't prevaricate. Must have an abortion. What will your brothers-in-law say? Who was it? You must know. Don't be impertinent. Where did it happen? Might be *black*. So many sacrifices, gave you everything. Don't dare to speak like that. Don't lie. If it were not so public you would have it on the National Health. What d'you mean too late? How many months? Of course you know. Think of our friends. I am *not* shouting. Your sisters. You've made your grandmother cry. At least be civil. After all we've done for you. All the right people. Who was it? Might have a police record. Might be diseased, might be a black. This is intolerable. Who – who – who –?'

She knew that if she could hang on the terror would dissipate. She would recover as though coming round from an anaesthetic.

'I am not mad.' She opened her eyes. She had spoken aloud, looked quickly to see if she had been noticed, then rushed up the street, forcing her legs to hurry, driving herself. Reaching her door, heart thumping, breath coming in gasps, she fumbled for her key, breathing in the illusive whiff. What was it? Imaginary or not, it brought solace after the horror, even a sensation of happiness which she attributed to relief from the paralysis of fear. It was imaginary. She was safe in the ugly familiar street, safe from the voices mumbling the familiar accusations in weird accents in the strange city, the nightmare background of prying eyes, claustrophobic walls, darkness and that smell mixed with the voices. If only she could control the panic she might recover the shaft of joy which was always out of reach. Finding her key, she felt shame for the envy she had felt towards the two women with their children, their buggies, their ordinary lives. Perhaps, she thought, putting on her glasses, it was envy which brought on the panic. She unlocked her door; the telephone was ringing in the house. Her heart slowed its beat. Somewhere behind the dead fish eyes, bullying questions, was gaiety, illusive, poignant, almost blotted out by that other fear. Epileptics must feel like this, she thought, and breathed in the smell of her house: garlic, flowers from the market, herbs. The telephone stopped.

Trip, her tortoiseshell cat, came to greet her, pressing her head against her ankles with sharp little pushes, prickling with her whiskers. She picked up the cat. 'Hungry?' Trip purred, pushing a paw against her cheek, flexing her claws, just not drawing blood.

Jim Huxtable, talking to Hannah Somerton further up the street, put the hat he was holding on his head, stopped what he was saying and stared.

'Who is that girl?'

'She's called Hebe. She's a neighbour.' Hannah claimed Hebe.

'Hebe, a young virgin crowned with flowers, arrayed in a variegated garment.'

'Oxfam shop anorak.' Hannah tried to retrieve his attention.

'Hebe, daughter of Jupiter and Juno.' She had opened the door, disappeared.

'Who?' What was the man talking about?

'Hebe is the Latin name for Veronica.' He looked at Hannah. 'She harnessed peacocks. Fell down in a position which –'

'I thought Veronica was a bush. A shrub,' Hannah corrected herself, fearing to sound lewd.

'Ah, yes.' Jim looked at Hannah, small, fair hair, lovely green eyes, rather like Maudie Littlehampton. He was tempted to get to know her, find out what she was like in bed.

'She's hardly a virgin, she's got a son of twelve.' Hannah laughed, showing her perfect teeth. 'She's a cook.'

'Really? Well, I must go. If you think of anyone with anything interesting to sell, here's my card. My telephone number's on it.' He lost interest in Hannah.

'Thanks, I'll get in touch if I think of anything.'

'Thank you.' He began to move away.

'Did you see my aunt's paperweights?' She tried to keep him talking; really attractive men were a rarity.

'Yes, she doesn't want to part.'

'Pretty, aren't they?' She would like to delay him.

'Very pretty.' He moved away. She liked the way he walked, a European lope, an American lope was quite different. His hair under the hat was grey, his eyes dark grey. Wish I knew more about antiques, she thought as she crossed the street, then I could have kept him talking. She looked at the card: 'James Huxtable.' A London telephone number, Fulham address. She opened Hebe's door and walked into the house.

'You came up the street in a rush.' Her statement held a question.

'It's good for the heart, they say.' Hebe snapped shut her mind, trapping her fears until the next time.

'What was the hurry?' Hannah pressed her, curious.

'I must get into dry clothes, I am soaked.' Why does she walk in on me like this? 'There were two idiot girls who pushed their children out into the street and nearly got them killed.' She took off her anorak and shook it. Trip moved hastily under a chair to avoid the drops. 'They had so many children.'

'Not single parents, like us. Shall I put the kettle on?' Hannah moved to pick up the kettle, take it to the sink, turn on the tap. Hebe wished she would not treat her kitchen and her kettle with such familiarity.

'I must change my clothes.'

'Where have you been?'

'For a walk.' She had no intention of sharing the joy of her walk. The tramp across fields and moorland, the sound of water dripping from trees, the rustle of wind, cries of sheep, shriek of buzzards, the delicious solitude.

'I would have come with you if you'd said.'

I dare say you would, thought Hebe, climbing the stairs without answering.

'There's a lot to be said for single parenthood,' Hannah called after her.

'Yes.' She pulled off her jersey.

'Edward's late with my maintenance,' Hannah called up the stairs.

'Always is,' Hebe shouted back.

'I've written to my solicitor.'

'You always do.'

'What?'

She writes every month, thought Hebe, brushing her damp hair. It's amazing the funds don't just dry up. At least I'm spared that hassle. She peered at her face in the mirror. I do not look like them, she thought, examining her face, nor sound much like them. It must be them behind those blind windows chanting their intolerable accusations. She stared at her high forehead, full mouth, dark eyes.

Bernard Quigley had said: 'Your face is an asset. You look honest.' And he had laughed his creaky old man's laugh.

'I've wet the tea,' Hannah called up the stairs.

'Thanks, I'll have coffee,' Hebe shouted, then reproached herself for snobbery. Why shouldn't Hannah say 'wet the tea' if that came naturally?

'Do you want real coffee, Nescaff or a bag? How was the job? Very boring?'

'A bag will do. It was lucrative.'

'When's the next job?'

All these questions. Hebe pulled on a jersey and rejoined Hannah in the kitchen. 'I haven't decided.' She took the proffered cup, and watched Hannah pour herself tea, resenting the way she made herself at home, sitting behind her teapot. Then, regretting her surly reaction, forced herself to be friendly.

'After the holidays when Silas has gone back to school.'

'And when does Master Silas grace us with his presence?' Hannah's lightness of tone failed to conceal the envy she felt of Silas at a fee-paying school, while her own son Giles was state educated.

'Day after tomorrow. When does Giles get back from the Paris trip?'

'Tomorrow.'

'I hope he enjoyed it. Silas is longing to see him.'

'Not grown too grand?'

'Don't be silly.' Hebe spoke sharply.

'Edward Krull could perfectly well afford –'

'Of course he could, but he doesn't want to. You've told me.'

Hannah sniffed, scenting a rebuff. 'Did you see that fellow I was talking to earlier on?'

'I didn't have my glasses on. I didn't see anybody.'

'A dealer. He was calling from house to house. Rather dishy. He visited Aunt Amy.'

'People like that are called "Knockers". Did she show him her things?'

'He saw the paperweights. She must have liked him or she wouldn't have taken them out of the cupboard. I was talking to him, getting friendly, you know how it is.'

'No.'

'You are so private. You never stop and chat. You miss a lot. I asked him to come in and see whether I had anything that might interest him. I thought he'd be someone I'd like to know.'

'Might be a thief.'

'He seemed friendly. Then he caught sight of you and he said, "Who is that? What's that girl's name?" It was as if he knew you.'

'I didn't see him, I told you. I hadn't got my glasses on.'

'He went on up the street but he stopped and stared when I came over to you. Pity you didn't meet him, you could have made friends.'

'I shouldn't think so.'

'He talked with that kind of voice, you know what I mean.'

'I don't.'

'You do. He talked like the people you go and work for.'

'How do you know how they talk?' Hebe was irritated.

'I guess, bet I'm right. You talk like them yourself.'

'Did he need a cook?' Hebe mocked.

'I told you, he was looking for antiques but' – Hannah narrowed green eyes – 'he gave the impression of –'

'Rich?' Hebe was laughing. 'Stately homes?'

'Confident.' Hannah smiled, not resenting the mockery. 'He seemed confident until he clapped eyes on you, then he seemed disturbed, sort of puzzled.'

Hebe wondered whether the stranger was a friend of one of her clients. 'What was he like?' she asked suspiciously.

'Tall, pepper and salt hair, grey eyes. Until you appeared I thought he was interested in me. Oh, I said that –'

'I expect he was. You are beautiful.'

'Do you really think so?' Hannah looked delighted. 'Honest?'

'Of course I do,' said Hebe warmly.

'Another thing about him, he knew Latin and wore a hat.'

'Latin?'

'Said Hebe was the Latin name for Veronica, the shrub. You don't often see men in hats. And something about driving peacocks.'

Hebe finished her coffee in a hurried gulp.

'You aren't interested, are you? Sometimes I wonder whether you are a lesbian.' Hannah probed.

Hebe took her mug to the sink, standing with her back to Hannah to hide a broad smile.

'I suppose Silas' father was your one great love.'

'Have you been reading Mills and Boon?' Hebe asked coldly. Then – for she did not wish to hurt – she said, 'I am busy making a living. Look, love, I have to get the place ready for Silas so –'

'Can I help? D'you want me to leave?'

'It's just that I have rather a lot to do.' Difficult to get rid of Hannah, who thought nothing of staying for hours. How much easier life had been before Amy Tremayne's niece had come to live in the street, imposing friendship regardless.

'Okay, I'll leave you to it. Let me know if I can help in any way.' Hannah stood up. Hebe reached for the teapot. 'No, no, I'll do that.' Hannah snatched up the pot, emptied and washed it with meticulous care. 'Just give a shout, I've only got Giles and Aunt Amy.' Would she never leave?

'Perhaps I should have asked him where he is staying. Invited him for a drink, or something. He seemed to be alone.'

'Some people like being alone.'

'I could have asked him to meet George Scoop.' Hannah ignored the hint.

Hebe refrained from asking after George, not wishing a fresh line of talk.

'I've been out with George while you were away. The only thing is, he spends his days gazing down gullets. Would his being a dentist, dontologist, actually, put you off?'

Hebe remained silent, noting that Hannah was now on Christian name terms with her dentist.

'He is good-looking.' Hannah was determined to discuss George. 'He is in a good practice. I got to know him while he was fixing my teeth. He is about forty, a bit careful with money.'

'You told me.'

'He takes me out to dinner. I ask him back. We watch telly but he – well, I suppose it's because he is so keen on his work, he keeps making remarks.'

'Such as?'

'People's teeth, he notices their fillings when they laugh, whether their dentures fit, whether the teeth are dirty. He doesn't use the word "dirty", he calls it –'

'Tartar.'

'That's right. He admires Mrs Thatcher and Monsieur Mitterand for having theirs fixed. He never gets away from his work.'

'Wedded to it.'

Not liking Hebe's ironical tone, Hannah checked. 'Well, let me know if I can help.' Still she lingered.

'Thank you.' Hebe edged Hannah towards the door, closed it after her. Oh, the joy of being alone! The telephone pealed, shattering with its intrusion the welcome quiet. The cat leapt bristling on to the windowsill. Hebe picked up the instrument.

'Hello.'

' 'Allo, 'allo, vot colour knickers you wear?' A thick French accent.

'Wrong number.' Hebe put the telephone back in its cradle.

Higher up the street Jim Huxtable sat on the seat a town councillor had given in memory of aged parents who had lived in the street when it was first built. They had complained of aching legs and breathless struggles up the hill. After their death their son had given the seat, inscribed with his parents' names. Rude boys had carved coarse words and passing dogs did worse. Jim Huxtable waited in case the dark girl should come out of her house, hoping to get another look at her. Pretty name, Hebe, Cup Bearer to the Gods. Not many peacocks to harness in this awful street. What was the indecent posture she had fallen into that got her into trouble, if memory served him right? The mores of the ancients were not so very different from those of the present. He wondered how Bernard had known about the old woman's collection of paperweights.

Down the street a door slammed and the girl with green eyes came out. He didn't want to talk to her again. Tired and hungry, he walked fast up the hill to his car and cursed when the engine stalled.

As Hebe closed her door Hannah crossed the street with a hop and a skip. Between the hop and the skip she decided to remarry.

Thinking of Hannah, Hebe let laughter erupt. A Lesbian! What would Hannah dream up next? She thought of Silas, who would be home tomorrow, his brown eyes mercifully not short-sighted, his arc of a nose, hair the colour of a bay horse. Where did the nose and hair come from? Not from me, not from them. She remembered carrying Silas and her love for the unborn child. She had been happy, then, in a precious intimacy which was no longer theirs. Was it envy of those women that brought on her panic? Did they feel for their unborn babies as she had felt for Silas? Perhaps not, since they each had in their buggies the reality babies turned into. I am no baby lover, thought Hebe, yet I loved Silas as a baby with passion.

She considered Hannah's relationship with Giles; a comfortable intimacy. She envied Hannah but Hannah invented for her 'a great love'. How banal.

Trip sprang up by the sink, making it clear that she was still hungry. Hebe reached into a cupboard for a tin of cat food. She sat watching Trip eat, then wash herself before going out on her night prowl. The cat sat listening to the sounds from neighbouring gardens, making sure there was no danger. Hebe watched the little animal, thinking, Silas loves that cat. Trip rushed to the back fence and vanished over it. Hebe went up to bed, where she lay mentally totting up her income. The total was healthy. If she continued work on the present basis the years of Silas' education were assured, although the very nature of her work was insecure. Old ladies do not live for ever and other work inclined to be impermanent. Fun, though, she thought, luxuriating in the solitude of her large bed, kicking her legs under the duvet; enjoy tonight without some Hercules thrusting himself between her thighs.

2

Downstairs the telephone was ringing. Hebe let it ring, pealing its jarring note over and over again until at last it died. She lay looking forward to tomorrow and Silas, planning his holidays.

Trip desecrated the neighbour's garden, making a neat little scrape, and, covering her excrement with tender paw, climbed back over the fence. It was raining. She leapt from the fence on to Hebe's windowsill, dropped into the bedroom, padded across to the bed to insert herself under the duvet. Feeling wet fur against her face, Hebe put on her bedside light.

'I shall never get to sleep.' She fetched a towel and wiped the little animal who, purring, burrowed into the warmth. 'Silas taught you that. You can snuggle up to him tomorrow.'

For the third time the telephone rang. Irritated, she ran downstairs and picked up the receiver.

'Yes?' she said tersely.

'You got big tits?' A strong cockney accent.

'I told you wrong number,' she said irritably.

'Vot colour knickers?' pleaded the French voice.

'You don't even get the accent right.' She put the instrument back and covered it with a cushion. She went back to bed where the cat made room for her.

Midnight was striking from the town clock when she was disturbed yet again by a scrabbling at her window, a thud as feet hit the floor, the sound of material tearing.

'Sod it! I've torn my skirt.'

'God, Terry, I told you wrong number, I told you twice. Twice!'

'Just look at my skirt.'

Hebe switched on her bedside light. 'Terry, I'm trying to sleep. Silas is coming home tomorrow.'

Terry was examining the tear. 'D'you think it will mend?' he asked.

Slender with cropped hair, wide shoulders and long legs. His skirt was pleated red cotton, worn with a fuchsia sweatshirt. 'D'you think it will mend?' he asked, stroking Hebe's shoulder.

'I shan't mend it for you.' She lay back, pulling the duvet up to her chin.

'Listen to why I rang you. I made it with another girl, no trouble at all.' Terry spoke excitedly. 'It's all due to you.'

'Couldn't it have waited?'

'Listen –' He was taking off the skirt and inserting himself into the bed. 'What you got in here? Trip, it's only me, don't scratch. Bloody little beast, give over, make room. She's wet.'

'Terry,' she protested. 'I told you –'

'Listen, love.' He put his arm round her, settling in the bed, stretching his legs.

Annoyed by the disturbance Trip scrabbled out of the bed and perched on the chair where Hebe had laid her clothes.

Terry snuggled up to Hebe. 'I haven't come here to sleep with you.' He kissed her neck.

'Sleep is just what one doesn't do.'

'It's the crappiest expression for it. Give us a kiss.'

'Sleep is what I want at the moment.'

'Didn't you hear what I said? I made it with another girl. No problem. You were right. No skirts. No knickers. I did like you taught. I came to thank you, thought you'd be glad to know.' Terry was aggrieved.

'I am glad. It's just that I want to sleep. I told you it's all in the mind, now will you –'

'Okay, now listen to this:

She can present joyes meaner than you do;
Convenient and more proportional.
So if I dream I have you, I –'

'That's Donne and the verse ends – "And sleep which locks up sense, doth lock all out." That's what I want now.'

He laughed. 'You are not really angry.'

'Are you in love with this girl?'

'She was just a fun girl for an evening. I've got other ideas.'

'Someone specific?'

'Maybe.' Terry leaned from the bed to pick up a book from the floor. 'Could we read a bit? Would you read to me, for the last time?'

'You read.' She gave in.

'Okay.' Terry began reading. 'I sing the progresse of a deathlesse soule –' his young voice rising and falling in gentle cadence. Hebe remembered when she had first met him installing burglar alarms in the Midland Bank, noticed him reading Milton, started talking about poetry, an interest which had evolved into reading aloud to each other after lovemaking. He was taking a course in English at night school. She did not know what connection poetry had with women's clothes. The skirts and knickers were a harmless aberration, the skirt, she suspected, a ploy to rouse her interest. Now it seemed this phase was ending. She had enjoyed the poetry, coming from a boy who looked as though he would be more at home in a disco than reading Donne to the cat, for I am not listening, thought Hebe, and Terry has read himself to sleep. She listened to his breathing, remembering his discovery of ''Tis the Arabian Bird alone lives chaste for 'tis but one, But had kind nature made them two they would as the doves and sparrows do.' For a while he had called her his Arabian Bird. Perhaps that's what I am, she thought. The town clock struck the half hour.

'Have a heart, Terry.' She shook him. 'Wake up.'

Terry woke staring at her, puzzled.

'Time to go, Terry.'

He was sleepy, his mind far away. Reluctantly he got out of bed. 'Don't happen to have any Y-fronts?'

'Silas' would be too small.'

'Then I'll go without. Lend us your jeans. I'll see you get them back.'

'Are you sure you won't need –'

'Yes. I'll leave my skirt with you as a memento, and the panties now, it's okay without them.' He had forgotten Donne.

'I am glad.' Hebe watched him struggle into the jeans she had taken off when she went to bed.

'Fit a bit tight, but what the hell. I'm – what am I?' He stood looking down at Hebe, exultant.

'Normal,' she suggested, smiling up at him.

'That's about it.' He searched in his skirt pocket. 'This is for you.' He thrust a wad of notes into Hebe's hand. 'You earned it. Can't think how you did it. From now on I can be like anyone else.' He bent down to kiss her. ''Bye, love.'

'Thanks, Terry.' Hebe looked at the money. 'It's far too much.'

'No, it's not. I've got this girl in mind. Don't you want to know who she is?' She could see he wanted to tell her.

'No.' He must manage on his own.

'She will be the first to get the straight treatment,' he said, zipping up the jeans.

'Without frills.' She was amused.

He gave her a friendly hug. 'Sending me up.'

'Go now. I must sleep.' She pressed him to leave.

'But I had to tell you. Analysts tried and you did the trick in just two years.'

Hebe was counting the money. 'This is an awful lot, Terry.' She was shocked by the amount.

'I shan't see you again, not like this. I want you to have it.'

'Thanks.' She did not trust herself to say more.

'I'll take care of Trip when you go away. Keep in touch with you.' He bent to kiss her again. 'Goodbye now.' He moved to the window to climb out. 'This is a lot easier in jeans.' He gave a snort of laughter.

She heard him land in the flower bed, switched off her light and went to the window to watch him put on his shoes, climb the fence to the alleyway behind the gardens and break into a run, the sound of his feet beating a tattoo.

'There goes a satisfied customer,' she said to the cat as she dropped the skirt and the discarded briefs into the wastepaper basket. 'God! I must sleep.' She got back into bed. She would miss Terry, miss the poetry reading. Buy herself a treat with part of his goodbye money, perhaps; put the rest towards Silas' education. She felt a rush of affection for Terry. Will his new girl make him happy, will they read poetry together as we have? Why should I worry, she thought, as she lay listening to the cat purring. I taught him:

As freely as we met we'll part
Each one possest of their own heart.

If he has learned that lesson why can't I abide by it? We are friends. Restoration poems are not essential for survival, not essential for Silas. She dozed, thinking of the good times with Terry during the past years – quite a course in Eng. Lit., a profitable spell of work, a success. She remembered thinking him farouche until she had discovered his troubled spirit, grown fond of him for himself not only for the colour of his skin, which in some lights resembled a Mars Bar. So much for you. Briefly she permitted a vision of her grandfather, quickly banishing him from her mind.

Then she reproached herself for not making Terry promise to tell his new girl about his little ways. He would never tolerate Y-fronts, never really change. The girl was on to a good thing if she did but know. Terry was intelligent and caring, which was more than could be said for most fee-paying lovers. The word 'fees' brought to mind Silas. Would the term away have changed him?

3

Hannah sat in front of her mirror to do her nails. She wore rubber gloves for rough jobs, thought Hebe mad not to bother. Hebe had said, 'Making pastry cleans them. The dirt lends zest to the pastry.' Hannah wondered what the Cordon Bleu would say to that and remembered Hebe remarking that she had been given the best tips by the French chef when she worked at the hotel on the cliff. Saying this, Hebe had laughed, as though the tips were humorous. Painting her nails, Hannah wondered whether the antique dealer was staying at the hotel. She had dined there with George. It was perhaps too expensive for the dealer. He had climbed the street knocking at doors. Surprisingly, Amy admitted him. Hannah had been watching at her window, hoping to see Hebe return. It had been easy to talk to the man when he left Aunt Amy's. She brushed her hair. Had the stranger noticed it? She lifted her lip like a horse sneering, admired her teeth, straight as a regiment of guards. George had done a good job. Would Jim Huxtable be interested in her year's sessions with George who had gloriously brought to order her set of snaggles? Would he be interested to know she had flogged her only good piece of jewellery, Edward's engagement ring, to pay for her teeth? Annoyance spoiled the joy of her teeth. Edward never sent her alimony on time. His dilatoriness kept alive the tie when she would rather forget him. New teeth, new life, damn you, Edward. But she was pleased with her adoption by deed poll of the name Somerton. Would Giles stop being obstinate and change his too? He hung on to Krull to annoy, to be able to threaten he would run away to his father. She hoped he would soon realise that Somerton sounded better than Krull. Perhaps he would latch on to this through his friendship with Silas and also perhaps get the hang of Silas' and Hebe's vowels. Eyeing her image in the glass Hannah mouthed A-E-I-O-U as taught at the elocution lessons she preferred to call speech therapy. Hebe's vowels came naturally and Silas' were perpetuated at his school. Hannah's thoughts veered to Hebe's odd life working as cook to rich old women. She never discussed the people she worked for. She never talked about Silas' father, had not responded when Hannah told her about Edward, did not, as other women would, tell her own tale. Hannah's mother and Aunt Amy had been sisters. Her mother had married higher socially than Aunt Amy, who had some undiscussed connection with Hebe, who was thick with Amy and like Amy secretive. Hannah realised that she knew as little about her aunt as about Hebe. She had been referred to by her parents as 'that poor old maid living alone in that house. You should go and see her, she's your only relative.' A year ago, finding herself in the neighbourhood with Giles, she had visited, been welcomed. With no roots after living in America, it had seemed natural to settle here, send Giles to school, keep an eye on her aunt. She had grown very fond of Amy. Hannah's thoughts wandered.

'I must marry again,' she told herself. 'Have another bash.' Though the marriage to Edward had left her bruised and there was much to be said for independence, marriage was what Hannah preferred. Hebe seemed to manage her life extraordinarily well for someone whose income of child benefit and single-parent benefit was only augmented by temporary cooking jobs. What did those old women pay? Hannah blew on the varnish, which was dry at last. What did she do about sex? While enjoying her relationship with George, Hannah had yet to decide whether to make it permanent. George's line in pillow talk was mundane. Dontology does not turn me on, she ruminated. There must be somebody more amusing than George.

Time to see whether Aunt Amy was okay for the night. She looked across at Hebe's house. There was no light.

Up among the hills Jim Huxtable sat with Bernard Quigley outside his house finishing the claret they had drunk with their supper.

'I was wondering how you knew that old woman had that collection of paperweights. They are immensely valuable.'

'What?' The old man put his hand to his ear.

'You are not deaf,' said Jim patiently and waited for an answer.

'I wanted to know whether, if she still has them, she is prepared to sell,' said the old man grudgingly.

'She invited me to come again, she may change her mind.' Jim looked at his host, sitting with his cat on his knee, stroking it with gnarled fingers. The cat's purring was loud. The damp air, heavy with the smell of honeysuckle, was counterpointed by Bernard's dog, Feathers, who lay at his feet. 'Your dog smells a bit high,' he remarked.

'Rolled in a pong. You may bath him tomorrow.'

'Thanks,' said Jim, ungrateful at the prospect.

'She won't sell,' said the old man complacently, reverting to the paperweights. 'She's too fond of them.'

Jim thought of Bernard's idiotic trick, making him call from house to house. 'I don't buy at the door.' 'Nothing to sell here, not even the balls from a brass monkey.' Rebuffs.

'If you knew that, why did you suggest that charade?'

The old man did not answer.

'There was a girl, a few doors up from your friend's house. A talkative girl, gave me an oeillade.'

Bernard laughed. 'That's her niece.'

'Another girl came up the street, reminded me of someone. Who would she be? Lives opposite your Miss Tremayne, seemed short-sighted. She was carrying her spectacles. You know her, by chance?'

'I do not know her.' In the old sense to know a girl was to make love, thought Bernard, as he had made love in the old days, tenderness and laughter mixed with passion. How delightful to have such an experience with Hebe. She was born too late, he thought, jealous of the younger man's interest. He remembered his dealings with Hebe, taking advantage of her naivety by paying her twice the worth of her mother's jewels. He took a snuff box from his waistcoat pocket, measured, inhaled, sneezed. The cat jumped off his knee.

Watching Bernard, Jim thought the light of dusk, usually so

kind, made the old man look like a fossilised bird. 'Why did you never marry?' he asked.

Bernard sat thinking. 'Impossible to make up my mind. Wasn't prepared to give anything up. *Embarras de choix*. What about you? If you are not careful you will end up a bachelor, not that I can't recommend the state. Got lots of girls, have you?'

'You could say that.'

'Don't want any of them to be permanent?'

Jim did not answer.

'If you get a chance to buy those paperweights –'

'Yes?'

'I am off to bed. See you in the morning before you go.' Bernard heaved himself out of his chair. Jim stood up. Bernard snapped his fingers at the dog. 'Come boy, bedtime. You could give them to the girl. She probably carried her spectacles because she did not want to see.' There was tenderness in the old man's voice.

'So you do know her.' Jim expected no answer. He decided to call on the girl called Hebe and ask whether she had any antiques to sell, see why she was worthy of the paperweights. That way he could get a look at her. He could still get to London by evening if he did not dally on the way.

Also thinking of Hebe, Hannah let herself into Amy Tremayne's house.

'It's me, auntie, how are you?'

'Still alive.'

'Can I come in?'

'You usually do.'

Ignoring this unpromising start, Hannah said, 'What did you think of the Knocker?'

'I thought he was rather interesting. Comes from London.'

'Did you sell him anything?' Hannah looked round her aunt's cluttered room, absolute hell to dust.

'No.' Amy was grumpy. 'I saw you talking to him.'

'Why shouldn't I? Did you show him your paperweights?'

'They are in the cupboard.'

'I know. I put them there. There is such a lot to clean.'

'Stopped talking to you when he saw Hebe,' Amy chuckled.

'Do you think he knew Hebe?' Hannah quizzed her aunt. 'He seemed more interested in her than me.'

'Say anything?' The old woman looked up suspiciously.

'He just stared. Perhaps he knew Hebe's husband.' Hannah fished.

'She doesn't wear a ring.'

'D'you mean she wasn't married?' Hannah seized the chance of discussing Hebe, persuading her aunt to talk.

'Wouldn't be strange these days,' said Amy drily.

'Oh, auntie!'

'Oh, auntie,' mocked the old woman.

'Perhaps he died before he could marry her, her lover.'

'Did she tell you that?' Amy raised an eyebrow.

'She never tells me anything. I imagined she had a great romance who died soon after they were married or even before they could.'

'Perhaps she disposed of him like you did poor Krull.'

'Rich Krull.' Hannah corrected her aunt, laughing.

'You girls. Chuck a perfectly good husband. Can't stick to anything.'

'If she isn't married, perhaps Silas is adopted?' Hannah pressed Amy.

'With those eyes? Perhaps he's her brother.' Amy was heavily humorous. 'I'm off to bed if that's all you have of interest.' She pulled herself up from her chair. The white hair framing her face was thick, her eyes, surrounded by wrinkles, were still beautiful.

'Like a hot drink? Cocoa? Horlicks?' suggested Hannah, still hoping for gossip.

'I'll have a toddy. Make it strong.' Amy went up to bed. If Hebe chose to mind her own business, she was not the one to broadcast it. Amy felt contempt for Hannah, who told every Tom and Dick her life story. Stories grew in the telling, it was only sensible not to tell them. Climbing out of her directoire knickers, which were getting difficult to get these days, Amy sighed, wondering whether she had been wise to give Hebe introductions to Lucy Duff, Louisa Fox and at the beginning to that old bastard Bernard. Too late now and the child – she thought of Hebe as a child – had to live. Give him his due,

Bernard had not cheated. He had introduced her to the hotel on the cliff and the French chef and she could not approve of that though it had proved useful.

Hannah brought the hot toddy. 'I made it strong.'

Amy drank, sipping through pleated lips, sitting propped by pillows. Hannah watched with affection.

'She works to pay for Silas' school; it must cost a bomb.'

'If you'd stayed married to Krull your Giles could have gone there too. If you marry again you will lose your alimony.' Amy grinned over her glass.

'Who said I wanted to?' Hannah was on the defensive.

'It's on your mind. You weigh the pros and cons. Shall I, shan't I?'

'I thought we were talking of Hebe,' said Hannah huffily.

'But I was thinking you might marry again. I saw you this afternoon. You can't sit around for ever taking money from Krull, giving nothing. It's not right.'

'You can't talk,' shouted Hannah, erupting in anger. 'You've never been married, you've always been alone, you don't know what it's like.'

The old woman was silent. Then, peering at Hannah, she said softly, 'None of us should be alone, it's not natural.' She looked tiny in her large bed.

'It's better than being stuck with someone you don't want,' muttered Hannah, not intending her aunt to hear, annoyed that she must defend herself.

'I heard you. You're as bad as a tart I heard in Paris, she –'

'I didn't know you knew Paris,' exclaimed Hannah, surprised.

'This tart' – Amy stressed the word – 'this tart said to another tart about a man who had just paid her off, this tart said, "*Et moi, je soulage moi-même*". Perhaps you don't.' The old woman mocked her niece. 'How that girl laughed!'

Hannah giggled. 'I hope Giles isn't learning that sort of French on his school trip.'

Amy raised an eyebrow. 'When does he get back?'

'Tomorrow.'

'Send him to see me.'

'No need. He loves you as much as I do.'

'Ho.' Amy switched off her light and lay back on her pillows, not waiting for Hannah to reach the landing.

'Old bitch.' Hannah fumbled for the light switch. 'I might kill myself falling downstairs,' she called but Amy did not answer. Searching for the switch Hannah thought of Giles growing up so quickly. He would soon be gone.

Courting sleep, Amy considered her afternoon visitor, questioning whether he had come by chance. He had admired her treasures, talked knowledgeably, known their value. Refusing to sell, she had put a tacit invitation in the manner of her refusal. They had talked about France. He had held the paperweights in his long fingers so that their brilliance caught the light. 'Glass flowers last longer than bouquets,' he had said.

But are they as sweet? Thinking of her paperweights, she thought of the secret trapped as the flowers were in the glass. Let Hannah pity her as the old spinster aunt who had spent a dreary life. She need never know of the period when she had been *la fille Anglaise*. Later she had had no heart for it, had gone back to work in England, a dully secure secretary.

Amy had watched Hannah waylay Jim Huxtable, watched them talking until, looking down the street, he had seen something which had caught his interest. Maybe, thought Amy, if he comes again I will sell him one. Considering her treasures, her mind went back to the Hôtel d'Angleterre fifty years ago. What fun it had been, waking to light filtering through the red plush curtains, the hugging and kissing, the cosiness before coffee and croissants. The warmth, the laughter, the presents. She was unwilling to think of the presents as payment since she had not in that instance wanted payment. It amused her that Hannah, who longed for romantic love, should think of her as 'a poor old thing' whereas Hebe, who thought of love with detachment, as an indulgence for others, should long since have correctly assumed her to be a retired lady of pleasure.

Further up the street Hannah restlessly debated whether she should marry George. She had planned to marry a man who pronounced regatta 'regattah'. George said 'regatter'.

4

Mungo Duff had difficulty finding a parking space in the multi-storey car park and was infuriated that he had no loose change for the meter. It was a hot day. He was weary of the cathedral crawl Alison had insisted on for her friends the Drews from Santa Barbara, over on a two-week trip. By the time he had found change, tracked back to the ticket machine, stuck the ticket on the windscreen, he was more eager for a drink at the bar of the Clarence than the prospect of trailing round Exeter Cathedral, listening to his knowledgeable wife and her even more knowledgeable guests. However, duty calls, he told himself. Yesterday Winchester, Stonehenge, Salisbury and Sherborne, tomorrow home and put one's feet up. Crossing the street on the way to the Close he caught sight of swirling skirts. There was something familiar in the swinging stride and lift of buttocks. Searching his mind to fit a face to the buttocks, he joined his wife and guests, who stood in the centre aisle gazing up at the minstrels' gallery. By tonight Alison would be complaining of a stiff neck and serve her bloody right. Mungo sat down in a chair, stretched his legs and waited. Let Alison do the work, it was she who had angled for an invitation to Santa Barbara, not he. Mungo sincerely hoped the Drews would keep her for a long visit. Why, he mused, could they not be content with Oxford, Cambridge, Anne Hathaway's cottage and Westminster Abbey, like any other decent Americans? Viewing his wife from behind as she wandered up the aisle, he compared her bottom and her friend Patsy Drew's with the bottom viewed briefly in the street.

'Oh, Mungo.'

Damn! Alison had seen him just as memory was about to yield.

'Yes?' He went to join his wife.

'Stay with them, darling. I just want to nip into that shoeshop on the corner, they've got a sale,' murmured Alison.

'They are your visitors, not mine,' he hissed.

'Darling, don't be mean.'

'Isn't it nearly lunchtime?' he prevaricated.

'Soon, soon. Be an angel. I won't be long.'

'Oh, God!'

'If you're not here when I come back I'll meet you in the bar.'

'That means you'll be ages.'

'No, no.' She left him, walking swiftly in her expensive sandals to use her eye for a bargain and buy at reduced price a pair, more likely two, of exquisite shoes to flaunt in California. When, years ago, they had been in love, he had jokingly called her a shoe fetishist. Now he called her a shopaholic. He had loved her jaunty walk, comparing her to a Shetland pony, but now, as he watched her go, he wondered whether her legs were not too short and whether in middle age her body, all right at present, would become barrel-shaped. Sulkily he joined their guests.

'A very lovely cathedral. We were comparing it to Durham and Lincoln.'

Patsy Drew never seemed to feel tired. What did Alison see in her?

'This is much cosier.' Mungo made an effort.

'Cosy?'

'Friendlier. Smaller. Less far to walk.'

'Are we tiring you, Mungo?' Eli was concerned, younger, more spry than Mungo, a lot fitter; all that jogging.

'Lord, no.' He rallied his manners.

'It's all new to us. You see it all the time.' Patsy was apologetic.

'Actually I've never been to Exeter before.'

'You don't expect us to believe that.' Must she be arch?

'I've been through it in the train.'

'But it's so close to your home.'

'Two hundred miles isn't close to an Englishman.'

The Drews laughed, appreciating his English wit.

'Why don't we skip the rest and have lunch?' Eli suggested. 'Then we can do Bath on our way home, perhaps fit in Wells too.'

'Certainly Wells,' said Patsy. 'Wells is a must.'

'So is a drink.' Mungo headed towards the cathedral door. 'Alison said she'd meet us in the bar.'

As they walked across the Close to the Clarence Hotel, Mungo glimpsed the mystery bottom. It vanished through the door but the hall was empty when they reached it.

In the bar Mungo ordered drinks and settled his guests in comfortable chairs. The bar was full of strangers. 'I had better go and reserve a table,' he said and made his way to the restaurant. As he went he looked about but saw no familiar face. He peered into the other bars and the buffet but to no avail. Returning to the bar after reserving a table he met Alison.

'Bought anything?'

'Three pairs.'

'Oh God!'

'Just what I need for the States.'

'Want,' said Mungo sourly.

'Want, too, of course. Have you ordered me a drink?'

'Not yet. Didn't know what you'd have.'

'I always drink vodka.'

'You don't, you often drink sherry and when you are feeling continental you drink Campari.'

'Mungo darling, don't be so marital.'

When Alison called him marital there was a row in the offing. Mungo apologised. 'Sorry, sorry, sorry.'

'Patsy, love, wouldn't you like to freshen up?' Alison bent to kiss Patsy as though they hadn't met for a week. Mungo flinched at the Americanism.

'Order me a vodka on the rocks while we are gone,' Alison said to Mungo.

Mungo said 'Of course', resisting the urge to say 'Sure'. He wondered whether Alison was having it off with Eli, or had it in mind for the future.

The women went in search of what Patsy called the john. Mungo took a swallow of whisky and waited for the feeling of rejuvenation which would get him through lunch and the afternoon. 'The wine waiter says they have a good Bordeaux,' he said to Eli. This was one of the days he must get a bit drunk if he was to survive.

In the ladies' lavatory Hebe took off her clothes. The only annoying thing about Marks & Spencer was the absence of anywhere to try things on. Over the years, when shopping in Exeter before meeting Silas off his school train, she had formed the habit of taking her purchases to the Clarence, trying them on in the ladies' cloakroom and returning such things as did not fit immediately. The fact that Marks & Spencer now had places where it was possible to try on clothes had escaped her, thanks to her myopia. The cloakroom was empty. Hebe left her clothes and bag on hooks in the lavatory and stepped out into the room to try on bikinis. She had tried on two and was about to try on a third when Alison and Patsy came suddenly into the room.

Alison stared. Patsy's mouth formed an 'O'. Hebe stepped back into the lavatory and bolted the door. She stood petrified with embarrassment. She listened.

Alison and Patsy went to other lavatories. She heard them go in, bolt the doors, pee, rustle paper, flush water, unbolt the doors, come out, wash their hands, leave the cloakroom and a burst of chatter in the corridor.

Her hands fumbling, Hebe dressed, put the bikinis back in their bag. She could not now remember which fitted her. In the confined space she combed her hair, adjusted her glasses and stood listening. Would they say something to the hall porter, complain at the desk? She had never been to the Clarence for a drink or a meal; she was not known. Assuming nonchalance she strolled into the passage which led to the hall. As she went she adjured herself, look natural, don't hurry. She had not expected to meet Mungo hurrying down the passage on his way to the gents. She dropped her parcels as she put up her hand to shield her face.

'What are you doing here?' Mungo had had two double whiskies and couldn't believe his eyes. He stooped to pick up her parcels. Their faces came close as Hebe too bent down. 'What are *you* doing here?' she said accusingly. 'Why aren't you at home?'

'Alison's got these Americans staying. They are into cathedrals – Winchester, Stonehenge, Sherborne yesterday; today Exeter, Wells, Bath and if they notice how close they are to Glastonbury it'll be that, too –'

'You're drunk.' She snatched her parcels from him. 'Your breath stinks.'

'Only a little. Do you live here?'

'No, no, no.'

'Near here?' He loomed over her, taller than she remembered.

'Certainly not.' She was in retreat.

'Alison's going to America on a long visit. Got her eye on the husband.'

'So what?'

'So we can be together, darling,' said Mungo loudly.

'Don't call me that,' Hebe hissed.

'She won't hear, she's in the bar.' He snatched at the hand holding the bikinis and found himself grasping the bag. 'Oh,' he followed her, 'here, this is yours.' He caught her arm. 'It was your bottom I saw earlier on. I couldn't place it.'

'What are you talking about?' She took the bag and hurried on.

'Since when have you worn glasses?'

'Goodbye.' Hebe crossed the street in great leaps and on to a passing bus. Looking back she saw Mungo, a head taller than anyone on the pavement, black hair ruffled, staring after her, a wild look in the blue eyes squinting down his highland nose.

Left on the pavement Mungo remembered that he was on his way to the gents. When he rejoined his wife and guests they were laughing as Patsy described her consternation at finding a naked girl in the ladies' rest room.

'She wore nothing except a pair of glasses.' Patsy and Alison shook with laughter.

Eli chortled. 'Life in a cathedral town. Beats Trollope.'

'She's not a trollop,' said Mungo, mishearing.

'Who isn't?' Alison took him up quickly.

Mungo sensed danger. 'That girl,' he said. 'You know who I mean, that girl who cooks for mother. Thought I saw her in the street just now. What's her name, can you remember?' he asked Alison. 'Does she come from these parts?'

'I think she comes from London. I can't remember what she's called.' Alison appeared uninterested. 'Don't order more drinks, darling; shouldn't we have lunch?'

'Of course, of course, and we'd better look sharp if we are doing Bath and Wells. We could do Glastonbury too, why not?' cried Mungo, his voice hearty with relief.

Alison, whose intake of alcohol did not match her husband's, took the wheel on the drive to Wells and Bath. They decided they would after all give Glastonbury a miss. Patsy had heard that it was the haunt of hippies and drug addicts. 'We have our own in California.'

Feigning sleep on the back seat, Mungo wondered what the hell Hebe was doing in Exeter. Secretive girl, he loathed having to communicate via her forwarding address. Did she perhaps live hereabouts? Why had he not hung on to her and forced her to tell him her address? The moment he was sure of Alison's dates for Santa Barbara he would write, get her to join him. It might be possible to take her abroad, she had had a bagful of bikinis. For a while, speeding towards Wells and Bath, he planned a Mediterranean holiday, but as the wine he had drunk at lunch on top of the whiskies began to wear off, he ruminated sadly that it was Hebe who called the tune, not he, that it was she who would choose dates and locale as she always did, a service flat off Sloane Avenue.

Alison, in the driving seat, switched the driving mirror to get a glimpse of herself. She was dissatisfied with her appearance. Her hair, naturally the colour of golden-shred marmalade, needed styling. Cornflower blue eyes were fine but would be better if she had her sandy eyelashes dyed, as Patsy had suggested. Time I bothered more, she thought, sweeping on to the M5 motorway. She twitched the mirror again to look at Mungo on the back seat. She thought with amusement, as she often had before, that he had all the assurance of an old Etonian without having actually been there, whereas she herself felt unfulfilled and insecure in spite of her natural bossiness. I must put that right, she told herself, moving into the fast lane. She wondered how often Mungo had been unfaithful. He had looked shifty at lunch when his mother's cook had been mentioned. Aha! Alison said to herself, sticking out her lower lip. Oho! 'I shall get my hair restyled in the States,' she said over her shoulder to Patsy, and 'We are sending the boys to Eton,' she said to Eli, sitting beside her.

'Is that so?' said Eli, unimpressed. 'Our speed limit in the States is fifty, what's yours?'

'Seventy.' Alison increased speed, pushing the speedometer up to eighty.

5

Hebe swept a mile down through Exeter on the bus and walked back up the hill cursing Mungo. She did not think Alison had recognised her; it was years since they had met when she had first gone to work for Mungo's mother. In those days she'd had a fringe, now her glasses were an added disguise. With an effort she dismissed Mungo and his wife from her mind. The day, which she had planned as a peaceful shopping day, had lost its appeal. What mattered was to be in time for the train bearing Silas from school and his other life. She just had time to return the bikinis and get her money back. She forced herself to be patient, not to hurry getting her car from the car park, not to drive too fast to the station, to park tidily, to comb her hair, adjust her skirt, relax, concentrate on Silas.

Always after the separation of term Hebe feared Silas would be changed, no longer hers, that he would not accept her. She was afraid of embarrassing him by too great a show of affection. She paced the platform in painful anticipation.

When the train arrived on time she was surprised. She had persuaded herself it would be late. When Silas hugged her she nearly wept with relief. When they had piled his belongings into the car and he sat beside her as she drove he said, sounding heartfelt, 'It's great to be home.' She felt overwhelming joy at having so miraculous a child. She loved his chestnut hair, his wide mouth, his nose jutting large, his slightly haughty expression which his eyes belied.

'You have grown,' she said.

'What do you expect?' he answered. Her euphoria evaporated.

'What do you want to do these holidays?' she asked. She had

been about to ask, 'What shall we do these holidays?'

Annoyed with himself but anxious to assert his independence, Silas said, 'I thought Giles and I could go exploring. There are places we have not been to.'

'I could take you in the car.' Involuntarily Hebe included herself in his life.

'We rather like going by bus, if you don't mind.' Silas looked at her sidelong.

'Of course I don't mind,' Hebe said sharply. 'Why should I?'

She thought my role is to cook, give him pocket money, be there when needed, if needed. For God's sake, she adjured herself, don't cling, don't be possessive.

'One of the boys offered me a lift down. His father's taking him to Cornwall,' said Silas. 'The Scillies, actually.'

'Why didn't you accept?'

'I'd rather come by train. I look forward to seeing you waiting on the platform. I like this long drive home with you.'

'Oh, darling.' Her heart leapt.

'Of course it would have saved the train fare.'

'To hell with the train fare,' cried Hebe and they both laughed, mocking the ruinous train fare.

'How are the jobs? When did you get home? Do you mind that sort of work?'

'It's the only work I'm any good at, it pays. Do you mind me doing it?' She feared his criticism.

'Why should I?' Silas was genuinely surprised. 'One of the boys has a sister who cooks for shooting parties. He says some of the guns try and lay her.'

'Oh.' What did Silas know about laying? Academic knowledge, surely.

'I told him you specialised in old ladies because they pay more and he said he'd tell her. Would it spoil your market, Ma?'

'Of course not. There's room for all.'

'D'you never get asked to do jobs in the holidays?'

'I wouldn't take one,' said Hebe quickly. 'Holidays are my only chance of seeing you.'

'You could take a quickie, go for a week, I wouldn't mind.'

'What do you mean?'

'If you send me away to school I could quite well stay at home while you work.'

Oh my God! What a deadly barb.

Silas, who had been meaning to say something of the sort for some time, thought perhaps he had said too much.

Hebe wondered whether she was losing touch, whether she had ever been in touch with Silas.

'Are you happy at school?' Ask a silly question.

'It's all right.'

'What sort of answer is that?' she cried in distress.

'I'm perfectly happy, Ma,' Silas lied, already at twelve adept. 'I've lots of friends,' he added, knowing that such a statement would assuage her fears. 'How is the street?' he asked sweetly, conscious that she thought it ugly.

'As ugly as ever.' Hebe glanced at him, wondering where he got that large nose. 'But you used to like it.'

'I do like it. It's full of secret people.'

'Hannah, Giles, Amy Tremayne.'

'And other people. You never seem to get to know them. Don't you think you might like some of them?'

'Not really.' Hebe spoke truthfully. 'I'm not sociable. I'm never at home long enough.'

'You think the street's too ugly to have anyone interesting living in it. I heard you say so to Hannah.'

'You make me sound snobbish.'

'We wouldn't be any different if we lived in another street.' Silas felt protective towards the street, which he found fascinating in its dark conformity.

'I would be different in a Georgian square or a country cottage,' said Hebe, thinking how different she was while away on her jobs. 'As long as it was beautiful.'

'It's home, you are there.'

Hebe was afraid to speak. One minute he snubs, the next he gives me courage. She wished she knew her mysterious child better.

'I am happy you like it,' she said. 'And,' she joked, 'if by some miracle a job turns up in mid-holidays you can see how you get on by yourself.'

'I'd get on all right.' He was serious.

'They always pay twice as much.' She hardly believed it was herself speaking. Would it be good for him to find out what it's like to be alone? 'You'd be alone,' she said, expecting him to protest.

'I'd get meals off Hannah or Amy if I needed to.' Silas mocked her, thinking that being alone would be wonderful, very different from the loneliness of school.

Nearing the steep street, Hebe feared she would never really know Silas. Then she remembered the nightmare of the day before and realised, as she stopped at her door, that she seldom experienced her panic when away working. She thought with amusement of her meeting with Mungo and was laughing as she drew up at her door, enjoying her fondness for Mungo.

'Here we are, my old Miracle,' and Silas too laughed, delighted to be back, glad that his mother was apparently unhurt.

'I'll change my clothes,' he said as they carried his luggage upstairs, 'then find Giles.' He was anxious to slot back into his home environment.

'I will get tea.' Hebe wished she was not shy with Silas, that he did not keep her at arm's length. He has inherited my secrecy and reticence, she thought. Then, remembering her unfortunate rencontre with Mungo, she wished it were possible to share the joke.

Silas came down wearing jeans and a T-shirt. 'D'you mind if I go and find Giles now?'

'There's a letter for you on the mantelshelf.'

Silas opened the letter. 'Oh, great!' he exclaimed. 'Magic! Michael Reeves' mother is asking me to stay. How brilliant!'

'Who is Michael Reeves?' Hebe felt a chill.

'A boy at school. They've taken a cottage on the Scilly Isles. They sail. You won't mind, will you? It's only for three weeks.'

'Three weeks?' She tried to keep her voice level. 'When?'

'That'll be terrific.' Silas was overjoyed. 'Three weeks' sailing. Just imagine, I've never sailed.'

'When?' She felt cold, he was sure he was going.

'She says to say what date suits you. She's quite nice. She came to the sports at half-term.'

'I was working and couldn't get away.' Hebe avoided school functions.

'You don't mind, do you?' Silas looked anxious. 'It's the boy who offered me a lift down.'

'I see.' She was stunned by disappointment.
'Sure you don't mind?' Silas assumed he would go, did not question.
'Of course I don't. It's very kind of Mrs Reeves.' I must not cling, she told herself. 'I must write to her. It will be fun for you.'
'Can't we telephone?' Silas was in a rush to fix a date, seize the opportunity, pin it down.
'Yes, love, we will telephone tonight.' She surrendered.
'Good. I'll be off now and find Giles.' Silas left the house, leaving all the doors open as he ran, hungry for life.
For several minutes Hebe was in misery. Then she made her decision. She would work. Not Mungo, that would be too soon, he would think he'd won a point. Mrs Fox would do, no complications there and quite good money. She was smiling when Silas came back, bringing Giles with him.
'And how was Paris?'
'Wonderful.' Giles was a masculine version of Hannah.
'Tea?'
'I've had mine.' Giles smiled, showing crooked teeth. Would George Scoop fix these for free if Hannah married him?
'Have another.'
'Thanks.' Giles was fond of his friend's mother, considered him lucky. 'I wish my mother was a cook.'
'It's a useful trade.' Hebe offered Giles cake. 'I shall go to Mrs Fox in Wiltshire while you are in the Scillies,' she said to Silas.
'Who is Mrs Fox?'
'One of the old ladies who can afford a cook now and then to jolly her up.'
'Will you be back when I come back from the Scillies?'
'I will be back,' she said. 'Of course I will.'

6

Mungo Duff quarrelled with Alison when Eli and Patsy left, perversely accusing her of selfishness in planning to leave him alone. While he was anxious that she should go to Santa Barbara he did not wish her to enjoy herself, though he hoped she would deceive him with Eli. She must go, feel grateful to him for parting with her, and return to cherish him with a guilty conscience. If he could find Hebe he would welcome Alison home with open arms; if he failed he would be in a strong position to play the injured husband. He hoped Eli would disappoint her in bed. Alistair and Ian were to visit friends, another source of recrimination. Alison had arranged their holiday without consulting him.

'They will grow up without knowing their parents,' he had protested. 'We might as well be divorced.'

'I often think,' Alison had answered, 'that children of the divorced see more of their parents than those of the undivorced, but is it a good thing? I can't see what benefit they would derive from you in your present mood. It is important,' she had added purposefully, aggravating, 'that they should make useful friends, then they will meet the right kind of girl. They can't start soon enough.'

'All right, go off, enjoy yourself. Leave me on my own.'

'You were invited too.' She had said this before.

'You know perfectly well I can't leave the office just now.'

'I do not. You often leave the office and pop down to London. Your office manages all right then.'

'I keep in touch. I am on business, anyway.' Mungo thought of how little business he did when he 'popped', as Alison called it, down to London: a token telephone call, a business lunch, the rest of the time spent with Hebe. He cursed Hebe's fiendish one-way system, her casual telephone call suggesting a date. Why did he put up with it, he asked himself, not bothering to answer, for if one thing was sure Hebe called the tune. 'And I pay,' he groaned.

Alison took him up. 'You know perfectly well I am paying for myself.'

'I didn't mean in money terms. I meant I pay in loneliness.'

'Go and see your mother, she's lonely, if anyone is.' Alison was unsympathetic. 'She'll probably have that woman she gets to cook for her.'

'I don't suppose so.' Mungo had already checked with his mother that Hebe was not coming until the autumn. 'No, dearest,' his mother had answered his next question, 'I don't know where she lives. Miss Thomson writes to a forwarding address in London. She comes three times a year, as you know, so that Miss Thomson can have time off.'

'Miss Thomson,' said Mungo to Alison, 'isn't due for a holiday.'

'Why can't you go when Miss Thomson is there?'

'Visitors are too much for her.'

'I don't believe that. She is always very welcoming to me.'

'And I don't believe that.' Mungo was determined to be disagreeable.

'Believe what you like. I am not going to let you spoil my trip.'

In bed Mungo lay thinking of Hebe. What had she been doing in Exeter? Had she not said, the year before, when, after her stint cooking for his mother she had let him take her for a week to Devonshire, that she had never been there? Had she not exclaimed with delight as he drove her through lanes frothy with cow parsley, bright with campion and bluebells? Had she been putting on an act? What had she been doing in the Clarence? Was she staying there with another man? Mungo groaned, remembering Hebe's long arms and legs wrapped round him in her lovely but casual embrace.

'Got a stomach ache?' Alison, half asleep in the next bed, roused herself.

'No, no.'

'Let a woman sleep, then. You drank too much at lunch yesterday. It always upsets you.'

'I can't wait for you to go to America,' Mungo shouted.

'All right, all right –' Feeling herself valued, Alison stretched in her bed, thinking it would do Mungo good to be without her. She was glad he minded her leaving him alone. She was unaware that for years Mungo had spent six weeks a year with Hebe, weeks when he was supposed to be on business in London. She had heard from friends that he was seen about with a girl, but since he came home sweet-tempered she had long since decided that London was good for him. Whoever he saw there presented no threat. She herself, when Mungo was absent, either had a room in the house decorated or went abroad with a friend to look at pictures and cathedrals. It was high time she altered the pattern. If Mungo could step out so could she.

While Alison slept Mungo searched his mind for ways to find Hebe, momentarily considering employing a private detective, deciding against as it would be too embarrassing. Hebe had not wronged him, all that was wrong was her bloody mysterious way of conducting their affair. Unable to sleep, he thought back to his first encounter with her years before. As he savoured the memory, Alison in the next bed snorted, turning away from him. It was thanks to Alison he had met Hebe and, oh God, Mungo groaned, having to be grateful to Alison was hard, for Alison was a good wife, albeit bossy. A wonderful manager, a good mother, a particularly good daughter-in-law, and this, combined with her bossiness, had brought Hebe into his life. His father, long dead, would have been amused, thought Mungo. His father who, satisfied with his own marriage, never strayed, had found the straits his friends got themselves into vastly amusing, recounting unfortunate incidents, illegitimate children to be provided for, abortions arranged, risky ailments – he always referred to venereal disease as a risky ailment – the expensive upkeep of mistresses hilariously funny. Mungo's father had strayed, thought Mungo, into sudden death, leaving his mother rich and lonely in their large house which he would in due course inherit and, the taxman permitting, pass on to his two sons at present at preparatory school, heading for Eton, Alison not considering his old school good enough.

Mungo lay listening to his wife breathing and thought of the time of his father's death, when Alison had taken charge, arranged the funeral, not bothering to make it look as though Mungo had arranged it, had written and answered letters, had comforted and consoled effortlessly, found a cook-housekeeper to run the large house, live-in with colour TV, her own car, regular days out and long holidays, for a modest salary. It was the holidays – a fortnight three times a year – which did the trick of keeping Miss Thomson happy, Alison emphasised, when describing her mother-in-law's arrangements. Then, Alison would explain to incompetent daughters-in-law, then the splendid extravagance of a temporary cook during Miss Thomson's absence, so that Lucy could entertain all the people she wished without annoying Miss Thomson, who liked a quiet routine. 'And here,' Alison would say, 'here I was in for a stroke of luck. I was recommended a woman. She comes when Miss Thomson goes away and everybody's happy.'

'Is it expensive?' Alison would be asked.

'Well worth it,' Alison would reply, not divulging the cook's salary. 'One is sometimes very lucky,' Alison would say in a satisfied voice which made Mungo choke, for Alison's good luck was also his. When seven years ago he had visited his mother without warning, she had said, 'Darling, how lovely to see you. Go and tell the cook you will be here for dinner. Miss Thomson is on holiday.'

Mungo had been bemused. 'Do we have cooks in this day and age?'

'Didn't Alison tell you? You will find her in the kitchen; tell her you are here.'

And there in the kitchen had been Hebe. The only bloody nuisance, thought Mungo, listening to Alison in the next bed, was that Hebe only appeared when Miss Thomson went away, not when Alison decided to go to Santa Barbara, thus giving him a gorgeous opportunity of seeing her, a golden chance he looked like missing. Mungo wondered whether his mother did, possibly, have an address other than the forwarding address he had himself. He could say he had a friend who had a mother in similar circumstances who needed a temporary cook. He could, perhaps, extract Hebe's address in some other crafty way. It did seem so stupid not to know where she lived. Unable to sleep, he remembered Hebe as he had first seen her.

He had gone into the kitchen expecting a middle-aged frump and found Hebe rolling pastry, intent. She had not heard him. He had time to take in the sight of a tall girl in a pink striped dress and white apron, a parody of a cook. She had glossy dark hair cut shoulder length and a full mouth. She had the largest, darkest eyes he had ever seen. She smiled and he quite simply fell in love and determined to seduce her.

This had not proved immediately easy. To start with, Mungo questioned his mother after dinner – the best dinner he had ever eaten under her roof – as to where she had found so excellent a cook. He had been surprised that she was Alison's discovery, though not surprised that he had not been told about it.

'Dear Alison,' said Mungo's mother. 'She took so much trouble. She interviewed at least six people. This girl was the only one who would agree to fit in with Miss Thomson. Miss Thomson plans to go away in spring, summer and autumn. Apparently her plans suit Hebe. Alison took a lot of trouble. Now she does not have to trouble any more.'

Mungo noted the repetition of the word 'trouble' and wondered if his mother was as fond of Alison as she professed.

'So all Miss Thomson has to do is make her own arrangements.'

'I should think she'd do that anyway.'

'Yes, dear.' Mrs Duff did not rise further than a slight swirl in the conversational pool.

'Where does she come from?'

'I have not asked. I do not believe in prying.'

'Did she have references?'

'I believe Alison found she was connected in some way with a woman who worked for your father, all very respectable. She is obviously –'

'Obviously what?' Mungo knew what his mother hesitated to say. He wanted to see whether she would describe Hebe as one of us, a lady, or some similar euphemism such as a nice girl.

'Well, darling, educated.'

'Lots of girls are educated.'

'You know quite well what I mean.'

'Even servants.'

'She isn't a servant,' Mrs Duff protested.

'Then what is she?'

'Darling, don't be boring.' Lucy Duff had changed the subject.

During the two days he spent with his mother Mungo made frequent attempts at conversation with Hebe. She was polite but busy. She did not eat with his mother as Miss Thomson did and when not at work vanished in her car. Mungo ran out of excuses to visit the kitchen and left after two days determined to put the girl out of his mind. She remained in it and a week later he came back to see his mother using the excuse of a hiccup in her income tax. Lucy Duff was not deceived and secretly wished him joy. While taking advantage of Alison's bossiness and capability, she did not like her any the better for it. Let Mungo have some fun.

Finding Hebe preparing dinner, Mungo rushed straight to the point. 'I have come back to ask you to sleep with me.'

Stirring the sauce she was making, Hebe glanced up and said, 'I won't sleep with you here.'

'Why not?'

'Not in your mother's house.'

'But you will?' Mungo stared at her.

'When I leave here we can go to an hotel.'

'You will – oh my God!' Mungo felt exhilarated, couldn't believe his ears.

'I'll see what it's like then –'

'You'll see what what's like?'

'I'll see,' Hebe was patient, 'whether I like sleeping with you. We can come to an arrangement if I do and you want to go on with it.'

'Oh.' He was deflated by her calm tone.

'I can't do it for nothing. I have to earn my living. I am very expensive.'

'Are you a prostitute, then?' Mungo was puzzled, excited.

'I'm a cook but if you want I'll give you a try.'

'Give *me* a try!' Mungo exclaimed.

'It's you who asked me, not me you.' She seemed so calm, so detached.

'Please.' Mungo put his arm round her and tried to nuzzle her neck.

'Mind my sauce.' She pushed him away with her elbow. He saw she was smiling. 'We will spend a few days together, see how it goes.' She stirred the sauce. 'Then, if I'm happy, we will discuss money.'

'If *you* are happy.'

'You will be happy all right. I have to think of me.' Had she been mocking him? 'I am a very expensive cook,' she said. 'The same applies to bed.'

Mungo did not grudge her a penny. All he minded was her secrecy. He was no wiser now than when he first met her. He did not know where she came from or where she went when they parted. Meeting her in Exeter was the first clue he had in all the years. Why was she wearing spectacles? What was she doing in Exeter, he asked himself, as futilely he wooed sleep. He knew she did other cooking jobs, that she had other lovers. He groaned with anger and frustration.

'Do stop waking me. If you can't sleep go to the dressing-room,' Alison scolded. 'Take a digestive pill.'

'Your snorting keeps me awake.'

'I don't snore.'

'I said snort, silly bitch.' Mungo got furiously out of bed and made for the dressing-room. Would Eli put up with Alison's snorts? Hebe never snorted or snored. Trying to settle in the dressing-room bed he resolved once more to pump his mother. She must know of something of Hebe's background.

7

Louisa Fox recognised Hebe's voice when she picked up the receiver. 'Hebe, how nice to hear your voice.'

'I wondered whether you would like me to come during August. I have a cancellation, so I just –'

'Thought you might come to me?'

'Yes, I –'

Louisa was enthusiastic. 'What day will you come? It will be a treat.'

'Would the seventh to the twenty-first suit you? Have you got your little book handy?'

'Not necessary. August is a month when I lie low. We shall be on our own.'

'Oh good. I'll arrive in the evening and bring a dinner to cook.'

'I shall look forward to it. You can tell me your news when you come.' Not, thought Louisa Fox, that that girl ever has anything to tell. She switched on the television for the news and wondered whether to ring Lucy Duff. While she thought about this the news reader led her through world disasters to the weather man. She dialled Lucy's number.

'Lucy, that you? Listen, I have the treasure coming in August. Am I not lucky?'

'I thought you never got her in August. I can't. I supposed she had a child for the holidays or another job. I never get her at Christmas or Easter. Miss Thomson has to arrange spring, summer and autumn. She was here in May. Two blissful greedy weeks. Can I come and stay?'

'I don't think so. I will get her to stuff my deep freeze; come later on. Did Mungo visit you while she was with you?'

'No, Alison had him on the lead.'

'Really tied?' Both women laughed.

'How do I know?' said Mungo's mother. 'Maggie Cook-Popham's Dick swears he saw Mungo with Hebe in London.'

'Did he indeed? Where did he see them?'

'Walking in Kew Gardens.'

'When was she with Maggie? Don't tell me her boy –'

'I bet he tried, though if he had succeeded the whole world would hear and that wouldn't suit –'

'Wouldn't suit Hebe. Does Mungo ever –'

'Never breathes a word. Wouldn't dare say anything in case I let something slip to Alison, as if I would.'

'As if you would.' The old women, separated by miles of wire, laughed.

'We are not like Maggie,' said Lucy. 'Though for news that doesn't matter, telling Maggie certainly saves stamps.'

'Wouldn't it be a good thing if you could get Hebe to come in the holidays? Your grandchildren would love her food. If she is coming to me in August it may mean she is not tied in the holidays, as you thought,' suggested Louisa.

'I am not having the little beasts to stay,' cried Lucy. 'Not until they are a lot older.'

'Heavens, why not?'

'They picked all the buttons off my Victorian chairs.'

Suppressing her inclination to laugh, Louisa said, 'How dreadful. What possessed them?' Lucy must have annoyed the little beasts in some way.

'Alison is going away. I gather she is sending them to stay with friends. Mungo is hopeless with them, he shouts and they laugh. She is sending them to people who stand no nonsense.'

'They will be better when they grow older,' opined Louisa.

'One hopes so.' Lucy was doubtful. 'We must remember your telephone bill,' she said, hinting that Louisa had talked long enough.

'Goodbye,' said Louisa, ringing off. It takes the rich to remind one of bills, she thought. Mungo would one day be rich. Louisa considered him fortunate if he was having an affair with Hebe. It was old history now, and it would hurt Lucy to know she had been second choice. Mungo's father had asked her to marry him before he asked Lucy. Mungo might never have existed, since I am barren, and if I am right and Hebe is Christopher's grandchild she might not exist either. Louisa was surprised that Lucy had never noticed Hebe's extraordinary likeness to Christopher Rutter, starchy, pompous, upright, who had long ago proposed marriage and had been surprised and angry when she refused him. He had married a girl as upright as himself. Calculating dates, Lucy decided Hebe was probably a granddaughter, child of the daughter killed in the air crash. Suspecting Hebe's provenance, Louisa forbore telling her friend, since Lucy, who reproached others of gossip, could gossip with the best, and Hebe, for reasons best known to herself, never spoke of her family or friends, not even of Bernard who, by coincidence, knew Hebe since he lived in the same part of the country. Louisa did not think it necessary for Hebe to know of her friendship with Bernard. Bernard was amused by Hebe, she knew, and loved her. Lucy would be fascinated by any connection with Christopher Rutter and gossip. Recommending Hebe as a temporary cook who also worked for Maggie Cook-Popham, Lucy had said, 'Not only is she the most marvellous cook, but she's a lady,' using the expression which Mungo deplored. Since Hebe never discussed her clients Louisa respected her reticence, believing she travelled from one post to another. While she joked about Mungo with his mother, she would not have credited him as a business transaction. If she considered Hebe's and Mungo's affair, she thought of it as a bit of fun for the girl and for Mungo, married to managing Alison, a well deserved treat. She would have been astonished to hear the difference in the rates for mistresses compared with cooks.

Looking forward to Hebe's cooking, Louisa welcomed Hebe's visit, blessing the day when Lucy had suggested she should give her a trial. Lucy, thought Louisa with a pang of envy, could afford permanent Miss Thomson whereas she herself could only just manage Hebe's exorbitant fees once or twice a year. She was quite unaware that Hebe, liking her, charged her less than Lucy and charged Maggie Cook-Popham, whom she neither liked nor trusted, very much more.

While Louisa telephoned Lucy Duff and looked forward to Hebe's cooking, Hebe enjoyed the short time there was with

Silas before he went to the Scillies, happy to watch him relax from the taut boy back from school, glad that he had a friend in Giles. Though hurt at first by Silas' defection, she found herself looking forward to a fortnight in Wiltshire; better to be busy than sit at home wondering how he was enjoying himself. Meeting Mungo in Exeter had alarmed her. It was possible he might find some lead to her whereabouts. If she was away in Wiltshire it lessened his chances of finding her. She was fond of Louisa Fox, loved her house, enjoyed working for her. But she reckoned without Miss Thomson, who resented hints that the girl who took her place provided imaginative meals and was not opposed to Lucy entertaining her friends, a thing she was not prepared to do, feeling martyred if anyone came for a drink, morning coffee or tea. She feared Hebe, resenting Lucy referring to her as 'a treasure' or, worse, 'my lady cook'. Listening on the extension to Louisa's conversation with Lucy enraged her. The jealousy she already felt of Hebe lit a latent talent for mischief. Preparing the supper she would presently share with her employer, Miss Thomson considered the theory she had hitherto dismissed as absurd of Mungo and Alison divorcing, of Mungo marrying Hebe and of Hebe either superseding her permanently or losing her job in some sly way. Miss Thomson was saving to retire to a flat on the Spanish Costa. Fearing any interference with her plan, she decided to poke an apparently innocent spoke in Hebe's wheel. She chose a postcard, addressed it to Alison and wrote:

'Dear Mrs Duff: Should you wish to contact H. Rutter, the temporary cook, she will be working for Mrs Fox in Wiltshire from the 7th to 21st. Yrs. Truly, A. Thomson.'

Reading this, Miss Thomson hoped that Alison would wonder, What on earth does this postcard from Miss Thomson mean? Is it a warning? She would grow more alert, with luck make trouble for Hebe, leave Miss Thomson in peace to complete her savings. It can do no harm, thought Miss Thomson, opening a can of soup, it doesn't exactly say anything but in Alison's shoes I would have a little think.

The card dropped through the letter-box an hour after Alison's departure for the States. Reading it, Mungo whooped with delight.

8

Hebe let herself in to Amy's house, her spirits lifting with affection.

'Hullo, love.' She kissed Amy. 'I've sent the boys out for the day. Gave them sandwiches.'

'In the rain?'

'Never mind the rain. Have you seen Hannah?'

'Gone to her elocution lesson.' Amy grinned. 'Teeth, name, now it's her speech has to change.'

'If it makes her happy.' Hebe sat beside Amy. She looked round, noticing that Amy's paperweights, banished by Hannah, were back on the windowsill where the colours caught the sun.

'Where did you buy those lovelies?' She stroked the old woman's hand.

'Given to me, I did not buy them.'

'Ah.'

'Valuable now, you know.' Amy was complacent. 'Where are you going tomorrow?'

'To Mrs Fox. It's better to earn a bob or two than sit around moping while Silas is away.'

'Who will mind Trip? Would you like me to feed her?'

'Terry's going to feed her.'

'Ho, Terry,' Amy mocked. 'That one!'

'I've brought the rent.' Hebe handed an envelope to the old woman.

Amy counted the money. 'You paying a year in advance or something? This is far too much.'

'I got a bonus. Please take it.'

'Who from?' Amy looked at Hebe, black eyes glinting. 'Not that blackamoor?'

'A bonus from *Terry*.' Hebe grinned. 'A goodbye present.'

'Leaving you, is he?' Amy was curious.

'Still friends. He's – er – moving on.'

'Queer, isn't he?'

'A little fantastic –'

'You're fond of him, aren't you?'

'He makes me laugh. We read poetry.'

'So you've told me. Love poems.'

'And others, too. He's passed his O-level.'

'Failed last time, didn't he?'

'I failed mine!' Hebe looked distressed.

'Took him on to annoy the old man, didn't you? Couldn't resist the combination of a black boy with a failed exam.'

'It began that way,' Hebe said stiffly. 'He's become a good friend.'

'What's he do? Still burglar alarms?'

'He is self-employed, goes solo now.'

'Like you.'

'Like me.' Hebe returned Amy's look calmly and added gently, 'Like us.'

Amy squeezed Hebe's hand. 'I never set about it like you. Didn't read poetry and play backgammon. Didn't call the tune. I don't know how you get away with it.'

Hebe looked away, not answering.

'Lovely girls like you should get married. Hannah wants to re-marry.'

'Her dentist.'

'But she finds him dull. Edward Krull was dull, she doesn't want to repeat her error.'

'Oh, do you know someone who knows him?' Hebe was surprised into gossip, not surprised when Amy did not answer. She sat in the small sitting-room in the house which Amy had made home for her in her time of crisis, sheltering her until after Silas' birth, later renting her the house across the street. 'What would I have done without you, Amy?'

'You'd have managed.'

'You saved us.'

'Don't exaggerate. If not me it would have been somebody else. You had got yourself into a fuss, that's all.'

'Fuss.' Hebe thought fuss an understatement. She said, 'There was nobody else. No, Amy, you saved us all right, then started me on the right track.'

'Few people would call it the right track,' Amy laughed delightedly.

'You introduced me to Bernard.'

'The old bastard. We could have managed without him,' Amy sniffed.

'He bought my things, didn't cheat me, introduced me to the job at the hotel.'

'Some job. I grant he did not cheat. He had no business to let you meet that Hippolyte. You could have worked for Lucy Duff and Louisa Fox.'

'I do work for them.'

'Decent people. I worked for them when they needed a secretary before –'

'My grandfather.' Hebe spoke stiffly.

'Thought you didn't like him mentioned.'

'I don't.'

'Well, then. What did that chef teach you that you had not learned at the Cordon Bleu?'

'Soufflés.' Hebe remembered Hippolyte. 'You laugh, you relax, you enjoy, you rise, light, generous, delicious, ready for a second helping.' 'He taught me how to make soufflés,' she said gravely.

'Ho,' said Amy, doubtful still. 'Ho.'

Changing the subject, Hebe said, 'I'm dropping Mrs Cook-Popham, Amy. I don't like her son. I'm okay with Mrs Fox and Mrs Duff and the odd job.'

'I distrust the odd jobs.'

'I enjoy them,' said Hebe, blithely thinking of Mungo and Hippolyte, regretting Terry. 'It's the odd jobs that make the money as you –'

'As I should know. Odd jobs don't last,' said Amy sadly, remembering in old age the delights of waking up in the double bed in the Hôtel d'Angleterre, the laughter, the rising sun glinting through the red plush curtains, the coffee and croissants. 'They don't last,' she said in bitter recollection of the lonely journey home to London, the quack doctor in Battersea, the pain and anguish. 'They don't last. That's why I became a secretary.'

'And worked for the Duffs and Foxes and my grandfather,' said Hebe sombrely. She could remember Amy the secretary, but found it hard to visualise Amy in her career in Paris. Who was the man who let her down, she wondered, and heard for a second those other voices asking, 'Who was the man?' and 'Have an abortion.'

'Shall I make us some tea?' She stood up to break the spell.

'Yes, love.' Amy watched Hebe put on the kettle, lay out cups. She wondered for the millionth time who Silas' father could be. One would think, if one had not seen the child born, that the man had never existed. She tells me about her lovers, thought Amy. Those grandparents had not found out. Fools, always on at the child, 'Don't mumble, don't interrupt,' always 'Don't'. And 'Hold yourself up,' 'Don't stoop.'

Hebe, warming the pot, spooning tea, reaching for the kettle, thought, So Amy had an abortion. If she hadn't her child would be older than me, middle-aged. She handed Amy her cup.

'I keep my life narrow. It's better that way.' She was defensive. 'I stick to business.'

'Yes.' Amy took the cup. 'I suppose it is best.'

'I save a lot of money.'

'A bank balance is nice,' Amy agreed.

'I am getting Silas educated. That's what is important.'

'Yes.' Amy's thoughts were years away. Why did I panic? she asked herself. Out loud she exclaimed, 'The bastard!'

'What?' Hebe was startled.

'I loved a bastard. He was not the marrying kind.'

'As you know I think love should be avoided.' Hebe's tone made Amy laugh.

'Well,' she said, 'I have you, I have Silas and now Giles and Hannah, Hannah believes in love; that's why she has changed her name and her teeth and is learning to talk posh. Hannah believes in marriage, but she ain't got *chien*. Perhaps in marriage you don't need *chien*.'

'What's *chien*?'

'It's indefinable, sort of smell, what was called sex appeal in my day.'

'Smell?' Hebe looked thoughtful. 'I bet you had *chien*.' She searched Amy's face for the girl concealed by old age.

'Not enough to hold him,' said Amy. 'He loved somebody else.'

'At the same time?' Hebe was shocked.

'You're a fine one to talk, with your collection.'

'But I don't love. Love's disaster. I am an entertainer.'

'You certainly entertain me. I live a vicarious life these days. Got Silas' address in the Islands in case of need?'

'I have it for you. The people are called Reeves. They sound all right.'

'In what way?'

'Oh, you know.' Hebe looked away.

'The right sort?' Amy's tone made Hebe flush.

'Yes, I suppose so.' She stood up, hesitating, unwilling to leave Amy's atmosphere of serenity. She bent to kiss the old woman. 'You would have made a wonderful wife.'

'Not to him. Some men should never marry. I realise that now.'

Hebe wondered how much Amy had suffered to acquire wisdom. 'Some women, too,' she suggested. 'Perhaps I am one.'

'From the way you are shaping you may well be. Your career –'

'Now, Amy, don't start on "my career".'

'Certainly not my sort.'

'Hannah will marry George Scoop.'

'Hannah may not be as sensible as you think,' said Amy. 'I rather hope not. That dentist does not deserve Hannah.'

'Not good enough for her?'

'She is not right for him.'

'Gosh! Why?'

'She would treat him as she treated Edward Krull.'

'How do you know?'

'You have to be a saint to tolerate bores. She is set on marriage though.'

Hebe stood, considering Hannah's relatively simple life. 'I must fly.' She kissed Amy goodbye.

'Goodbye.' Amy was comparing Hannah's intention of

marrying with Hebe's mode of life, which to her mind did less damage. She chuckled, thinking, She does enjoy herself. She said out loud, her eyes reflecting the glint of sun on her paperweights: 'She entertains, she enjoys variety.' She spoke to the paperweights as to a living person. 'And she makes people happy.' Amy kept these thoughts to herself, having no one to share them with.

9

It is against my nature to confide more than the minimum to Amy, thought Hebe, sorting Silas' clothes for him to take on his visit. She wondered whether there was someone somewhere from whom it would not be necessary to guard her tongue. She piled Silas' clothes on the bed and took what was necessary to iron down to the kitchen. Putting up the ironing board, plugging in the iron, she thought of Mungo. Amy approved of Mungo, she was obviously doubtful about Terry. Was it not Terry who had encouraged her to call her clients The Syndicate, finding the joke in dubious taste. But would she approve of Mungo if she knew how foul his language could be, that he boasted ridiculously of the size of his member. Testing the heat of the iron, Hebe thought of Mungo with tolerant affection. Amy likes it when he takes me to Wimbledon, she thought, and the movies and the opera. He is very generous, always pays up without a murmur when I beat him at backgammon. I jolly him along, she thought, ironing Silas' T-shirts. I make him more fun for his family, better for his wife. Go home and practise, I say, you've had a nice change. Hebe folded the T-shirts, reached for some pillowcases, squirted water to damp them. She likes Mungo's class, she thought, smoothing the pillowcases, she knows Hippolyte was born a peasant, refers to him slightingly as Hippo. I call him Hippo to show fondness. He enjoys me, finds me funny. Hebe pressed the iron on the pillowcase. He gives me free lunches in his restaurant on my day off when I'm working for Maggie Cook-Popham, pretends he doesn't know me when I appear in his restaurant. Hebe chortled in recollection of Hippolyte's face when she had come not alone but with a potential client. He succeeded very neatly in putting me off the poor man. I was not planning to do more than tease. I was bored with the man, that was all. Who had it been, what had been his name? Folding the pillowcases Hebe racked her brain. There had been quite a number of potential members tried and found wanting. '*Il y a toujours l'un qui baise et l'autre qui tend la joue.*' Grandfather used to say, 'Well, old man, it is I who *tend la joue.*' I am making a pretty profit in this career you suggested for me and getting Silas educated. There had been failures, Hebe admitted to herself. There was the man who had taken her to Rome for the weekend, dined her in the Piazza Navona: *prosciutto con figi*, a marvellous risotto, mountain strawberries. But he drank too much Soave, did not know its fatal effect. He had become alarmingly drunk, uncontrollably tiresome back at the hotel. I am not proud of that one, thought Hebe, switching off the iron. It was a dirty trick to throw all his trousers, shoes and pants out of the window, but what else could a girl do? I had to get away. I told Hippolyte about that one, she thought. He was so pleased he invited me to dinner with his partner. I never told Amy. I can't remember what he looked like, she thought, leaning on the ironing board. Some sort of English outdoor type? She shook her head, remembering Edward, head clerk in a solicitor's office, who did his wife's ironing every Saturday, ironing out the clients' marital dramas in imagination. There had been something sinister about him; she had not wanted him to start ironing out her troubles. Hebe folded the board and put it away. 'Keep them keen,' she said to Trip, who came mewing through the cat-flap. 'Limit them to two weeks at most. With Mungo three times a year, four or five trips to Paris with Hippolyte and my cooking we are okay. I shan't really miss Terry. I can still see him. Can't put so much aside for the rainy day or Silas' university, that's all. It's a far cry,' she said, picking up the purring cat, 'from flogging my mother's pearls and Social Security. Not that I ever intended to depend on that!' The cat jumped out of her arms to lap milk from her saucer. 'It's an enjoyable life,' Hebe said to the cat, 'but I wish Silas wasn't going away.'

'Who is this you are taking me to see?' Sitting in the bus beside Silas, Giles wiped the steam from the window with his sleeve.

'An old man in a cottage miles from anywhere. He's got the

most fabulous things. He is very old. He is called Bernard Quigley. He has a dog called Feathers and a cat. He's my friend. I found him when I was exploring across country.'

'Is he a relation?'

'I have no relations.' Silas stared at the passing country.

'You must have. I've got lots of relations in America and Amy's Mum's aunt. Everybody has relations.'

'We don't.'

'You must have. Why don't you have relations?' Giles persisted.

'Don't be boring. I don't have any.'

'Ask your mum. Doesn't she tell you about them? My mother tells me all about her father and mother, what they did and everything.'

'Boring. We get off here.' Silas led Giles out of the bus at the stop near a telephone kiosk forlornly posed at a crossroads. Rain was pelting down; the boys pulled up the hoods of their anoraks.

'We go across here.' Silas climbed a gate into a field.

'Isn't there a path?'

'No.'

Silas led the way through wet grass. Water seeped into their shoes, which squelched. 'Should have worn wellies.'

Giles persisted. 'Surely your father had relations? Hasn't your mum kept up with them?'

'No.'

'Why? Hasn't she told you about them? My mother tells me about my father. She wants to put me off him.'

'We climb this.' Silas leapt at a bank and scrambled over it, dropping down into a field of kale. Giles followed. Silas trudged on, the tall kale brushing against his shoulders.

'Surely,' Giles nagged, 'she's told you about your father.'

'Nothing, I told you.' Silas let a kale plant swish back to hit Giles' face.

'But when you ask?' Giles mopped his face.

'I don't. She never brings up the subject, so it's not there.' Silas pushed on through the kale.

'Perhaps you were born in a test tube like those kids in Australia.'

'They didn't do it twelve years ago.'

'Might have done. What else could you be?'

'Son of a murderer? Artificial insemination?'

'Secret agent, titled bloke of some kind, pop star.'

'If I were I'd get maintenance, like your mum.'

'That's boring, too. Mine goes on and on about my father. One of these days I shall run away, live with him in America.'

'You do that. Here's Feathers.' Silas squatted down to greet the large wet dog who had appeared out of the mist. 'We have ham sandwiches. You like ham.' Feathers pranced back a pace then came forward and licked Silas' face. He had large ears with strands of hair round the edges. His tail, long and feathery, waved so that a swirl of drops swished from side to side of his chocolate brown body. 'This is Giles,' Silas told the dog.

Giles patted the dog then followed Silas to a clump of trees bent sideways by the prevailing south-wester. From the trees rose a drift of smoke. 'He's in.' Silas trotted to a wall and began to climb, putting his feet neatly between the stones. Giles followed. Silas called in his high child's voice:

'Mr Quigley, Mr Quigley, are you there?'

Bernard Quigley stood in his porch. 'I did not expect visitors on a day like this. Come and get dry by the fire.'

'I just thought we would visit. This is Giles Krull. I am going away tomorrow to the Scillies for three weeks.'

'What does your mother say to that?' Bernard peered into Silas' face.

'She's pleased for me. I shall be sailing. She's going to do a job for a couple of weeks.'

'Where?' The old man moved jerkily about his tiny sitting-room, pushing the boys near the fire, fetching glasses from a cupboard, a bottle of sherry.

'To some old girl called Fox.'

'Fox.' The old man glanced quickly at the boy. 'Get by the fire. Don't let the dog take up too much room. He's wet too. Have a drink, dear boys, a drink won't do you any harm. You're old enough. Eleven, are you?'

'Twelve.' Silas held his hands towards the fire.

'Well then, drink up.'

The boys tasted the sherry, trying to hide their distaste.

'You'll like it when you are grown up.' The old man

observed them as he drank, emptying his glass in one gulp, quickly refilling it.

Giles was fascinated by Bernard Quigley. He was small, stooping and old. His face had fallen in in some places and filled out in others so that the original proportions were lost. His nose, once an aristocratic curve, had taken hold and jutted out above a gentle mouth, putting large hooded eyes into shaded misproportion. His hair hung wispily round his collar. He wore brown trousers, a collarless shirt and braces which hung down over shrunken shanks, like the harness of a horse too old to work waiting for the knacker. His straggling moustache was stained with snuff.

'I knew your father,' he said to Giles. 'Edward Krull.'

'Oh, did you?' Giles, beginning to steam, moved away from the fire. 'When?'

'When he was at university.' The old man took a snuff box from his waistcoat pocket and said: 'Edward Krull, so dull, dull, dull. They sent him to America.'

'Who did?' Giles was not used to bluntness from the old.

'His friends.' Bernard Quigley searched Giles' face for a likeness to his father. 'But you don't look like him,' he said, adding, after a pause, 'fortunately.'

'I thought he was supposed to be good-looking.' Giles was defensive.

'I grant you that.' Bernard Quigley dismissed good looks. 'He was good-looking all right, but what's the use of that in the dark, ask your mother?'

'In the dark?'

'In bed, dear boy. Perhaps you don't know about bed yet. Have your balls dropped?'

'What?' Giles retreated towards the fire.

'Your voice hasn't broken. Never mind. Think what's ahead of you, all that glorious copulation.' He eyed Giles speculatively. Giles grew pink.

'That's a lovely snuff box.' Silas, anxious for his friend, tried to distract Bernard's attention.

'George II. Belonged to my grandfather.' The old man showed the box to Silas, snatching it back before he could touch it. 'I will show you my things when we have had lunch. I have a lot of food in the house.'

'Can I help?' Silas offered.

'No, no, get dry and give your sandwiches which your lovely mother gave you to the dog.'

Silas laid the sandwiches in front of Feathers, who sniffed cautiously and began to eat, more it seemed from good manners than hunger.

Giles looked round the room. Chippendale chairs elbowed Sheraton, occasional tables overlapped one another, laden with porcelain, silver, jade. Every wall space was hung with paintings and mirrors which reflected the light from the fire. There was barely room for an oil lamp on the table near the old man's chair. Several candelabra stood on the floor, messy with candle grease.

Across the hall they could hear Bernard moving about.

'Do you think he likes snuff or just wants to use his snuff box?' Giles whispered, overawed.

'I should think he made himself like it, just as he likes this.' Silas poured the contents of his glass on to the rug.

'Won't he smell it?' Giles felt uneasy as he copied his friend.

'The smell of the paraffin lamp will drown it.' Silas watched Feathers sniff the wet patch then return to his snack.

'I never knew my father was dull.' Giles mulled Bernard's insult. 'My mother's said a lot of things. She never said he was dull.'

'Puts you off America, does it?' Silas asked, cheerfully spiteful.

'Come and have lunch,' Bernard called. Silas and Giles joined him in the dining-room which was as crowded as the sitting-room. Giles, counting the chairs, noted there was a set of ten with carvers. Some of the chairs were stacked, giving the room the appearance of a sale-room. Bernard had laid three places. Giles looked at the silver and cut glass. 'Is all this very valuable?'

'You don't ask the value of things, you admire their beauty, rarity, workmanship.'

'Sorry.' Giles was abashed.

'You'll learn. Now eat up, the food's delicious, not like the stuff Hebe put in your sandwiches.'

'What a wonderful ham.' Silas regarded a ham Bernard stood poised to carve.

'Sent by post.' The old man carved rapidly. 'Girlfriend of mine sends it from Wiltshire, it's specially cured. The pig's right buttock is more tender than the left, it scratches with the left.'

'How does the postman get here? There's no road.' Giles accepted a plate of ham, wondering meanwhile about the pig's buttocks.

'The man has feet. He walks.' The boy is like his father, thought Bernard.

'In all weathers?' Giles persisted.

'Of course he walks. I have my coffee posted, peaches in syrup, Stilton cheese, all the things that matter. Have some salad, make your bowels work.'

'They do, thank you.' Silas helped himself to lettuce. 'My mother's a good cook.'

'Get constipated at school?'

'Sometimes,' Silas answered gravely.

Giles, disconcerted by the train of talk, asked, 'Did you never have a road?'

'Of course there was a road.' Bernard Quigley was crushing, shooting a sharp glance at Giles, wondering whether he was going to like this boy sitting there looking so healthy and young opposite himself, so haunched and shrunken, his life behind him.

'What happened to it?' Giles felt impelled to ask.

'I let the grass grow. People might use it. People might visit me.'

'We are visiting you,' Silas said, grinning.

'But you've taken the trouble to jump a few banks, get yourselves wet. Your mother comes.'

'I didn't know.' Silas looked surprised. 'I thought you only knew me.'

'I know lots of people. Keep them separate, that's all. Your mother's like that. Makes life easier.'

'How?' Giles' mouth was full of ham, Bernard noticed. A bad mark there. Surely table manners still mattered.

'They do not discuss you behind your back if you keep them separate. Silas' mother may find her life easier to manage that way; other people such as your dull Krull father are gregarious. Have some figs in syrup or cheese. You can have both, of course.'

The meal continued in quasi-silence, Giles ill at ease, Silas content. As he ate Giles looked round the room. 'You have no electricity,' he observed.

'Right. No electricity. Well water. No drains. No road. Any other queries?' Bernard stared at Giles offensively.

'He wasn't exactly querying.' Silas felt Bernard Quigley was about to badger his friend. 'I like your house as it is,' he said.

'Sure?' The old man looked suspicious.

'Quite sure.'

'Then I'll show you some of my treasures. Sit by the fire.' Bernard led the way into the sitting-room with his braces flapping.

'Your braces are hanging down.' Giles was diffident now.

'More convenient,' said the old man ambiguously as he opened a drawer in a Sheraton desk. 'You can look at these things while I have a snooze.' He handed a box to Silas, sat back in a wing chair and fell asleep.

Crouching in front of the fire, the boys inspected rings, watches, early sovereigns, diamond brooches, a large emerald set with diamonds, medals, Battersea boxes wrapped in tissue and jewelled bracelets.

'Must be worth a bomb,' whispered Giles. 'These medals alone.'

Bernard Quigley woke and observed the children.

Giles sat back on his heels and stared at his host. 'Where does all this come from?' He waved his hand round the room.

'My work. I live in my bank.'

Giles' eyes widened. 'A burglar?'

'Certainly not. I am a dealer. You look very pretty.' He smiled at Silas, showing beige teeth, amused by the boy who had put the rings on his fingers and the bracelets round his wrists. 'Wait a moment,' he said, jumping up. 'I've got a tiara in the kitchen drawer.' He left the room.

'What did he say?' Giles stared at his friend.

'A tiara,' said Silas.

'What's a tiara?'

The old man came back carrying a plastic bag from which he took a tiara. He set it on Silas' head. 'Keep still or it will fall off.'

Silas, cross-legged by the fire, sat looking at the old man. The diamonds and emeralds twinkled in the firelight. Giles gasped.

'Beautiful.' The old man snatched the tiara off Silas' head and put it back in its wrapping. 'Now,' he said in a practical tone, 'would you chop me some wood before you go? Stack it in the shed.'

'Of course.' Silas stood up, took off the rings and bracelets, putting them back in their box, which he placed on Bernard Quigley's knee. 'Thank you.' The boy and the old man looked at each other. Giles felt excluded.

'Trot off home when you've chopped the wood. Come and see me again.' Giles felt the invitation was not for him.

'Thank you for lunch,' he said. Then, unable to repress his curiosity, he said, 'In what way was my father boring?'

'He talked about money, he was respectable, he was conventional.' The old man spat out the epithets then, noticing Giles' stricken face, he relented. 'A bit of cross-pollination has done you no harm.' He edged the boys to the door and pushed them out into the rain, shutting the door behind them.

'Come on, chop, chop.' Silas led the way to the wood pile and set about chopping wood, stacking it in a neat pile. Sulkily Giles helped him. When they had finished they set off across the fields towards the bus stop.

'If my father's a bore,' said Giles, the cruel description rankling, 'what's yours?'

'A mystery,' Silas answered shortly.

'You mean you really don't know?'

Silas turned on his friend and hit him on the nose. Taken unawares, Giles sat down, getting wetter than before. His eyes watered.

'There's the bus.' Silas began to run. Giles got up and followed.

'Perhaps you are adopted,' he yelled as he ran, the rain mingling with blood from his nose, which had begun to bleed. 'I thought you were just a bastard,' he shouted as he followed Silas on to the bus. Silas fought his way forward and sat beside a tourist so that there was no room for Giles, who stood miserably in the crowded aisle, jostled by strangers. Seeing his plight, a woman handed him a tissue which he held to his nose.

When they reached the town they walked up the street on opposite sides. As Silas came level with his door Giles called out, 'See you when you come back?' in questioning tones.

Silas called back warmly, 'Of course,' and went into the house.

Giles found he was still clutching the blood-stained tissue and threw it into the gutter.

'Litterbug.' Silas had reappeared as though about to say something. He stood in the doorway smiling, then shrugged as though he'd changed his mind and went in again.

Late in the evening the rain stopped. Bernard Quigley, followed by Feathers, picked his way through the fields to the call box.

When Louisa answered the telephone she sounded breathless, 'Hullo.'

'Are you all right?' Bernard spoke without preliminary. 'Having trouble with your heart?'

'I rushed in from the garden. There's so much to do. Why are you ringing up? Has something gone wrong? Are you well?'

'Hebe's boy was here today, told me she is coming up to you –'

'She is. She said she had a cancellation, whatever that means.'

'The boy's going on a visit to the Scillies for three weeks. Schoolfriends.'

'That explains it. I did wonder.'

'Can you afford her?'

'No, not really.'

'Want some money?'

'Yes, I suppose so. I had not thought. I had not worked it out. She offered to come and I was so pleased I –'

'I'll arrange it.'

'Bernard, should I?'

'Don't be silly. What is the point of keeping things for that nephew? He's never going to marry, from what you tell me. When did you see him last?'

'Weeks ago. He doesn't always come into the house, he's shy. He comes to fish in the evenings.'

'I'll send you some cash.' Bernard listened to Louisa's small protest. 'Wait, I have to put in more money.' He inserted the coins. 'Are you there, Louisa?'

'Yes, I'm here.'

'You must pay her more. Lucy Duff pays a much higher rate.'

'Oh dear,' Louisa protested. 'How shaming.'

'The girl likes you so she charges you less than Lucy.'

'She cooks wonderfully, helps me in the garden. I don't entertain.'

'I will send the money by hand. You will get it in a few days.'

'Thank you. Shall I send you more things?'

'No, don't bother.'

'Your voice has not changed,' cried Louisa in Wiltshire.

'But the rest of me has. Goodnight, darling, get back to your garden.'

Bernard rang off. The telephone box smelt of tobacco and urine. How disgusting is the human race, thought Bernard, dialling another number, inserting coins.

Louisa's voice had grown old. Forty years ago it had a lilt. 'That you, Jim?' The voice at the other end affirmed that it was. 'Listen, I want you to sell some things for me. Shall I send them to you or will you collect?'

'I'm coming your way, I'll collect. There is someone I want to see near you.'

'Ah. Meanwhile I want you to get five hundred to Louisa Fox. This is her address.' Bernard named house, village and county. 'Got it?'

'Yes, okay. See you soon.'

'Are you buying or selling from this person you want to see?'

'I don't know yet,' said Jim Huxtable. 'It's just a hunch I am following.'

Bernard walked back to his cottage following Feathers, who trotted, tail aloft. As he walked he considered love in its various aspects. It was probable that he loved Louisa as much as he had forty years before, when they met secretly to love and part; now there was no guilt, no pain. They had not met for thirty years; to do so now would embarrass them. As he reached his door he wondered what Jim Huxtable's hunch could be. He paused in his porch, looking at the fading sunset, remembering Silas in the tiara. Who was it the boy looked like? He cursed his unreliable memory. Indoors, fumbling for matches to light the lamp, he caught sight of his reflection in one of the mirrors. Forty years ago in Louisa's arms, he thought, I wore the mask of youth. This may be the real me. I am still thin, he thought, recollecting the moment when her maid had come in unexpectedly with a message and he had laid flat under the bedclothes until she left the room. Bernard remembered their laughter had led to renewed lovemaking. Love affairs are much easier nowadays, he thought, applying the match to the wick, steadying the flame, but less exciting. Of all of them now only Lucy Duff had anyone who lived in and she had never had much to hide, seldom lapsing from virtue and not enjoying it overmuch when she did.

Giles, in his bed in the house Hannah had remodelled as George Scoop had remodelled her teeth, knocking rooms together here, making it open plan there, thought of Silas and that Silas would go tomorrow to other friends. The friends had fathers, probably their fathers were with them. Indeed he remembered Silas had said Michael Reeves' father had driven him from school to Cornwall, offering Silas a lift. Giles, puzzling about Silas' fatherless state, was seized by inspiration. He got out of bed and tiptoed downstairs, and wrote a note to Silas.

'Perhaps your mother is a Hermaphrodite.'

Opening the street door with stealth, he darted across the street in his pyjamas and posted the note through Hebe's letter-box.

10

Having watched Silas take off in the helicopter Hebe went back to her car to drive to Wiltshire. Silas would slip her from his thoughts until it was time to come home. I will never know what has gone through his mind, she thought. I love him but I seldom know what he is thinking. She wished she possessed the easy relationship some women had with their children. Hannah never bothered about what she said to Giles. Yesterday there had been a row because Giles said he'd been told his father was a bore and Hannah had shouted, 'He's all sorts of things I don't like but he's not a bore. Can you imagine me marrying a bore?' making it clear by her denial that it was true. She had taken the suggestion as an insult to her intelligence and Silas, listening and watching, had not asked, as other boys would, 'Was my father a bore?' There was no father with whom odiously to compare, for Hannah, when angry with Giles, would often cry, 'Giles, you are just like your father.'

I should have invented one, Hebe thought, as she drove towards Mrs Fox in her elegant house and lovely garden, but it is now too late. She concentrated her thoughts on Mrs Fox and what meals she would cook during the next two weeks.

In Salisbury she stopped to stretch her legs, parking the car and strolling round the Close to look at the beautiful houses, wondering what sort of people deserved these privileged surroundings. Were they especially virtuous or just very rich? She crossed the grass to the cathedral to sit and rest before the last lap of her journey. She resented having to pay to go in, feeling it made the atmosphere secular. Influenced by the secularity she took biro and paper from her bag and wrote Hippolyte, Mungo, Terry, Louisa, Lucy, Maggie, crossing out Terry and Maggie.

The sums represented by the list of clients amply covered the cost of Silas' education. No need these days of help from Amy or to accept the frequently offered help from Bernard. She let her mind dwell on Bernard, grateful that she could love him without payment. From now on she would be free too of the financial tie to Terry, and Maggie Cook-Popham could be dropped.

On her way back to her car she sighted a hat shop and stopped to stare. Lucy Duff had told her that when young if depressed she would buy a hat to cheer herself up, an infallible cure, advised Mungo's ma, for the mopes. I'll give it a try, thought Hebe, joking with herself, and she went into the shop. If tempted she might spend some of Terry's bonus.

At the sight of her the owner of the shop felt a lift to his despondent heart. What a head to bedeck. Laying down the *New Statesman* he rose from his chair.

'May I look round?' Hebe saw a young man carelessly assembled. Short legs, body leant back from the hips, large hands at the end of long arms, receding hair curling at the back, hazel eyes set in a face which resembled a hare with a long indented upper lip.

'Please look round, yes, do look –' He stepped back, knocking over a wastepaper basket, sweeping the *New Statesman* off his desk. 'Do you read this?' He retrieved the magazine, hoping to engage her in talk.

'Not very often.' Hebe looked away. He seemed nervous. She studied the hats, at first glance disappointingly Conservative Fête or Conservative Conference, depending on the season they were destined for. A second look revealed rogues in the gallery, a beret, a red hat with a wide brim. She picked it up.

'I'm afraid that's not for –' The shopkeeper moved forward anxiously. 'It's just for –' He seemed unable to finish his sentences. 'But if you –'

Hebe put on the hat and studied herself in the glass.

'You look marvellous in – of course if you'd like to – I mean it's not for sale because it's –' He spoke like what Lucy Duff would call a gentleman, what 'they' would call public school, though public-school vowels were not always like 'theirs' any more. The mirror reflected people passing in the street. Hebe, hands up to tilt the hat, froze. She should have remembered.

'It's much best worn straight.' The young man had got a whole sentence out. 'It belonged to my great-aunt, she bought it in 1939 at the outbreak of –'

But Hebe was hearing 'long-haired yobbo', 'dirty feet', 'Communist', 'workshy', 'whore', 'abortion', 'black', 'who, who?' Her eyes followed them as they walked down the street, that familiar limp his, the bag carried over her left arm hers, a new younger Labrador at their heels. Her legs crumpled and she was sitting on the floor.

'I say, just a minute, I'll –' The owner of the shop sprang to fan her with the *New Statesman*. 'Here, let me –' He helped her to her feet. 'Just sit –' He sat her in a chair. 'Half a mo, I've got a –'

Hebe put her head between her knees. The hat fell off. 'So sorry. Stupid. No lunch. I –' She could not finish her sentence either.

'Here, have a swallow.' She felt a glass knock against her teeth, smelled whisky. She sipped, swallowed.

'So sorry. Have I hurt the hat?'

'Of course not.' He fanned with the *New Statesman*. 'I'm not really Left –' He was staring at her with his hare's eyes.

'Left what?' She clutched at her composure. They hadn't seen her. They shopped in Salisbury. She felt a fool. It must be Thursday. Their day.

'Wing.' He gazed at her; her colour was creeping back. Was she perhaps pregnant, to feel faint? He couldn't very well ask. 'Not Left Wing,' he assured her. 'It's just to counter the hats.'

Hebe smiled. 'How intelligent of you. I'm all right now,' she said. Better not explain, just be casual.

'– so very glad.' He did not seem able to begin a sentence either.

'I must be on my way.' She stood up.

'But you must take the hat,' he urged.

'How much is it?'

'Nothing, it's just it's –' He was putting the hat in a paper bag, striped red, green and white like the Italian flag.

'But how much – I must –' This is infectious, she told herself.

'– part of the décor. It wasn't for sale. I'd like you to –' he handed her the bag, 'have it.' He smiled triumphantly.

'I can't take it,' she said firmly.

'You must. You look super in it. My great-aunt would be so –'

'Is she dead?'

'No, just old. She gave it me for –'

'What?'

'Fun.' The hare's eyes lit up. 'For encouragement.' He gave Hebe the bag. 'And now I am –'

'What?' She felt a creeping friendship for this young man.

'Encouraged. You should see what –' Hebe waited '– they buy. Petals, feathers, gauze, but you took the one good hat with unerring eye. Please keep it, it will give me so much –'

'Pleasure.' Hebe finished the sentence for him. 'Thank you very much.' She accepted the hat.

'Are you going –'

'Another ten miles.'

'So you don't live –'

'I'm going to a temporary job.'

'I see. I hope you enjoy –'

'I shall. I've been there before. Goodbye.' She held out her hand.

'Oh.' He took her hand in a large dry grasp. She would have expected it to be damp.

'Thank you very much.'

He went to the door and watched her go down the street. She turned, laughed, and shouted, 'I bet your father was a General.'

'He was, he –' She'd gone. He hadn't asked her name. She would read his on the bag, Rory Grant, Hatter. His Great-aunt Calypso had said, 'Be bold about it, don't let them put you off, always do what you want to do in life.'

Hebe put the striped bag on the back seat and drove the last ten miles to Louisa Fox. It had done her good to find the hat, done her good to see them walk by. They had not seen her, no harm was done. Her eyes hurt. She looked forward to an early bed and taking out the contact lenses. She exposed her eyes to the world when working, a counterfeit penance, disguising herself at home with her large glasses.

As she drove she puzzled over her grandparents. Why was she still afraid of them, was it habit? Why had she not smelled the smell which usually accompanied the panic? Trying to assemble her thoughts, to sift fact from fiction, what she already suspected became clear. The smell had nothing to do with the two old people walking down the street in Salisbury. She wondered what the dog was called. The old dog's name had been 'Smut'.

Hebe drove slowly, feeling safer with every mile. They would have been in Salisbury to have their corns cut, go to the library, prowl in the bookshops without buying, walk back to their car, drive away south to the house on the edge of the New Forest.

They would not go into a hat shop on impulse and allow the hatter to give them a hat. They would walk in the centre of the pavement, unseeing, not noticing their errant granddaughter. There was no room in their lives for frivolous hats, no room for girls who consorted with long-haired, bearded, bare-foot layabouts. It seemed so very long ago, yet nothing about them had changed. Except, thought Hebe in joyous surprise, catching sight in the driving mirror of the striped bag on the back seat, except that I am no longer afraid. Perhaps that will be the last time I hear their voices, the last time I fear them. Her spirits soared as she turned the car off the main road to drive the last miles to Louisa Fox.

She drew up by the front door. Three mongrel dogs rushed, barking, from the house. The door was open; the hall would be cool and smell of roses.

'Quiet, boys, quiet.' Louisa Fox came round the house, a slight woman in a cotton dress, wearing a gardening apron. She held up her face to kiss Hebe.

'I am too dirty to touch you.' She showed earthy hands. 'Can you manage your bags? Oh my word, you've been to Rory's shop. How comical. What did you buy?' She scanned Hebe, the contents of the car, the paper bag, with bright black eyes. 'Rather a brave man to start a hat shop in Salisbury. His father's furious. Show me what you bought. I'm surprised you found anything fit.'

Hebe took the red hat from its bag.

'But that's one of his antiques. I know it well. A friend of mine gave it to him.'

'He gave it to me.'

'I'm glad you accepted. Come in and have a drink and I will tell you about the garden. There's been a disaster or two since you were last here. Bring your stuff in. Down!' she shouted at the dogs who were leaping and wagging round Hebe, 'But there are lots of raspberries and the tobacco flowers smell delicious.'

'I brought some sauce for pasta which I thought you would like tonight and if you have raspberries –'

'Don't start talking of food straight away, have a drink first. I've put you in your usual room. What would you like to drink, wine?'

'Yes please.'

'There's a bottle in the fridge. We will have it on the terrace. Come along.'

This is the kind of house I like, thought Hebe, following Louisa through a paved hall where her feet alternately clicked on stone and shuffled on worn rugs. Louisa led her through her drawing-room to the terrace. 'Sit down. I will fetch the wine.'

'Can't I?'

'No.' Louisa left her.

Hebe sat on the white iron seat and looked across the garden to the meadow beyond the fence, where cows swished their tails by the chalk stream, bottle green water, trailing weeds and the sharp cry of a coot.

'Here we are.' Louisa brought a tray with wine and glasses, the bottle beaded. She poured, tasted. 'Just right.' She handed a glass to Hebe. 'There.'

The dogs lay down sighing, flicking an occasional ear, glancing up to wag a gentle tail, closed their eyes, slept.

Sipping her wine, Louisa watched Hebe. She looked vulnerable and wary.

'I am glad you have that hat,' she said. 'Rory needs encouragement. He makes lovely hats.'

'I thought they looked rather conservative.'

'So they pretend, but did you try one on? No? If you had you would have found that each one has some wicked exaggeration. He uses his hats to mock the Establishment. He guys his customers.'

'Rather cruel.'

'No, never cruel. His father tried to push him into the Army. He went on strike.'

'I wondered.' Hebe laughed. 'His shop struck me as some sort of protest.'

'He comes here sometimes to fish the stream. He's an honorary nephew. I knew his father and grandfather.'

'Are they dead?'

'To me.' Louisa considered Hebe. Would she ever relax completely? It seemed unlikely. 'Rory's grandfather was one of my beaux. Or thought he was,' she amended. 'It was hard to decide whether he or another man was the most trying. Such a tedious fellow.'

Hebe glanced quickly at her employer. 'Surely there was no need for you to know bores?'

'Many eligible men were boring. Rory's grandfather was one. His older brother, whose widow gave Rory that hat, by the way, was far from being boring. Alas, not a beau of mine. Once I had a date with Rory's grandfather in the Ritz and at the same time a date with another man in the Berkeley. In those days,' Louisa grinned at Hebe, 'the Berkeley was across the street from the Ritz.'

'I wouldn't know.' Hebe was polite.

'Not your line of country?'

'Above my station.'

'Mine too, now. Anyway, both these men wanted to marry me. I told the one I would dine with him at the Ritz and the other – he was called Rutter by the way, might be a relation of yours' – Louisa did not look at Hebe – 'that I would dine with him at the Berkeley. Then, with both tied down, I rendezvous'd with someone else and spent the night with him.'

'Did you marry that one?' She is telling me she knows my family. Hebe grew alert.

'He was not the marrying kind. They were both jealous of the man I did dine with, so I tied them down waiting. Later I married someone else.'

'Not a bore,' Hebe grinned.

'Not at all. Both these bores live within twenty miles of me. I never see them. I forget they exist. It just happens that I like Rory.'

'Because he annoys his father?'

'That is probably why.' Louisa put her empty glass on the table, hoping Hebe would feel a little safer if she knew she would not meet her grandparents, would feel liked, as Rory was liked.

'What happened to the man you spent the night with?'

'We talk sometimes on the telephone.'

'Doesn't he visit you?'

'No. Now come, let's get some punnets and pick raspberries. It is a treat for me,' said Louisa, leading the way to the fruit cage, 'not to eat my supper on a tray watching television. Either I can't eat because there is a nature programme with beautiful beasts eating other beautiful beasts, or our Prime Minister is making a speech which upsets me.'

'Surely you are a Conservative?' Hebe was surprised. Was Mrs Fox a rebel in these Tory surroundings?

'I was brought up to be one as surely you were.' Hebe nodded. 'But there are times when I wonder whether the government is not entirely composed of moles from Moscow.'

Hebe giggled. 'That's why you approve of the Hatter?'

'Yes,' said Louisa. 'I like rebels and I dislike hypocrisy.'

'Were the bores hypocrites, then?' Hebe suggested the nail for Louisa's hammer.

'Terrible hypocrites,' said Louisa. 'Oh, poor bird. Can you help that blackbird out of the cage?'

Hebe gently chivvied the blackbird towards the gate held open by Louisa. She felt grateful for Louisa's ambiguity.

'There!' she exclaimed as the bird flew free. 'Thank you.'

Hebe unpacked, changed her clothes and cooked a delicious meal. They finished the bottle of wine and Louisa, enjoying herself, opened another. She spoke of her garden and was grateful when Hebe offered to weed. Hebe went to bed early and Louisa read late, hoping the telephone would ring so that she could have a long talk, reverse the charges so that he would not have to search for coins, but the instrument remained silent. She regretted fate had prevented her marrying Bernard, although her marriage had been happy. As a lover he had been delightful, as a husband he might have failed and, Louisa reminded herself wryly, Bernard had never proposed marriage.

Listening to the night's sounds, an owl hooting, a distant train, a cow cough in the meadow, Hebe thought of her grandparents. They had looked old and proud, impregnable in their prejudices. She cursed her inability to communicate with them. I must communicate with Silas, she told herself. I must stop being afraid of him otherwise it will be a repeat story. Sleepily she considered her family, God-fearing, incomprehensible. How marvellous, she thought, that they had chanced in her childhood to employ Amy who had proved her salvation, defending her when the older sisters had tormented and teased, older sisters who had conformed to the family mores, willingly adapting themselves to the proposed pattern. Six, eight and ten years older than herself, Hebe remembered them as giantesses in riding clothes who demanded service in confident voices, manipulated their grandparents, never lowered their voices when telephoning, thought it a joke when the men they were engaged to and subsequently married arrived back from a party tipsy and shouted, 'Let's roger the slave,' as they lumbered towards Amy's bedroom. Hebe remembered her terror at the sound of their voices and the charge of heavy feet turning to exuberant delight as Amy delivered adroit kicks and a parting push which sent them tumbling downstairs.

Inexplicably the grandparents had approved of the young men, admiring them for their prowess on the rugby field, the hunting field. Now Robert fielded a Conservative majority in a safe seat; Marcus carved a niche in merchant banking; Delian manufactured microchips in Brussels.

Hebe remembered Amy's refusal to stay another day, her deadly politeness. She had watched her pack, offered her face to be kissed, sad at the pending separation, heard Amy's bright voice, 'See you again some day, love!', watched her get into the waiting taxi, seen her burst out laughing as the taxi rounded the bend in the drive.

Amy must have been at least fifty at that time, thought Hebe, which makes her well over seventy now, much the same as Louisa Fox and Lucy Duff. If Amy had been working for either of those it would not have been Amy who left the house but the boy friends. Hebe recollected her arrival years later on Amy's doorstep. Amy had said, 'You'll be all right with me,' and she had been all right and Silas was all right, really. If only I can be to Silas what Amy was to me, she thought. She remembered her spirits surging up from the depths as Amy drew her into her house, and of how at last she had been able to weep.

As she listened to the night sounds, she was glad that she would have two weeks with Louisa while Silas enjoyed himself sailing. It was good for him to have a wider horizon than the hideous street. She was glad he was having a good time with an ordinary family. Well, not an ordinary family, she thought, wincing at her inbred snobbery, people who were what Lucy Duff called 'gentlefolk'. 'Oh God!' she cried aloud and remembered Hannah saying 'Wet the tea' and cringed, reminded of her upbringing by 'them' whom she had disowned, the old white ram and his white ewe whose daughter had borne her. She suddenly missed Terry with his knickers. His life is uncomplex compared to mine, she thought, remembering the chocolate skin of silky texture.

11

Mungo Duff, a far from patient man, would have liked, the moment he read Miss Thomson's card, to leap into his car and speed across country to Louisa Fox, find Hebe, snatch her up and take her to Venice. The Highlands? To Yugoslavia? But why waste time travelling? There were delightful country hotels in England and Wales. Ireland, too, for that matter. Would she like Ireland? he asked himself, standing irresolute in the hall.

'I say, Dad, have you seen my snorkle? I left it with my goggles. It's disappeared.'

'Confound you!' shouted Mungo. 'Can't a man even –' He stared at his elder son standing a yard away, his younger brother at his elbow. Both boys looked startled. 'What the hell are you doing?' Mungo yelled. Thinking of Hebe, he had forgotten his children.

'Packing, collecting what we need at the Reeves.'

'Oh, God!' Mungo's dreams fell about his ears. He cursed Alison for departing so blithely to Santa Barbara. Alistair and Ian had to be packed off to the Scilly Isles. Until they left he was shackled by parental responsibility.

'Got bad news, Dad?' Alistair eyed the postcard in Mungo's hand.

'Of course not. Don't pry,' he snarled at Alistair. Why did one burden oneself with children, what lunacy, what a hazard to happiness. He looked again at the postcard. She would not yet be there, not until the 14th. There was time to plan. Then doubt gripped his heart. 'What day are you two leaving?'

'Day after tomorrow. Dad. The twelfth. Ma told you.'

'Of course.' What relief.

'She told us we were old enough to pack for ourselves and that you would put us on the train. It's all right, isn't it, Dad? I mean, if necessary we can go in a taxi.'

'Don't be stupid,' Mungo snarled.

'We are only trying to remember to pack everything. Ma said if we left anything behind we were not to bother you to send it on.'

'Very sensible of her,' Mungo grunted.

'So have you seen my snorkle?'

'No, I have not seen your snorkle. If you are old enough to pack you are old enough to find your fucking snorkle.'

The younger boy gave a high giggle. 'Fuck' was not a word his mother allowed in the house. ('I will not allow that word in the house.') This applied to most four-letter words. Seeing Mungo's expression he suppressed his giggle. Mungo stared at his sons, fruit of his loins, he supposed, though there was no proof, he thought sourly; they both looked exactly like Alison. 'Get on with it,' he said, 'and don't make a mess.'

Ian and Alistair turned and ran. From the back premises Mungo heard an explosion of laughter. Bloody little bastards, they had no respect. Mungo remembered his own father and grinned. He used to give one a clip on the ear and his mother would cry, 'Mind Mungo's eardrum'. Mungo stooped to pick up the rest of the letters. There was one in his mother's hand. He opened it, tearing pettishly at the envelope.

> Darling Mungo. I have to see you on a private matter. When you have got the boys off to the Scilly Isles I would be grateful if you would come and see me so that we can talk. The matter is too delicate to discuss on the telephone. I must ask you to come here. It will not take long. All my love, Mother.

All her love. What about my love? Mungo screamed with inward rage, threw the letter on the ground and stamped on it. Then, glancing round to see whether he had been observed, picked the letter up and put it in his pocket.

That evening, the boys safely in bed, the snorkle found on a shelf in the greenhouse, Mungo telephoned his mother.

'Mother, what's up?'

'I told you, darling, I won't talk about it on the telephone.'

'Are you sure?'

'Positive.' He knew that tone of voice; there was no budging her.

'Very well. I can't come before the boys go on the twelfth. I'll come on the thirteenth.'

'A suitable date.' Was she laughing?

'I won't be able to stay.' Mungo was defensive.

'I wasn't asking you to, darling. As you know, Miss T. rather hates me having visitors.'

Did she think if she referred to Miss Thomson as Miss T. she would not hear?

'Is she listening?'

'She has so few entertainments,' said Lucy, amused. 'See you, then, on the thirteenth. I'll ring off now, you must mind your bill.'

Mungo thought, She is obsessed by bills. Tearing up her letter he noticed she had put a second-class stamp on it.

On August 12th Mungo put Ian and Alistair on the train to Penzance where Jennifer Reeves had arranged for them to be met and taken to the heliport. During the afternoon he arranged with Alison's daily lady to come and feed the cat while he was away, thankful that Alison refused to have a dog. He would not trust a dog to Alison's daily lady. The cat was able to fend for itself if she forgot it. Mungo always thought of the daily lady as Alison's, not his or the boys' adjunct. Her regard, when she bothered to notice him or the boys, was distinctly insubordinate. With Alison she was servile and intimate.

The boys gone, he set off north in his car, stopping to dine on the way at a highly recommended restaurant to fortify himself for any bad news his mother had to impart. As well to stoke up with the good things of life, he told himself, before she broke the news that she had cancer or had lost all her money. As he ate his steak and drank his claret, Mungo let his mind wander. If it was cancer he must get his mother into a hospice, it would be far better than all the hassle of finding a decent nursing home. She belonged though to BUPA so perhaps that side might not be too difficult. On the other hand, if she insisted on dying at home, Alison must come back sharpish and get down to finding private nurses. A terrible bore, but Alison would manage. Mungo ordered another bottle. This really was a good restaurant. If he took Hebe to Scotland they could have a meal here on the way. On the other hand, if his mother had not got cancer but had somehow managed to get into a financial bog, he shuddered to think what to do. One thing he would not do, and here for once Alison would be in complete agreement, would be to have his mother to live with them. No fear, thought Mungo, drinking his claret and ordering Stilton. It was hazardous enough arranging sessions with Hebe without his mother spying on him with those sharp eyes. Mungo sighed, thinking of Hebe's eyes, enormous like a woodmouse, long lashed. He suddenly realised he was intoxicated and broke into a sweat at the thought of the police stopping him as he drove north and using their dreadful new gadget.

'Waiter?' Mungo enunciated with care, even two syllables could betray –

'Yes, sir,' falsely obsequious.

'Is there anywhere I can stay the night? I don't feel like driving on.'

'Here, sir, why not here? The restaurant is part of an hotel.'

'Is it? Thank God.' He groaned with relief. 'Book me a room.'

He spent a sleepless and worrying night and appeared at his mother's house at lunchtime the following day distinctly hungover.

When Mungo saw his mother looking remarkably well, bearing down like a battle cruiser to embrace him, his heart, *malgré lui*, sank. Alison, he decided, would have to find a cottage to suit reduction in circumstances, comfortable of course, or a flat, a flat would do, but not within fifty miles.

'Fifty miles of what?'

He had not realised he was thinking aloud. 'I said "your nifty smile". Are you growing deaf, mother?'

'Certainly not.' She wore a curious expression, amused, sardonic.

'Ill? Are you ill?' He looked at her keenly.

'Why should I be? I am as strong as a horse.'

'Is it money, then, have you lost it all?'

'Darling, are you crazy? I am perfectly well and very well off, as you well know, thanks to your father. Come and have lunch. We will talk about your troubles afterwards.'

'My troubles?' He stared at his mother.

'What else? Come and have a drink.' She headed towards the dining-room.

'Oh, God, no. Well, perhaps yes. A whisky, then.'

'Like that, is it? Stiff with lots of soda. Would you like an aspirin, too?' She peered up at him, gimlet-eyed.

'Yes.' Mungo was sheepish. His mother had a fondness for weakness which his father had never pandered to. But I oblige her, he thought disconsolately, sipping his whisky while she fetched the aspirin.

During lunch, at which Miss Thomson was present, Mungo listened to his mother's opinions on the government – not real Tories, no proper background; on the weather – pretty good; her garden as affected by the weather; the iniquities of industrialists polluting the air with the puffs from their chimneys. His mother still talked to him as though he were a child, Mungo thought morosely as he ate his roast chicken. 'Puff', indeed.

'What about the rivers?'

'Darling, that's for somebody else to worry about. My plants are not affected by the rivers.'

'Your income comes from industry.'

'Oh no, Mungo, it does not. Your father would never invest in industry.'

'Ask your trustees.' Mungo was sulky and nervous.

'I shall leave well alone.' Lucy shifted from uncertain ground. 'Shall we have our coffee out of doors?'

'I will bring it out on the patio for you, Mrs Duff.' Miss Thomson rose from the table and left them.

'Maddening woman, she insists on calling the terrace a patio. It's so common. Come on, let's go into the garden. She also refers to the lawn being manicured.'

Following his mother on to the terrace, Mungo reflected that she must be one of the last to dare call somebody 'common'. He wished he had her ghastly self-assurance.

They sat in the sun, not speaking, looking at the view in the distance of which a factory chimney could be seen, puffs of pollution belching. Miss Thomson brought the coffee tray and retreated. Mungo watched her back, her thick efficient waist, strong plump shoulders, solid legs ending in flat, sensible shoes on inward-turning feet.

'What's your trouble then, Mother?' If it wasn't cancer or money what could it be?

'Not mine, darling, yours, I told you.'

'What?'

'Yours.'

'Explain.' He gulped scalding coffee. What did she mean? What the hell was she up to? 'What's up?'

'What's up is that Alison has left you. She asked me to break it to you.' Lucy's eyes glinted.

'I don't believe it.' Mungo burst out laughing, delighted that his mother neither had cancer nor was going broke. He was really very fond of her.

'She has apparently decided to form a *ménage à trois* with those friends of yours in Santa Barbara.' Lucy watched her son's face with curiosity. He could be a bit slow on the uptake.

'Not my friends, they are Alison's.' The full impact of his mother's news was slow to sink in. 'She met them when she took the boys skiing at Mégêve. They have been staying with us.'

'So I gather.'

'Do you mean to say she was carrying on with him under my nose?'

'With them, I told you, it's a threesome. I wonder what your father would say.' Poor fellow, thought Lucy. It makes him look so ridiculous. To go off with a man understandable, to go off with a woman quite frequently done, but with a pair, unusually esoteric.

Mungo finished his coffee and sat thinking. Lucy pursed her lips, watching him. Who was it who had said, when she was about to marry Mungo's father, 'He's a delightful fellow but the kind of man who has stupid children'? That dreadful little friend of Louisa's, Bernard Quigley, who had once made a pass at her, more than a pass if she dared be honest. Lucy blushed in shamed recollection. He'd been rather fun, made one laugh. It had only happened once, in France; she had liked the hotel.

'Well?' She broke the silence lying between her and her only child. 'Well?'

Mungo noticed her raised colour. 'You may be upset,' he said, 'but I think it's absolutely marvellous.' He let out a shout of laughter. He saw himself speeding down the motorway, snatching Hebe from Louisa Fox, marriage in a registry office and happy, happy ever after. Lovely, lovely Hebe. Noticing his mother's expression and unable to fathom it, Mungo stopped laughing and said, 'I shall divorce her.'

'What for?'

'Adultery, of course.'

'With whom?'

'Um, both I suppose. Oh, come on, Mother, why not desertion, incompatibility? There are all sorts of causes for divorce these days.'

'Who will care for the boys?' A deadly sentence. Mungo felt a shiver of fear. 'You will help me, Mother?'

'No.'

'Good God, Mother, you are their grandmother, you –'

'I know I am.'

'So you will –'

'Won't.'

'Mother!' Mungo was aghast, his joy dissipated, alarm rushing into the vacuum. There was a long pause while mother and son confronted each other. Mungo was the first to look away.

'Alison is your wife,' said Lucy. 'We may neither of us be particularly fond of her –'

'Mother!' He was shocked by her honesty. It was all right for him to be disloyal, not for her.

'After your reaction to my news just now, I think you had better listen. As I was saying, we may not be fond, but my word, dear boy, she is useful. She looks after you and the boys faultlessly. You are fed, exercised, have your holidays arranged, your bills paid. She arranges the servicing of your cars, she plans your social life and that of the boys, she sees that they go to the right schools, spend their holidays with the right people.'

'She's a dreadful snob.'

'So am I, so are you. If that pretty girl who comes to cook for me were not a lady do you suppose you would pursue her so briskly?'
'How do you know?' Mungo shouted furiously.
'Don't be silly, Mungo. You may think it secret, so perhaps does she. There is such a thing as the grapevine. Maggie Cook-Popham's boy saw you with her twice.'
'Does Alison know?'
'Probably. Anyway it wouldn't bother her, she would not care.'
'Oh.' Mungo felt his mother had kicked him in the teeth. 'When did all this happen?' he asked weakly.
'Quite suddenly. Alison telephoned me. She has also written. She had never been unfaithful to you before, by the way. This is an arrangement arrived at on the 'plane going over. Alison telephoned me on arrival. Her letter came yesterday, dotting the "i"s. She used the word "finalised".' Lucy sniffed.
'She must have been drunk or drugged.'
'I gather neither. She has been contemplating some such move for a long time and it happens this American couple are offering her exactly the life she has always longed for.'
'What utter rubbish.'
'Read her letter.' Lucy handed Alison's letter to her son. A practical, lucid deposition. Alistair and Ian's holidays over, Mungo was to assume responsibility. Alison would, if necessary, advise from Santa Barbara, otherwise it was up to Mungo. Her lawyer, who was also Eli and Patsy's lawyer, would be in touch shortly. Lawyer's address attached.
'My God, my God!' Mungo felt like weeping. 'She cannot know what she is doing. She cannot have made up her mind so quickly.'
'She went snap when she clapped eyes on you,' said Lucy drily. 'Your father said he'd never seen such a fast worker. She saw you and, as I say, went snap.'
'I thought it was me.'
'You were supposed to, darling.'
Some people love their mothers, thought Mungo.
'Are these people, Eli and Patsy, rich?' asked Lucy.
'Seem to be rolling.'
'There you are, then.'

'I shall have to make the best of it.' Mungo did a rapid rethink. He would get Jennifer Reeves to help with the boys. She was an able woman with a boy of her own; two more wouldn't matter one way or the other. He could still marry Hebe, still live happy ever after. His mother was talking. 'What did you say?'

'I said we had better get to work at once.'

'Doing what?'

'Getting her back of course.'

'Why, for God's sake?'

'For mine if not for yours and the boys. I cannot possibly do without her.'

Mungo stared at his mother. When she spoke in the deadly tone she had just used resistance was sheer waste of breath.

Noticing her son's alarm, Lucy explained. 'Dearest, some day I shall get cancer or some such nuisance and need looking after.' Mungo winced. 'Who other than Alison do we know capable of coping? Not you, dear boy. Some day I may have a financial worry or two, need to move house, be too old to manage. Who do we know other than Alison capable of taking charge of me?'

Mungo buried his face in his hands. His mother was a horrible old bitch, he loathed her. How could people be so utterly selfish? It was damnable.

'So what?' he muttered through clenched teeth. 'So what or just so.' That was what Alistair and Ian said when they wished to be annoying. 'So?' Never, of course, to Alison; they wouldn't dare.

'So we get to work,' said Lucy calmly. 'You grovel, I blackmail. We use the telephone and spare no expense. We begin, let's see –' she looked at her watch, 'in half an hour. Catch her asleep. You will talk to Alison and I will talk to this Eli and Patsy.'

'I thought they were just rather boring Americans who were into intensive sightseeing.'

'My poor innocent.' Lucy laughed at Mungo as though he were ten years old. 'Come now, let us try and enjoy this. Grovel, grovel, grovel, tongue in cheek.' She was enjoying the situation.

Mungo made a last desperate appeal. 'Mother, please, there must be some other way.'

'I am not changing at my age and nor are you at yours. Do you imagine I would ever have had a child if it had not been certain I would have a Nanny who would take charge of you, if you had not been certain to go away to boarding school when you left the nursery?'

'I was miserable at my prep school,' Mungo muttered sulkily.

'I notice you send your boys to the same one. People like us did not put up with the horrors of having children at home, which even quite nice people do these days.'

People like us, nice people, must she? Mungo writhed.

'And you,' Lucy fixed Mungo with her clear eyes, 'are just like me. If you had not had Alison to manage, direct and bring up your boys you would not have embarked on having a family.'

Mungo made a choking sound of protest.

'I do not mean, darling, that I do not love you. I do very much. I might not if I had had to change your nappies and nurse you through mumps. In principle I also love my grandsons.'

'I am not sure I do.'

'Nonsense, of course you do. They have not had mumps yet, have they?'

'I don't know. I can't remember. Alison –'

'There you are, you don't know. Measles? Chickenpox? Athlete's foot? Those little mites that burrow into your – er – your, you know what I mean.'

'Crabs. Mother, must you?'

'Are you prepared to tackle all that on your own?'

Mungo was silent, thinking of Hebe. He did not want Hebe tackling the care of Alistair and Ian, dealing with their crabs. He wanted Hebe to himself, her undiluted attention. Tears came to his eyes. He gulped.

Perhaps he loves Alison, thought Lucy. No, he can't, it's the shock.

'When do we start? What do we do?' Mungo gave in.

12

Silas, catching a foreshortened glimpse of his mother from the helicopter as it swung away towards the Scillies, wondered what a Hermaphrodite could be; whether Giles, who liked useless bits of information, had discovered some new religious sect – whether Hermaphrodite was an esoteric dish like Moussaka, or an autonomous republic of the USSR. Giles particularly treasured gems such as 'It takes three years to digest black pepper', and had eagerly taken note of Bernard's information about the pig scratching. Silas promised himself a trip to the Public Library to rummage among the dictionaries.

He settled in his seat to watch Land's End disappear and peered ahead to catch a glimpse of the islands. He looked forward to meeting Michael and wearing the denim shorts Hebe had bought him. They had never seen one another in anything other than their school uniforms. He wondered what his friend would be wearing. Looking down at the choppy sea, he hoped the weather would clear and that the sun would show more enthusiasm than it had during the last fortnight. His fellow travellers in the helicopter seemed to be prepared for the worst, carrying yellow oilies and rubber boots. Arrived, Silas shook his head to free his ears of the din of the helicopter, followed the other passengers on to the tarmac and looked around for Michael. A female voice hailed him. Mrs Reeves waved. Silas waved back and went to meet her carrying his duffle bag.

'Hello, Silas.' She had large teeth and showed her gums when she smiled, which she was doing now. She was tall, with thick fair hair pulled back in a bun, which made the sou'wester she wore look peculiar. Her face was red from the wind, her eyes blue. She wore a yellow oilskin with a velvet collar, an old

Guernsey jersey, a denim skirt. Her legs were bare. She wore blue ankle socks and trainers. Her handshake was firm.

'Nice to see you, Silas.' She was not as he remembered at the school sports, he must have confused her with some other boy's mother.

'How do you do, er, hullo.' Silas looked around for Michael.

'They are all sailing. I had some shopping to do in St Mary's so I said I'd meet you.' Her voice had carrying quality.

'Oh, thank you.'

'They will be back for supper. Come and help me load my stuff in the boat. Alistair and Ian only arrived yesterday and were keen to get cracking. They knew you wouldn't want them to wait.'

'Oh, oh no.' Bugger Michael, thought Silas. It's not lunch time yet, what am I supposed to do stuck with his mother till supper? 'Of course not.'

'D'you know Alistair and Ian, Silas?'

'No, no, I don't. Who are –'

'You wouldn't, I suppose. They are at a different school. But you might have met them in the holidays.' She looked brightly enquiring.

'I don't think so.' Where was he supposed to have met them? Silas followed his hostess. Who were they, anyway?

'Hadn't you better put on a mac?'

'Yes, of course.' He unzipped his duffle bag and found his anorak.

'Does nothing but rain here,' she said.

She seemed frighteningly competent, guiding him to a mountain of shopping, getting him to stow it in large baskets. 'There's a fantastic basket-maker in Totnes who makes these. I can't stand plastic bags, can you?'

'Er, no I can't.' Silas had never thought about it.

'D'you know Totnes? Delightful place. These baskets come from there. He makes every conceivable European shape. No Eastern rubbish.'

'Rather heavy,' Silas ventured.

'But last for ever. Their being heavy shouldn't worry a strong boy like you.'

'Of course not.' They had reached the quay.

'That's right, stow them. Not like that, not all on the same side, the boat will sink. Here, like this.' She rearranged the baskets, grouping them in the middle of the boat.

'Sorry.' Silas felt foolish.

'Done a lot of sailing, Silas?'

'Er, no.' Ask a silly question.

'Alistair and Ian make a useful crew, Julian says. Julian is my husband.'

'Oh.'

'My name is Jennifer. Call me Jennifer, everybody does.'

'Thanks.' I shall call her 'You', he mutinied.

She had the boat stowed to her satisfaction. 'Sit on that thwart.'

What's a thwart? he asked himself.

'Cast off, can you?'

Silas managed that.

Jennifer Reeves started the engine and steered the boat into the rain, phut-phutting over the waves. 'Soon be there.'

Silas kept silent. They were apparently going to another island.

'When you've helped me get all this to the cottage I expect you'd like lunch and then you can explore the island.'

'Thanks, yes.'

'Know the islands well?'

'I've never been here.'

'Goodness, and you live so near.'

'Well.' He felt put down.

'Lots to do on the mainland, of course. Didn't Michael say you live in the town?' She sounded unconvinced.

'Yes.'

'Oh.' She savoured this. 'Like it?'

'Yes. We live in a street.'

'Really?' It sounded 'reahly'.

'It was built by a crazy old man who hated Cornish granite so he imported these dark red bricks from Devon and built a street of brick houses, dark brick with yellow bricks round the windows.'

'Yuk!'

'That's what my mother thinks, but it's so ugly I love it. It's hideous and frowning and secret and built up a very steep hill.'

'Reahly.' He could see her uvula.

'All the houses have nylon curtains and gardens at the back, and there's an alleyway between the gardens and the backs of the houses in the next street, which is built of granite like the rest of town. Ours is called Wilson Street.'

'Reahly,' said Mrs Reeves, sitting at the tiller, steering the boat across the water to Trescoe.

Silas sat quiet after his outburst, listening to the snap and crunch of the boat on the water, rather enjoying the bouncy movement but disliking the smell of stale fish. He wondered whether the oily, smelly bilge would slop up as it threatened to and wet his hostess's feet. It did not.

'Here we are,' she said, quelling the engine.

Silas helped carry the baskets to the cottage which the Reeves had rented for the holidays. Jennifer Reeves moored the boat and carried her share of baskets without showing any strain. Silas followed her into the cottage, deciding she was a good ten years older than Hebe.

'If you unpack the baskets I will put everything away.' Gosh, what efficiency. Not that Hebe wasn't efficient, Silas told himself, she just didn't make it so obvious.

'Put the baskets in the porch. I shall have a drink and get us some lunch. That be nice?'

'Thank you very much.' He stacked the baskets in the porch.

'Not there, silly, everybody will trip over them. Up on the shelf.'

'Sorry.' He stacked them on the shelf. Why hadn't she said 'shelf' in the first place.

Jennifer dripped drops of angostura and poured herself a generous gin.

'My father was in the Navy,' she said.

Silas looked blank.

'Pink gin, Silas, pink gin.'

He watched her take a swallow, wondering what she was talking about.

'That's better. Now for lunch. There's a stew – baked pots and fruit. Do you?'

'Lovely.'

'Shocking of me. Didn't offer you. Would you like a Coke?'
'No, thank you.'
'The boys always help themselves. Want to go to the loo? Like to see your room?'
'Thank you. Yes, please.'
'I'll show you.' She led the way. 'You're all in this big room together, you won't mind that, will you?'
'Of course not.' Just like school, he thought. Hope I like them. He looked doubtfully at the four beds.
'When you're ready come and eat. Here's the bathroom. Mercifully there's another loo downstairs. I'm not keen on people peeing in the garden, one might sit – kills the grass, too.'
Silas rejoined her. In silence they ate a very good stew, baked potatoes and fresh fruit. He helped her clear the table, stack the dirty plates in the dishwasher.
'All mod cons in these cottages.'
'Yes,' he said, putting in the last plate.
'Right, then. You unpack and explore. I'm going to have my rest. They will be home for supper, if not before. You'll be all right?'
'Yes, thank you.'
Jennifer Reeves went upstairs. He heard her drop her shoes, gentle thuds on the floor and her voice saying 'Aah' in relieved tones. She turned on a radio for Woman's Hour. Silas crept upstairs into the assigned bedroom. Three beds were rumpled. He put his duffle bag on the fourth, searched for a jersey and trainers, put them on. He looked out of the window. It was still raining and he debated whether to keep on his jeans or change into shorts. He changed.
He followed a path uphill from the shore to find some sort of view. The path was bordered with tamarisk and fuchsia, the air soft and salty. He began to enjoy himself.
He explored, finding Trescoe Abbey Gardens, wandering dazed by the exotica, loving the surprises, avoiding other people. Presently he left the gardens and, after a long tramp, found a sickle-shaped beach empty except for birds. He sat on a rock and watched the water, a blue-green he had not seen in Cornwall. A boat rowed by a girl came slowly into view. A man

sat in the stern with a fishing rod, casting a fly. Silas watched as the man caught and played mackerel as though he were on a lake fishing for trout. The man and the girl talked in low voices. Silas was not the only watcher, for seals' heads bobbed inquisitively quite close to the boat. Silas had never seen seals. The boat went slowly out of sight, the man and the girl still talking in quiet voices. Silas watched the seals watch them go. The rain had stopped. He undressed and walked down to the water and waded in. He did not want to splash and alarm the seals, who might still be close. He swam out from the beach, then turned to look back at the white sand, grey rocks and the low cliffs ornate with purple heather. Near the shore there were overhanging clumps of thrift, their grey seed heads like the woolly heads of pantomime footmen. The water was cold; he swam for the shore. He had no towel and liked the way his clothes clung stickily to his body. Carrying his shoes he walked inland. Presently the sun came out. He lay in the heather listening to the gulls, watching a kestrel hover. Lulled by the sound of gulls and breakers thudding on rocks round the headland, he fell asleep. When he woke the sun was hot on his face and the salt from his bathe drew the skin tight. He rubbed his hands on his cheeks, making a small dry noise, echoed close by; beside him on a flat rock was an adder. Silas lay watching the beautiful creature as it moved away into the heather, making a thin papery sound. He closed his eyes. The ecstasy of the adder on top of the sighting of seals was almost too much. Feeling hungry, he got up to walk back to the cottage. He had come further than he thought; the sun was slanting from the horizon and gulls flew towards their evening haunts.

Coming up from the jetty he met Michael Reeves with his father and two boys of about his and Michael's age. They were talking in loud voices, carrying bits of impedimenta from the boat and their day's sailing. Michael hailed Silas loudly.

Michael's father said, 'Hullo, how are you? Nice to see you. Got here all right, I see. Hope my wife looked after you, fed you and that sort of thing. Been exploring, have you? Sorry to leave you, we couldn't miss a good day's sailing, knew you wouldn't mind,' in a louder, deeper voice than Michael's.

Nobody introduced him to the two other boys, whom he later knew as Ian and Alistair.

Michael and his father wore crushed and dirty linen hats which had once been white. Ian and Alistair wore blue denim hats which were too small for them, having borne several seasons. Michael's father wore red Breton fisherman's trousers with patched knees and all the boys wore very tight denim shorts like Silas, but old and dirty so that he felt awkward. The whole party wore Guernsey jerseys like Mrs Reeves and smelt of boats and sweat. Silas wished Hebe had not said, 'Your jerseys will do but take my old white thing if you want to.' The old white thing was a Guernsey. Silas felt vaguely resentful towards Hebe. His own jerseys were serviceable but not Guernseys.

Michael and his friends jostled in the porch, talking loudly, shouting about the day's sailing to Jennifer in the kitchen, who shouted back, and above the cacophony Julian Reeves boomed that what he needed before anything else was a stiff whisky.

'Help yourself, then, I'm getting the nosh.' Jennifer clattered pans, ran water into the sink. 'Boys, boys, put your filthy boots in the porch, the floor was washed this morning.'

Michael and his friends kicked off yellow rubber boots and threw them down in the porch. A reek of hot feet drifted into the cottage.

'Take your boots off, darling.' Jennifer addressed her husband. 'Mrs Thing did the floor.'

'Okay, okay.' Julian Reeves stepped out of his boots and stood pouring whisky into his glass. Silas silently took the boots and put them with the others.

'Brought boots, did you?' Michael addressed him.

'No, I didn't know I'd need them.'

'We can lend you some, I expect.'

'Go and change your filthy shorts before supper and for God's sake wash,' Jennifer shouted at Michael who was standing close beside her. Michael muttered. Silas followed him and the other boys upstairs. They started rummaging in the chest of drawers.

'Quite glad to change,' the boy Silas would subsequently know as Ian said, stepping out of his shorts. 'These things squeeze my parts.'

Alistair and Michael laughed.

'Large parts run in the family,' said Ian encouraged. 'Father says his are much admired.'

'Who by?' enquired Silas, feeling left out.

'Our father has a mistress, thinks we don't know. Haven't heard mother's opinion, suppose she takes them as they come.'

'As they come.' Alistair, younger than Ian, laughed lewdly.

'My mother continually expects Pa to have a mistress. It's her constant dread,' said Michael, intent on keeping his end up. 'Actually he wouldn't dare. He gets slapped down if he so much as looks at a girl.'

'Supper's ready,' Julian Reeves shouted up the stairs in a foghorn voice. The boys pattered downstairs in bare feet. Silas slipped off his shoes and followed them.

Jennifer doled out large helpings of a stew similar to the one they had eaten at lunch on to Habitat plates and everybody started eating.

Julian Reeves opened a bottle of wine and helped his wife and himself, then offered the bottle to Silas.

'Thank you.' Silas held out his glass. Julian filled it three quarters full. The other boys helped themselves to Coke. Silas felt he had made a *faux pas* and shyly gulped his wine.

Julian and the boys regaled Jennifer with their day's sailing, constantly interrupting and contradicting one another.

'We thought we'd sail round the Bishop's Rock tomorrow if the weather holds. Like that, Silas, eh?'

'Oh yes, lovely.'

'Silas tells me he lives in a very interesting street.' Jennifer was refilling her glass. 'Apparently he lives in the town. I hadn't realised.' She fitted an aitch into the word, 'reahlised'.

'What's the street called?' Julian asked in an expansive voice.

'Wilson Street. It was Lord Kitchener Street but they changed it to Harold Wilson Street a few years ago.'

'Golly! Under the Labour government?'

'He's got a bungalow at St Mary's, you know.' Jennifer was deprecating.

'What a funny thing to do.' Ian's mouth was full of stew.

'I wonder why.' Passing cheese and Bath Oliver biscuits, Jennifer eyed Silas speculatively, as though he were responsible for the renaming.

'He did something for the town. It was a way the Council had of saying thank you.' In the ensuing silence Silas refused a Bath Oliver and helped himself to bread.

'Takes all sorts, I suppose.' Jennifer buttered a biscuit, munched, caught her husband's eye. 'Early to bed tonight if you are Bishop's Rocking tomorrow. Clear the table, will you, boys.'

'Okay,' said Michael, Ian and Alistair. 'Okay.'

Silas opened his mouth and shut it again.

Jennifer stood up. 'Pub?' she signalled her husband.

'Of course.'

Silas watched his host and hostess stroll out into the dusk.

'Let's get this done.' Michael started clearing the table. Silas helped. Ian and Alistair made vague movements without contributing.

'Your family Labour, then?' Ian enquired.

'Labour?' Silas was puzzled.

'Ya, Labour not Tory. You know, Wilson Street, I ask you. Goes to show.'

'What?'

'Reds under the bed and so on.'

'Don't be stupid, Ian.' Michael hedged his bets, remembering he was host.

'I have a pot under mine.' Alistair was gleeful. 'Used to wet my bed.' He sounded almost proud.

'Kiddo.' Ian was dismissive.

'What's on the box?'

They moved into the next room to sprawl and watch a Western on ITV. Ian turned up the sound but carried on a desultory conversation with Michael. To the accompaniment of saloon doors swinging, guns firing, the rattle of the stagecoach and galloping hooves, Silas learned that Michael's family often joined forces with Alistair and Ians' in the holidays, that they regularly skied at Mégève, that they had spent last summer holidays in the Canadian Rockies and that there were plans afoot for a trek in Ladakh the following year, although it was possible that Alistair would be considered too young to go.

'You can always go to Uncle H in the Highlands,' Ian consoled his younger brother.

'Piss the Highlands,' shouted Alistair above the background music of the film, voicing the anger and frustration of younger brothers. It all sounded very glamorous beside holidays spent in the dark brick Harold Wilson Street and expeditions to see Mr Quigley with Giles.

'Why the hell are you not all in bed?' Jennifer Reeves shouted when she came back from the pub.

'It's their holidays,' Julian was alcoholically amiable.

'Up, up you all go,' cried Jennifer, as though addressing recalcitrant dogs.

Silas took a long time going to sleep. He would have liked another blanket. He would have liked his duvet and Trip nestling furry and purring against his stomach in his own bed in his mother's house in the absolutely hideous street called Wilson Street. He wondered whether the rumour that the street had not been renamed out of gratitude but out of spite might not be true. He woke twice from his uneasy sleep to listen to the wind buffeting the cottage and to the sea growling.

13

Availing himself of Louisa's open invitation to fish, Rory Grant, having eaten a solitary supper, took his rod and drove the ten miles to the point where Louisa's stretch of water began. He parked his car, tucking it into the side of the road, pulled on his gumboots and, standing in the quiet of the August evening, put up his rod. Choosing a fly from his flybox, he listened to the gurgle of water flowing under the bridge and the evening sounds, the imagined rustle of bats hunting over the water, the rhythmic chewing from a group of recumbent cows who watched him benignly as he climbed a stile and began his slow progress along the river, casting his line over the water with the flick of wrist and movement of arm of inborn talent. As he cast his line he cast his cares. The mesmeric flow of the water brought solace and comfort to his insecure soul. When a trout rose to the fly and he struck, excitement took over until he had landed it, killed it with a sharp knock on the head and put it in his bag. He almost resented the interruption to his peace. By the time he had fished up the river it was nearly dark. He had caught four good fish. He stood looking up at Louisa's house, debating whether to go home without calling on her or whether to visit. He decided on the latter.

He cleaned the fish by what light was left, wrapped them in leaves and, walking through the garden, went round to the back entrance. He found the key Louisa kept hidden near the back door and let himself into the kitchen. Feeling for the light switch in the dark, he was aware of a delectable smell of cooking lingering in the warmth of the Aga and of tails thumping a greeting from the heap of mongrels lolling against the stove. He switched on the light.

'You're a fat lot of good as watchdogs.' He crouched down to stroke friendly heads and pat silky flanks. 'Suppose I'd come to mug Aunt Louisa? What about that, then?' The dogs seemed mildly amused. The largest got up and went to sniff the fish Rory had put on the table.

Rory stepped out of his boots and padded to the dresser for a dish. He laid the fish neatly head to tail and took them to the refrigerator.

'She in the drawing-room watching TV?' The dogs looked at him brightly. 'Or has she gone to bed?' They wagged their tails, mouths slightly open. 'I'll go and see, you stay here.' But as he opened the door into the hall one of the dogs, Rufus, pushed past him and ran ahead. Perforce he had to follow.

The hall was in darkness, a grandfather clock tic-tocked in the silence. Rory went to the drawing-room and found that dark also.

'Hell, she must have gone to bed. Where's that dog?' He stood listening, not wishing to disturb the sleeping house. He could leave a note or ring up in the morning, but the dog had gone upstairs, presently it would scratch at Louisa's door. The animal would wake her if she were asleep. Rory snapped his fingers, whistled softly. The dog did not wish to hear. Rory switched on a light at the foot of the stairs and made his way to his aunt's bedroom. To his surprise the dog was not standing outside Louisa's room or anywhere to be seen.

'Curse it.' Rory tiptoed past Louisa's door and set off in search. No dog on the first floor. He climbed the next flight.

Outside a bedroom he considered his own, since he had spent many happy holidays in it, the dog sat, head raised in expectation. Rory snapped his fingers. Rufus wagged more briskly. Rory, seeing light under the door, knocked, opened, walked in behind Rufus.

In front of the cheval glass he had known all his life, a glass before which he had pranced, draped in his bathtowel pretending to be a Roman Emperor when he was eight, stood the girl he had given his Great-aunt Calypso's hat. The girl was trying on the hat, posing in front of the mirror. She hadn't a stitch on.

'Oh, hullo,' said Hebe, surprised.

'I was trying to –' Rory gasped. Gosh, what a girl! – 'to

catch the – he ran ahead up –' Wasn't she going to cover herself? 'I was afraid Aunt Louisa might have –'

'What?' Hebe removed the hat, reached for a slip which she slung round her waist.

'A headache.' Rory gazed, fascinated.

'No, she hasn't. She went to bed early. She's been gardening all day.' Hebe was putting the hat back into its striped bag. 'She was tired. Do you want the hat back?'

'Oh no!'

'What are you doing here then?'

'I'm only – I was fishing – I put some trout –' Rory still stared in stupefaction.

'Where?'

'In the refrigerator.' She was stroking that bloody Rufus. He watched her hands fondling the animal's head.

'Good.' She watched him. Was he aware he was getting an erection?

'Could you put that hat on again?'

'Of course.' She took the hat out of its bag and put it on. Rory watched her back, her raised arms putting on the hat, her reflection in the mirror. She turned round.

'Why don't we?' With a gentle gesture she indicated the bed. Rory had no recollection later of taking off his trousers or Hebe taking off the hat. Rufus sniffed round the room then, finding an armchair, settled in it to sleep.

Waking with the sun shining through partly drawn curtains, Rory was aware of eyes watching an inch from his face.

'I'm very short-sighted,' said Hebe.

'Oh, ahh, I've never ever been able to do –' He tried to speak. 'Not properly so that I – er – not like –'

'Well, it's lovely, isn't it? And you can, can't you?'

'Yes, oh yes, it was simply –'

'Once more then before I get up? How would that be?' She was not laughing at him, not mocking him as others had.

'Wonderful. Wonderful. Wonderful,' he sang.

She gentled him. 'Take it slow.'

'I've never been able – then suddenly seeing you in the hat I –'

'Did your great-aunt wear it in bed?'

Rory laughed, holding Hebe in his arms. 'My great-aunt didn't need hats to get her going.'

'Nor will you now.'

Presently Rory asked, 'Who are you? What are you doing here?'

'I'm a temporary cook, one of your aunt's indulgences. Has she never told you?'

'No, well, yes. I've heard she sometimes –'

'I'm also –' Hebe paused.

'What? Tell me. Also what?' Sudden gloom seized him.

'I'm also a prostitute. I do this for money.' He would now leap out of bed, causing a draught, and flee. Hebe sighed, turning away, but Rory said, 'I like the word courtesan better.'

'Oh.' She was surprised by his tone.

'I can pay you. I'm quite well off.'

'Let's discuss that later if you want to. I have to get up and get breakfast. We could have trout. Does your aunt like trout?'

'She says so, when I bring them.'

'Come and talk to me while I bath.' Hebe slid out of bed and disappeared into the adjoining bathroom, an old-fashioned room, once a dressing-room converted at some pre Great War period. The bath had a mahogany surround; the lavatory also. The walls were papered with an exuberant pattern of roses. There was a small fireplace in a corner, an ottoman and an armchair covered in cretonne to match the walls; a marvellous background for Hebe, filling the bath, feeling the temperature, stepping in, lying back.

'Why don't you sit down?' She indicated the armchair. Rory, a bathtowel round his loins, sat.

The dog Rufus came and leaned on the mahogany surround and stared at Hebe's face through the steam, his intention to lick, if possible, taste soap. Hebe stroked his nose with soapy fingers.

'You spoil him.' Rory felt a pang of envy for the dog's proximity, his casual acceptance of Hebe's kindness.

'He's a dear good dog, I like him.'

Rory sat, watching her soap her neck, sponge her face, lift feet from the water, soap her toes.

'How did you get in?' she asked.

'I'm Louisa's nephew, I know where she hides the key.'

'I see.'

'She lets me fish her water whenever I feel low. My name is Rory Grant.'

'I know, it's on the bag the hat was in.'

'Of course, how silly of –'

'Why do you never finish your sentences?'

'I suppose they are not worth finishing.'

'It could become a very irritating habit.'

'I hadn't –'

'Thought. Say "thought". Say it.'

'You are mocking me. Thought.'

'Good. My name is Hebe.'

'Hebe, a pretty bush, I mean –' Rory floundered.

'What?'

'Shrub, I meant shrub.'

'You didn't.' Hebe stood up in the bath. 'Could you pass me my towel. You've got it wrapped round you.' She held out her hand.

'Oh, sorry.' He divested himself. 'I'd better dress.' He backed towards the door.

'Okay. See you downstairs. I'll give you breakfast.'

In the doorway Rory looked back at Hebe vigorously towelling. 'So beautiful.'

'Take Rufus down, he must be pining to pee.'

Rory pulled on his clothes, snapped his fingers at the dog and hurried downstairs. The dogs in the kitchen greeted him and Rufus with much wagging, yawns, chortling whines and growls. Rory let them out into the garden where they disappeared in the mist rising from the river, a bank of cotton wool with the sun's shafts angling through. He stood staring, unseeing, exhilarated.

In the house Louisa switched on the seven o'clock news, quickly dousing the volume.

The dogs came back full of jollity, jostling each other, prepared for another happy day. Rory groaned in disbelief. Was this event true? Behind him in the kitchen Hebe switched on the coffee grinder, a discordant screech.

'Ghastly noise.' She wore a pink cotton dress and a white

apron, her hair demurely brushed in its shoulder-length bob. She wore no make-up.

'Sit down, Rory, don't get in my way.'

'Can't I help?'

'No. Just sit while I get us breakfast.' She was terrifyingly efficient, setting the coffee to percolate, choosing a fish to cook, spreading a tablecloth, laying three places, forks, knives, spoons, cups, saucers, salt, pepper, butter, marmalade, all placed swiftly on the table, loading the toaster.

'When you said that –' Rory's sentence was strangled by his nervous throat.

'What?'

'That you are – that you – er – that –'

'That I'm a tart?'

'Er, yes.'

'I sleep with people for money. Got that? I have to earn my living. I have certain commitments like gas bills to pay.' And, she thought, school bills. 'The only things I'm good at, Rory, are cooking, so I take temporary cooking jobs and, as you've found out, fucking.'

Rory muttered in protest, 'Lovemaking.'

'No, Rory, not lovemaking. It's not lovemaking, it's –' Hebe paused, searching for a word which would suit him.

'What is it, if it's not lovemaking? You've made me love you.'

'This is not nineteen thirty.' Hebe poured him coffee. 'Milk, sugar?'

'Both, please. What was last night, then?'

'A free sample. If you enjoyed it and want repeats you'll have to pay.' Much better, thought Hebe, to get the financial bit over fast, then one could relax and enjoy. 'Them's my terms,' she said lightly. 'No money, no fuck.'

'Don't call it that!' He winced.

'Precious.' Hebe laughed, but her mockery was not hurtful. 'I feel very friendly,' she said, observing Rory's long upper lip and hare's eyes over the rim of her cup.

'Are there other – er – other men?'

'Yes.'

'Many?'

'That's my business. You are not likely to meet them and what you and I do has nothing to do with them, right?'

'Right,' said Rory bravely. 'So what – er – what happens?'

'I fit you in when I can.'

'Like a dentist's appointment.'

'More or less.'

They both were laughing when Louisa came into the kitchen. 'Hullo, Rory.' She kissed him as he stood up. 'You're up early. Any luck on the river? Oh, I see you've had a good morning.' She eyed the fish Hebe had ready in the pan. 'How delicious, trout for breakfast. I see you've met Hebe. Am I not lucky to have Hebe for a couple of weeks? All the glorious food without the bother of travelling to France.' Her quick eyes skimmed Rory's unshaven face. 'What time did you get here? The dogs didn't bark.'

'No, they didn't.' He looked embarrassed.

'Coffee?' Hebe held the pot aloft.

'Yes, please,' Louisa accepted. 'Someone at the door, I think.' Rufus growled and the other dogs set up a loud cacophony.

'Quiet!' shouted Louisa. 'Quiet, you beasts.'

Hebe went to the back door. A uniformed constable stood outside.

'Anybody here got a Volvo registration, er –' He consulted his notebook.

'Yes, it's mine,' said Rory, standing up.

'Parked in a rather dodgy place, if I may say so. Morning, Mrs Fox.' He saluted Louisa.

'Good morning, Constable. Like a cup of coffee?'

'No, thank you all the same.'

'I'll move it.' Rory pushed past the policeman.

'Quite a lot of traffic along that road, people going to work. You left the window down; the night dew won't have done it any good.'

'Or harm, either,' Rory shouted over his shoulder.

'Come back for your breakfast when you've moved it,' Louisa called after him. 'Goodbye, Constable.' She watched his retreating back then turned back into the kitchen. 'Well, now we can have breakfast in peace.' She smiled at Hebe, cooking the trout. She did not expect Hebe to answer and Hebe was obligingly silent, thereby rising several notches in Louisa's esteem, one of her beloved husband's maxims having been 'Never explain, never apologise'.

14

'I was wondering' – Louisa put down her napkin – 'whether I could ask you to do my shopping, Hebe. I do so hate Salisbury when it is full of tourists. Would it be very selfish to ask you to do it?'

'Of course not.' Hebe, who had been silent through breakfast, wondering whether her new acquaintance with Louisa's nephew would endanger her job, met Louisa's eyes. 'Have you much to be done?'

'One or two things I have ordered and my library books changed.'

'Could I do that? I hardly know your taste in reading.'

'I read thrillers,' Louisa answered. 'Crimies – the more complex the better. I never understand the plots but find them excellent soporifics, better than Mogadon. You will be more than able to choose for me. Not American, though.'

'And not bacon and egg.' Rory, who had reached the erroneous conclusion that his aunt believed he had got up early, spoke with the knowledge of years. 'Louisa objects to traces of other people's breakfasts in library books, bits of egg, tea stains, crumbs.' His eyes swivelled from Hebe to Louisa.

'I also object to the prudes who cross out four-letter words like "shit" and "fuck" ' said Louisa primly, 'and those who correct grammatical errors and write in the margins.'

'Tell you what,' exclaimed Rory, 'I could –'

'What could you?' Louisa watched Rory's surprise at his own temerity. He is going to offer to drive her.

'I could drive – er – Hebe in and – er – give her a lift back when I come back to fish.'

'Shall you be fishing this evening?' Louisa affected surprise.

'Yes,' said Rory. 'The weather's – er – propitious.'

'Splendid. How glad I am that I have a deep freeze. Would that arrangement suit you, Hebe?'

Hebe nodded. 'I might find something special for dinner,' she said.

'So you might.' Louisa stood up. 'I shall spend an uninterrupted day in the garden. Have a good time. No need to hurry back.' She left the kitchen followed by her dogs.

'I could give you –'

'What?'

'Lunch.' Rory forced the word out as though it were dangerous.

'Then say "lunch". Don't leave it in the air. I bet your father the General finished his sentences. If he hadn't, wars would have been worse.'

'Or better.' Rory thought of his father. 'He's still alive. Do you have a father?'

'I'll clear up the kitchen and get ready.' Hebe ignored Rory's question. They were not likely to be in Salisbury, she thought. They only go there once a month and I, she thought, have altered so much they would not recognise me. 'While I get ready, will you find Mrs Fox's books and get a list of what she wants? Make yourself useful,' she finished, rather cruelly, for she felt irritated that she was still rather uncertain about Rory. If only he were not Louisa's nephew he would fit perfectly into the gap left by Terry.

Having watched Rory drive off with Hebe, Louisa settled to enjoy a potter round her garden, her dogs strolling behind her, pausing to scratch, snap at flies, indulge in a little larking about, enjoy in their middle age the security felt by animals aware of their own worth, generous in their love for their owner, prepared when necessary to bark their heads off at strangers but rarely bite. Dead-heading her roses, Louisa anticipated her next conversation with Bernard, when she would regale him with the getting together of his one-time rivals Christopher Rutter and Algy Grant's descendants. Her peace was interrupted by the dogs' wild barking at a man coming round the house. He paid no attention to the dogs, who reared and rushed round his legs. Louisa watched his lips move. 'Quiet!' she yelled and the dogs subsided. The man came up to Louisa.

'Mrs Fox? I've brought you a packet from old Bernard Quigley. My name is Jim Huxtable.'

Louisa shook hands. 'Is he so very old?'

'*Façon de parler*. I thought as I was driving past I might be quicker than the post.' He took from his pocket a thick envelope and gave it to Louisa. 'Will you count it?'

'I don't think I need.' Louisa liked the look of Bernard's messenger. 'Shall we go into the kitchen and I will give you a drink.'

'Thank you.' He fell into step beside her.

'Or a snack. We could have a snack before you go on your way. Have you far to go?'

'Cornwall.'

'To Bernard?' Her face lit up.

'Yes.'

'You must tell me how he is. It is ages since I saw him, ages.'

'I think he is well.' Jim Huxtable paced beside Louisa. 'Have you known him long?'

'More than fifty years.'

'That's quite a long time.'

'It depends how you look at it.' Louisa looked back along the telescoping years to see herself and Bernard young, she twenty, he rather older. 'How is he keeping? Do you see much of him?'

'When I am in Cornwall I stay with him. Do you know his house?'

'No. Tell me about it.'

'It's very isolated. He lives in it with his cat and his dog.'

'Feathers.'

'Yes, his dog is called Feathers.' Jim looked with interest at Bernard's old friend. 'He has a great collection in his house. He sometimes buys from me, occasionally sells.' She was beautiful once, he thought.

'So he's still an active dealer?'

'You could say that. Sometimes he asks me to sell things for him.'

'Then he trusts you.' Louisa looked at Jim with interest.

'I hope so.' Jim suffered her glance.

They went into the house.

'Let's see what we can find to eat. Is it too early for you to have lunch? My cook is in Salisbury.' She did not wait for Jim to answer but flitted about the kitchen emitting little cries of pleasure: 'Ah, bread. She makes bread – delicious. Ah, pâté, here we are, she makes this too. And wine, here is a bottle and salad, she makes the most gorgeous dressing, here it is, and if we have any room left we can eat fruit and cake. How would that be? Are you hungry?'

'I am beginning to be,' said Jim, appreciating Louisa.

'Sit down, then.' Louisa found plates and glasses, poured Jim a glass of wine. 'We can finish with coffee, though I cannot make coffee like my cook.'

'Perhaps you'd let me. I learned how to make coffee in a bar in Italy,' Jim offered.

'Certainly, that would round off our snack. Tell me more about Bernard. How is age treating him?'

'He keeps it at bay; he has some trick.'

'He walks across country to the telephone. That keeps him fit.'

'It's a long walk, very long in rough weather. I have begged him to have the telephone put in.'

'He won't,' said Louisa, spreading pâté on crusty bread. 'From Bernard originated the expression, "Don't call me, I'll call you." He is fierce in the preservation of his privacy, always was.'

'It's inconvenient.' Jim remembered with irritation times when to get hold of Bernard had been impossible and necessitated the long trip to Penzance. 'He does not answer letters. Does he ever write to you?' Jim asked, then wished he had not, sensing her pain.

'No.' Louisa was expressionless. 'Have some more pâté? No? Fruit, then.'

'Lovely pâté. It was excellent. Your cook has talent.'

'I'll tell her. She is only here for a fortnight. I treat myself to a cook once or twice a year. At my age travel is an effort and to be honest I don't care for it any more, so I have this splendid girl. She cooks divinely and when she is here she fills my deep freeze so that for a long time I have treats. Do you not think this a good idea?'

'Brilliant.' He tried to imagine this woman and Bernard in their prime.

'There are other considerations,' said Louisa. 'I don't have to leave my garden or my dogs.' She looked at the dogs lying by the

Aga. 'And if the telephone rings I am here to answer it.'

She is still in love with Bernard, thought Jim, fascinated. How does it work in old age? Is it purely cerebral? 'Shall I make coffee?' he asked. 'I'm sure I can't compete with your cook but I'll try.'

'Thank you. She's gone to Salisbury with my nephew. He was here fishing. We had trout for breakfast.' Louisa smiled, remembering Rory's unshaven appearance. 'He must have got up very early. He is fishing again tonight.' She laughed, thinking of Rory. 'I am sorry you missed them,' she said, watching Jim make coffee. Then, 'Perhaps you can stay. Would you like to stay the night? It would be no trouble since I have my cook. She is bringing back some delight from Salisbury for dinner.'

'Alas, I can't, I must push on.'

'Would you take one or two things to Bernard for me, since you are going his way?' I can trust this man, thought Louisa, and he's jolly attractive.

'Of course.'

'Bernard sells things for me. When we have had our coffee let me see what I can bear to part with. It is a question of balance; cook versus things.'

'I see.' Jim felt distress.

'Cooks are expensive,' said Louisa. This man would be much better for Hebe than Rory, she thought, and I wonder whether he is married.

'Yes.'

'But she gives me so much pleasure.' She watched him make coffee, pronounced it delicious, 'Even better than cook's.' She amused herself referring to Hebe as 'cook'. Then she led him through the house and, while he envied her furniture, she opened a drawer and exclaimed, 'Ah, this', and again, 'Ah, this and this', producing pieces of jewellery, a snuff box, a watch, putting them into his hand. 'Put them into your pocket so that I do not see them,' and seeing his surprise she explained, 'If I hide things I may sell and forget them then I feel less wrench at parting. I think that should do for the present.'

'I'll give you a receipt,' Jim said.

'No, no. Bernard trusts you, that's enough.' But Jim wrote a receipt while she watched him.

When she stood by Jim's car to say goodbye she said, 'I enjoyed seeing you. Tell him to telephone me.'

'I will do that.' It is important; Bernard is not a stale old man to her.

'I wish you could have stayed and met my cook.'

'Thank her for my lunch. I will tell him to telephone.'

A lonely old thing, Jim thought, driving away. What would I want to meet her cook for? He switched on his car radio and settled himself for the long drive to Cornwall calculating, as he listened to the afternoon concert, the value of Louisa's 'things'. However much the cook cost Louisa could afford to pay her quite a few more times.

Weeding her herbaceous border with the sun on her back and the sound of bees among the flowers, Louisa thought Bernard's friend a handsome man; tall – she liked tall men – nice hair, must have been that rare colour she liked before it went grey – good eyes, a humorous mouth. He was the type she admired, the type she had married. Why then the tug at her heart when he spoke of Bernard, why after nearly fifty years was Bernard, who was small and had never been good-looking, so special. 'Ah,' said Louisa, sitting back on her heels and pushing her hair back from her forehead, 'he made me laugh.' The dogs wagged their tails, glad that she was happy. Remembering the big bed in the Hôtel d'Angleterre in Paris so many years ago, with the light shining through the chinks of the red plush curtains and the breakfasts of croissants and coffee, Louisa grinned. 'He was a rascal,' she said to the dog Rufus who was her favourite, 'a rascal but he still makes me laugh.' Rufus bowed down, inviting her to play, waving his plumy tail. 'But I couldn't be part of a team, could I?' she said to Rufus, voicing the suspicion she had taken care never to verify that she was by no means the first girl Bernard had taken to stay in that hotel room in those long ago days which in old age seemed clearer than yesterday, infinitely more real than the present.

15

Jennifer Reeves believed in her menfolk, as she thought of her husband, her son and his friends, starting the day with a good breakfast. Silas ate what was put in front of him, a bowl of porridge followed by bacon and eggs, washed down with tea, and listened to Michael arguing with Julian about the merits of a boat they had had the previous year compared with the boat they were to sail that day. As they talked it dawned on him that his hosts thought nothing of sailing to France or Holland and that Julian and Jennifer had sailed down the coast from Sussex during the summer term, taking several weekends to bring the boat to the Scillies, returning to London after each trip. He was impressed by so much effort. It became clear as he listened that Mrs Reeves was giving him her place in the boat on the day's expedition. When he politely protested, Jennifer cried, 'No, no, Silas, I don't mind at all. I have lots to do here and you have never been to Bishop's Rock. You must go, you will love it. I have been often, haven't I?' She appealed to her husband and son, showing her fine teeth and healthy gums.

'Ma's a great sailor,' said Michael with his mouth full. 'Pass the marm, Pa.' Julian pushed the marmalade towards his son. 'Are we taking our lunch?'

'Mrs Thing has made pasties. Super for sailing.'

Silas wondered what Mrs Thing's name could be.

'Mind you all take lots of sweaters, it can be cold out there. Has someone lent Silas boots?' asked Jennifer.

Michael said, 'He can wear mine, I've got two pairs.'

'When's the off?' enquired Ian.

'Half an hour.' Julian's voice grew louder at the prospect. 'If you're not all ready by then I'll go without you.'

'Time to empty our bowels.' Alistair, the younger brother, left the table. 'Bags I the upstairs loo.' Nobody commented.

Presently, wearing Michael's spare boots, which, too large, made walking difficult, wearing his favourite sweater and carrying Hebe's Guernsey for spare, Silas stood waiting for the others. He noticed that the wind had not dropped during the night and that the sea between Trescoe and St Mary's was choppy. When the boys and Julian were assembled they proceeded down to the landing stage, carrying lunch baskets and a variety of objects strange to Silas which would be needed on the boat. Julian handed him a life jacket and Alistair officiously showed him how to put it on. At the landing stage they clambered into an inflatable dinghy and set off across the water to St Mary's where the Reeves' boat was moored.

Silas had never been in an inflatable boat and enjoyed the crossing; the wind made his eyes water. When they reached the boat in which they were to sail he clambered in after Michael and sat down where Julian told him, out of harm's way. Michael, Alistair and Ian busied themselves about the boat, obeying Julian's orders. Silas surreptitiously put on Hebe's sweater over his own and flexed his toes in the too large boots to keep warm while he readjusted his life jacket.

Julian and the boys exchanged shouted greetings with people on shore. Silas sat hoping his ignorance of sailing would not show, wondering if he would ever learn which rope did what. He wondered belatedly whether he had the guts to say he would rather stay on shore and watch birds and as he wondered Michael cast off and they moved out into open water.

From time to time Julian shouted at Silas, pointing out to him St Agnes. 'That's St Agnes. Splits in two at low tide,' and 'Shags, d'you know the difference between a cormorant and a shag?'

'Yes.'

'Interested in birds, are you?'

'Quite.'

'Like to take the tiller?'

'Oh, thank you.' Silas felt tremulous pleasure. Was he now responsible for all their lives?

Pleasure was succeeded by anxiety. Suppose somebody

shouted 'Port' or 'Starboard', what was he supposed to do? 'Port on the right is never left,' he remembered. Julian had gone below. He could see him putting on another sweater, balancing with his legs apart. Alistair and Michael were further up the boat near the mast, Ian right in the bows. The boat was crashing along on her side. Ian shouted something and pointed. Silas looked up. Coming in from Penzance was the *Scillonian*, a familiar friend moored in Penzance harbour but out here doing a chopping roll, sending up a steep wave at her bow, menacing. Silas watched with interest as she drew nearer. 'Watch out, you shitty idiot!' Julian snatched the tiller, tipping Silas off balance so that he sprawled backwards. Julian, white and furious, altered course, ignoring angry shouts from the *Scillonian*.

'What d'you want to give him the tiller for? He's never sailed in his life,' Michael yelled. 'Ma would have a fit,' he raged at his father. Julian shouted 'Shut up!' and chopped at his son. Michael dodged. It began to rain viciously, coldly, cruelly. Silas, on his feet again, wondered where he could go to be out of the way. He felt futile, ashamed, small.

'Why don't you go below?' Michael suggested, but Silas shook his head. He was supposed to be enjoying this. He would not ask how far to the Bishop's Rock, how long before we get there. He stared at the sea and braced himself against the movement of the boat, wishing his feet in the two big boots were not so terribly cold.

When they reached it the Bishop's Rock was scary in its defiant loneliness. Julian, who had been silent after his spat with his son, laughed as he steered. Silas, watching Michael, guessed that they were far too close for safety and that Julian was punishing Michael as he drove the boat close in where the sea surged and sucked at the black rocks.

It was Ian who suggested lunch and fetched up the basket of pasties. They were now tacking for home. Silas had seen boats tack in Mounts Bay but had never realised how much work it entailed. It seemed crazy for Julian, Michael, Alistair and Ian to be trying to eat pasties as they worked the boat, dodging and ducking the boom. The wind had increased and Julian yelled that they must shorten sail. Silas caught snatches of incomprehensible jargon and admired the boys as they nimbly obeyed.

They looked serious now and Silas saw Julian look up at the sky, frowning.

Clouds bulging with rain were surging in from the west. A black mass suddenly sheeted rods of water, as he remembered seeing in a Rembrandt print in a book of Hebe's. The squall hit the boat, drenching them in the few minutes it took to pass. In his fear, Silas gulped and gobbled his pasty, noticing with one cell of his brain that the pasty was greasy, had been made with fat meat, was in no way comparable to the pasties made for him by his mother when he went picnicking with Giles, nor had Mrs Thing put in any turnip.

The sensation that he had a stone in his stomach, that he would never be warm again, that he was going deaf, assailed Silas so suddenly that he barely had time to reach the side to be sick. To compound his misery the wind blew the vomit back on to his chest, splattering Hebe's jersey, and down into Michael's boots. Pasty, porridge, bacon, egg and tea in a greasy agonising rush. Oh God! I wish I could die.

'He's thrown up into my boots,' yelled Michael, and Ian, who never became a friend, laughed.

16

With the courage many timid men acquire behind the driving wheel, Rory found himself able to speak to Hebe sitting beside him in a butcher blue cotton dress, her shoulder-length hair tousled by the air from the open window. Her legs were long and bare. He noted with relief that she had not painted her toenails and that her rather large feet were beautifully shaped.

'When last night I came into your room,' he began.

'Yes?' She looked at the road ahead.

'When I came into your room, were you surprised?'

'Of course.'

'What puzzles me is that you didn't scream.'

'What good would that have done?'

'You didn't cover yourself up.'

'I had nothing to hide.' Hebe looked at the road. Soon they would see the spire of Salisbury Cathedral, the tallest in England.

'You – er – the words you used – I –'

'Would you rather have me say I saw something stirring in the undergrowth of your trousers? That it?'

'No, it's just –'

'Too well brought up? What about your aunt and her library books? She isn't afraid to use four-letter words.'

'She shocks my father and mother.'

'You needn't.' Hebe turned to look at him. 'You needn't, if I shock you, have anything more to do with me. It's no skin off my nose.'

'Hebe, you know I –'

'What?'

'I want to. I – er – want – I –'

'Do you *never* finish a sentence?'
'Only short ones.'
'Tell me what you want, then?'
'You. That short enough?' Rory said with a burst of spirit.
'You want to join the Syndicate?'
'Is that what you call it?'
'For want of a better word.'
Rory was silent. He was both excited and horrified. Presently he said, 'It sounds so cold.'
Hebe sniffed and said, 'Businesslike.'
'How can you?' Rory protested in anguish.
'Look,' she was growing impatient. 'My body is my business. Business is buying and selling – right? You sell hats.'
'Not many,' he sighed.
'Don't interrupt. I sell. If you want to buy, you buy. There's no obligation.'
'Oh – I –'
'I enjoy my business. Surely you noticed that last night?'
'Oh, I did.' Rory's cry was heartfelt.
'Well, then.' She was smiling now.
'How do I set about it? How do I join?' Rory capitulated, looking sideways at Hebe, trying to see the eyes he had woken to find watching him at close range.
'Keep your eye on the road, love, you nearly had us in the ditch.'
'Oh.' His eyes swivelled back to the road. 'Sorry.'
'This is how it works.' Her voice was dry. Inwardly she cringed, loathing this part of the transaction. 'I tell you when I am free. We decide a place to meet and I meet you there for a weekend or a week.'
'Not longer?'
'Not longer. We decide in advance how much you will pay, you give me a cheque or cash if you'd rather, and it's up to me to tell you when I will come.'
'You decide that, why can't I?'
'I should think that's pretty obvious.'
'Fitting me in with the rest of the Syndicate.' Rory bristled with jealousy.
'Yes.'

'Why don't you sack them and marry me?'

'Marriage is not on the menu, that's one thing you must get into your head.'

'Are you married already?' Rory was appalled by the thought. Hebe married to some brute, forced to make pin money as a cook, as a, ah me, he groaned inwardly, a tart.

'No.'

Rory felt the conversation coming to an end, that Hebe sitting beside him was some sort of female oyster clammed shut. He mixed metaphors in his muddled mind.

'Do I have a choice of venue?' he asked.

'Yes, you can have that,' she conceded.

Driving the last three miles into the city, Rory wondered whether to have Hebe to stay in his house behind the shop; he was happy there and had a garden which was pretty and not overlooked. Or whether he dared take her to a cottage his Great-aunt Calypso occasionally lent him in the middle of her wood famous for its flowering cherries, daffodils and bluebells. He steered the car thoughtfully through the maze of streets, with their infuriating one-way system, to the place he parked his car. Beside him he noticed with baffled rage Hebe was calmly checking her shopping list.

Rory had never before found shopping fun. They went first to the fishmonger, where Hebe discovered grouse flown from Scotland. 'Why not buy grouse?' She felt the breasts of the dead birds, murmuring, 'These had pitifully short lives.' Rory volunteered to pay, since he felt this might repay Louisa's hospitality. They stood discussing the matter, annoying the fishmonger, holding up a queue of people. Hebe explained that she always bought extra for Louisa's deep freeze, which she filled with pâtés and preserves. The birds were piled into the shopping basket. They went to the delicatessen, argued over cheeses and bought German mustard and a bottle of Greek olive oil. They carried their shopping back to Rory's shop before returning to the market to buy vegetables and fruit. Rory watched Hebe choose, setting aside the unripe or slightly off, regardless of the fury of the stallholders. 'In France they don't respect you if you just take what you're given. Look at that peach, a Saturday night bruise, and that banana's lame.' Her shopping done, she turned to Rory. 'Shall we do the library before lunch?' They fetched Louisa's books from the car.

In the library Rory took over, collecting armfuls of crime from the shelves, sitting on a bench to look them through. 'You help,' he said to Hebe. 'She used to get home and find she'd taken out a book she'd already read. She puts a little sign, look, here's one, a dot in a circle. Discard that, check for the purely American, she can't read the language, and lastly for other people's breakfasts.'

'What about the rude words crossed out?'

'That, too.' Rory laughed.

The librarian from her desk pointed to the sign which said 'Silence'. Hebe whispered to Rory, 'I am enjoying my day,' filling him with joy.

They chose four books and added them to their pile of shopping.

'Why don't we have lunch here? What have you got in your fridge?' Hebe peered into the refrigerator.

'Don't you want to go to a restaurant?'

'Not particularly. Here's a nice wine.' She held up a bottle of Muscadet. 'Why don't you run to the fishmonger and buy prawns or something. There's brown bread and butter here.'

Rory came back with a lobster and a lettuce. Watching Hebe make mayonnaise, he knew he had never been happier.

During lunch he told Hebe of his life, his parents, his schools, his stand against going, as his father wished, into the Army, his sudden declaration that all he had ever wanted was a hat shop, an inspiration based on his resemblance to the March Hare, about which his family teased him.

'I bet that floored them.'

'It did. Then I had to have one. That's how I started. I had never really considered such a thing.'

'And your Aunt Louisa backed you up?'

'Yes. She doesn't like my father, and my Great-aunt Calypso helped me too.'

'The aunt who gave you my hat? That aunt?'

'Yes. Her husband planted the wood where I want to take you when – er – when it's my turn. There's a cottage.'

'What a long sentence, Rory. You finished it and several others.'

'You are mocking.'

'Only a little. Let's go to bed and you tell me about your great-aunt's wood.'

'Oh, I will.' Rory got up from the table. As they went upstairs he said, 'I hope you'll find – er – find the bed –'

'Comfortable?'

'Yes and er –'

'And you can tell me about your other girls.'

'I'm not much good with girls. They – er –'

'Don't know what they're missing.' Hebe caught her dress by the skirt and whooshed it up and over her head in what seemed to Rory one waving movement. 'Come on,' she said, climbing into his bed, 'let's enjoy ourselves.'

Should he enjoy himself? Should he not feel the puritan shame his parents had instilled?

'Work up an appetite for dinner,' urged Hebe cheerfully.

'You are so prosaic,' he cried. 'So –'

'Practical.'

'Perfect.' He was delighted.

'Not that.' Suddenly she held him. He sensed fear in her and feeling her vulnerable held her close. When she slept he watched her until she woke. 'We should be getting back if I am to cook dinner. This has been quite a long day off and a lovely siesta.'

Rory wanted to ask how it came about that she was a tart, guessed she would not tell him. Standing under the shower, watching her dress through the open door of the bathroom, he realised she had told him nothing about herself.

'Rory,' Hebe called, 'you still haven't shaved. What will your aunt think?'

'My aunt,' said Rory thoughtfully, 'may not – er – may not –'

'What may she not?' Hebe came to sit on the edge of the bath to watch him shave.

'May not expect me to stay.'

'You mustn't stay.'

'But last night – er –'

'Last night was exceptional. Really, Rory, it was. I never mix my cooking commitments with my tarting.'

'Don't say –'

'All right, but it's true I never mix the two. Today's a day off.'

'You mean I've got to wait?' Rory, with his face covered in lather, looked slightly mad.

'I shall have to see when I can fit you in.'

'When do you leave Louisa?'

'On the twenty-first.'

'So then we can –'

'I have other commitments.' In Hebe's mind a vision of Silas coming to greet her off the train. Only this time he would be getting off the helicopter, his wonderful visit over. 'I'm sorry,' she said gently. 'I really do have other things to do.'

Disappointed, Rory shaved, his anxious eyes trying to catch sight of Hebe in the glass.

'I could drive you.'

'I have my own car.'

'Where do you live?'

'I never tell anyone where I live.'

'Blast!' shouted Rory. 'Blast you!'

'That's the way it is. That's the only way I can manage. You must put up with it.'

'You give, then take it all away,' he wailed.

'If it's any comfort to you, none of my clients knows where I live. Your aunt doesn't.'

'Even she?'

'Even she. I ring her and suggest dates. You will just have to trust me and if you find someone better, well and good.'

'But I want to be able to telephone – er – talk to you, write to you.'

'Sorry, Rory, you can't. I have an address in London which forwards my mail. I'll give you that. I don't mind if you write.'

'I can't bear it!' Rory shouted through the lather. 'I really don't –' Clumsily he mopped his face.

'Then stop now. No need to go on. Forget the whole idea.' Stupid of me, thought Hebe, to think this man could take Terry's place. This is a clinger.

'But I – I – want –' Rory cried like a deprived child. 'I do so want.'

'Think about it. No need to hurry. There's no rush. I don't

blame you if you don't want to go on. I see your point of view. It's just that I pay more attention to mine.'

In silence they collected the parcels, in silence they drove back to Louisa's house. He grew sulky, almost surly. Hebe felt oppressed, her cheefulness left her. She reproached herself for encouraging him, for enjoying herself, for accepting the hat, for inviting him into her bed. She felt sad.

Louisa's dogs greeted them with barks and yelps, leaping up on Hebe as she stood with her arms full of parcels, Rufus jumping up to her face, bumping her with his wet nose.

'Down!' shouted Louisa, coming out of the house, 'Down, you beasts.' She took one of the baskets from Hebe. 'You clever girl, grouse. Shall we have a grouse for dinner? Quiet!' she shouted at the dogs. She followed Hebe into the kitchen where she was putting her parcels on to the table.

'What's the –' Hebe sniffed the air. 'There's a –'

Louisa looked at Hebe; she seemed odd. Rory, catching sight of her face, saw her as he had first seen her in his shop and wondered whether she was about to faint.

'Here.' He pushed her into a chair. 'I'll get a glass of – put your head between –'

'It's all right.' Hebe took his hand. 'I'm not going to faint, just for a moment I imagined I smelt something that,' she buried her face in his sleeve, 'reminded me.'

'Of what?' whispered Rory.

Oh dear, he's fallen in love with her, thought Louisa, watching them. Poor dear Rory.

'I don't know. I don't know what it reminds me of, that's what worries me.' She tried to laugh. 'I'm just being silly. It's like coffee or wood smoke, something of the sort.' She let go of Rory. 'I feel a fool, like when you can't remember a word which you know really well.'

'I'm often at a loss for a word,' Rory comforted.

'I had a visitor today. He made coffee after lunch, perhaps that is it,' Louisa volunteered. 'A friend of a friend of mine brought me a packet I was expecting. He made the coffee. It was even better than yours, Hebe.'

'That must be it.' Hebe looked relieved, though still puzzled.

'Smells are very evocative.' Louisa watched Hebe anxiously.

'And it's a tease when you can't remember what they remind you of,' she gabbled on, while Hebe collected herself.

Although the grouse were delicious, conversation at dinner was strained. Louisa was not surprised when Rory decided that it was not after all a good evening for fishing, a lie which he took little trouble to hide. They watched the news on television and Louisa thought of Bernard in his tiny isolated house when the weathermen forecast gales coming in from the Atlantic, knowing that when the wind blew and rain pelted down Bernard was loath to adventure across country to the telephone. She would have to wait to question him about Jim Huxtable; wait to tell him about Hebe's meeting with Rory. He was always interested in Hebe's visits, a subject which almost superseded their gardens. Her thoughts took her away from the young people who presently took the dogs for a run. She tried to visualise Bernard, old and pottering in his garden, and failed, only seeing him young with no interest in flowers other than to order in quantity at a florist and send with a card: 'Louisa, my love, Bernard'.

They had walked by the river and back to Rory's car. 'Goodbye.' Hebe held out her hand.

Rory bent to kiss her. 'When shall I –?'

'I have written down my forwarding address; here it is. I will get in touch, I promise. Are you sure you want me to?'

'Of course I –'

'I don't want to make you unhappy.'

'I will take the risk.' He got into his car and Hebe watched him drive away. She looked up at the threatening sky, hoping that Silas' pleasure would not be spoiled by storms, and forgot Rory as she tried to visualise Silas in the company of strangers. As she sniffed the scent of jasmine and tobacco plants and watched moths fluttering round the flowers, she wished herself away from Rory, so easily hurt, bruised, as she herself was by the world they had both been born into, had both escaped. And yet, she thought, part of me wishes it for Silas. Why else do I send him to that school, encourage him to stay with those people? Do I still believe he should have that chance? Do I believe in that mould which I fought to escape? Am I not as hypocritical as they were? They brought me up to be like them, to marry a man with money as my sisters did. Am I not tarting with Mungo and Rory to pay for Silas to have what I rejected? Am I misusing the Syndicate money?

In bed she lay reading Rory's copy of the *New Statesman*, finding cheer in the Heartsearch column. 'Attractive Intellectual - Well worn - Unconventional colour-blind male/female - passionate - scrawny - happy - myopic - Nigerian - non-sexist - tallish - working class background - jazz media orientated - educated - divorced - academic.' None of these paying propositions. She had once answered an appeal from a lonely Hampsteader in a bedsitter. He had needed to have a girl walking beside him across the Heath. I must look him up some time, she thought, when I am doing a stint with Mungo. It had been an agreeable sexless interlude. After the walks they had eaten chocolate éclairs and drunk camomile tea. He had given her ten pounds a time. She turned the page. Ah, here goes! She took note of an advertisement. 'Love Lingerie, Ultimate in Undies, slinkiest pure silk, cut to dazzling American minimum.' The illustration showed a lady with her pussy slung in the sort of bag Leni Riefenstahl had made for the Nazi athletes when filming them for the Olympic Games. Must send for one for Terry, a parting gift; his neat little apparatus would fit into that pure silk job nicely.

Consoled by cheerful memories of Terry, she turned off the light.

17

The storm, which in infancy had made Silas sick, grew that night to monster proportions unusual even in the South-West. The gale gusted in from the Atlantic, bringing rain which lashed the streets, racing down the gutters. At high tide waves leapt across the sea wall, scattering stones and kelp over the promenade. Ships made for the shelter of Mounts Bay. Lifeboats from St Ives and Sennen battled to the rescue of a French trawler. Rogue water, gaining speed as it travelled, swept cigarette butts, lolly sticks, cellophane wrapping towards drains which, already blocked, refused entry. Gathering force in the alleyway behind the houses, the water found a weakness in a wall, sucked until it discovered a chink then, crawling through, gained entry into Amy Tremayne's garden, travelled to the back door, spread through the house, souping wet the rugs in her sitting-room until they could hold no more, reformed and found the way out to the street.

Disturbed by the ferocity of the gale, Amy got out of bed to close her window. Reaching up to pull down the sash, a fierce pain in her chest assailed her. She collapsed in a chair, sick and dizzy. Her pills, out of reach, mocked her from the table by the bed. The telephone was on the ground floor. How often Hebe had begged her to have an extension. She tried to breathe, willing the pain to go, willing time to pass so that daylight would bring help. Rain driving in at the window drenched her knees. If Hebe finds me dead she will be upset. I can't die yet. She willed herself to live, sitting huddled in the chair by the window. As time passed she dozed, forgetting that Hebe was away working for Louisa Fox.

Terry, on his way to feed Trip, hurried up the street in the dawn, his chin tucked into his upturned collar, looking about him fascinated by the violence of the weather. Level with Hebe's door he noticed muddy water across the street, investigated, looked up at Amy's window, saw that it was open, looked more closely, saw the huddled figure in a chair. He tried the front door, found it locked, water seeping through.

He called up, 'Hi, Miss Tremayne, you're flooded.'

The old woman jerked awake. Terry saw her face. 'Christ, she's dying.'

He leapt on to the low wall which separated a strip of flowers from the street, gathered all his strength, sprang, catching the window ledge, hauling himself up to fall head first into the room at Amy's feet.

'Don't be afraid.' He picked himself up. 'Let me get you back to bed.' He gathered the old woman in his arms. 'You are cold.' He laid her on the bed, propped her with pillows, pulled up the bedclothes. 'Have you got pills? Is it your heart?'

'Yes,' she whispered.

'These the pills?'

'Yes.'

He tipped out the pills. 'One? Two?'

'One,' she whispered.

He put the pill in her mouth, held a glass so that she could drink. She gripped his hand.

'You are Hebe's black revenge.' He could hardly hear her.

'What?'

'Hebe's black –'

'You need something hot. Don't move, I'll see what I can do. Okay if I leave you a moment?'

He ran downstairs, splashed into the flood. 'Christ!' Hurried into the kitchen, put a kettle on the gas, rummaged for brandy, found a half bottle of whisky, saw a hot water bottle hanging on the back of the door, filled it, made tea, poured in a dollop of whisky, carried them upstairs.

'Don't try and talk.' He tucked the hot bottle in by her feet. 'Soon get you warm. Drink this.' He sat beside her spooning hot tea into her obedient mouth. 'That better?' He willed her to live.

'Yes.' She felt better for the tea, the hot bottle was warming her feet. Terry put the empty cup aside and started rubbing her hands between his.

'I must telephone your doctor.'

'No.'

'Surely –'

'I don't want a doctor.'

'Okay.' He went on rubbing her hands. Should he tell her the downstairs was awash? Would it set her heart off again?

'Did you say flood?' Her voice was stronger.

'Yes. It's coming in at the back. I should –'

'Stay with me.' She held his hands. 'Hebe's black revenge.' She stared at his anxious face, liking his fine high-bridged nose and sculptured mouth.

'I'm not with you.' He was puzzled.

'Hebe's black joke.' What a spit in the eye for Christopher. She had never seen Terry close up, only catching an occasional glimpse from a distance. 'Hebe never told me you were so beautiful.'

Terry looked embarrassed. 'We're still friends. The other's over.'

'I know.'

'I was on my way to feed her cat. What d'you mean, black revenge? Black joke?'

Amy began to laugh.

'Don't laugh, mind your heart,' Terry exclaimed, but she looked better, a lot better.

Amy grinned, thinking of Christopher Rutter, how furious he would be, his worst accusations come true. Why had she never had the enterprise that Hebe showed? Where had Hebe found him?

'Where d'you come from? What's your job?'

'I met Hebe up country. I make burglar traps. I'm self-employed. I was adopted by liberal whites. I dropped out of a posh school they sent me to. It's my own invention.' If he went on talking she might go to sleep, then he could get the doctor. 'I make a contraption like an abacus with marbles. It's set under a strip of carpet to match what's in the room. When the burglar treads on it he feels insecure, scarpers.'

'Do you sell many?' Keep him with me for a bit longer, she thought.

'Quite a lot. A friend of Hebe's gave me introductions, lists of names, old fellow called Quigley.'

'Oh, him.'

'Do you know him? He made this list of people all over the country. Some bought.'

'Tell me who he sent you to.'

Terry recited a litany of names, his pleasing voice lulling her until suddenly she grew alert. Among the names were Robert, Delian, Marcus. Did Hebe know this?

'Did he send you to anyone called Rutter?' she asked sharply.

'Yes, an old bloke called Christopher Rutter, same name as Hebe's. Mr Quigley says everyone is interconnected. It's a common name, he says.'

'Did you tell Hebe?'

'I don't think so.'

'How did you get on with him, old Christopher? Did he buy?'

'He did, said my quotation was cheaper than most.'

Amy began to laugh.

'Hey, don't laugh, this isn't the time.'

'*Ce n'est pas le moment*.' Her mind wandered.

'What?'

'In the Hôtel d'Angleterre he said' – Amy remembered the tone of voice – 'he didn't want to know, thought it would sound easier in French. He left and I left soon after. Bloody Bernard.'

Terry frowned. What was Amy on about? He was trapped. She was hanging on to his hand. He should have got the doctor straight away, or the niece, the blonde across the street. Hebe had not said Amy was gone in the head. His eyes, roving round the room in search of escape, hit on Amy's clothes.

'Hey! Do you wear those things?' Amy followed his glance.

'They keep the draught out.' She eyed her directoire knickers. 'They are to my taste.' She turned to look at him. 'And yours is different.'

So Hebe had told her. 'Yes,' he said, looking Amy in the eye. 'Yes,' he repeated. 'Knickers for comfort, skirts for a lark.'

'Good lad,' she said unexpectedly. 'And you and she read poetry.'

'She talks to you a lot.' He grew suspicious.

'She must talk to someone. Recite me something before you go.'

'I'll try. What do you like?'

'The one about the chestnut tree, know it? Great rooted something?'

'Blossomer. Chestnut tree. Yeats?'

'That's the one. Then fetch Hannah. Do you know her?'

'I'd like to.'

'Chestnut poem first,' Amy insisted.

Terry cleared his throat and began. As he recited he saw the rain had stopped and the sun was shining. 'O chestnut tree great rooted blossomer.' Amy held his hand and closed her eyes. When he reached, 'How can we tell the dancer from the dance,' Amy lay quiet, her hand in his. Terry looked at her face, no longer twisted with pain. Sitting beside her, examining her face, he thought he understood why Hebe loved this old woman. It was peaceful in the room. Soon he must get help, but he was loath to break the peace between himself and Amy. She opened her eyes.

'Better now.'

Terry stood up. 'Will you be okay if I leave you and wake your niece?'

'Yes.'

'I should get the doctor.'

'No. I hate fuss. I'll be all right.' Her voice suddenly peevish, she said, 'You want to get away. Thank you for coming. Just fetch Hannah.' She was annoyed with herself. She had betrayed Hebe. 'I'm very grateful,' she said stiffly.

Puzzled and hurt, Terry let go her hand, stood up awkwardly. 'I'll go.' He left Amy's room and ran down the stairs, splashing into the flood. He had forgotten the flood water, had concentrated on Amy. Now, ankle-deep in water, he forgot her. The flood was urgent. He pulled open the front door and water surged into the street. He ran to Hannah's house and hammered on the door.

Opening the door in her dressing-gown, Hannah stared at Terry, her mind foggy with sleep, filled with an unexpected and strange exhilaration. Wow! Terry was talking, his voice eager; he too was excited. She heard, 'Your auntie's flooded, muddy water is coming in from the back.' But his eyes conveyed another message. He pushed past her into the house, towering above her so that for a moment all she saw was his neck and throat.

Hannah yelped, backing away. 'Who are you? What do you want?' She stared at the ebony youth.

'Name's Terry, friend of Hebe's. Get some clothes on, for Chrissake, you silly female. The old girl's awash.' His excitement was infectious.

'What's the matter, Ma?' Giles, in pyjamas, called from upstairs.

Terry shouted the situation to Giles. In minutes they were in Amy's house. Giles dialled 999 on Amy's telephone. Terry went to the back of the house to find the source of the flood. Hannah arrived wearing yellow boots, jeans and a green jersey.

'What's it like out there?' she asked.

'Job for the Council. We telephoned. Got a spade so we can divert the water?'

'No, we haven't.'

'I'll get one from Hebe's. Got to feed the cat, anyway.' He darted out into the rain.

'Who is that? He sure is bossy,' said Hannah to Giles.

'Friend of Hebe's. Lucky he found the flood. Hurry up, Mum, stop staring.'

'That you, Hannah?' Amy's voice from upstairs.

'I'm coming up.' Hannah went up, expecting Amy to make a fuss.

'You all right, Auntie?' She stood by Amy's bed.

Feeling ill but unwilling to show it, Amy said, 'Just a bit tired,' unconvincingly.

'You don't look well,' Hannah was anxious.

'I shall stay here until the mess is gone. That boy can help you. He's been reciting poetry to me.'

Hannah glanced out of the back window at Terry, stripped to the waist, digging a ditch to divert the water. 'Doesn't Hebe know him?' she asked.

'Lovely, isn't he?'

'Lovely?' Hannah stared at Amy. 'How did he get in?' she asked suspiciously.

'Jumped. He's a jumper.'

'You're joking –'

Amy closed her eyes. Hannah looked more closely at Terry. He was lovely. He was also making Giles laugh. Hannah's spirits soared. Mm, she thought, why not? 'I'd better go and direct operations if you are comfortable,' she said.

'I'm comfortable.' As Hannah left the room Amy chuckled, pleased at the prospect of vicarious entertainment. Time Hannah loosened up, she thought, and who better than Hebe's joker to do the loosening. She knew Hebe's standard to be high, but this one was superb. She quite understood Hebe breaking her unwritten rule never to have a local involvement.

By the end of the morning Terry and Giles had stemmed the water, the ground floor of the house was ready to be scrubbed, Council workmen had unblocked the drain. Hannah, filling the kettle to make tea, was almost sorry the crisis was over. As she handed Terry his tea she looked at him appraisingly. Waking her in the morning and grubbing at the back of Amy's house with Giles, she had thought him not much older than Giles. The look he was giving her now was in another league. Her eyes widened when he advanced on her, catching her round the waist so that the cups in her hands joggled.

'Watch out, you'll spill the tea.' She showed her toothy regiment as he pushed his face close to hers.

'How about a quick little screw before din-dins?' he suggested.

She pulled away from him, laughing. 'I must look after my aunt.' She tried to look disapproving.

'After, then,' he pressed.

'And look after Giles. Let go, Terry.'

'I'll wait.' He let go. 'I'll show you a thing you'll enjoy.'

'Cheeky.' She could not help laughing. Then, 'That's enough,' slightly nervous. She tried to snub him.

'It will be,' he leered, looking lascivious.

'Will somebody bring me my treasures?' Amy's voice came in quavery descant from upstairs.

'I'd forgotten her. What treasures she got? Nothing like yours, I bet.' He put his hands over her breasts.

'Hey, hands off.'

'Treasures,' came Amy's voice. 'My treasures,' on a higher note.

'Coming,' shouted Hannah, backing away from Terry. 'Terry can bring them up.' She thrust a tray into Terry's hands. 'Stand there.' She opened the cupboard and started arranging its contents on the tray.

'They real?' Terry looked in wonder.

'She thinks they are.'

'Baccarat, Clichy, St Louis, my, my!' He stared in surprise.

'Don't drop them. Take them up to her. Give you something to do with your hands.'

'Worth a fortune these, they're the real McCoy.'

'What?'

'Your boobs, luvvy.' He was irrepressible.

'I'm going to ring George and tell him what's happened.'

'Who's he?' Terry's eyes, reflecting the multicolours of the paperweights, were jealous.

'George Scoop, he's a dentist, a dontologist,' she corrected herself.

'Scoops the tartar off your gnashers? Scoops you into bed, does he?' Terry, his face close to Hannah, mocked. 'What a name for a dentist!' He leant across the tray which he held between them to kiss Hannah, his tongue flicking across her teeth.

'Keep off.' Hannah pushed. The tray slanted and the paperweights began to slide. 'Watch it!' she cried. 'They'll smash.'

Terry righted the tray. 'I'll take 'em to her, you telephone your fella.'

Hannah watched him leave. He had a beautiful back. As she dialled George's number she compared it with George's whitish lardy version.

'Can I speak to Mr Scoop?' she asked the receptionist called Jean.

'Do you want an appointment?' Jean recognised Hannah's voice.

'It's Mrs Somerton. I want to talk to him.'

'He's busy, Mrs Somerton, can I take a message?' Jean giggled.

'Just see if he's free.'

'Well, Mrs Somerton –' Jean's impertinent voice set Hannah's teeth on edge.

'Just try, girl.' She used asperity. 'It's important.'

'Just a minute, Mrs Somerton.' Hannah listened, heard the receptionist say, 'Tell Mr Scoop, Evie, Hannah Somerton wants to speak to him, says it's important – to her.'

'Hallo?' George came on the line, suspicious. 'Who is it?'

'George, my aunt's flooded, oh, George, water all over the ground floor.'

'Have you rung the Council?'

'Yes, but I –'

'Did they come?'

'Yes, but it –'

'They'll take care of things. Look, I'm busy, Hannah.'

'I thought you'd help, I thought you'd like to know.'

'But you've got help, love, what could I do?'

'I thought,' Hannah cried, 'that you –'

'I'm a dentist, Hannah, not a labourer. Can't the neighbours help? Your street's full of idlers.'

'Only because they can't find work.'

'But I can. Hannah, I have a difficult extraction to do. I can't waste time rabbiting to you.'

'I'm not rabbiting,' Hannah shouted.

'Yes, you are. I'm busy. I don't like being interrupted when I'm in my surgery. I'll ring you some time.'

'Some time!' Hannah yelled.

'Look, love, I'm sorry, it's a compacted wisdom tooth, it's –' but Hannah had replaced the receiver.

'Not rushing to your aid, Scoop?' Terry was back in the room. 'Your auntie says she'd like a sandwich. Hey, you're crying.' He put his arms round her. Hannah laid her head against his shoulder. He smelt of warm flesh and fresh perspiration. Suddenly she hated George's deodorants, his aseptic body. Terry tipped her head back and licked her tears away.

18

Jim Huxtable left his car in the pub car park and went into the bar, ordered a pint of bitter and stood drinking it, glad to stretch his legs after the long drive. 'Got any sandwiches?' he asked the landlord.

'Brown bread with crab, brown bread with beef, brown bread with turkey.'

As he ate he listened to the talk of the storm, the street up the hill flooded. He pricked his ears. So, Bernard's friend of the paperweights was in trouble. As he finished his sandwich he watched a black youth and a white boy arguing with the barman.

'Ya, ya, he's under age. Beer's not for him, it's for the helpers,' the youth was expostulating to the barman. 'Council blokes who helped at Miss Tremayne's. His ma wants to give them a beer.'

'So long as you know under eighteens can't be served.'

The youth burst out laughing. He nodded towards Jim. 'He's a dealer, not a copper. Come on, Giles.' He loaded Giles with beer cans. 'See you.'

'Have to be careful,' said the barman to no one in particular.

Jim walked up the street. The wind was drying the surface of the road. A magpie from a nearby park hopped beside the gutter, searching for titbits, flew off sideways. Jim stopped outside Hebe's house, hesitated, rang the bell. If she came to the door he would get the pang of disappointment he had grown to expect. He pressed his thumb on the bell, saw a curtain move. Was she nervous? What was she afraid of? He turned his head. The curtain moved again. A tortoiseshell cat peered out, fixing him with a green stare. Jim gave up.

Across the street the door of the owner of the paperweights

was propped open. Jim knocked. A weak voice from upstairs called. 'Who is it?'

'Jim Huxtable. I came to see you a while ago. Friend of Bernard's.'

'Come up.'

She was in bed, the paperweights on a table beside her. She looked frail.

'I see you've had a flood.'

'The boys and Hannah mopped up. I'm waiting for something to eat. Sit down.'

Jim sat by the bed. 'Still not for sale.' He eyed the paperweights.

'Not for sale.' She smiled, observing him.

'Know me the next time,' he said. 'Are you ill?' It seemed strange that with her ground floor in a mess she should lie so calmly in bed.

'Just a bit. Better now. The chocolate boy climbed in and saved me. A little bit of heart trouble, that's all.'

'Is the doctor coming?'

'Don't want him, my niece –'

'The dark girl?'

'No, Hannah, the fair girl. Do you know Hebe, then?' Amy's voice was suddenly sharp.

'No, I don't. I just wondered whether she had any antiques to sell. I called at all the other houses. I thought I'd –'

'Hebe has no antiques. She wouldn't sell antiques, not now.' Amy was weakly aggressive.

'Did she once?'

'Sandwich coming up, Auntie.' Feet on the stairs, Giles hurrying into the room. 'Mum says would you like anything else.' Giles caught sight of Jim. 'Hullo, saw you in the pub.' He put the plate of sandwiches beside Amy. 'She'll be over soon. This enough?'

'So she's called Hebe,' Jim reminded Amy, ignoring Giles.

Amy answered Giles. 'Yes, love, that's plenty, tell her and thank her.'

Giles stood poised to leave. 'You okay, then?' He watched Jim with suspicion.

'Yes, love.' Amy reassured him.

'Some of us are going to the beach for driftwood, it's low tide.'

'Have fun.'

'Bye, then.' Giles sprang away, his trainers going thud thud thud on the stairs.

'So Hebe was selling things at one time.' Jim tried to place her. Camden Passage? Some antique shop in the provinces? Portobello Road?

Amy munched her sandwich. 'She sold some things to an old scoundrel, that's all.' Why was she telling him this, she wondered, champing on her sandwich. Because I like the looks of him, that's why. 'Give him his due, he gave her a good price.'

'Bernard?' Jim hazarded. 'D'you know him?'

'Hebe's a cook.' Amy ignored Jim's question. 'Cordon Bleu. Hannah, who made this sandwich, isn't Cordon Bleu but she's a good cook too. I saw you talking to her.'

'Yes, very pretty. Green eyes.'

'That's right, Hannah Somerton. Her name was Krull but she changed it. Changed her teeth, too.' Amy snorted.

'Beautiful teeth, I remember.' Jim was polite. How did one get back to the dark girl?

'They were,' Amy leant forward staring at Jim, 'snaggle every which way.'

'Oh.'

'Didn't prevent her catching Krull. He's rich. She wants someone else now, though.'

'I'm not rich.' Jim drew back from the old woman blowing crumbs.

'You're safe, then. Take this tray down when you go, there's a dear. I'm now going to have a nap.' She looked old, ill, wanted him to leave.

Jim took the tray. 'Put it in the back kitchen. Nice of you to call. Goodbye.' She drew the sheet up, pursing her lips, the movement matching the folds of the sheet, dismissing him, slipping away into old age.

Jim took the tray down. He could report the safety of the paperweights and, if Bernard was interested, come again. In the street he wondered whether to renew acquaintance with

Hannah, glanced at her door, decided against and went back to his car. The old woman had choked him off. Why?

'Now then.' Terry drew the curtains of Hannah's bedroom. 'Let's get down to business.' He cleared his throat, pushing Hannah gently back on to the bed. 'D'you like it under the duvet or on top of the duvet?' His voice was husky. He cleared his throat again. 'Suppose you take off your panties and I'll take off mine.'

'Panties!' Hannah gasped. 'Do you wear –'

'Nice, ain't they, and this,' he was on top of her, 'is nice too.'

'I didn't know men wore them.' She was interested.

'Real silk. I'll buy you a pair. Now pay attention.'

She was half amused, feeling the silk. 'Are they satin?' This was unusual, exciting.

'I am.'

'You are.' She touched him. There was something about a very young man. Now George, she forgot what she had been about to think of George. 'I don't usually –' she began.

'Shush. Come on, get cracking, it takes two.'

Presently Hannah, watching Terry asleep, breathing silently through his nose, remembered George who had been known to snore. George had money. She shook Terry gently.

'What do you do?' she asked.

'I'm self-employed.'

'Doing what?' But Terry wanted sleep. She remembered she must scrub Amy's filthy floor. She lay for a few more minutes considering George. Would he or would he not come and help her? Like hell he would. He would say that his hands were precious. Rubbish, she thought resentfully, he could wear gloves. The expression 'rabbiting' rankled. She turned to reach for Terry's hand, smooth, firm, nice nails. George, under stress, bit his.

'Terry?'

'Yes?' Terry woke, glinting a dark eye at her. 'Hullo, goosegogs.'

'Say "regatta".'

'Regattah.' He was smiling. 'Received pronunciation suit you? I regattah, you regattah, she begat her. You on the pill?' A flick of anxiety.

'Yes.' She blushed at the admission. George had insisted.

'Ah – Ah –' He stroked her face gently.

'I have to scrub auntie's floor.'

'I'll help you.' He sprang up. 'Where's me knicks, then?'

'On the floor.'

She watched him put them on. They really suited him. Much nicer than George's baggy boxers.

19

Walking Louisa's dogs along the river after dinner, Hebe felt pleased with life. She was enjoying her work for Louisa, revelling in the countryside so different from the dark brick street in which she lived. If Silas were with her it would be perfect, she thought, but if he were it would not be possible to arrange the addition of Rory to her troupe. She considered Rory. He was endearing but against this he was Louisa's nephew, a potentially embarrassing connection. She liked to keep her cooking and tarting separate. It might be difficult, with Rory living so close to Louisa, to manage this. But why not, she encouraged herself. My old home is not far away and they, my grandparents with their new dog, don't know I am here. Amy would approve of Rory. Hebe smiled to herself. Rory was unmarried, belonged to the strata of society Amy envisaged as Hebe's. Amy, a romantic, would see Rory as the Mr Right she secretly hoped for her. Thinking of Amy, she felt a surge of love and gratitude. It was ungrateful to hate the hideous street. Amy had provided a loving home in it. In the street she had found refuge when filled with apprehension, waiting for Silas, experienced exuberant joy when he was born, reshaped her life, destroying the person she had been brought up to be, plotted her survival, planned her cooking career, found friendship with Bernard and through him discovered Hippolyte and the formula for survival she had carefully planned. Strolling by the river, pausing to throw sticks for the dogs, hearing a water vole plop, watching it swim close to the bank then vanish, seeing the swirl and rise of secret trout in the bottle green water, Hebe counted herself fortunate, congratulated herself on the profitable career which with balanced planning was so enjoyable a way of keeping herself amused while educating Silas. She dismissed a tiny cloud of whingeing doubt which occasionally assailed her as to whether she had truly chosen the right education for her child.

Hebe peered at her reflection and that of Rufus in the darkly waving water. Hippolyte, founder member of the Syndicate, had urged her to put a high price on herself, had taught her about bed. It was after learning 'The Soufflé System' that she had enlarged her horizon when occasion arose and became a tart as well as a cook. Mungo was the most profitable of her lovers, Hippolyte both friend and lover, constant. Latterly there had been Terry, a delightful novelty, and now Rory. She stroked Rufus' wet head. 'Everything's fine,' she said to the dog, whose reflection in the water wagged its tail. 'I like my work. I am giving Silas the chance to be whatever he likes. A few more pleasurable working years, Rufus, old dog, and I can retire.' She leant forward to watch a trout sliding under the weed, its movement so beautiful she held her breath. 'It's a wonderful evening,' she said to the dogs. 'Run, run, you must get dry, run.' Hebe ran with the dogs along the river, fleet and happy, for she would soon be home with Silas for the rest of the holidays.

The sun had set. From the French windows of Louisa's drawing-room yellow light streamed into the garden, alive with moths, the sound of the news on the television, jasmine and tobacco plants scenting the air.

'What a perfect evening,' said Hebe, coming into the drawing-room from the garden, carrying flowers, accompanied by the dogs.

Louisa, sitting on her sofa opposite the fire, where a log glowed even though it was August, looked up, smiling.

'We are just listening to the news,' she said.

In armchairs on either side of the fire sat Mungo on Louisa's left and Rory on Louisa's right. Both looked at Hebe expectantly.

The news announcer was saying, '– to be unveiled by Her Majesty – happily the rain – informality mixed with pomp – the umbrellas have come down – generations represented here today – now the Queen – one might almost say – pulse of history – roll of Gotha – inspiration – pride – the

Queen's walkabout – adversity – hope – affection – great man – Prince and Princess of Wales – great –'

'Great philanderer, had a lot of affairs, they say. I don't call that much of a likeness.' On the screen Her Majesty had pulled the string and the statesman was revealed in bronze. Louisa went on talking. 'You've met Rory, of course, and I believe you know Mungo.' She was enjoying the situation.

'Yes, of course. How do you do. Hi!' said Hebe, who never said 'Hi'. 'Is there anything you'd like?' she asked Louisa. 'I am on my way to bed.'

'No, thank you, my dear.'

Mungo and Rory had risen to their feet.

'I thought I'd take Rufus to sleep in my room tonight,' said Hebe, looking her employer in the eye. 'He was very noisy last night.'

Rory gasped.

'So he was. A good idea. Goodnight, my dear.' Louisa exaggerated cheerfulness.

'Goodnight, then. Come along, dogs.' Hebe left the room, followed by the dogs.

'Switch off the television, Mungo. Would you draw the curtains, Rory, as you are on your feet?' Louisa turned to Mungo. 'Now tell me how dear Lucy is. Your mother, Mungo. Do pay attention.'

Mungo stopped staring at the door which had closed behind Hebe. 'My mother's all right,' he muttered.

'And Alison, how is dear Alison, hasn't she gone to America or something?'

'Or something,' said Mungo heavily. 'She eloped to form a troika.'

'Goodness!' exclaimed Louisa. 'But you will get her back?' she teased.

'Unfortunately *yes*,' cried Mungo. 'My mother –' He stared at the door. Why the hell had Hebe gone off like that, taking a pack of dogs with her as though she needed protection? He knew the dog Rufus, it had once bitten him. Did she imagine he would rush up and rape her in front of this crowd of people? Of course he wanted to rape her, wasn't that what he'd come for?

What the hell was that fool Rory doing here, anyway? Why was Louisa acting so funny?

'Your mother, you were saying?' Louisa pried.

'She's said something, implied something. Oh, I don't know but Alison is coming back.' In his fury and pain Mungo was almost shouting. 'Coming back on the first flight she can get.'

'What did your mother say to her?'

'I don't know,' Mungo moaned weakly.

'I expect she told her the man had AIDS. Alison wouldn't like that.'

'Christ! Do you think he has?' Mungo was shocked.

'I should be surprised if he has, but I cannot see your mother managing without Alison. She depends on her.' Louisa grinned. She did not add, 'And so do you.'

Rory, who had arrived at the house simultaneously with Mungo, and was a-bubble with suppressed rage at the advent of his cousin, let out a loud guffaw. He had never liked Mungo, who was ten years older, had the advantage of a richer background than his own and had been held up to him as an example by his father. 'Your cousin Mungo fits into the family business, follows in his father's footsteps. Why cannot you join the Army? You would be made welcome in the old regiment.' Rory's hesitation over joining the Army had been welded into determination by Mungo's willingness to join his father's firm. If he had not been in such a rage with Mungo he would have felt grateful for this negative influence. As it was, watching Mungo's behaviour since arriving in Louisa's house, the way his eyes wandered in obvious search, a feeble excuse to fetch water from the kitchen, his restless inattention to Louisa's small talk, he had guessed that Mungo was a member of Hebe's Syndicate. When Hebe came in through the French windows, surrounded by dogs, carrying flowers, looking in her light cotton dress like some latterday Diana, Rory's heart had leapt, and so, quite obviously, had Mungo's. Hebe had barely glanced at either of them but with a barefaced lie about feeling tired had swept out of sight to lock herself no doubt into the bedroom he considered his, where so lately he had lain in her arms and she brown, soft, warm had – Rory closed his eyes in an effort to blot out the intruding vision of Hebe in Mungo's arms. Oh,

God, Oh, God! Rory cried to his maker, I cannot bear it. His fury switched from Mungo to Louisa. She was tormenting Mungo about Alison, his mother and his schoolboy sons Ian and Alistair. Rory overheard odd words which did not make much sense but, forcing himself to pay attention, became alert.

'Not really, Mungo, none of the beds are made up.' Mungo, it appeared, was inviting himself to stay. 'I can't ask Hebe to do housework. She comes here to cook, nothing else. She is tired, as you no doubt saw.' Looking the picture of bounce and energy, thought Rory. 'I suggest' – Louisa was swinging into her stride – 'that you ask Rory to put you up for the night. You will gladly do that, Rory, won't you?'

'What?' Could one really choke with emotion, Rory wondered.

'You will have your cousin Mungo for the night. He has to leave early so that he can be home when Alison telephones the time of her arrival from California. The west coast of America,' Louisa added, as though Rory were some idiot child who knew no geography.

'I don't think –' began Rory.

'A good opportunity to see something of each other. You are, after all, cousins, even though perhaps you may not have very much in common.'

'I – er –'

'Perhaps you have more in common than you think.' Was she being purposely malicious? 'You are of the same generation. I am sure you will find mutual interests.'

'I had hoped –' began Mungo querulously.

Louisa stood up. No need for Mungo to voice his hopes. 'It was lovely of you to visit me on your way, and you, too, Rory. Come and fish whenever you like. Now you must forgive me, I am feeling my age – rather overdoing it in my garden while Hebe is here. Such a cook, such food! I am sorry I cannot ask you – But of course Alison is a wonderful cook, too, and such a good manager. Next time you come' – Louisa was moving towards the door so that Mungo and Rory had perforce to follow – 'next time, ring me up and give me notice. It will be so nice.' It was possible, thought Rory admiringly, to gather that it was not nice now.

'I always enjoy seeing the young.' Louisa had the drawing-room door open, was leading them across the hall. 'You must bring your boys to see me, Mungo. So lovely for Lucy to have grandsons.' Was that malice in her voice? She had hold of Mungo's arm. Does she think he is going to sprint upstairs after Hebe? Rory wondered. 'Did you bring anything with you?' Louisa asked. 'No?'

'No,' said Mungo, who had his suitcase in his car. I used to love Aunt Louisa, he thought bitterly. The old viper.

'Then goodnight. God bless.' Louisa put up her face to be kissed. 'And goodnight, Rory. Lovely to see you, lovely.'

Mungo and Rory walked to their cars.

'I'll put you up for the night,' said Rory, with unexpected pity for his cousin.

'Oh, go to hell.' Mungo got into his Jaguar and slammed the door.

Rory got into his Volvo and shut the door quietly before switching on the engine.

Louisa watched the cars drive to the main road. 'What a pantomime!' She burst out laughing.

Leaning from her open window with the dog Rufus beside her, Hebe grinned. Louisa stood on the steps until the sound of the cars died away then went in, closing the front door. Hebe saw the light in the hall turned off. She listened to the soft sounds of the August night, a roosting bird in the creeper resettling itself, distant traffic, the cow with a cough in the meadow. 'Come, Rufus.' She got into bed, followed by the dog. 'Your mistress is a lovely lady.' She put an arm round Rufus, who groaned with pleasure. 'I am not going to worry about it tonight,' she said to the dog and lay hoping for sleep, without dreams or voices chanting dirty fingernails – Communists – earrings – abortion – bare feet. She switched her mind to other moments when things had not gone exactly right: the embarrassing episode in the Clarence at Exeter; Rory walking in when she was trying on the hat; Hippolyte, surprised by the sound of his wife's return from shopping, leaping from the bed to pull on his trousers, exclaiming, '*Il faut sauver les convenances*' before glissading out of the window. 'You don't worry about "*les convenances*",' Hebe said to the dog lying beside her. Rufus braced his feet against the wall and heaved his back against Hebe. 'You take up more room than any lover,' she said.

Refusing to review the tangle her carefully ordered existence was faced with, she slept surprisingly well.

20

'Don't be such an oaf, Michael, wash them out, there's a tap by the back door – yes there *is*, use your eyes, you nitwit – I will give you some Jeyes, that will get rid of the smell – yes, it *will*. The sooner you do it the better – don't be so *wet*. How dare you talk to me like that?' The sound of a slap, a cry of indignant pain from Michael. 'I have never known anyone make so much fuss, everybody's seasick some time –'

'Not into my boots.' A whimper.

'Shut up about your fucking boots, stop beefing.' Another blow sounded.

'That hurt!' Michael yelped.

'It was meant to.' Jennifer Reeves' voice spitting venom. 'He is your visitor, you insisted on inviting him.' There was the sound of another blow and Jennifer saying something Silas couldn't catch.

Changing his wet clothes, Silas peered out of the window as Michael, holding the boots into which he had been sick, approached the tap under the window, dribbled Jeyes fluid into each boot and turned on the water. Silas saw that Michael's cheek flamed red and that he was crying. Pulling on dry socks he felt pity for Michael, even though he had been foul and unsympathetic on the boat. Ian and Alistair had laughed high shrieking laughs until, looking at Julian to see whether he too was amused, they had abruptly sobered, realising something more than Silas' seasickness was afoot. Julian was angry at his own temerity. The weather, far rougher than he had bargained for when they set out from St Mary's, punished the boat. He would need all his expertise on the run home without being bothered with a seasick child. 'Get below,' he had shouted at Silas, 'out of the way.'

Silas had crept unsteadily below, crawling into a corner of the cabin. It had seemed for ever before the bumping, crashing, heaving and jolting had stopped. Listening to Julian shouting orders at Michael, Alistair and Ian, he was glad, if this was what fathers were like, that he had none, and now Mrs Reeves (less than ever could he think of her as Jennifer) was steamed up.

Silas reached for a dry shirt and put it on. Standing in socks and shirt, he looked down at Michael. The boots were full of blue-white water. Michael stirred with a stick and emptied them down the drain. Silas craned out to see if there were any identifiable bits of pasty, then began to search for dry pants and jeans and his one dry jersey.

'Bring your wet clothes down with you when you have changed, Silas. I will wash them,' Jennifer called.

Silas called back, 'Thank you very much,' and went back to the window, one arm in the sleeve of his jersey, pulling the rest over his head. 'Are the boots spoilt for good?' He leant out of the window.

Michael looked up. 'Only unusually wet.' He was grudging.

'I will stuff them with newspaper,' suggested Silas. 'That's what my mother does.'

'Good idea.'

'I am awfully sorry.'

'Forget it.' Michael's cheek was fading.

'Your mother's –'

'Got a filthy temper,' muttered Michael. 'They both have.'

'Hot tea,' shouted Jennifer up the stairs, falsely cheerful. 'Hot tea, Silas.' Then, changing tone, 'For heaven's sake, go and change, Michael, don't hang about, you'll be catching cold. Tell Alistair and Ian to change too. You are too old to need a nanny.'

'Nanny never hit me.' Michael came up the stairs at a run, looking as though he had dodged another blow. 'Take your wet clothes down to her,' he snapped at Silas. 'Give her something to do. She can put them in the machine.'

'Thanks.' Silas collected his clothes. Hebe's white Guernsey smelled of vomit. 'I didn't mean –'

'Nobody means to be sick.' Michael was pulling his jersey over his head. 'Does your mother create?'

'No.' Hebe seemed very distant from the Scilly Isles. 'No,

she doesn't.' He tried to imagine Hebe shouting like Mrs Reeves. The idea was ludicrous.

'Ours does.' Ian and Alistair, who had joined them, were also pulling jerseys over tousled heads. 'Our mother makes fury, our father makes sound.'

'They all do.' Alistair was philosophical.

'Today was all my father's fault,' Michael said, searching for dry clothes. 'He knew sailing round the Bishop's Rock would frighten him, he was showing off.'

'Oh.' Silas stood in the doorway holding his wet clothes.

'Tea,' Jennifer Reeves called up the stairs. Silas ran down to the kitchen. Jennifer took his bundle from him. 'Ugh!' She held it at arm's length as she crossed the room to the outer kitchen. Silas heard her open the washing machine and say 'Ugh!' again.

Julian, already changed, sat at the kitchen table. 'Tea?' he offered Silas.

'Thank you.' Silas watched Julian pour tea into a large cup. He had a heavy jowly face; he was scowling.

'Milk? Sugar?'

'Yes, please.'

Julian poured in milk and added lumps of sugar. Taking a flask out of his pocket he added a dollop of whisky. 'That will settle your stomach.' He winked at Silas. 'Drink it up and you will feel better.'

Silas drank, thinking the mixture disgusting. He hated being winked at and wondered morosely whether he would throw up again. Julian clearly hoped he would. Instead he felt a revivifying glow. The cup empty, he held it out and asked for more.

'Oliver Twisting?' Julian stopped scowling. Jennifer came back into the room, shutting out the sound of the washing machine as she closed the door. She said, 'Really, Julian,' in mock reproach, then sat at the table to drink tea and eat buns. Julian switched on the radio, muttering, 'I want to hear the weather forecast.'

'You should have listened last night,' said Jennifer sarcastically. Her husband raised his eyebrows in mock resignation. Somebody was interviewing a politician.

'Mumble, mumble.'

'That's a very good question,' said the politician.

'Fuck. Bloody watch has stopped. Missed it.' Julian switched off the radio, wound his watch, stood up. His stomach sagged over his trousers. 'What time's supper?'

'Same time as usual?' Jennifer did not look up.

'Same old stew?' asked Julian nastily.

'Mrs Thing doesn't have a large repertoire,' said Jennifer snappily.

'Time for a drink. I'll ask them whether they heard the forecast at the pub. You coming?'

'Get me some cigs, I am running out. No, I'm not coming. If you'd listened to the forecast last night instead of trying to pull that girl in the pub, you wouldn't have –'

'Oh, Christ!' shouted Julian.

'Here we go,' muttered Michael *sotto voce*.

'She was hardly likely to look at you, she's on her honeymoon.' Jennifer's voice rose.

'You stupid cow, shut up.' Julian left the cottage, banging the door. Jennifer began clearing the table. 'Put on mackintoshes if you are going out,' she said. It was an order.

'I will help you hang the clothes on the line.' Silas had noted the cessation of sound from the washing machine.

'Thank you, Silas,' said Jennifer.

Michael, Ian and Alistair put on boots and oilies in the porch and went out, leaving Silas with Jennifer.

'Come on, then.' She sounded martyred.

The rain had almost stopped. Silas piled the damp clothes into a basket and took them to the line. Jennifer shook each garment and pegged it up. Silas helped, observing as she stretched up that her heavy breasts wobbled and that where her jersey parted from her skirt there was a roll of white skin. He compared it with his mother's taut brown body. Jennifer's blonde bun came loose and lopsided on to her neck. Silas thought of Hebe's brown bob.

'I am going to rest before supper. Shall you go for a walk?'

'Yes.' Silas took off his shoes and set off up the hill barefoot, hoping to retrace the way he had walked on his first day. Perhaps he would see the seals again, find the little beach.

He climbed until he could look across the water to Bryher.

The wind had dropped, the sea was subsiding. Between the islands the water was pewter-coloured in the evening light, smoothing itself calm. He watched the sunset begin its spectacular. Yellow light seeping under storm clouds gave the impression that golden treacle had been spread over the sea between the islands. As he watched the colours changed from gold to pink. The heather at his feet was spun with spiders' webs, raindrops reflecting the reddish purple of the heather and occasional blue of Devil's Bit. There was no sound other than the soughing of the wind, gulls and the sea pounding on the rocks. Away from the voices of his hosts Silas felt comforted. Then the raising of his spirits begun by the whisky in his tea ceased. It had been an awful day. He hated sailing. He loathed the Reeves family. Ian and Alistair were awful too, but he promised himself he would buy a postcard and post it to Hebe: 'Having a wonderful time. Wish you were here.'

Below him two people walked along the path talking in quiet voices. He recognised the couple who had been in the boat on his first day. Silas felt a pang of envy at their happiness, quiet voices, gentle pace, so different from the strident aggressive Reeves. He watched them move out of sight, then looked back at the sunset. He had missed the beach off which he had seen the seals, where he had swum and later seen the adder, but here was the sunset. He watched the clouds roll away and the sky blaze; tomorrow would be fine. His feet were cold. He stood up. Would he be late for supper?

Silas ran, arriving back at the cottage panting and out of breath.

'I'm sorry I'm late.'

'It doesn't matter, we started without you.'

'Have a glass of vino.' Julian poured Silas a glass of wine and pushed it towards him. Jennifer compressed her lips and handed Silas a plate of stew. Michael glanced anxiously at his mother. Ian and Alistair smirked. The stew was the same as the stew of the night before.

'This food's bloody monotonous,' Julian said aggressively. He ate with a spoon, shovelling the stew into his mouth, crouched over his plate, heavy shoulders bulging in his jersey, green quilted waistcoat hanging open.

'It's a very good stew,' Silas ventured.

Julian looked up and stared at Silas. Silas shyly gulped some wine and looked at his plate.

'I didn't say it was bad, I said it was monotonous,' said Julian.

'Yes.' Silas swallowed more wine.

'Monotonous. Comes from the Greek. Means lack of variety, sameness. Don't they teach you Greek at your establishment?'

'No.' Silas felt confused.

'Not taught Greek? What sort of school is it, then?'

'We don't learn Greek,' said Michael.

'We don't learn Latin, either.' Ian joined the conversation.

'You know they do not take Latin,' said Jennifer. 'They take modern languages.'

Julian ignored his wife.

'We opted for German,' said Alistair.

'What's that to do with the stew? Why can't you ask Mrs Thing to give us a bit of variety?' Julian glared at Jennifer.

'I have. It doesn't make the slightest difference.' Jennifer helped herself to bread. Julian looked away from his wife and glared round the table at the boys, who studied their plates. Silas decided not to ask for a second helping. He crumbled his bread and drank more wine.

'Do you get stew at home?' Julian was glaring at Silas, masticating with open mouth.

'Sometimes.'

'Not as good as Mrs Thing's, I don't suppose. Mrs Thing's a stew artist. Have some more. You need a refill after today.' Julian laughed abruptly.

'No, thank you, sir.' The 'sir' slipped out. The atmosphere was so like school.

'The boy calls me "Sir" now. Have some more stew, I say. Give the boy some more, Jennifer, give us all some more.' Julian held out his plate. Jennifer spooned stew on to it. 'Don't suppose you get stew like this at home. Make the most of it while you can. Mrs Thing's excellent stew. Hah!'

'Silas' mother is a cook,' said Michael.

There was a pause while Silas drank wine, Julian masticated and Ian and Alistair passed their plates for second helpings, exchanging covert glances.

Jennifer Reeves, spooning stew on to the plates extended towards her, said lightly, 'One of my uncles married his cook.'

'Blotted the old copybook there, didn't he? Wasn't even pregnant, was she? Still, think what it must have saved in wages. Quite a good idea, when you think on it. Marry a cook, good idea, good idea.' Julian ate.

'Must you use a spoon?' Jennifer exclaimed.

'Yes, I must. Knife and fork are okay, but for Mrs Thing's stew a spoon's the thing.' Julian's truculence was almost tangible.

'You are drunk.' Jennifer spoke through clenched teeth.

'Not very. Mrs Thing's stew will soak up the surplus alcohol. So Silas' mother is a cook, is she? Well, I never. How, ah, did that come about? I mean in these days it's pretty rare to find a cook. Endangered species. Clever of your father to find her.' Julian stared at Silas. Silas drank his wine, emptying the glass, reaching out his hand towards the bottle to help himself to more.

'Let me.' Julian took the bottle and poured wine into Silas' glass. Jennifer sighed. Michael, Ian and Alistair sat watchful. 'So this endangered species married your father. What does your father do?'

'Julian.'

'All I ask is what his father does. No need to say "Julian" in that tone of voice.'

'Silas' mother is very beautiful.' Michael's voice gave its first pubertal crack.

'Beautiful, is she? Hah! A beautiful endangered species. She must have been something before she was a cook.' With the doggedness of intoxication Julian worried his prey.

'My mother is a Hermaphrodite,' said Silas proudly, 'and you are disgusting.' He flung his wine in Julian's face, stood up, threw down his napkin and left the cottage.

21

Looking at the clock on the dashboard, Mungo noted the lateness of the hour. Too late now to find a bed for the night. He had been driving at random, angry and frustrated since leaving Louisa's house. My dreams have fallen about my ears, he thought morosely. Where the hell am I? He had been travelling fast along unknown roads; the petrol gauge was dangerously low. 'That's all I need,' Mungo muttered, driving slowly now, on the lookout for a signpost.

Presently he came to one which said 'Salisbury 5 miles'. There would surely be an all-night garage. He nursed the car, glancing at the gauge which arrowed the red line. It seemed an age before he was on the outskirts of the city, passing one closed petrol station after another. Soon he was in the one-way system designed by clever councillors to entrap tourists. Close to the centre the engine sighed to a halt. Mungo drew into the kerb. He was tired, fed up and far from home. He got out of the car, locked it and started to walk. Rounding a corner he sighted a bay window in a small Georgian house, a white front door with a fanlight above it, a highly polished dolphin knocker. Light shone through the fanlight. Above the bay window the words 'Rory Grant, Hatter.' If only I had a brick to hurl through the bloody window. Mungo used the knocker – bang, bang, bang.

'Hang on, I'm coming. What's the –' Rory opened the door. 'Oh, it's you.' He recoiled.

Mungo shouldered past his cousin. 'I've run out of petrol.'

'Come in, then.' Rory looked at Mungo anxiously. 'I may have – a –'

'Have you got anything to drink? I'm done in.'

'– can in the garage. Yes, of course. Coffee? Whisky? Come

into the –' but Mungo was already in the kitchen and slumped at the table.

'You are up early,' he said in a surly voice.

'I haven't been to bed, I was too –'

'Upset. Me too. I've been driving in circles.'

'Here's some –' Rory produced a bottle of whisky, poured half a glass and pushed it across the table towards Mungo, then helped himself. Mungo drank, eyeing his cousin, who looked rather ahead of him in the drinking stakes.

'You drunk?' he asked.

'Not yet. Would you like some soup?'

'Oh, God,' said Mungo. 'Soup.'

'You look hungry.' Rory busied himself finding bread, butter, heating soup.

'I haven't come to stay.' Mungo put down his glass with an aggressive clunk.

'Of course not.' Rory pushed a bowl of soup towards his cousin, handed him a spoon. 'We can hate each other better when we've eaten.'

Mungo ate his soup, buttered his bread. 'Got any cheese?'

'Yes, I, yes, I have.' Rory got up, lurched to the larder, came back with Stilton in a jar. Mungo dug with his knife with vicious jabs, disgusting Rory at the combination of soup and cheese.

'She is an absolute bloody bitch. I was going to marry her. I *am* going to marry her. This come from Fortnum's?'

'So am I,' said Rory, pushing his soup plate from him with a jerk. 'Yes, it does.'

'I was first, I have first go,' Mungo growled.

'You are married to Alison.' Rory peered sagely at Mungo. 'While you get, while – er – start again. While you get shot of horrible Alison I will marry Hebe. Me first.'

'Don't call my wife horrible,' Mungo roared.

'There we go,' Rory let out a crow of laughter. 'Horrible Alison and,' he shot a glittering look at Mungo, 'you have two horrible little boys.'

'True.' Mungo spooned soup. It was delicious, revivifying, probably also Fortnum's. Bachelors could afford such luxuries.

'Got to think of them.' Rory was uplifted by whisky.

'Can't bear to. Never have children,' Mungo advised Rory. 'Millstones, total millstones.' He stared at Rory. 'What she see in you? You are such a funny shape.'

'Okay in bed,' Rory answered cockily, 'and she, oh Mungo, she is so, so, so –' Tears began to gather.

'So marvellous,' said Mungo, moved too. 'So soft, so warm. Not a bit flabby. So tender, just the right weight. I could eat her.'

'You talk as though she was a prime steak,' cried Rory, indignant, lachrymose.

'I shall if I want to, she's my mistress.' Mungo tried to whip his rage into fresh life.

'We are just members of her Syndicate.'

'Her *what*?' He glared at Rory.

'Syndicate. That's what she calls it.'

'Oh, holy Jesus Christ, oh, the cow, what an absolute cow!' Mungo yelled.

Rory, leaning across the table, slapped his cousin. 'I have wanted to do that for years, ever since –'

'When? Mungo stared at his young relation with interest.

'You said I looked like the White Rabbit.'

'Only your expression. I don't think it's going to bleed, is it?' He fingered his nose.

'I fear not. More whisky?'

'Why not? We'd better finish the bottle or it will feel lonely.' Mungo pushed his glass towards the bottle. Rory poured, squinting.

Mungo felt an improbable stirring of friendship.

'What shall we do?' Rory cried, sensing an ally.

'If you knew that girl as well as I do you would say what will Hebe do,' said Mungo gloomily. 'Any more soup? It's good, what is it?'

'Game. She made it. We found grouse at the fishmongers. Aunt Louisa gave me a thermosful to bring home.' Rory poured the remains of the soup into Mungo's plate.

'We should not be drinking whisky with this. Haven't you any claret?' asked Mungo aggressively.

'Oh, God.' Rory got up and disappeared through a doorway. Mungo listened to his uncertain steps on stone stairs and vague mutterings in the cellar below. He reappeared carrying a bottle. 'I was saving it for, saving it for –'

'Hebe.' Mungo took the bottle, rummaged in a drawer and found a corkscrew, uncorked the bottle. 'I would like to strangle her.' He set the bottle on the table between them.

Rory looked appalled. 'What has she done to deserve that?'

'Cheated.'

'No, no, she is absolutely –'

'Fair,' Mungo grunted. 'Why don't you finish your bloody sentences?' He snatched at the bottle and sloshed the wine into his empty whisky glass.

'That's what Hebe says. Oh Hebe, oh hell.' Rory helped himself to wine. 'It hasn't had time to –'

'Breathe.' Mungo was morose. They sat in gloom, sharing something akin to comradeship.

'How long?' asked Rory.

'Six years,' said Mungo. 'Six years. Six weeks a year for six years. Three lots of two weeks, always when it suited *her*. I've a service flat in London she comes to. I take her to the theatre, to bloody highbrow films, to exhibitions. I let her shop. *She* sends me to my office or my club when *she* gets bored, we play backgammon.'

'You make her sound like a feminist virago.'

'She's a pimpless tart, a soloist. I tried to instal her in a flat of her own, but no, she wouldn't hear of it, too bloody independent. For six years I've been trying to find out where she lives. D'you know, if I want to get in touch with her I have to write to a fucking little shop in Earl's Court which forwards her letters.'

'Won't they –'

'Clam up. It's a Pakistani family, they just laugh.'

'Where did you – er – where –'

'Meet her? In my mother's kitchen. She goes and cooks when the housekeeper is on holiday. Alison's arrangement, can you beat it?'

'Your mother, Aunt Lucy – great chum of Aunt –'

'Louisa's. Yes.'

'Does your mother, does Aunt –'

'Neither of them know,' Mungo was perversely proud, 'where she lives.'

'It can't be true.'

'It bloody is true,' said Mungo, adding, 'I hope.'

The cousins sat drinking the chilly claret, their soup plates pushed aside. Mungo dug his knife into the jar of Stilton, fishing out crumbs of cheese which he conveyed thoughtfully to his mouth. Rory, too depressed to protest, decided to put the remains of the cheese on his bird table. He did not fancy Mungo's spittle.

'What arrangement have you got?' Mungo asked in a threatening tone.

'I shall take her to Aunt Calypso's cottage in the wood when the cherries are in flower.' Rory was not prepared to admit there was as yet no arrangement. 'Of course she's very happy – er – happy –'

'Happy?' Knife loaded with Stilton half way to his mouth, Mungo repeated, 'Happy?'

'Happy here.' Bravely Rory spoke. He watched his cousin, ready to spring out of reach should he attack.

'She's expensive.' Mungo put the cheese into his mouth. 'She costs.'

'I can afford her – I –'

'Rich bachelor.' Mungo was contemptuous, also envious. 'I suspected you of poofery.'

'Must be a drain on your resources, what with Alison and the boys,' said Rory nastily, 'quite a –'

'I dress some of it up as expenses.'

'What a good idea. I could say she –'

'What?' Mungo was instantly alert.

'Models my hats.' Both men began to laugh. Rory refilled the glasses.

'Do you know who the other members of the Syndicate are?' Mungo enunciated carefully.

Rory said, 'No, I can't bear –'

'Nor can I. Doesn't bear thinking of.' Mungo dropped his knife on the table with a clatter. 'What say we keep her in the family?'

'Share her?' Rory was startled.

'Yes. Let's go and put it to her. You half, me half, fair do's, eh?' Suddenly he felt friendly towards this young cousin with his hare's eyes. 'And when the boys grow up they can join the

Syndicate. Put their names down now as you do for Eton. Brilliant. That's what we'll do.'

'Disgusting!' shouted Rory.

'Do you think so?' Mungo was still amiable. 'I thought family Syndicate – er – like Rothschilds or something, junior partners, Marks and Sparks.'

'Certainly not,' said Rory, shocked.

'Okay, just you and me then.'

'I am going to marry her,' said Rory, enunciating carefully.

'Not that again. Listen, if there is one thing I know about Hebe it is that she won't marry us.'

'Not you, perhaps.'

'Nor you.'

'Then why did you say –'

'What one wants and what one gets are totally different things,' said Mungo philosophically.

'Ah me.' Rory picked up the bottle. 'Empty.'

'Tell you what.' Mungo stood up and began lurching round the kitchen. 'Tell you what, we had better go back and have a confrontation.'

'At Aunt Louisa's? What for?'

'Clear the air,' said Mungo. 'What's the time?'

'Five o'clock.'

'Better shave first.' Mungo started towards the stairs. 'Have a bath.' He seized the banisters. 'This your bedroom?' He had reached the landing, rocking up the stairs.

'Yes – er –'

'Your bed? Where you and Hebe?'

'Yes, we –' Rory followed his cousin.

'What say we have a nap first?' Mungo caught Rory's arm and they fell together on to the bed.

'I say –' Rory felt he did not know what he wanted to say. He felt dizzy.

'Just a nap, then bath, shave, go together to fix the bloody Syndicate, fix Hebe. Lie still, can't you.' Mungo kicked off his shoes.

'I don't like being in bed with you.' Rory sniffed, hoping for a faint reminder of Hebe on the pillow then, remembering he had changed the sheets, felt desolate. It was horrible having his great lump of a cousin sprawling on his bed. It was also impossible to sit up, get off the bed, stand up. Rory surrendered to exhaustion, alcohol and Mungo's bullying.

As Mungo began to snore Rory reviewed his dreams. He had seen himself wandering with Hebe through the wood, the cherries in flower, at their feet bluebells and late primroses, early pink campion, birds singing their spring chorus, the sun would slant through tender leaves of oak, beech, ash, in the depth of the wood the cuckoo – Oh God, the cuckoo! He turned away from Mungo, away from the light now streaming in from the world outside. How could he defeat Mungo, what arguments could be used? Alison, Ian, Alistair, seemed to carry no weight. Would the sentence so often used by his parents to thwart him – 'What would the family say?' – be of the slightest use?

22

On the way from the heliport Silas rehearsed what he would say to his mother. He carried Hebe's Guernsey sweater. He pulled up the hood of his parka, shielding his face from cars passing along the road who might recognise him, stop, offer him a lift, ask with kindly curiosity whether he had a good time sailing. On the beach the high-tide mark was a line of weed wrenched from the seabed by the storm. Along this children ran shouting to each other as they gathered driftwood into a pyre, building a bonfire which would burn with blue flames from the lumps of coagulated oil. To the debris they would add refuse – plastic containers which would explode in the heat, adding a tinge of risk to their pleasure. People would complain about the smoke which would drift inland to sully their nylon curtains. Silas watched. Many times he had collected driftwood, taking armfuls home to burn in the sitting-room fire. He felt a sharp desire to join the girls and boys. Then he saw Giles was with them. He did not at all want to see Giles.

His thoughts reverting to Hebe, Silas recited to himself: 'It was marvellous. They have asked me to come again. I am home early because Mrs Reeves' father is ill. They are all going back. They sent you all sorts of messages – the food was very good – my clothes were just right – I'm afraid I spilled something on your Guernsey. We sailed round Bishop's Rock lighthouse – no, not dangerous at all, it was thrilling – I liked the other boys – a terrific family – it was brilliant.' A load of cock, he told himself. Cock was an expression fancied by Alistair. She will know it's cock when she smells the sick on her jersey. What am I to say? he asked himself for the hundredth time. Perhaps she will take it for granted the visit was okay, just as she believes what I tell her about school. About the only thing I've got from the Scillies is to use the word 'cock' and the seals and the adder and the colour of the sea. Should he 'lose' Hebe's jersey, drop it over the sea wall? Then she would not smell the vomit. No good. He remembered that she had paid a lot for the jersey and justified herself by saying, 'You will be able to wear it, it will come in useful when you've grown a bit.' God, how he hated the thing. And what was he to say about his duffle bag, how to explain its loss? Silas urged himself on. She would be so pleased to see him she would forget to ask questions. She never questioned him much, that was one of the marvellous things about her. Silas broke into a run.

Swinging round the corner, starting the stiff climb up the dark brick street, he forced his pace, his spirits rising. Soon he would be with Hebe. She would look as she looked on the station platform when he arrived back from school, eyes large, wearing a rather mad expression. She would hug him, he would put his arms round her, lay his head against her chest, they would laugh with relief at being together. It would be all right, Silas told himself, nearly there. He ran, arriving on the doorstep in a rush of joy.

The door was locked.

Silas was stunned. Peering from the window Trip, opening her mouth in a silent mew, showed her needle teeth and pink palate. Silas ran round to the back of the house. The back door was also locked. He rattled the handle. Trip came out through the cat-flap and wound herself purring round his legs, nudging him, turning in and out so that her whole body, including her tail, was part of the caress. Silas picked her up and held her close to his face. He remembered. He was to have been three weeks in the islands. She had said she would do a job in Wiltshire for a fortnight while he was gone. Silas sat down on the wet doorstep. He had guessed when Hebe told him about the job that she was only going because he was robbing her of a chunk of his holidays. He had blocked the knowledge. He had wanted to go to the Scillies. He had not cared. He had known perfectly well she was only filling in the time because he would not be there. Holding the cat against his face Silas wept; the addition of guilt to the shame and mortification he was suffering was too much. His eyes streamed, his nose trickled, he disgusted the cat, who jumped away, going back into the house through the cat-flap. Silas put his head between his knees and sobbed. He decided to throw himself over the cliff and have done with it.

'Can I be of any help?'

Silas saw feet, legs in jeans, tweed jacket over a dark sweater, above that a face he had not seen before. He struggled to his feet. He was cold and stiff from squatting on the doorstep. The man wore an old felt hat, rain dripped from its brim. 'Who are you?' he asked and was ashamed of his tearful voice.

'Name is Jim Huxtable,' said the stranger. 'Rather wanted to see the girl who lives here.'

'She's not here.' Silas started to cry again. He was cold, tired, hungry, wet. He wished the man would go away. He wanted to die. Failing that, he wanted his mother.

'And you are shut out?'

'She's away.'

'Who has the key?'

'Terry or Hannah or Amy but I –'

'Don't want to ask them.'

'I *can't*.'

'Who feeds the cat?'

'Terry or Hannah.'

'When will she be back, your mother?' What a bedraggled child.

'Not for days and days.' Silas' voice rose in lamentation.

Jim took stock of the situation. If the child knew people who had the key it was their business to help. The sensible thing would be to take him to one of them, let them take over.

'Do you happen to know somebody called Bernard Quigley?' he asked vaguely, thinking Bernard might help were he here.

'Yes!' Something about the boy's eyes, the way they lit up, touched him. 'My mother does and I do too but it's a separate friendship, it's nice to –' How to express, how to explain that it was nice to see old Quigley by himself without Hebe being there?

Jim thought, Really, these latchkey children, how irresponsible people are. 'I am staying with Bernard Quigley,' he said, watching the boy's face. 'Been doing his shopping. Would you like to come and see him? Perhaps you could tell him your trouble.'

'Yes, please,' said Silas adding, 'there's nothing to tell.'

'Come on, then.' Jim led the way to his car. Silas followed. Jim wondered why he was angry, why he was behaving in this mad way. This boy was no business of his. But as he drove out of the town with Silas beside him Jim thought, This will help me to meet that woman. Knowing her boy I can call later to ask whether he is all right. To see her would get rid of the niggling idea he had had since he had first seen her. Just one more who isn't, this one is obviously a bitch of the first order.

They did not speak on the drive. Jim thought small talk unnecessary. Silas was sunk in nervous gloom. When they reached the lonely call box Jim asked Silas to open a gate into a field. 'The farmer lets me leave my car here.' He locked the car.

They walked across the fields in Indian file, Jim leading the way, carrying the shopping. Silas followed. If I run, thought Silas, it's only a half mile to the cliff. I could jump, there would be no need for explanations. He mulled this dramatic vision. Commonsense told him the man walking ahead would run faster than he, would catch him and he would look even more idiotic, an even greater fool. He followed Jim sulkily through the wet field. Half way to the house Feathers met them, bouncing and bounding, wagging his tail, yelping with joy.

'I have brought a friend of yours to lunch.' Jim greeted Bernard who stood in his porch, watching them walk towards him through the rain. 'Got himself locked out.'

'Come in and get dry.' Bernard expressed no surprise. He put his hand on Silas' shoulder and guided him into the sitting-room. He was moved by Silas' appearance. Someone had hurt the boy.

'We must find you dry clothes,' he said. 'You had better change. But have a drink first. Just a spoonful of brandy. You hate sherry, you won't like this either but it will warm your guts.' Bernard poured a small measure of brandy and handed the glass to Silas. 'Don't pour that on to the rug. Drink it.'

Silas blushed and swallowed the brandy obediently. Bernard kept his hand on his shoulder. Silas stopped feeling he must throw himself off the cliff. Bernard waited until Silas' shoulder muscles stopped feeling like a wound spring. In the kitchen Jim was moving about unpacking the shopping, talking to Feathers, who, being a vocal sort of dog, rumbled and groaned in response. Bernard said, 'Now go upstairs, first door on the left, take off your wet things. Jim,' he called, 'find clothes for Silas to wear until his are dry.'

Jim brought a towel. 'These will keep you warm.' He handed Silas a T-shirt and a heavy sweater. 'Put them on. Socks.' He handed Silas socks. 'Can't do anything about trousers. Try this, wrap it round you.' He took a shawl off the bed.

'Thank you.' Silas stripped off his clammy clothes and pulled on the T-shirt and sweater, which reached his knees. It was warm and smelt delicious. He wrapped the shawl round his waist like a sarong, pulled on the socks.

Bernard called up the stairs. 'You had better stay here until your mother comes back.'

'Can I?' Silas was amazed.

'Of course. Come down and sit by the fire with Feathers when you're ready.'

Jim beckoned from the kitchen. Bernard joined him.

'There's something badly wrong,' Jim whispered to the old man. 'What sort of people are they? I've heard about children being locked out and what it leads to.' His voice rose. 'What does the child's father do? He should be prosecuted –' He was blazing with righteousness.

'There is no father. Keep your voice down.'

'And the mother's a prostitute I suppose,' Jim sneered.

'Yes, she is.'

'Then *she* should be prosecuted. It's criminal leaving a child alone. I found him shivering and crying, shut out, afraid to go near the neighbours. What sort of bitch is she?'

Bernard was wheezing in an effort to stifle his normal cackle.

'What the hell's funny?' Jim snarled.

'Silas is supposed to be staying with some rich school-friend in the Scillies. His mother is consoling herself for his absence by working as a cook for my friend Louisa.'

'Mrs Fox, who you sent me to? That one?'

'Yes.' Bernard used his snuff-stained handkerchief. 'The boy has an adoring mother who slaves to –'

'Prostitutes, you mean,' said Jim nastily.

'If you like. To educate him at a lamentably expensive prep school. When not, as you put it, prostituting, she takes jobs as a cook with old ladies. I assure you whatever happened to Silas happened in the Scillies and more than likely he has brought it on himself. Since when have you been so puritanical?'

Jim was deflated. 'He will tell you what happened?'

'I doubt it, knowing his mother. She makes an oyster look like an open safe. Silas takes after her.'

'What shall you do?'

'Keep him here. Telephone Louisa presently.'

'Here he comes.' Jim listened to Silas coming down the stairs.

'It was unforgivable of me to tell you what I have just told you.' Jim saw that Bernard was distressed by his indiscretion.

'I too can oyster,' he said, listening to Silas approaching.

As Silas reached the bottom step, Feathers, a dog with a sense of occasion, jumped up, putting his paws on his shoulders, knocking him back into a sitting position, licking his face. Silas laughed. The old man and the younger man exchanged relieved smiles.

Eyeing Silas' feet, Bernard said, 'You'll break your neck in those socks. See what you can do about them, Jim. Sit down, Silas.'

Silas sat by the fire and Jim showed him how to tuck the socks back so that he would not trip. Feathers huffled and snuffled round him, noting that Jim's smell was now joined with Silas'.

'Lunch,' cried Bernard. They followed him into the next room. 'Sit here by me.' Silas sat beside Bernard. He was furiously hungry. Jim put a bowl of soup in front of him. 'Start eating,' said Bernard. Silas obeyed.

'Wait a minute,' Jim said to him. 'It's out of a tin, let me add a drop of sherry.'

'I –'

'It improves it no end.' Jim poured a little sherry into Silas' soup. 'Try it.' Silas sipped.

'Like it?'

'Yes, thank you.' Silas had never met a friend of Bernard's, imagining him forever solitary. He drank his soup, feeling safe with Feathers' chin pressed on his knee, wriggling his toes in Jim's socks.

Then they ate fish baked with fennel. 'Tonight,' said Bernard, 'we are eating grouse which clever Jim found in Salisbury. Ever eaten grouse?' he asked Silas.

'Never.'

'I would have bought more. There was only a brace left, some greedy woman had bought nearly the whole stock. She was filling a deep freeze, the fishmonger said. I shall make soup from the carcasses.'

'Fancy yourself as a cook.' Bernard was mocking. 'Silas' mother is a paragon, you can't surprise him.'

Silas looked down his nose. There was a drop in the temperature. Jim caught Bernard's eye. Bernard, using his great age as armour, asked, 'Were you proposing to kill yourself when Jim found you?' Not waiting for Silas to answer, he turned to Jim. 'When did you last wish to do away with yourself, Jim? I can't remember when I last had the impulse. It's something which dims with age. It must be thirty years since I seriously considered it. Come now,' he was looking directly at Jim, 'tell us.'

Sensing the appeal (did Bernard hope to cauterise Silas' wounds?) Jim rose to the occasion.

'Quite some time ago I imagined myself in love.'

'You!' mocked the old man, encouraging Jim. 'In love?' he scoffed.

'In Italy,' said Jim. 'I was taken to a party. It was a feast day, you know the sort of thing, a procession, statues of saints carried wobbling, priests, altar boys swinging censers, people singing and chanting, smell of garlic, wine, incense, children shouting, getting over-excited, their mothers slapping them.'

'Italians don't slap their children,' interrupted Bernard. 'But go on.'

'I was watching the procession. It was at night, did I tell you? There were brass bands, tumpity-tump.'

'Carry on.' Bernard watched Silas' interested face.

'The dark town lit by candles, candles stuck in all the windows of the town, lined along ledges. It was Lucca. Ever been to Lucca?'

'No.'

'I was watching from a balcony. The procession wound through narrow streets which make the houses seem tall when they are not really tall. By the light of all those candles they did seem tall –'

'Where was the girl?'

'What girl?'

'The one you fell in love with.'

'She was down in the street with a group of hippies. There were stalls selling necklaces of hazelnuts. I saw she wanted one. I ran down and caught up with her. We walked together. I bought her necklaces and put them round her neck.'

'What did she look like?'

'Very long brown hair, long dress, could hardly see her face. You know how it was at that time, one didn't see people's faces, there was so much hair. I had a beard.'

'I remember you, a sad sight.'

'It was the long hair and beard era.' Jim was defensive. 'Flower Power and so on, tremendous crops of hair on both sexes.'

'Go on.'

'We spent the evening together. She was lovely.'

Silas was absorbed. He was with Jim in Lucca walking with the candlelit procession, he could hear the people singing, the bands. It was wonderful.

'She had brown eyes, a wonderful walk. We were happy. Then she went wild, it was quite hard to keep up with her at times, she moved so fast.'

'And then?'

'Then' – Jim spoke fiercely – 'the night went sour. There was a fight of some sort. I lost her. Everyone was running to get out of trouble.'

'So you didn't make love to her –'

'I had, before the confusion, the fight, the running away. She vanished. It was as though she'd never been. Can you understand? Perhaps,' Jim said, 'she was an illusion.'

'Yes,' Bernard sighed, 'perhaps she was.'

'When I could not find her I felt like killing myself.'

'Ah,' Bernard sighed. 'You had not known her before that night?'

'No, I told you.'

'So you have been seeking her ever since.'

'Sometimes I think I see her,' said Jim, 'catch a glimpse.'

'And it's never the girl.' Bernard snapped his fingers. 'I would not have believed you capable of such flights of fancy. Shall we have coffee by the fire?'

'All very well to mock.' Jim got up to make the coffee. 'Some of us, not you of course, are romantics.'

'I have had my moments.' Bernard was dignified.

Silas burst out laughing. The idea of Bernard in a romantic situation was hilarious.

Bernard looked satisfied. 'I was never so stupid as to mislay them,' he said, stooping to put logs on the fire. 'When I was no longer in love with a girl I arranged matters so that love turned into friendship. In that way I have kept up relationships with nearly all my amours.'

'And how do you manage that?'

'When you are – er – on the wane, you work it so that it is she who thinks she is cooling. She keeps her *amour propre*, you keep yours and you remain friends. It works,' said Bernard smugly. 'In every case except one it has worked with me and even that one – well, we were talking about you. What was your girl called?'

'I don't know. I asked the people she had been with. They said she wasn't of their party. I was not surprised, they were not her kind of people – into drugs, I'd say.'

'So she had no name. What nationality?'

'We spoke French. Her Italian was poor. She said "Do you speak French?" I remember that. She may have been French.'

Bernard was laughing. 'A girl without name or nationality. You are inventing her.'

'I would not wish to kill myself for a myth,' said Jim stiffly.

'You have not even described her appearance.'

'I told you, she had long hair, brown eyes, brown skin. If I saw her now as she was then I might know her, but by now I might not recognise her. We met at night, by torchlight. I made love to her in darkness. It was quiet, near the church, the noise of the procession muted. There is a black Christ in the church.' Jim was back in Lucca.

Silas looked at Jim's face lit by a sudden blaze from the fresh logs. 'What happened?' he whispered.

'I searched for days. I was working in a bar to earn money. Nobody admitted seeing her. I described her as a girl running. They said a lot of people were running that night. It was a disgrace to have a fight on the Saint's day. It was the fault of foreign hippies. I suppose she left the town.'

Jim poured coffee into cups, handed it to Bernard, offered it to Silas.

'Silas?' It was the first time Jim had called him by name. Silas accepted coffee, helped himself to milk and sugar. Bernard sneezed. 'It is quite refreshing to find that people still fall in love. What happened?'

'I decided against suicide, had an affair with an American blonde, became a philanderer.' Jim spoke flatly.

'But you still look for her,' Silas suggested.

'Exactly.' Jim looked at the boy. He is recovering, he thought, feels safer now, not safe enough for us to ask what happened, probably won't even tell his tarting mother. Perhaps he won't tell anybody until some occasion arises like today, when I have told him about my love in Lucca to distract him. 'Sometimes I see a woman who reminds me of the girl. It never is her.'

'That must be tantalising.' Bernard was almost sympathetic.

'It keeps me young.' And single, Jim thought, surprised.

'Perhaps she is still looking for you,' Silas suggested, liking the idea.

'I doubt it. Last seen in full flight,' said Jim. 'She was a fast mover.'

They sat drinking their coffee, Bernard by the fire in his wing chair, Jim opposite him, Silas, Feathers and the cat at their feet. Outside the rain poured pitilessly, soaking the peninsula from the Atlantic rain clouds. Feathers licked his chops in a dream. Bernard put his cup into its saucer with a clink.

'I have never before told anyone about that girl.' Jim caught the old man's eye.

I am supposed to believe it never happened, thought Bernard. He is as vulnerable as the boy. 'It was generous of you to tell us,' he said. Presently, he thought, I shall stumble across the fields to the telephone and alert Louisa about Silas. She will tell Hebe. I must wait as late as possible; I have not the strength to stump across the fields twice. We must see that Hebe does not take fright and drive recklessly on her way home.

23

From the call box by the bus stop Bernard dialled Louisa's number and listened to the ringing tone which would rouse her in Wiltshire.

Many years before, knowing that she was in London with her husband, he had visited the house, prowled round, explored the garden, posing as the man who was calling about fire insurance. He had asked the maid to accompany him round the house so that no suspicion would be aroused. Thus when he talked to Louisa he could picture her in her surroundings, enduring grief when her husband dropped dead (quite a shock) and the change to widowhood, pushed for money but enjoying her garden, her dogs and latterly the joyful treat of Hebe's cooking visits. He could visualise her in the drawing-room with the view of the garden through the French windows. When he rang up at night he saw her in bed, library books, clock, pills, spectacles on the bedside table. Sometimes he forgot that she had grown old and imagined the girl who had shared bed and breakfast in the Hôtel d'Angleterre with such zest.

'Hullo?' Louisa's voice was clear. 'Bernard?'

'Yes.' She always guessed right.

'Darling Bernard, I have so much to tell you that will make you laugh.' She bubbled with delight.

'You have Hebe with you?' He cut her short.

'Of course I have. What's the matter?'

'Her boy. You know she has a boy?'

'She doesn't know I know. You know I am discreet.'

'Louisa, I have the boy here with me.'

'With you? Why? How strange.'

'Hebe let him go and stay with smart schoolfriends in the Scillies.'

'I know. You told me that was why she has come to me. What's happened?'

'Jim Huxtable, our go-between –'

'Yes? I liked him. I liked his looks. Nice manners, too.' She would have liked to discuss Jim.

'He found the boy sitting on the doorstep, his mother's you understand, locked out, blubbing. The man doesn't know what to do, the boy won't tell him what's the trouble, so Jim brings him out to me. He is here in my house.'

'But what happened? What –?'

'Child doesn't say. Just like his mother, a clam. I have not asked.'

'Was it something terrible? Was he raped? One reads such awful things in the papers.'

'No, no, nothing physical. He's run away, that's all I know, and needs his mother.'

'Of course he does,' she cried.

'Will you then, darling, tell Hebe to hurry home but to drive carefully.'

'Of course I will. No need to use that tone of voice.'

'Can't think why people have children, they are nothing but grief,' Bernard grumbled.

'Come now, Bernard, just because we –'

'Let's stick to the point.'

'Very well.' Louisa was quiet.

I have hurt her, thought Bernard. She always wanted children. Supposing we had married – 'Are you still there?' he asked.

'Yes. I was thinking that although it's worrying for Hebe she will be glad of an excuse to leave me.'

'Why? She enjoys going to you enormously.'

Louisa told him – the tale growing with the telling – of Mungo and Rory calling at the same time. 'If you had telephoned before I would have told you about Rory. She wandered into his hat shop on the way here. He is *épris*, everything going very nicely and then Mungo appears and, oh Bernard, she was splendid, such aplomb, an example to any girl in her situation, such nerve.'

'That's one way of looking at it.'

'I will tell her in the morning. She must get some sleep.'

'If what you tell me is true she will not be sleeping, she will be worrying.'

'I did my best, I turned them out.'

'They will come back, Louisa, they won't stay away. One might but two together won't. Neither will trust the other not to steal a march.'

'Do you think so? Is that what you would do?' She was amused.

'Go and wake her, Louisa. She must come back, the child needs her. Make haste.'

'I will, I will.'

'I can't keep him indefinitely.'

'How selfish you are. What about Amy Tremayne and that Hannah girl?'

'Jim says he refused to go near them. Probably afraid of being laughed at.'

'Very well, I will rouse her. Bernard, darling?'

'Yes, Louisa.'

'Keep in touch, tell me –'

'That I love you?' Bernard laughed. 'You know I do. I love you,' he said.

'Yes, that, but tell me what happens, what upset the boy.'

'I will if I ever find out. Goodnight, Louisa.'

'Goodnight, my love.' She rang off. Bernard laid the receiver back in its cradle. Time was, he thought, we said, 'Goodnight, my love' and meant it. Has time robbed me of feeling? How this call box smells. Bernard stood with the door of the box open, breathed in the wet night air, took a pinch of snuff and set off across the fields sneezing luxuriously.

As he walked he saw Louisa spring out of bed, put on the lace dressing-gown with satin lining which they had chosen together, run along the passage and up those stairs (hung, he remembered, with quite interesting prints) to knock on Hebe's door, wake her. What would she say, how would she put it? Bernard laughed grimly. She was old, the dressing-gown would be of wool, Louisa had changed. In the old days she had not liked other women; she had feared potential rivals. She was right, he conceded, when once meeting unexpectedly he had been with another woman. She had been right to be jealous. But I always loved her best, he thought, trudging through the wet grass, or almost best. She need not have made such a fuss about that girl; I only slept with her once, can't even remember her name. Now, he thought, as he caught sight of his house in the moonlight, she likes other women, she is friends with Hebe's lover, Mungo's mother – she never knew about my caper with her – and she loves Hebe. As he scrambled through the gap in his garden wall he was pleased that, while he could visualise Louisa in her house, she had never seen his. He was one up on her there. Time was, he thought, letting himself in, stroking Feathers' soft head, time was we talked of love all night, now we discuss our beloved prostitute. I hope she drives carefully. It is a long way, she will worry. Should I have sent Jim to fetch her? I may not have wanted children, he thought, pushing his cat aside with his foot so that he could put a log on the dying fire, but I love Hebe as a father might or a grandfather. I am not, thank God, a dirty old man who pinches bottoms, fumbles up skirts. I did pretty well in my prime. I have memories enough to carry me to my grave. 'You still awake?' he called softly to Jim in the next room.

'Yes. The boy is asleep. Is his mother coming?'

'Yes, Louisa is telling her.'

'Shall you tell the boy she is coming?'

'No. He may fret if she is delayed.'

'I am going to bed. Goodnight.' Jim went upstairs.

Bernard sat in his wing chair, Feathers at his feet staring into the fire, twitching his ears when the fresh log caught and sparkled. Bernard listened to the prickle of burning wood, watched the flames. He thought of Louisa. Had she been happy? Would she have been happier if he had insisted that their love was large enough to flout convention. The opposition had not been insuperable; he had used it as an excuse to save the single status he enjoyed. She had married conventionally. He knew she had loved her husband. But not as she loves me, he thought jealously. Bernard stroked the cat as she leapt on to his lap. 'She still loves me best,' he murmured to the uninterested animal. 'Things are best as they are. We are old, I am rich, I help her.' Bernard liked his role. He thought, I send her money. She does not know that the things she has parted with when really short are here, that I kept them for her, pretended I had sold them. Some day when I die she shall have them back, the rings, the ridiculous but valuable tiara. I have left them to her; a farewell surprise. Thinking of Louisa, Bernard cursed old age, its tricks of memory, words, people growing illusive and ephemeral. Who, for instance, was the girl Louisa heard he had been dining with the time he told her he had 'flu – he had spent the night with her in an hotel afterwards. She had not been up to much, he remembered that, but not her name, nor could he put a face to her. Louisa had made a scene. It had not been the first girl.

'One often had 'flu,' Bernard said to Feathers, who laid his head on his master's knee. 'Alas, one never gets it now.'

Feathers groaned sympathetically.

'I loved her so much.' Bernard stroked the dog's muzzle. 'But I could not stop having 'flu. It wouldn't amuse her, even now.'

24

Not a nice thing to leave them in their party clothes, stuck there until somebody takes pity. Not nice at all. Holding the steering wheel tightly, Hebe drove west to get back to Silas. She cursed herself for working at Louisa's when she should have waited at home in case he needed her. She had been apolaustic. Absorbed by self-reproach, she missed the turning which led to the faster, less winding road to Exeter. She had driven several miles before she realised this calamity. More time would be wasted going back, better to go on, praying that the holiday traffic would not be too diabolical. She told herself, He will be with Amy or Hannah and Giles. They will look after him until I arrive. Try not to fuss, she adjured herself. She was sitting upright, the safety belt cutting into her shoulder, tense. She made an effort to relax, to drive less fast. It would not be nice to have an accident.

Nice – now there was a word which didn't apply. She drove feeling jolted and shocked by the meeting she had just experienced.

They have not changed; they are no nicer than they were. What a terrible hat she was wearing, and he all dressed up for some function. They are still my grandparents, she thought, with the mixture of love and hurt she had long suppressed. Have I not watched the obits in *The Times,* hoping they would die? She was amazed by the strength of her feelings. What a ludicrous coincidence that they should also use the short cut. If I had not I should be well on my way to Silas. This is the last thing I need. She stopped her car by a telephone box and leaned on the steering wheel, reliving the scene which had just taken place.

The old people's Rover interlocked with a Land Rover. The farmer abusive, her grandfather furious. She had asked if she could help. They had not recognised her. He had said, 'We could ask this young woman to telephone a garage for us.' How pompous his voice sounded; it had changed. Did he have new teeth which fitted better than the old? And the new dog. It had come wagging. She had asked its name, seen the old man's head jerk up, known that he recognised her, heard him call the dog back in the tone he used when the dog was about to roll in a smell. It was as if he thought I would contaminate it, she thought, horrified. She had said, 'I will ring the AA for you.' She had been polite. 'I like your dog,' she had said, and, 'Good-bye'. Why, she thought angrily, did I not say, 'I will find a black layabout, drug addict with dirty nails to fix your car.' She looked at the call box, turned the key in the ignition, started the engine. Let someone else find them. I am wasting time, I must get back to Silas. The telephone is probably vandalised, she excused herself, treading on the accelerator, speeding away.

They brought me up to be nice, she thought. I was not nice leaving them sitting there. I bet they trusted me to phone the AA. Someone else will come along and be nicer. An involuntary gust of laughter seized her. Louisa Fox had been nice waking her when she had just got to sleep. Really nice. Hebe smiled, remembering Louisa.

'Sorry to wake you, Hebe. There is a message that your boy has come back on his own from the Scilly Islands. He is all right. Naturally he wants you. No, of course you must go to him.' She had been seized by manic anxiety.

As she scrambled out of bed to dress and pack, Louisa had given her money, far more than she was owed, waved aside protests, said something about it being perhaps a blessing in disguise that she had to cut her stay short; a hint, of course, to the Mungo-Rory duet, the disarray of the Syndicate. She had seemed amused, murmured something about having had less cooking but greater entertainment.

Yes, Louisa had been very nice. Not nice as 'they' would be, but nice from the bone. She had made her eat breakfast, stood in her dressing-gown on the front steps holding Rufus, who had indicated that he would like to come too. He had got into the car and had to be dragged out. Louisa had held him by the collar and waved with her free hand, calling, 'Let me know how he is. Come again. Drive carefully in the holiday traffic. Take the short cut to the main road.'

'Damn the short cut. If I had not used it I would not have met them. They probably also thought themselves clever using it.' Hebe talked to herself. 'It was not nice meeting them. Nice, not nice. Nice people. The right sort of people.' She could hear their voices.

Louisa was nice and the right sort. She does not like my grandfather. Hebe remembered the dropped hint; she had casually accepted Silas' existence, asked no nosey questions.

Should she have telephoned Amy or Hannah? Why had she not done so? It would have been so simple to telephone one of them. This is what being crazed with anxiety means, thought Hebe. All I want is to be on the road on my way back to him. I shall not stop fussing until I see him. Why did he send me that postcard, 'Having a wonderful time, wish you were here'? What does it mean? Try and think of something else.

What else? What would block out her need to see Silas' brown eyes, arched nose, russet hair, to hold him close, to hug him? I shall have a crash if I don't think of something else. She was near tears.

Deliberately she set herself to think of her grandparents – her childhood, her upbringing. Forcing herself she recollected the intolerable boredom of long meals, wondering what to talk about, what subject would be neutral and not cause an argument. No politics other than Tory; literature tricky, too many writers were Left Wing or not nice in their private lives or wrote about people who were not nice; gardening safe but might lead to one being asked to weed or plant out the Canterbury bells, so boringly tedious. She had not been horsey. Horses. Her sisters, before they married, had talked almost exclusively of horses, hunting, eventing, racing or point to points through those meals. Dogs, tennis, golf, bridge all safe but wrapped in a pall of platitudes. Parties? Okay if they were nice people's parties where one met the right sort, the euphemism for a marriageable man, the benefit acquired from a nice upbringing. So I suggested the Cordon Bleu cookery school when I failed my O-levels, suggested I would meet nice girls. It never occurred to them that I saw cooking as an escape. It was good of them to send me; I should be grateful. Why did someone not tell him he got cabbage stuck in his teeth? Hebe, driving as fast as was safe, perhaps too fast, muttered, And the relations! Who was related to who, through whom, by whom, and always they were potentially nice, or related to the right sort. Failing the gentry bit, titled. Hebe grinned, pressing her foot on the accelerator. So why the surprise when they exploded about dirty nails, beards, guitars, bare feet, blacks, earrings, Communists, long hair? Why the surprise, Hebe wondered as she drove. Were they not terrified by the Permissive Society? How naive she had been at sixteen and what a prig, Hebe mocked herself. I thought they were fond of me. Not as fond as of my sisters, but fond enough to stand by when I became pregnant. I had thought I would be original, I would keep my virginity. Oh, the irony. Talking to herself she fretted, caught in a long line of cars, held up behind three lorries all impossible to pass, just as many cars travelling east as west, the traffic crawling to a halt. She drummed her fingers on the driving wheel chanting, 'Virginity, Virginity, when, where, how did I lose it?' The traffic going east had halted also. Hebe sang, 'Virginity, where did I lose you? You don't lose it like dropping a purse, for God's sake.'

'Did it hurt?' A man driving a Ford Cortina towards London asked across the gap between their cars.

Hebe wound up her window. That's all I need, a pick-up. I shall get myself arrested. The traffic moved on. He called me a whore, she thought, he called me that. Perhaps he remembers, sitting by the roadside in his morning coat and top hat, perhaps he remembers what he said, perhaps she in her flowered dress remembers too. They were not nice that day. Remembering her grandparents, Hebe's tears coursed down salt as she caught them with her tongue. The traffic increased speed, it was possible to overtake the lorries. There was the respite of a dual carriageway. She hurried on; it was imperative to reach home and Silas.

As she sped down the A30 Hebe was glad she had made herself think of her grandparents. She had bottled them away too long. I should have had the guts to tell them they have a beautiful bastard great-grandson. Then later she thought I am a fool, I am educating him in the way they educated me. I too am a snob. I despise Hannah's vowels; I didn't want Silas to talk like Giles. I sent him to a school where he makes friends with the right sort of people, who invite him to stay in the Scillies and something has happened to him, something not nice. During the long drive she experienced the catharsis which left her weak but with a clear mind. She even recovered enough to think wryly of Mungo and Rory as the right sort of nice men to have in her Syndicate, and of Lucy Duff's and Louisa Fox's houses as the right sort of houses in which to work.

Tired and anxious, impatience overwhelmed her on the last stretch into Penzance, but she felt relief as she left the traffic to swing uphill into the steep and hideous dark brick street, roar up to her house, jam on the brakes and jump out. She let herself in, calling, 'Silas, I am back, darling.'

Trip looked up from an armchair, showing displeasure at being disturbed. No sign of Silas. The house was slightly dusty, everything exactly as she had left it, in her bedroom an indentation on the bed where Trip had slept. Silas' room was neat, empty. She opened windows, letting in the August air. He would be with Amy. She filled the cat's bowl with fresh water, bent to stroke her. Trip moved into the garden with a preoccupied air. Hebe ran across the street to Amy's house and walked in.

'Hullo, Amy.' Amy was resting in her armchair.

'You are back early.' Amy kissed her, reaching up to hold her.

'Is Silas not with you?' Hebe drew back.

'Silas?'

'Staying with Hannah, is he?'

'He is in the Scilly Isles, not due back. Why have you left Louisa so soon?' Amy got up from her chair. 'I expect you'd like a cuppa.' Then, looking closely at Hebe, 'Something wrong?'

'You telephoned. I rushed back. Is he with Hannah and Giles?'

'I never telephoned.'

'Then it must have been Hannah, he must be there. I will go round to her.'

Amy caught Hebe's hand. 'What am I supposed to have telephoned about? What was the message? What's wrong?'

'The message was that Silas had come back and wanted me. Naturally I thought it was you. He must be with Hannah.' Hebe was filled with incipient panic.

'Hannah doesn't know where you were. Unless she has second sight.'

'I will go and ask her.' Hebe ran out of the house leaving Amy's door open, raced up the street to Hannah, anxiety treacherously transforming itself into blind fear. She let herself into Hannah's house. Empty sitting-room, kitchen and garden. She took the stairs two at a time, sounds of Bach from Hannah's bedroom. 'Hannah!' Hebe burst into the room. Curtains drawn across open windows, the joyous sound of Bach, Hannah and Terry lying contentedly in bed listening to the radio.

'Is he with Giles?'

'Is who with Giles?' Hannah switched off the radio.

'Hi, Hebe.' Terry, lying with his head cushioned on pillows, an arm round Hannah's shoulders, smiled up at Hebe. She scarcely noticed their happy faces, their nakedness, the clothes scattered on the floor. 'You are standing on me best knickers.' Hebe kicked away the knickers and in so doing caught her heel and tore the garment. 'There now, you've torn 'em.'

'Where is Silas?' Hebe stood over them. 'You sent me a message. I've come back. He needs me.'

'Sit down.' Terry reached out and pulled Hebe down on to the bed. 'You look as though you'd lost your marbles.'

'I've got to find him. You sent a message,' she pleaded with Hannah.

'No, love,' said Hannah, sitting up, beginning to worry.

'Then who?' Hebe's voice rose.

Terry held her wrist. 'Why not tell us what this is in aid of?'

Hebe told them of the message and her drive.

'Somebody being funny?' suggested Hannah.

'Couldn't be. I thought it was Amy but she says not. She's the only person who had my number.'

'Didn't Silas have it?'

'Of course he did, but the message wasn't from him, it was about him.' Hebe's voice wobbled.

'We had better get dressed.' Hannah got out of bed. 'Look sharp, Terry.'

Hebe sat on the bed watching them.

'You don't mind, do you, Hebe?' Hannah zipped up her skirt.

'Mind what?'

'Terry and me.'

'Why should I? Oh, sorry. I hadn't taken it in. I'm glad for you.'

'Told you she wouldn't mind.' Terry spoke across Hebe to Hannah. 'She hoped you would be jealous,' he said to Hebe.

Hebe smiled wanly.

'You both up there? I've made a pot of tea,' Amy called up the stairs.

'Tea!' Hebe almost screamed. '*Tea!*'

'Yes, tea.' Terry took her arm. 'Come to Amy's while we think what to do next. Amy's not been well, her ticker.' Hebe appeared not to take in what he said. Amy gestured to him to shut up.

As they reached Amy's house Giles appeared at the bottom of the street, his arms full of driftwood.

'Giles may know something,' said Hebe.

They waited for Giles walking slowly up the street. Terry ran to meet him, taking some of the driftwood. The women saw Terry question Giles, Giles shake his head.

'Come and sit down, you look done in.' Amy led Hebe into her house. 'Sit down.' She poured tea and gave it to Hebe. 'Drink that.'

They watched her drink.

'That better?'

Hebe shook her head. 'Not much.'

'Why don't you ring up Mrs Whatsit in the Scillies?' suggested Giles. 'She would know why he has left, if he has.'

'What a fool I am.' Hebe sprang up. 'I will telephone from home, it's easier.' She ran out of the house.

'Hadn't we better –' Hannah stood up, ready to follow.

'No, leave her.' Amy was firm. 'It's a private conversation.'

'Jennifer Reeves speaking.' The line to the islands was clear. Invisible Jennifer Reeves sounded as though she stood next to Hebe.

'This is Hebe Rutter,' said Hebe.

'I see.' The voice was chill. 'About time,' it said mysteriously.

'I got a message about Silas that –'

'Does he want to apologise?' Sharp, chill.

'I don't understand.' She was mystified.

'So he has not told you? I am not surprised. What excuse does he give? We do not usually put ourselves out to have strange boys to stay.'

'Strange boys?' Hebe felt blood rushing to her face.

'Very strange, and that's putting it mildly. Poor Michael asked to have him as we were also having two very nice –'

'Nice?' Hebe felt anger and suspicion.

'Very nice boys. The right sort, not at the same school as Michael and your boy, of course, though how –'

'Right sort?' Was this woman really speaking like this?

'Of course they will all be at the same school soon. I am talking of Ian and Alistair, not your son. I don't know what school will take him – not Eton, naturally.'

'I –'

'I would suggest you teach him some manners, make him write and apologise for –'

'For what?' Hebe restrained a shout.

'For his behaviour, his language, the inconvenience to say the least. His rudeness to myself and my husband –'

'What are you trying –'

'I am trying to tell you that we were quite worried until the Harbour Master at St Mary's told us he had been seen getting off a boat from Trescoe and going up to the airport to the helicopter. We thought something unpleasant might have happened to him.'

'It obviously had,' said Hebe grimly.

'What did you say?' Jennifer tripped in mid-stride.

'I said it obviously had. Something very unpleasant.'

'Mrs Rutter –'

'Did you send me a message?'

'Of course not. The boy is message in himself.' Jennifer Reeves laughed, pleased with her witticism. 'By the way, he left most of his luggage behind. Not a very good packer, either.'

Hebe felt fury at the word 'either', cast brutally into the murk.

'If you like to be at the heliport on Thursday we are cutting the holiday short, you can collect it. I take it you will be there.'
Hebe put the receiver back in its cradle. She was shivering.

'So who sent the message?' Terry put his arms round her.
'You were listening?'
'No need for a loud hailer, has she?' He kissed the top of her head.
'Oh, God!' Hebe leant against him. 'What can have happened? Where can he be?'
'We had better go back to square one, telephone the old lady you were working for, ask her to tell you again.'
Louisa did not answer when the telephone rang. She was at the bottom of the garden, feet up on her garden seat, surrounded by adoring dogs enjoying the afternoon sun, listening to the Bach concert on her transistor radio.

25

Mungo surfaced to the sound of cathedral bells, light filtering through closed curtains, an unfamiliar room. He closed his mouth, parched from snoring. An attempt to breathe through his nose was partially successful. The scent of hair roused his curiosity and a response in his half-waking state of sensual arousal. The smell was not Alison's, which he had been used to before they slept in separate beds, nor was it Hebe's. With shock he remembered he was in Rory's house, in Rory's bed. And here lay Rory, asleep with his head on Mungo's shoulder, breathing sweetly, relaxed and peaceful. As though aware of Mungo's gaze he snuggled closer, turning trustfully towards him, nuzzling close.

Recollecting the evening and night before, listening to the bells, Mungo remembered. It must be quite late. There was action to be taken, plans to make, but what action, what plans? He remembered his mother, her appalling direct approach to what she called Alison's elopement. Sending him out of the room while she telephoned to Santa Barbara, she had said, 'Leave it to me. You cramp my style if you listen. I will call you if I want you.' He had gone downstairs to listen on the extension but Miss Thomson had been sitting by the telephone. His only consolation had been that while in the room with Miss Thomson she had not been able to eavesdrop either. Mungo envied his mother's lack of hypocrisy. She is right, he thought, she cannot manage without Alison and neither can I. Fourteen years of Alison's competent bossiness had unmanned him. The drive across country to sweep Hebe off her feet into Happy Ever After was poppycock. He would be fortunate if he could keep the arrangement with Hebe which had worked so well up to date.

Rory stirred, mumbling in his sleep. Mungo began a manoeuvre to extricate himself from Rory without waking him. If he could get to Louisa's without Rory he could see Hebe and arrange to spend time with her soon. But before that, thanks to his mother, he had to meet Alison, see that she was settled back at home in her role of wife, mother and daughter-in-law. He would have to spend a little time with her. Mungo tried to calculate how long. Since Alison had never defected before the question was academic. He squinted at his watch. Eleven thirty-five. He reared away from Rory whose hair was tickling his nose. Rory woke.

'Hullo.' Rory smiled cheerfully. 'Good morning.'

There was nothing good about it. Mungo swung his legs off the bed and tottered to the bathroom. His head was throbbing, his mouth felt like a grouted roof, he felt dizzy. Rory joined him. 'I'll get some tea.' They urinated together. Rory flushed the lavatory. Rory looked bright-eyed, alert, healthy. He said, 'You look revolting.' He appeared concerned.

'I feel it,' Mungo grunted.

'Go back to bed while I dress, then I will get breakfast.' Rory guided Mungo back to bed. 'I'll get you an aspirin.' Mungo lay back with a groan. Rory brought a glass of water and aspirin. 'Take two, come on, swallow.' He had taken charge.

Mungo lay hoping the aspirin would work, listening in disgust to his cousin shave, shower, whistle, sing, clean his teeth, gargle. Rory had hit him the night before and now this. Mungo felt middle-aged, resentful, jealous. Rory brought strong Indian tea, sat beside the bed and persuaded him to drink two large cups. 'You are dehydrated, you must –'

'I must go to Louisa's,' Mungo muttered.

'We will go together,' said Rory firmly.

Mungo was too weak to protest.

'There's no hurry.' Rory still looked concerned. 'We will have something to eat and go to – er – gether. I won't – er – I won't sneak off without –'

'Me?'

'No.'

Mungo felt a vicious desire to do something unpleasant to Rory for playing so fair. Had he not had the intention of doing just that, reaching Hebe first? Drinking his tea he sneaked a look at Rory, who looked young and, oh God, spry in clean jeans and white T-shirt which flattered his hazel eyes. His freshly washed hair, though thinning in front, curled jauntily at the back. He looked what he was, young.

'Take your time,' said Rory, in the voice of one talking to an invalid. 'Have a bath, borrow anything you want.'

'My bag is in my car,' said Mungo grumpily.

'Give me your keys; I will get it for you. When you have had a bath and changed you will feel better.'

'There's nothing wrong with me,' Mungo shouted.

'No, no.' Rory took the car keys and disappeared with the tea tray, presently returning with Mungo's bag. 'It's a beautiful day. We will eat in the garden when you are ready. There is no hurry.'

How dare he be so nice? Mungo was consumed with self-pity. Trying to whip up his hatred he only succeeded in breaking into an alcoholic sweat. One way and another he had overdone the booze during the last few days. I am not a real drinker, he told himself.

When Mungo came downstairs Rory had laid a table under a tree in the garden. 'Brunch,' he said to Mungo heartily.

They sat down to orange juice, kidneys and bacon, fresh rolls, butter, bitter marmalade and strong coffee. They ate in silence, watched by a robin which ventured on to the table, helping itself to crumbs. Mungo felt a pang of envy for his cousin's mode of life.

'You live very comfortably,' he said grudgingly. Rory looked at him, nervously cleared his throat and said:

'Alone.'

'But you do what you want.'

'Within reason.'

They had finished their meal. Mungo felt almost human. They sat watching the robin hop among the plates, flash back into the tree, return when Rory crumbled a piece of toast.

'Tell me,' began Rory, 'um, tell me about –'

'Hebe?'

'Yes.' Rory blushed. Sure of himself with Mungo hungover, he was unsure with Mungo recovered. 'Six years?' He shied away from the thought.

'Alison,' began Mungo, 'was looking for someone to cook for my ma when the dragon housekeeper has her hols. She found Hebe, recommended by an old girl who had worked for Aunt Louisa at one time. I met Hebe in her capacity of cook. I fell in love with her.'

'Love.' Could one in charity imagine Mungo in love? It seemed doubtful to Rory.

Mungo helped himself to more coffee. Rory waited.

'I found,' Mungo went on, 'that she was willing to sleep with me if I paid, that her conditions were like any other tart.'

'She isn't a tart.'

'She *is*. Conditions, money in advance. Fair enough, I said, to that, but the other conditions make her different. I don't call her as I would any other call girl –'

'I wouldn't know,' said Rory primly.

'Actually I don't either,' Mungo admitted. '*She* would arrange dates. *She* found the flat we go to. *She* tells me when and for how long we may be together. *I* haven't the foggiest idea where she lives, there's only this Pakistani shop which forwards –'

'She sounds as bossy as –' Rory hesitated.

'Alison. I know, but not the way she sets about it. It took me three years before I realised she had suggested, planted the seed if you like, of anything she wanted to do. When *she* wanted to go to Greece I found *I* wanted to take her there. My firm has connections so it's easy. Same with Venice and Rome. She never suggests Paris for some reason. I have suggested Paris but no, she won't.' Mungo sighed. 'I go to Paris alone or take Alison.'

'Nice for Alison.' Rory's voice was downbeat.

'Alison doesn't really go for French food. Now Hebe, you can't fault her on food.'

'She is a cook, she –'

'I know, I know, but she *knows*, she talks about food like a restaurateur.'

'Perhaps she comes from a –'

'No, no, Hebe's what my ma calls a lady. One of us, you know what a snob she is.'

'Almost as bad as mine.'

Rory, momentarily distracted, thought of their mothers. Mungo thought of the joys of Hebe in London, Rome, Venice, that island in Greece. He sighed. 'I love the girl,' he said heavily.

'So do I.' Rory stated his feelings obstinately.

'We read aloud to each other,' said Mungo. 'We play backgammon.'

This piece of information disturbed Rory dreadfully, revealing a depth of intimacy infinitely more alarming than sex.

Mungo shifted his chair, disturbing the robin. 'One doesn't like to link money with love,' he said, 'but if one does I warn you, Rory, keeping Hebe is like having a third son at school. Six weeks a year. For that I could have another son.'

'Do you want another son?'

'God forbid.'

'I have no sons. I'm not bothered. Besides, you say you charge her to expenses. That's pretty sordid and morally wrong.' Rory was on the attack.

'Last night you were all for it.'

'Last night I had a few drinks and last night you were suggesting your sons, your well educated sons, should join –'

'The Syndicate? Does she really call it a Syndicate?' Had Rory been pulling his leg?

'Yes,' Rory admitted sadly.

'I wonder who the other members are?'

'We may know them.' Rory was not pleased with this thought.

'Aren't we wasting time? Are we not going to see the girl, was not that the idea last night?'

'Last night we were both going to marry her, today you seem to be content to keep her as your mistress. I still want to marry her.' Rory began clearing the breakfast table. 'Help me with this,' he said sharply to his cousin.

Mungo helped stack the remains of their meal on to a tray which Rory carried into the house.

'Suppose I make you an offer, buy you out?' Rory brought out the sentence in a rush. Could he borrow from the bank perhaps, a sexual mortgage?

'You must be joking,' said Mungo haughtily.

'She might be – er – she might be –'

'What?' Mungo snarled.

'Pleased,' Rory stacked the plates in the dishwasher, 'to get rid of you.'

Mungo tried a sarcastic laugh. This was an awful thought not to be voiced.

'What about the forty-six weeks a year she is not with you?' Rory mustered courage. If only he could undermine Mungo's self-confidence.

'She cooks.'

'Only occasionally for your ma and Aunt Louisa, Louisa told me. Six weeks with your ma, that leaves forty, and about three to four with Aunt Louisa, that leaves thirty-six for the rest of them.'

'Who?'

'The Syndicate, you fool,' Rory shouted in exasperation. 'Just think, she –'

'She must be a millionaire,' said Mungo in admiration.

'All you think of is money.' Rory, outraged, stared at his cousin.

'All I think of,' Mungo stared back at Rory, 'all I think,' he said quietly, 'is what I may lose.'

The two men looked at one another, full of unvoiced thoughts of Hebe's skin, eyes, mouth, hair, thighs, her laughter, her manner of giving, her voice, her talent for making them feel supermen.

'Come on,' said Mungo.

'Right,' said Rory.

They drove out of Salisbury in silence. To Mungo, the unspeakable thought of his clumsy young cousin fucking Hebe was distracting. Never allowed to swear or use four-letter words by Alison, he habitually used them to himself and outside her ambience. To Rory, the vision of Mungo lying on top of Hebe with his, with his, oh God, with his thing up her was an obscene vision which would not go away. As he drove he wondered vaguely whether it would be first-degree murder if he killed Mungo, if he had the guts to do so, how to set about it.

'There's a hell of a lot of traffic on this road,' said Mungo, remarking on what was obvious, a heavily congested road.

'The races. Salisbury races.'

'More like an air-show. Anyway, can't we get off this bloody road? You live here, you ought to know.'

'No short cuts, only very –'

'Very what?' How can Hebe consider this ass? It's crazy, I must tell her it's madness, he can't churn out a single sentence.

'Only very long cuts. You know, narrow and – er – winding.'

'Are they full of traffic?'

'No – nothing because you can't –'

'Can we get to Louisa that way?'

'Yes, but –'

'Then get us off this road. Can't you see, it's jammed for miles. We will never get cracking along here.'

'You can't pass anything on the narrow –'

'You said there was no traffic on them. There will be nothing to pass.'

'Oh, all right.' Rory swung the car into a narrow lane which wound charmingly along a flattish valley. The lane ran back and forth, crossing and re-crossing a graceful chalk stream. Cows looked up in ruminative surprise, Rory slowed to let a pheasant pass. It was a lane unchanged since the era of the horse and cart.

'What shall we say to Aunt Louisa? I usually only turn up in the – er – '

'What?'

'Evening, to fish.'

'No good fishing in full sunlight, any fool knows that. Old Louisa's no fool.'

'She'll – er – smell –'

'She's already smelt it,' snarled Mungo. 'Don't be an oaf. She sided with Hebe last night, practically saw us off, treated us as though we'd come to rape the girl.'

'Wasn't that what you, what you –' Rory, who was driving, swivelled hare's eyes to look at Mungo.

'Watch where you're going,' yelled Mungo. Rory braked and stopped the car. The lane was blocked by a shiny Rover, its wings jammed into the mudguards of a Land Rover, the machines interlocked like fighting dogs.

'Accident,' said Mungo, stating the obvious. He opened the door of the car and got out. Rory followed.

The Land Rover contained some bales of hay, bags of fertiliser and a pitchfork. There was no sign of a driver. By the side of the road, sitting on the grass, an ancient couple and a Labrador dog. The Labrador wore the customary expression of such dogs – just say what you want and I will try to oblige if it is within my humble capacity. The couple stood up, expunging from their faces exasperation, anger and impatience, to greet Mungo and Rory with the reserved half-smiles of country gentry. They were dressed for a function. The woman wore a longish dress of flowered silk, over it a thick silk coat of navy blue, white shoes, white gloves and a hat which made Rory flinch. If there was one thing which upset his sensibilities it was plastic cherries. She wore a double row of pearls, a diamond brooch and good rings. Her husband wore morning dress of dated cut.

'See you have had a bit of a smash,' Mungo suggested, moving towards them.

On hearing Mungo's impeccable vowels the elderly couple smiled with less reserve.

'Driving too fast, always in a hurry these fellows,' said the elderly man.

'I see. Anybody gone for help?'

'A – er – a young woman went for help,' said the man. His hands trembled as he pulled a handkerchief out of his pocket, then smoothed his trousers which had grown uncomfortable as he sat. Mungo wondered whether the old-fashioned expression 'adjusting his dress', which was what the man was doing, was still used. He noted with interest that the old fellow's trousers had fly buttons, not a zip.

'Where's the driver of this?' Rory slapped the Land Rover with a comradely hand.

'We have waited hours.' The elderly lady looked at her watch. 'We have been here since dawn.'

'They won't want to know how long we've been here,' snapped her husband, putting her in her place.

'The driver of that thing got tired of waiting,' said his wife, her voice tremulous.

'She said she would tell the AA to come,' said the husband. 'They are usually reliable.'

'But *she* never was,' said his wife bitterly.

'So a friend went for help?' Rory brightened.

'She said she would tell the AA.'

'Well, someone will be along soon.' Mungo was impatient to get on.

'I told you nothing can pass along this lane,' Rory shouted at Mungo in exasperation.

'So only locals use it. I suppose the Land Rover's local?' Realisation was dawning.

'Yes,' they spoke in unison. 'Yes, he is.'

'I shall have to back all the way to the main road.' Rory was furious. Then, remembering his manners, he said, 'We will tell the AA to rescue you.'

'We'd better write down the car numbers,' said Mungo, making an attempt to be practical, 'although your friend will have told them already.' He found a pencil and walked round the car and the Land Rover, writing their numbers on the back of an envelope.

'I expect your dog wants his dinner.' Rory made a feeble try at amiability.

'She drove away and left us on purpose.' The woman spoke through clenched teeth. Rory was startled to see tears in her eyes. 'She will not have told the AA.' Then, recovering, she said, 'He has his dinner at night.' Her smile was socially pure. 'I have it for him in the car. It is we who shall miss our luncheon. My husband was to have made a speech.'

'Where are you going?' Rory made conversation.

'Ledbury. That is why we made an early start. A wedding.'

'I have friends near Ledbury. They are – er – called –' Rory blurted out the name of a titled uncle and aunt. 'He's – er – my godfather.'

'That is near where we are going. I shall tell him you rescued us. My husband was at school with him.'

'Don't worry.' Rory was not liked by his uncle who, he had heard, referred to him as the poofter hatter. 'We will back away now and telephone the AA for you.'

Rory and Mungo got into the car and Rory, putting the car into reverse, began the drive back to the main road. 'This will rick my neck.'

'What d'you want to suck up to those people for?' asked Mungo. 'Boasting about your bloody godfather.'

'It was you who let us in for ringing the AA. I was just being normally polite. You wrote down their car numbers – pretty officious.'

'Who do you suppose they were? They looked like something out of a pantomime.'

'Poor old things, they were going to a wedding.' Rory felt a spasm of tenderheartedness. 'The dog was rather nice.'

'You can't judge people by their dogs,' said Mungo aggressively. 'Cats, now, are another matter.'

'I shan't invite you to my wedding,' cried Rory spitefully, twisting his neck as he reversed the car, 'to – er – to Hebe.'

Mungo refrained from hitting Rory, possibly causing another car crash and further delay.

26

Eileen Rutter walked away. She was afraid Christopher would lose his temper. She tried not to listen to the sound of tearing metal as the surly owner of the Land Rover wrenched the vehicles apart with scant respect for the Rover. All he had said, arriving with a mechanic and a breakdown truck, had been, 'Must get these apart before milking time.' The mechanic had got on with the job.

Her shoes pinched. She was conscious of looking ridiculous in these surroundings and that Christopher looked an old buffoon. She was glad of the dog's company. 'She recognised us,' Eileen said to the dog. 'That is the only chance we've ever been given. We missed it.' Thirteen years ago Christopher had refused to look for Hebe. For thirteen years she had been taboo. 'She looks lovely,' Eileen said to the dog. 'I wonder what her child is like.' She talked to herself these days, Christopher having grown as deaf as herself. 'He didn't hear the beastly thing blow its horn. He shouldn't really drive.' The dog walked beside her companionably. 'She's so different from the other girls,' Eileen cried. 'She always was.' The dog glanced up. One could have asked whether the rumours one had heard were true. Seen at Wimbledon by Beata with a male companion; in a restaurant by Marcus, also with a man; walking along Knightsbridge, again by Beata; at the theatre with a man he said he knew quite well by Robert; glimpsed briefly in the West Country with a black youth too old to be her child, by Delian. Did that prove anything? One met black people, like it or not. Christopher had liked the enterprising young man who installed those devilish burglar traps. None of the sightings added credence to Christopher's conviction that Hebe lived in Brixton in the black community. 'At least we know she is alive,' Eileen said to the dog. 'She was wearing good clothes, driving a decent car. Perhaps she is all right. Small thanks to us,' said Eileen bitterly to the dog. Her hat was pressing on her forehead. 'She lied, she deceived, she betrayed, she went her own way,' Eileen faltered. 'Was that so terrible?' she said to the dog. 'Might I have not done something to help her –' She felt as she had felt before in the sad watches of the night, a hesitant doubt. She looked at the hat in her hand. 'I could see she didn't think much of this,' Eileen said to the dog, and with all her strength she threw the hat towards the hedge. The hat sailed in the light summer air over the low hedge then, weighted by the cherries, fell. With a joyous bark the dog bounded to retrieve it.

'What on earth are you doing?' Christopher drove up in the battered Rover. 'You will teach him bad habits. Get in, get in,' he said irritably, opening the car door. 'That young chap keeps a hat shop in Salisbury. You had better try his wares.' He was sarcastic.

Eileen got in beside her husband. 'You might at least have told her the dog's name,' she said loudly so that he would hear, 'not called him away.'

Christopher Rutter drove forward with a jerk so that the dog slid off the back seat on to the floor. 'Careful, we shall have another accident.'

'Shut up, woman!' yelled Christopher in his cracked old voice. 'Shut up!' Eileen began to weep, tears smearing her sunken cheeks.

'If you had told her his name –'

'Shut up!' cried her husband.

Eileen stopped crying. From nowhere came an ancient memory. Who was it she had deceived Christopher with, on that one dubious delightful occasion? Some friend of that girl Louisa. What was she called now? One forgot names. He had been small but very attractive. He had made her laugh. Eileen searched her mind for his name. She realised with pleasurable surprise that she no longer felt guilty.

'She never meant to tell the AA about us.' Eileen Rutter experienced a fleeting admiration for her granddaughter. 'You should have let her pat the dog,' she goaded her husband. 'Look out, you'll have us in the ditch.'

'Shut up!'

'Then if those young men have not also forgotten us the AA can get us out of that.'

'Shut up!'

'You should have let her touch him, told her his name –'

'God!'

He had been a delightful little stoat. Eileen sat back, remembering the name. Bernard Quigley, that was it. She wondered whether he was still alive. She looked at her husband's profile. Good looks aren't everything. She leant back in her seat and fastened the seat belt.

27

In Amy's house they gathered to question Giles. Had Silas sent him a message? No. Had Silas said anything before he left to suggest that he was worried? No. Had Silas –

'Look, Mum, I'm hungry. Can I have some tea?' Giles felt oppressed by the torrent of questions. Should he protect Silas? Was there something Silas would not want told?

'I'll get the boy some tea.' Amy busied herself producing a meal, trying hard not to look anxious. She felt unwell, had felt wretched since the morning of the flood. There was no time for that now. It had been nothing, she told herself, she'd taken fright being alone. It had been all right when Terry appeared; the pain had eased off when she took her pill.

'He was looking forward to going. Sounded okay to me.' Giles filled his mouth with bread and butter, spread jam lavishly.

Hannah stood over him, hoping to extract some crumb of information. Terry, leaning against the wall, watched her appreciatively. Some girl. Lovely rhythm. Quite different to Hebe. Couldn't compare them, really. He liked the way her eyes grew dark when she came. Poor old Hebe was looking blotched with worry.

'You were with him the day before he went away, did anything happen?' Hannah stood over her son.

'We got wet.' Giles, munching, recollected the field of kale and Silas hitting him so that he fell back in the mud and got wetter. One couldn't tell her that, not in front of this crowd. 'No, Mum.'

'Did you have a row?'

'No.' Giles shook his head. His conception of a row was

plates flying as Hannah hurled them at his father. He remembered sheltering under tables and behind chairs until the storm spent itself.

'No row? You sure?'

Giles remembered Silas last seen waving across the street. 'He called me a litterbug.' Can't do any harm to tell them that.

'You were having a row.' Hannah pounced.

'It was a joke.' Giles helped himself to cake. 'He was laughing when I last saw him.'

'Nothing to do with the Scillies, anyway,' said Terry, hoping to get back to the point.

'I am going to try to telephone again.' Hebe went out. 'She may be back by now.'

As Hebe left the house she brushed past George Scoop in search of Hannah.

'Anyone home?' he sang. 'Hullo, Amy.' He walked in uninvited.

'Hullo, Mr Scoop,' said Amy, not wishing to call him George. 'Sit down. Cup of tea?'

'Thank you, I'd love a cup. Thought you might be here.' George addressed Hannah who, answering without her usual gusto, merely said, 'Yes'.

'Hebe's son Silas is missing.' Terry looked George up and down. So this was George. 'I am Terry.' He held out his hand, smiling. George shook hands, took note of Terry's lovely teeth, regular, not a single stopping. Often the case with blacks.

'Are the police informed?' George looked round the room. He had not been to Amy's house before. He noticed that it showed few signs of the flood. Hannah must have exaggerated the damage. It had been a ploy to get him involved.

'It's hardly a police matter –' said Hannah.

'Let's listen to the local news.' Without asking Amy's permission George switched on her television. 'Might hear something on the news.' He sat down opposite the set. Amy drew in her breath.

'You want the football results,' said Giles, guessing correctly, feeling hostile.

George registered a sensation he had had before. It would be dicey to be Giles' stepfather. He watched the announcer. 'I know that man's dentist,' he said. 'He has a practice in Wimpole Street.'

Amy watched George, sizing him up to his disadvantage. Terry smiled broadly.

The national news finished, the local announcer took over. 'Now he is a patient of mine. Gets troublesome plaque. I stopped three of his teeth last month,' said George. 'Saved a molar.'

Terry caught Hannah's eye. She grinned. Amy said, 'Well,' non-committally, then again 'Well,' on a downbeat.

'If I get it right and Silas sent the message, then it's not a police –' began Terry.

'No, no, Hebe got a message. We don't know that it was Silas that sent it,' said Hannah.

'My God, I wish I could get at him.' George leant forward to stare at a man being interviewed on a fishing boat. 'One could do a lot for that chap.'

Hannah burst out laughing. 'You don't watch telly, you watch their teeth. What did the man say, George, bet you didn't hear.' She crowed with laughter, catching Terry's eye, turning to Amy, who suppressed a smile. One should not make fun of visitors even when self-invited in one's own house. George looked discomfited, began seriously to doubt any future with Hannah, though in bed she was terrific. Who was this bloke Terry? A bit young for Hannah, and coloured, black, not to put too fine a point on it. A friend of Giles? Not exactly suitable. There were other things in marriage besides bed. He turned to look at Hannah. No, dammit, from the way she was grinning at Terry she and Terry had a thing going. Tricky bitch, how could she?

Giles, passing his cup for a refill, thought, None of them are concentrating on Silas. George is bothered by Terry. Mum is teasing George. Terry feels pleased with himself for some reason. Oh, high oop, Mum's switched to Terry, that's it, and Amy's just watching. They didn't notice when Giles left the room and crossed the street to Hebe's house. Hebe, sitting by the telephone, looked up. 'Giles.'

'Any luck?' He sat beside her.

'She must be out. I am ringing every five minutes. I know

what she is doing, she is gardening. She will come in when she is tired. I must be patient.'

Trip peered round the door and walked in, pressing her flank sensuously against its edge. She strolled across to Hebe, leapt on to her lap, pressing her head up under Hebe's chin with hard little jerks, purring.

'She wouldn't talk to me when I got home.' Hebe stroked Trip.

'Cats get affronted. We had one in the States. Very unforgiving.' Giles looked at the clock. 'When is the five minutes up?'

Hebe watched the second hand. 'About now.' She dialled. 'Try, try and try again.' She listened to the telephone pealing in Louisa's drawing-room in Wiltshire. 'Still out.' She put the receiver down. 'Oh, Giles.' She began to weep. 'What on earth can have happened to him?'

'Shall I get Mum?' Giles was near tears himself.

'No, I must just keep on trying until Louisa answers. Then, when she tells me who sent the message, I may get some idea of where he can be.'

Giles fetched a roll of paper towel from the kitchen and handed a strip to Hebe. Hebe mopped her eyes, loving Giles for his action, thinking, Small wonder Silas is such friends with him. Giles blew his nose, while outside on the rooftops the sea gulls shrieked and quarrelled.

'I must pull myself together,' she said, and remembered that when she was a small child she had heard her grandfather tell a man who had lost both legs to pull his socks up.

'It's pretty difficult,' she said, taking another piece of paper towel from Giles. 'I feel I am going mad.'

'Oh, no,' said Giles, catching his breath.

'Do you think he is dead?'

'Of course not,' said Giles stoutly. 'He may be anywhere. He has no idea of time.'

'You know that's untrue.'

'What do you think of Mum and Terry?' Could he distract her?

'What do you think? It's you that matters.'

'I'm pleased.' Giles grinned, thinking, Nobody can call

Terry boring. 'Try that number again,' he suggested.

'I must not be hysterical.' She started dialling.

Louisa, sitting on her garden seat, watched Mungo and Rory snipping dead heads off her roses. She was amused by their visit, their transparent show of solicitude and affection. Enjoying the late afternoon sun she laid bets with herself as to how long the two would stay.

They had arrived in Rory's car. They had been clearly disconcerted at not finding Hebe. Bound to secrecy by Bernard, Louisa was unable to tell them that Hebe had hurried to care for her child. Neither Mungo nor Rory knew she had a child. It had become obvious that they both thought Hebe had either gone out to avoid them or that Louisa, in spite of her denial when asked by Rory, knew where Hebe lived and could be tricked into giving her address. Since she only knew by accident through Bernard, Louisa would only say, 'She has a forwarding address in London, but it is she who telephones when she is free and might like to come. I can give you the address.' From the way they hedged and hesitated. Louisa guessed that Mungo at least knew of this address and knew it to be a dead end.

Since they showed no inclination to leave, Louisa set them to work in the garden. Rory had done some ineffective weeding and Mungo had tied back some prickly ramblers. Now she watched them snipping away with secateurs. Lying with her feet up, her dogs lolling around her, Louisa enjoyed the spectacle of them spinning out the day as their hopes faded, unwilling to give up, suspiciously watching each other. She rehearsed what she would tell Bernard when next he telephoned. 'Neither dared let the other out of his sight,' she would say, hoping to amuse him. Rory came and sat on the grass beside her.

'I thought Mungo had to go and meet Alison,' he grumbled. 'What can Hebe see in him? He is far too old for her, nearly fifty.'

'Forty-five, nice-looking, rich,' Louisa murmured.

Rory muttered under his breath, watching Mungo. Then, looking up, he hissed in a whisper, 'He says she's a – well, she says so, too, but I can't – it's not possible, it's –'

'What isn't possible?' Poor fellow, he looks so distressed. Louisa felt pity for Rory.

'What he says – what she – that she's a tart,' Rory whispered.

Louisa raised her eyebrows. 'I only know her in her cooking capacity,' she said delicately. 'That's what she does here.' Louisa hesitated, recollecting that Hebe had done other than cook with Rory.

'Could it possibly be –'

'True?'

'Yes.'

'What did she tell you?'

'That she is, but I – I can't –'

'You had better believe it.' Louisa raised her head, watching Mungo approach. 'What are you doing about Alison?' she asked him.

'I am going to telephone. I said I would meet her at Heathrow but she may have arrived by now. All this made me forget.'

'All this being Hebe?' Louisa pried.

'All this being Hebe, yes,' Mungo shouted in exasperation. 'Oh, bugger it!'

'Temper, temp –' Rory crowed.

'Shut up, you little jerk,' shouted Mungo.

Louisa's dogs began to bark, the barking started as usual by Rufus, seconded by the higher yapping of the smaller dogs. Louisa shouted, 'Quiet!' Dogs and men fell silent. When the cacophony died down Louisa said, 'I think, dears, you had better give up. Hebe has gone and you, Mungo, must sort yourself out with Alison.'

'Oh my God!' Mungo's reluctance was tangible.

'Go on, Mungo, get it done. You have your boys to consider. Stop chasing shadows.'

'Hebe's no shadow,' Mungo blurted in protest.

'Go on, telephone. Take Rory with you as moral support.'

'God forbid!' Outraged by this frivolous suggestion, Mungo shambled away into the house.

Dialling Louisa's number Hebe listened to the engaged signal.

'Perhaps it's out of order.' Giles suggested. 'Ask the operator.' The operator checked and said, 'The line is engaged. Do you want me to break in? Is it urgent?'

'I will wait.' She felt despair. She had often known Louisa, regardless of her telephone bill, gossip for hours with Lucy Duff, Maggie Cook-Popham, whom she professed not to like, or other old ladies referred to as girlfriends.

When Hebe's doorbell rang it was Giles who answered the door to Jim Huxtable, but Hannah arriving at a run brushed him aside.

'Quick, Hebe, come. Aunt Amy's collapsed, I think it's her heart. Terry's ringing the doctor.'

Jim watched the two women race to Amy Tremayne's house. Soon a doctor's car braked to a stop. The doctor, met by George, hurried into the house. The boy who had opened Hebe's door came out to stand on the pavement looking irresolute. Ill at ease in this hideous street, Jim walked up to the seat erected in memory of aged parents too puffed to climb the hill in one go. He sat leaning back against a lovingly carved obscene inscription. He wished he had the dog Feathers with him. He waited, watching the houses.

The doctor came out after twenty minutes, pausing for a last word with the girl with green eyes before driving off. Almost immediately George got into his car and drove away. The boy on the pavement made a two-finger gesture. George did not look back. Still Jim waited. A black and tan dog with curling tail came busily down the street, paused, sniffed the seat, lifted its leg, caught Jim's eye, looked doubtful.

'Hallo.' Jim held out a hand. The dog dropped its ears, allowed itself to be patted, looked up with a conniving expression, went its way with jaunty step. Feathers, had he been there, would have started a fight. Jim watched the street, taking in its remarkable ugliness, snatching at what he saw to steady his mind, attempting to come to terms with what he had seen. Should he go down the hundred yards which separated him from Amy's house, go in, introduce himself to Hebe? Did he want to? What should he say? Would she recognise him, would she think him mad?

'Her name is Hebe,' he said out loud in the horrible street.

It made the situation no better. Could he say, 'I am the man you met in Lucca. I made love to you.' By candlelight in Lucca he had been able to talk to her. He tried to remember what they had talked about. They hadn't said much, there had been too much noise, too much doing. He shivered, sitting on the hard bench, its slats cutting into his thighs. Suppose it was not the girl? Suppose he was wrong, after all? She had not lived with a dream for – how long? Thirteen years. 'Sod it, bugger it, what am I to do?' Jim muttered. The suspicion that he was opposed to reality, wanted to keep his search unresolved, niggled at him. He had lived with it for so long he feared its ending. It was a part of his life; to end it was a terrible risk.

From Amy Tremayne's house came the fair girl, a slim black youth holding her hand, then Hebe. The boy who belonged to the group joined them. They walked along the pavement to Hannah's house. Jim stood up. The black and tan dog was coming back up the hill. Jim walked towards it. They met outside Amy Tremayne's door. Would she be able to help? 'I wish I knew what to do,' Jim said to the dog, who looked sure of himself. The dog wagged its curled tail, flattened its ears. On impulse Jim tried the door, telling himself she had invited him to come again. The door opened, he went in. He listened in the narrow hall with the dog beside him, walked slowly to the back kitchen where not so long ago they had talked. There were remains of tea on the table, chairs pushed back. With the dog Jim climbed the stairs and went into Amy's bedroom. She lay stretched on the bed, eyes closed in a waxen face.

The dog went close to the bed lifting its inquisitive nose. Jim noted the paperweights on the windowsill, twinkling and glinting in the afternoon sun, delightfully alive. He was overcome with embarrassment. He crossed himself. 'It's just a gesture,' he said to the dog, fighting the panic and surprise. I cross myself when I see a magpie. He remembered a woman with whom he had had an affair mocking him in Normandy, where there are many magpies. The dog farted. The noisome smell reached Jim's nostrils. 'Come on,' he said to the dog, 'we have no business here. She's dead.' The dog followed him down the stairs and went up the steet without a backward glance.

Jim ran down the dark red brick street to the car park. He felt dazed. It was not until he was back in Bernard's house and saw Silas that he realised he had not fulfilled his mission.

28

Alison, on arrival at Heathrow, telephoned her mother-in-law, who greeted her with 'I hope you had an enjoyable holiday. You are back sooner than I expected,' as though there had been no crisis.

Alison understood that her elopement was to be ignored. 'I wondered whether Mungo was staying with you. He is not at home.' She tried the casual unconcerned approach.

'He is visiting Louisa. I was talking to her earlier. He seems to have taken up with Rory. I would not have imagined they had anything in common, would you?'

'No. Not that I don't rather like him,' Alison amended, since she was in no position to cast aspersions. 'What is Mungo doing there?'

'Fishing?' Lucy suggested, thinking fishing for Hebe.

'I doubt it. He has better fishing at home.'

'Neglecting his work,' said Lucy sardonically.

'He's by way of having a holiday, which reminds me we should fetch the boys soon. They are in the Scillies.' Give the impression of united parents, thought Alison.

'They have had dreadful weather.' Lucy was undeceived.

'I must telephone Jennifer –'

'Why don't you join Mungo at Louisa's,' suggested Lucy. 'It would be a neutral situation.' Which was as far, Alison realised, as her mother-in-law would venture on to the tricky ground she presently occupied. 'Take a taxi and surprise the dear fellow, it will save him the drive to the airport.'

'I might do just that,' said Alison gratefully. 'It should not take me long to get there.'

* * *

Lucy Duff went out to her terrace wet from recent rain. Miss Thomson brought the tray of tea things and sat beside her. 'Shall I be mother?' she asked in her flat voice.

'No,' said Lucy. 'No, thank you.' She looked at Miss Thomson with ill-concealed dislike. First 'patio', now 'Shall I be mother?' Irreplaceable Alison must be set to work replacing Miss Thomson. She poured tea. 'Mrs Mungo is back from the United States,' she said, well aware that Miss Thomson called Alison 'Alison' and would be affronted by the expression 'Mrs Mungo'. 'Mrs Mungo is joining Mr Mungo at Mrs Fox's in Wiltshire. I believe Mrs Fox has the lady cook there at the moment. Oh, must you go?' Lucy watched Miss Thomson retreat into the house to compose a letter of resignation. ('I know when I'm not wanted.') Lucy drank her tea, visualising life without Miss Thomson and the shortly to take place arrival of Alison at Louisa's. Surprise for her when she finds what Rory and Mungo have in common is Hebe, Lucy thought pleasurably. 'How I miss you,' she murmured to the ghost of her dead husband, who would also have been amused. She rose stiffly and went to apologise to Miss Thomson, to whom she had behaved despicably, pausing en route to look at her husband's photograph, so like Mungo and yet sure of himself. He had a theory, she remembered as she looked at the long dead face, that only his insecure friends got themselves into pickles with women. If that were true Mungo must be insecure, and from what Louisa said his cousin Rory also. On her way to be nice to Miss Thomson Lucy decided not to apprise Louisa of Alison's imminent arrival. It would give Alison a sporting chance to find Mungo making a fool of himself over Hebe. Lucy did not know that for equally suspect reasons her friend had not informed her Hebe had left in the morning.

Alison, paying the taxi in Louisa's drive, was surrounded by baying dogs. The driver drove away leaving her to fend off Rufus who leapt and bounced, scratching her legs, hoping to lick her face. Alison beat off Rufus' unsolicited attentions by whirling her bag and shouting 'Down, down, down' in a voice which rose higher and higher as she became infected by fear. Such a lot of dogs, brute of a taxi man to leave her to cope alone.

Mungo, coming out of the house, came down the steps in a rush, kicked Rufus, grabbed Alison round the waist and kissed her. Alison flung her arms round his neck and kissed him back, then leant back, holding his arms to look up into his face in surprise.

'Oh Mungo' – her carefully prepared speech lost. 'Darling,' said Alison, 'darling.'

'Darling,' said Mungo, kissing her again. 'How wonderful to have you back.' He was astonished to find himself acting pleased to see her. He was amazed. 'Heavens,' he said, 'you are looking pretty.' He looked at his wife with delight. Her pale marmalade hair caught the afternoon sun, her blue eyes were striking. What had she done to her eyelashes? 'What have you done to your hair?' He kissed her again. 'Have you had a good time?'

'No, I have not. Oh, Mungo darling.' She gripped his arms.

'You look like a Botticelli angel,' he said. 'Why have I never noticed?'

Alison said, 'You have forgotten what I look like. Let me look at you.' She looked up at him, her remarkable eyes admiring his thick hair, his dark looks. He seemed to have grown more lined since she last looked at him. 'I had my hair done in Santa Barbara.'

'It's lovely.' Will she admit she's had her eyelashes dyed? he wondered.

'And my eyelashes treated.' Her gaze did not falter.

'Treated,' murmured Mungo, smiling. 'Treated.'

'We have to meet the boys when they come back from the Scillies.' Alison looked up at Mungo. 'I talked to Jennifer from Heathrow. They are all coming back on Thursday because the weather has been so vile.'

'Day after tomorrow.' He examined her face. What else had she changed?

'I spoke to your mother. She told me you were here.'

'Good.' Mungo began to laugh.

'What are you laughing at?' She laughed with him. She looked even prettier laughing.

'We can cut all these prepared speeches. Come and see Louisa. Rory is here. Remember him? Rory Grant, my cousin.'

'Of course I do.' They were moving into the house, Mungo carrying her luggage.

'What speeches were you going to make?' she asked courageously.

'We can discuss our speeches on the way to meet the boys, if we have to meet them. It's a bit of a bore. Shall we take Rory along, if we go?'

'As an umpire? Why not.' Alison felt like a swimmer who, having swum too far, struggles weakly back towards the beach. With a bit of luck she would reach *terra firma,* retrieve her breath (for breath read marriage).

'Alison, dear.' Louisa was advancing from the garden, accompanied by the dogs wagging good-naturedly, no longer threatening. 'How lovely. You will stay the night, won't you? We were coming to see about tea. This is Rory, do you remember him? Put it all on a tray and take it out under the tree. There are scones in the kitchen, Rory. Hebe left a supply.'

'Hebe?' Alison felt a threatening whiff.

'The darling girl who cooks for Lucy. You were the clever one who found her. She comes to me, too. Unfortunately she had to leave today. Now come on, Rory, make yourself useful.'

Smirking, Rory went to the kitchen followed by Louisa's voice. 'There is Devonshire cream for the scones and strawberry jam.'

'Bought by me and darling Hebe in Salisbury,' Rory said to Rufus, 'as well she knows and she is making sure Alison does too, my old beauty. Everybody knows somethink but nobody says nuffink, not in so many words.'

Rory stacked cups and saucers on the tray, put the kettle on, found the scones, dropped one, found cream and strawberry jam. 'Alison won't let Mungo go,' he said to Rufus who, thin streams of greedy saliva swinging from the corners of his mouth, ate gratefully. 'What's more,' Rory told the dog as he made the tea and carried the tray out to the garden, 'if I smell right, something has happened to Alison to make her value Mungo.'

Rory put the tray on the garden table by Louisa, who looked up at him with an amused expression. She was savouring the undeclared peace between Mungo and Alison and looking forward to her next conversation with Bernard. She would describe the unlikely development of comradeship between her nephews. She would suggest that Mungo, much as he loved Hebe, was also attached to his wife, and lay odds on Hebe losing a customer. As she poured tea and passed cups she assessed Alison's appearance, new hair-do, make-up, clothes. She saluted Alison's nerve. Summoned back from an elopement by her mother-in-law Alison should by rights be embarrassed, apprehensive, apologetic, uncertain. She was none of these things. She was eating her tea and describing her visit to Santa Barbara with animation, entrancing both her husband and Rory. She was not, Louisa noted, giving many details of her hosts while she described the house, its setting, its furnishing, its pool. Watching Mungo, Louisa counted several occasions when pertinent questions came close to expression but each time Alison, dolloping cream and jam on to her scones, switched the talk to topics nearer home, rounding off bravely with the question, 'Shall we drive down and meet the boys, darling, as I suggested? It would be nice to see Jennifer and Julian. And it will save the boys that dreary journey they so hate.'

'I never heard them object to it.' Briefly Mungo reverted to the argumentative mood he used to counter Alison's bossiness.

'Love! They have to change trains at Exeter. It would be fun to meet them. Why don't you come with us, Rory?' She doubted whether Mungo had been serious in suggesting Rory.

Rory, meeting her eyes, recognised an appeal. She was really much prettier than he remembered. He said, 'I should love to.'

'You can make an early start,' Louisa chipped in. 'Come and help me make up a bed, Alison. You must have an early night to get over your jet lag.'

Alison sprang to her feet.

'Mungo stayed last night with Rory,' said Louisa, looking at Mungo. 'Would it be all right if you stayed one more night with him? It would save me the bother of making up another bed.' Without waiting for an answer Louisa led Alison into the house. 'You can tell him anything you may want to when you are less tired,' she said.

'Thank you,' said Alison, sensing an ally.

'What is she separating us for?' Mungo turned angrily to Rory.

'I imagine the idea is to get you – er – get you reunited.' Rory began to laugh. 'They don't know how we – er – how –'

'We spent last night.' Mungo finished Rory's sentence for him. 'I don't particularly want you on this drive to Cornwall,' he said with chill.

'But I am coming,' said Rory with unusual determination. 'I – er – want to –' He did not say that, remembering the number of Hebe's car, he had realised that her number plate was Cornish. 'I want to have a snoop round Penzance. Nice antique shops,' he added by way of excuse.

'If Louisa is mean about beds I shall stay in an hotel,' said Mungo, who was growing suspicious. 'There's a plot of some kind between these women.'

'Then stay with me and we can – er – can – er –'

'Stick together.' Mungo finished the sentence automatically. 'Alison is full of bounce,' he said thoughtfully, 'very full of bounce.'

'Perhaps she found you – er – found you bouncy when you came back from the – er – Syndicate.'

'Oh, God!' said Mungo. 'Do you think Alison knows?'

'It's probable.' Rory handed the last of the scones to Rufus. 'Do you – er – want to sleep with her tonight?'

'I had not planned to,' said Mungo stuffily.

'Gosh.' Rory began stacking the tea things on to the tray. 'You had better plan something of the sort. Better be – er – spontaneous,' he advised.

Mungo restrained his longing to kick Rory, to thump Louisa, to assault Alison, all spontaneous reactions. He even refrained from ringing up and insulting his mother. Hebe, he thought, never brought out the worst in him.

Back in Rory's house Mungo felt exasperation. He looked at Rory's possessions with loathing. The absence of vulgarity maddened him. Good silver, lovely glass, enviable pictures, a collection of good books. The whole set-up would appeal to Hebe. Rory was watching as he glared round.

'What's – er – wrong?'

'Nothing,' said Mungo sulkily. 'That's your trouble.'

'I put my evil spirit into the hats,' Rory said. 'You wouldn't find anything in the shop that would suit – er – Alison. Have a look.' Hebe had the only suitable hat for a beautiful woman, he thought. 'I made a good one for Louisa,' he said.

'Louisa.' Mungo stood undecided. Rory watched him. 'Louisa is manipulating me.'

'Yes – er – she is.' Rory tried not to laugh.

'She is keeping me apart from Alison.'

'Yes – er –'

'Why?'

Rory shrugged. 'To let her rest?' he suggested.

'I am going back.' Mungo turned on his heel and left the house. Rory listened to Mungo's car drive away, then went to bed and lay plotting how to find Hebe's car and Hebe in Cornwall, quite a large county.

Mungo let himself into Louisa's house and stilled the dogs. He went upstairs. A light showed under the spare room door. He walked in. Alison lay in the bed, her pale marmalade hair framing her face, dark blue eyes startled.

'Mungo,' she chirped.

'Shut up.' Mungo was undressing. He felt domineering, masculine, randy.

'Mungo!' Alison exclaimed again in a whisper.

Mungo got into the narrow bed. 'Move over.'

'I can't, I'll fall out. What do you want?'

'To fuck you.'

'Don't use that word. You know I cannot bear –'

'Oh, shut up,' Mungo grunted. 'Let's get on with it.'

Presently Mungo, holding Alison, said, 'We don't do this enough.' And Alison began to laugh in a way she had not laughed for a long time, so that he said, 'That's right, my love, one should laugh. Now I shall make love to you.'

Alison bit back the question 'Who else have you laughed with?' and whispered 'I'm glad I came back.' Mungo fell asleep taking up more than his fair share of the single bed. So far, so good, thought Alison, enduring the discomfort. Perhaps I can wean him away from whoever it is who laughs. Could it be that cook? She tried to remember what the girl looked like.

Sitting between Mungo and Rory as they drove the next day,

Alison felt a sense of levity usually alien to her nature. When Rory, sensing her high spirits, ventured to suggest, 'Tell us – um – er – tell us about your hosts, these – er – friends of yours –'

'Yes, do,' said Mungo, driving the car. 'What do Eli and Patsy do when they are at home? Come on, tell.'

'What time does the helicopter arrive?' Alison feebly tried to deflect the attack.

'Alison!' Rory protested. 'Come on.'

'What was this *ménage à trois* like?' Mungo met Alison's eyes in the driving mirror. 'This troika.'

'All right.' Alison took a deep breath. She tensed her shoulders, gritted her teeth.

'Go on,' said Rory and put his hand over hers which were clenched in her lap.

'Bed,' said Alison in a rather high voice, 'with him first. Then Patsy came and watched. I did not like that. Then she got in on the other side of me. I think it was what's called an orgy.'

'Go on,' said Mungo, scowling at the road ahead. 'Go on.'

'Well,' Alison's voice rose higher, 'I enjoyed it with him, it was different, a change –'

'A nice change,' said Rory in an unwarrantably plump voice.

'Well, it was. If it had been only Eli I might still be there.'

'Oh,' said Mungo, his face clouding, but Alison was back in Santa Barbara. 'He was far worse than you, Mungo.' She did not notice her husband's eyebrows rise. 'He used words I have never heard. Your language pales. That put me off a little.'

'Only a little.' Rory's voice betrayed no feeling.

'But Patsy did not like it. She did not like the Eli and me combination.'

'Fancy that,' said Rory under his breath. 'So what happened?' he asked, for he could see, glancing at Mungo's profile, that Mungo could not or would not ask.

'What happened,' said Alison, the words coming in a rush, 'what happened was that Eli suggested he and I should take a trip to New Mexico without Patsy. I said, "Fine, I'd like that." Patsy was getting on my nerves, alternately pawing me and being nasty to Eli. I got packed and as I was coming down to the car I heard a scuffle on the stairs. She had torn all the buttons off his shirt and was tearing at his trousers. Then,' Alison gasped, 'then she went down and bit him in the leg.'

'Oh' said Mungo. 'Gosh! How shocking.'

'Ah,' said Rory. 'Then what – er – what –'

'I got into Eli's car and drove myself to the airport. I had talked to your mother, as you know. I had lied, of course. I had no intention then of coming home.'

'You lied to us,' said Mungo.

Alison's voice was tired. 'Of course I lied. Your mother was so obvious. Eli has not got AIDS but your mother can't manage without me.'

'Nor can I,' Mungo blurted, red in the face.

Rory noticed that both Mungo and Alison were close to tears. 'I have never seen man bitten by woman,' he said. Then they were laughing with the unstoppable hilarity usually confined to adolescents.

29

Cramming her spectacles on to her nose, Hebe ran to her car, started the engine and roared down the street, swinging dangerously into the traffic as she joined the main road. The agony since Louisa had given her the message, the anxiety she felt for Amy, the resentment engendered by her grandparents, the cumulative distress waiting for news of Silas combined to feed the panic which had begun in Amy's house. She forced the maximum speed from the engine, nipping perilously through the traffic, so tense she almost forgot to breathe. Jim, following, flinched at the risks she took, hoped she would not lunatically crash, that he would not have to carry a corpse to the hospital, be harbinger of woe to Silas.

Hebe travelled into the country out of sight. Jim caught up with the car by the telephone kiosk, its door swinging open, engine running, saw Hebe racing across the fields towards Bernard's house.

He parked his car and ran back to Hebe's car, shut the door, pocketed the keys and started running after her. Twice he saw her leap at a bank and scramble over. Once she fell, but was quickly up and running. As he ran Jim muttered to himself, 'This time, this time, this time.' Hurdling the last bank into Bernard's garden he collided with Feathers, stumbled, fell, swore. Feathers made haste to greet, snuffling at Jim's face, delighted to find it within reach.

'Bugger off.' Jim pushed the dog away. 'Out of the way, damn you.' He was on all fours in the wet grass.

Bernard stood over him. 'Hurt yourself?'

'No.' Jim staggered to his feet. 'Out of the way,' he said to Feathers.

'Stop,' said Bernard, as Jim turned towards the cottage. He caught Jim's arm and Jim swung round nearly knocking the old man down.

'Why?' Jim cried furiously. 'Why?'

'They have to be alone.' Bernard held Jim by the sleeve. 'We are going out.'

'I have to see her,' panted Jim. 'I've got to.'

'Presently,' said Bernard. 'You and I are going to the cinema. Go home,' he said to Feathers. 'It doesn't matter you being here. Come along,' he said, 'we must go out so that Silas can talk to his mother.'

'I have to see that girl,' Jim shouted.

'Not now. She has to be alone with him, it's important.'

'It's important that I see her,' Jim insisted.

'Only to you.'

Jim stared at the old man, deflated. 'I had not thought of that.'

Bernard, old and shrunken, looked up at Jim. He said, 'She won't run away.'

'I have her car keys.'

'We will put them back in her car.' He led Jim towards the road. 'Did she recognise you?'

'I don't think so. When I went to her house she was talking on the telephone. I told her Silas was with you and she rushed off. I don't think she noticed me, just registered the message.'

They walked slowly. Jim helped Bernard over the banks. 'This is not a suitable progress for a man of my age,' Bernard remarked, 'but we shall sit in the cinema and be warm and dry.'

'Why the cinema?' Jim was rebellious.

'It is dark.' Bernard spoke stoically. They had nearly reached Jim's car. 'I can sit and mourn.'

'Mourn what?' Jim was ill-tempered.

'You seem to forget,' Bernard got into Jim's car and began tying himself in with the safety belt, 'that you went twice to the town. First you saw Amy dead and forgot to tell Hebe her boy is safe. I sent you back. Going to the cinema does not mean I am not shaken by Amy's death.'

'Are you? Why?' Unwillingly Jim started the car.

'Once we were in love. Very agreeable it was, too.'

Jim found nothing to say, his mind on Hebe.

'If we find a movie which is a weepy I can pretend I am moved by that.'

'Yes.' Jim began to pay attention.

'We were in the Hôtel d'Angleterre. It ended badly,' said Bernard. 'Long ago in Paris.'

'Why?' asked Jim.

'She discovered I was sleeping with Louisa. Why do women always expect this one-at-a-time business? It makes no sense. That is what upset her most.' In old age Bernard refused the memory of Amy's pregnancy.

'All these years,' said Jim, momentarily forgetting his own troubles. 'All these years I have never known you visit her.'

'We were not on speaking terms,' said Bernard. 'Latterly, since she befriended Hebe and I got to know the girl, I tried to make it up. Louisa and I have remained close. Amy was bitter. There was nothing doing.'

'Perhaps she had reason to be bitter.' Jim had never considered his old friend a particularly nice character.

'Hebe has no need of you,' said Bernard nastily, confirming Jim in his view. 'She is even more capable than Amy of managing on her own.' Then, as Jim did not respond, he said, 'It's the mode for women to live alone these days. You must have noticed, even you.'

'Why even me?' Jim asked, but Bernard was pretending not to hear, leaving Jim feeling he had in some way made himself ridiculous.

30

Silas clung to Hebe and Hebe clung to Silas. Too breathless from running, she felt, in the joy of relief, that it was enough to hold him. He was alive, in one piece. She feared if she spoke she might say the wrong thing. Silas, holding his mother, felt her heart thumping. They huddled together in Bernard's wing chair in the dark little room. The fire flickered and Feathers sank down at their feet with a grunt.

Silas, his face pressed against her chest, said, 'I was seasick. I had no boots. They all know each other well. Mrs Reeves is a sort of horsey woman. I felt stupid because they all knew how to sail. I went off alone. I saw seals and an adder and people in a boat. There were two other boys. They boasted about their father's mistress. Well, the younger one did and the size of his – Then he said he wet his bed as if it was clever. There was stew at every meal and Mr Reeves – he's called Julian – picked on Mrs Reeves. She said to call her Jennifer. I couldn't. He picked on her about the stew and they called the woman who came to clean and cook Mrs Thing. He niggled on at me about school. Why don't we learn Latin and he and Mrs Reeves quarrelled without saying anything – they are snobs about everything – it was like that all the time. He gave me wine before I noticed the others only drank Coke. I felt so stupid. I've been sick on your jersey. We had to share a room, the four of us. It was a lovely cottage, very pretty but I wished – I sent you a postcard, I didn't want you to know I wasn't enjoying – now when I go back to school it will be awful – I was sick into Michael's boots and all over the front of your jersey. They talk in loud voices – he niggled me about you and what did my father do. Mrs Reeves jumped in and said – and they looked down their noses because we live in a street. It's okay to live in a street in London but otherwise you have to live in the country – and Michael said you were a cook and Mrs Reeves said she had an uncle who married his – Mr Reeves said cooks are an endangered species – he was drunk – he kept giving me wine and there was a thick feeling in the room – then he asked what my father does and I hated him and said my mother is a Hermaphrodite and I threw my wine in his face.' Hebe's arms tightened. Silas drew breath. 'I looked up "hermaphrodite" in Mr Quigley's dictionary so now I feel stupider than ever. When I'd thrown my wine at his head I rushed out – I grabbed your jersey off the line where Mrs Reeves had hung it, she washed it but it still smells – I didn't know what to do, but I was lucky because the people I had seen fishing were going across to St Mary's. They gave me a lift – I am sorry I left everything behind I just brought the jersey – the people didn't ask anything – next day I managed to get back on the helicopter, the crew remembered I had a return ticket. When I got home you weren't there and I cried – I'm sorry. Amy or Hannah would have asked questions – Jim found me and brought me here – he and Mr Quigley have been kind. It's been great to be with Feathers and the cat – it hasn't got a name, he says cats don't need names, he doesn't even call it "Thing" like the Reeves call the cleaning lady. They said – no, they didn't say, but I felt they wanted to say I've got no bottle. Well, they haven't got all that much. Michael cried when she hit him and I felt – I felt Hermaphrodites don't hit their children – Giles started it, he asked if I was a test tube baby and I said I couldn't be because they didn't do it when I was born – we had a row – I hit him – he fell into the kale and his nose bled. Mr Quigley had said his father was dull which was awful for Giles – he pushed a note through the door which said "perhaps your mother is a Hermaphrodite" – I felt proud of that until the dictionary – it's all been so awful – have I got a father?'

'No.' Hebe felt terribly cold.

'Don't you know him?' Silas tightened his grip.

'No.'

Silas, sitting with his arms round Hebe, looked up at her face, put up a hand and gently removed her glasses.

'They are misted up.' He put the glasses on the table beside the chair, ran his hand through his hair. 'It's wet from your tears.' He looked at his hand. Then he said, 'Not even a Hismaphrodite?'

'Silas.' Now is the time for burning boats, she thought.

'Never mind,' said Silas. He felt the pleasurable relief at being with her, the contentment at having poured out his troubles. He wrapped his arms round her. She began to speak, now or never.

'I have never been able to talk to you because I didn't know how to begin. I was in Italy and after I came back I felt peculiar, so they sent me to the doctor and he said I was pregnant. They – I have never told you that I was brought up by my grandparents. When they found out they were furious – horrible. I still get nightmares. I hear their voices say, "Who was the man?" and things like "Long-haired layabout, yobbo or black or bare feet and dirty nails." They kept asking "Who was the man?" – I couldn't answer because I didn't know. They wouldn't believe me. I wanted you. They wanted me to have an abortion. Do you know what that means?'

'Of course I do. But you didn't have one.'

'I came to Amy who looked after me. I sold things I had to Bernard Quigley, we became friends. I learned to earn money. I have tried to think who your father could be, but I don't know. All I get is this panic, I hear voices going on and on about an abortion and calling me a whore and asking who the man was.' Hebe drew a shaky breath. Silas tightened his grip. A log shifted on the fire; Feathers groaned. 'When I get these panics I hear their voices and it's mixed up with running in dark streets, I run and run and the buildings all round me are taller than skyscrapers and people look out of blind windows. I hear that repetition, "Who was the man?" ' Hebe hurried on. 'I must tell you, otherwise someone else will. As well as cooking jobs I am a part-time tart to make money to pay for us.' There, she thought, it's out.

'Don't you realise,' Silas shifted in her arms and looked up, 'don't you realise that what happened was a bad trip, probably LSD.' He sounded older than twelve. 'Rather fascinating.'

'I have never taken drugs in my life.' She was horrified.

'What do you know about them?' She sat up and stared at him.

'You can be given LSD in your drink. People think it's funny.'

'*Funny!*'

'You don't know and you go on a "trip". A master at school gave us a lecture on drugs. Who were you with? It happens at parties. Was it Hismaphrodite?'

Hebe began to laugh.

'Then,' said Silas, laughing too, 'he seduced you.'

'Oh Silas, I don't know, I honestly don't.'

'Just this nightmare thing?'

'No, one other thing. There's a smell.' Hebe sat up. 'My God, Silas, you smell of it now, how weird, and I haven't told you. I quite forgot. Amy is ill. How could I forget?'

Silas gave a shuddering sigh. 'Will she die?'

'She had a heart attack. She is in bed resting.'

'I can hear yours. Amy won't leave us.'

Hebe kissed the top of the head laid against her chest. Time later to worry about Amy but for this moment she felt light-hearted, overjoyed by Silas.

'It's this jersey that smells, Jim lent it to me,' he said.

Hebe was not listening. Her relief at finding Silas, telling Silas, blocked all other thought. She filled her lungs with the smell of Bernard's cottage – woodsmoke, garlic, paraffin, herbs, coffee, wet salty air coming across the fields from the sea. She breathed it all in and let out an exhausted sigh. Silas could be right about LSD. She simply couldn't remember.

'What's the difference,' Silas was speaking, 'anyway?'

'What difference?'

'Between marrying for money and being,' he hesitated then, 'being a tart? I don't think there is any difference except –'

'Except what?'

'Except that you seem happier than a lot of people at school's mothers.'

'Oh.'

'We are happier, Giles and I, than people at school. Mr and Mrs Reeves don't seem happy. Do I have to go back to that school?'

'I –'

'You know Giles talks like us when he wants and when I am with him I talk like him.'

Hebe said nothing.

'Giles only talks as he does to tease Hannah and it's easier to be like other people. It's a waste of money, Hannah having elocution lessons. Who wants to sound like Mrs Thatcher?' Silas laughed. 'What is your nightmare about, do you think?'

'My grandparents trying to find out who your father was.'

'What did they say? Tell me again.'

Hebe whispered, 'Who was the man? Long-haired layabout, dirty feet, might be a foreigner, who was the man, abortion, might be black, earrings, cannabis, dirty fingernails, may have a police record, who was the man –'

'I'm not bothered,' said Silas.

31

'Take me to Wilson Street.' Bernard, who had sat hunched in silence during the drive, now spoke.

'I thought you wanted to go to a movie.' Jim, too, had been silent, prey to feelings of anger, anxiety and exhilaration, an uneasy mix which made him so inattentive of his driving that several times along the road there had been a near miss with another car.

'I've changed my mind. Stop at the corner, I want to buy flowers for Amy.'

Jim drew into the kerb. 'Wouldn't it be sensible to wait for the funeral?'

'Sensible!' Bernard snorted as he opened the car door. 'Shan't be long.' He darted across the pavement into the flower shop.

'We're on a double yellow line,' Jim yelled after him. He watched the inexorable advance of a traffic warden. 'This is all I need.' He drummed impatient fingers on the steering wheel, cursing Bernard. The traffic warden sauntered down the street slipping tickets behind windscreen wipers. 'Come *on*, Bernard.' Why am I in such a rage, what does it matter? Jim asked himself. 'Hurry *up*!' he shouted to the old man. Bernard, arms full of roses, emerged from the shop.

'Hullo.' Bernard and the warden met beside the car. 'Karen, isn't it?' Bernard bared his ancient teeth. 'You are looking very beautiful. How's your mother? I don't think I've seen you since you left school. You have your mother's looks.'

'I am married now, Mr Quigley,' Karen chirped.

'Goodness, how time – I say, were you going to put one of your *billets doux* on our windscreen?'

The warden laughed and held the car door open for Bernard.

'Courting, Mr Quigley?' she queried, eyeing the roses. Bernard showed his teeth again. The warden snapped shut the car door. 'Don't forget your seat belt, Mr Quigley.' Bernard leant back in his seat. 'I love women, can't do without them.'

Jim drove on, wondering why Bernard had not long ago got himself murdered.

At Amy's house he stopped the car, deciding he would play no part in whatever obscene pantomime Bernard planned.

'Come on.' Bernard extricated himself from the seat belt. 'Idiotic infringement of personal liberty, these things. Look sharp. Follow me.'

Reluctantly Jim followed.

Bernard crossed the pavement, pushed open Amy's door. 'Never locks her door. Get raped one of these days, the old fool.' He mounted the stairs, opened Amy's bedroom door. Jim heard a faint exclamation and Bernard said, 'Stupid ass told me you were dead, brought you roses. Don't tell me you've had a heart attack.'

Jim heard Amy's crisp reply, 'It's not only Louisa who has a weak heart.'

'Still jealous after all these years,' Bernard crowed. Then, 'Let's look at you. You don't look too bad, give us a kiss.' Then, raising his voice, 'Jim, come in here.'

Jim went in. Amy lay with an arm round the bouquet of roses. Her free hand held Bernard's old claw. She smiled at Jim. 'Thought I was dead, didn't you? Where's the dog?'

'He wasn't my dog,' Jim felt acute embarrassment. 'I must apologise for coming into your house like that. I wanted –'

'Sit down, both of you.' Amy indicated chairs. Bernard sat holding Amy's hand. Jim sat uneasily by the window. 'You came to see my paperweights,' Amy said to Jim. 'I've got real flowers, now.' The hand holding the sheaf of roses tightened its grip round the cellophane wrapping.

'Just because I thought you might be dead doesn't alter anything,' said Bernard loudly.

'I'm not deaf any more than I am dead,' said Amy angrily. 'It never occurred to me you would change.'

It seemed to Jim that here was confirmation of an old quarrel.

Amy went on, 'You are not getting the paperweights. I have left them to Hebe.'

'I don't want your paperweights,' Bernard shouted, his voice cracking.

'Then why are you here?' Amy's eyes watched Bernard. Jim felt her hostility.

'Can your heart stand a bit of news?' Bernard peered into Amy's face.

'Of course. Spit it out.' Amy had the upper hand in this subterranean feud.

'A surprise?' questioned Bernard on a rising note.

'Go on,' she said.

'This friend of mine, Jim, has reason to believe he is Silas' father.' Bernard stared at Amy, his mouth slightly open, as though sharing in the surprise he was causing.

'He looks very like him,' said Amy unsurprised. 'Same nose. Your hair was chestnut before you went grey, I take it.' She was talking now to Jim. 'Silas has Hebe's eyes, though.'

'Dammit it, Amy, must you be so calm?' Bernard yelped.

'Doctor told me to keep calm.'

'He's been looking for her for *years*.'

'Does he want to marry her? Do you want to marry her?' Amy tried to see Jim's face, sitting with his back to the light.

'I'm,' began Jim, 'I've –'

'He's in love with her,' Bernard volunteered.

'Ho,' said Amy. 'Love! You are in love with me.' Bernard made a clucking noise, 'And with Louisa. There was talk of love with Lucy and even Eileen. That's Hebe's grandmother,' Amy spoke towards Jim, 'and a lot of others. Used to take us all to the same hotel in Paris. Talked of love. It didn't mean a thing.'

'Rubbish,' yelled Bernard. 'Am I not here with roses?'

'You came to make sure I was dead and pinch my paperweights.'

'Unfair,' yelled Bernard. 'I came because I love you.'

Amy said, 'Fancy that.'

In the silence that followed Jim stood up, disturbed by these grotesque old people.

Amy said in accusation, 'You keep in touch with Louisa.'

'I telephone,' admitted Bernard, 'sometimes.'

'And why not?' Amy was magnanimous. 'But you don't let her see you, poor shrivelled old manikin.'

'No.' Bernard closed his eyes. 'I don't.'

'He didn't want to marry any of us.' Amy switched her attention to Jim. 'Not that it matters now. Do you want to marry Hebe?'

'I –' Jim felt distraught. What business was it of this old crone to question him?

'It's up to Hebe, isn't it?' said Amy.

Bernard opened his eyes. 'Only Hebe?'

'As far as I am concerned only Hebe matters,' said Amy, her eyes flicking from Jim to Bernard. 'And for Hebe read Silas, for Silas is what matters to Hebe. Wherever he is, he seems to be lost.'

'Silas,' said Bernard smugly, 'is at my house and Hebe is with him. That is why Jim is here. I tactfully removed him so that Silas could explain why he ran away from the Scillies without a problematical father getting underfoot.'

'I thought you came to visit the dead. Is Silas all right?'

'Perfectly,' said Bernard. 'We cherished him as I' – he squeezed Amy's hand – 'cherish you.'

Amy heaved with laughter.

'Mind your heart.'

'Actually,' murmured Amy, 'my heart is better.'

'All the better for seeing me?' asked Bernard slyly.

These outrageous old people are flirting, thought Jim. He wondered whether they would notice if he slipped away. They did not, he thought, need an audience for their reunion.

'Actually,' the word seemed to amuse Amy, 'actually yes.'

Hannah chose this moment to come into the room, followed by Terry and Giles, her green eyes sparkling, teeth aflash.

'Goodness! Is this a party?' She looked from Bernard to Jim. 'We came to impart our good news.'

'Impart?' questioned Amy, holding Bernard's hand.

'One of Terry's words. We wondered whether your heart was up to it.'

'My heart is fine.'

As he left the room Jim thought the good news is the white girl and the black boy are, for want of a better word, in love. As he ran down the stairs and out to his car he resented the almost tangible glow of happiness surrounding the ill-assorted couples. He had yet to confront Hebe.

* * *

Jim parked his car beside Hebe's. He walked fast across the fields, fighting the inclination to go back to London, recapture the shield which had effectively protected him from serious relationships for thirteen years. Skirting the kale field and climbing the banks he reviewed the girls of past years. Fun girls, pretty girls, clever girls and stupid, he had shielded himself from any depth of feeling, with the memory of the perfect girl in Lucca, the girl who had left him, running fleet of foot, disappearing into the crowd. Remembering Hebe racing across the fields earlier in the day, he thought, She still runs pretty fast. He gritted his teeth, forcing himself on. She is there in Bernard's house. I have to put an end to this one way or another, he thought, as he climbed the last bank into Bernard's garden. Put an end to my dream, he thought resentfully, face up to some sort of reality. It is destruction, he thought, opening the door and walking into the house. He felt desolation and regret for his loss, now that it was too late to run away. If I had had any sense I would have stopped looking years ago. Not finding her I would have had something to keep.

Hebe was sitting in Bernard's chair, her arms round Silas curled beside her, asleep.

Jim sat on a chair by the door. Feathers came wagging and grumbling to greet Jim, pressing his head on his knee, inviting attention. Jim stroked the dog's head and looked at Hebe, who peered at him over Silas' head.

'Is he all right now?' indicating Silas.

'Yes,' she said evenly.

Feathers wandered back to sit at Hebe's feet. Jim felt exposed. Hebe had Silas as protection and now the dog also. He cleared his throat, unable to think of anything to say. Minutes passed. Hebe and Jim looked at one another. Hebe said something in a low voice.

Jim said 'What?'

She said, 'It's the smell. I think I recognise the smell, it's – this jersey you lent him.'

'You mean *me*? I smell?'

'Yes.'

'I smell of coffee. I keep a coffee shop, my clothes are impregnated with it. Why?'

'I get panics, nightmares. Then there's this smell which is nice.'

'I'm glad of that.' He studied her. She had cut off most of the long hair, the eyes were the same, the face thinner. 'It's a coffee shop on one side and antiques on the other.' Must keep talking, he thought.

'Oh.' She was not giving him much help.

'I was working in a coffee bar in Lucca; do you remember me? Do you remember the fiesta, the nut necklaces, the candles along the window-ledges, the narrow streets? You ran away –'

Hebe watched him. What were her thoughts?

She said, 'My nightmare panic.'

'It's been a marvellous haunting memory for me,' said Jim. 'I'm sorry if it was a nightmare for you.' He was stupefied. After all these years all she remembers is a bloody nightmare.

'The smell is mixed up with something else. I see now it was you. It's the other, the result, the – the – I –' She looked at him, distressed. 'I tried to tell Silas and do you know what he said?'

'What?'

'He suggested I'd been on a "trip", that someone had given me LSD.'

'That would explain a lot,' said Jim. 'You were with a bunch of hippies, people said, when I tried to find you.'

'I'd just met them. I was living with a family as an au pair learning Italian. I didn't know them.'

'In Lucca?'

'I was going home next day. I remember now. I must have blotted it out when the horror came later. I am sorry.'

'I am Silas' father,' said Jim, making the effort. There is no retreat now, he thought. For years my dream has been her nightmare. 'I think, I mean it's obvious, look at his nose and hair, he's my son.' Hebe said nothing. 'He has got your eyes,' said Jim. 'Perhaps we could get to know each other.' Still she said nothing. 'We seem to have put the cart before the horse,' he said. 'I don't want to bother you but Silas seems to be the result of our encounter. Perhaps if we –'

'The result.' Hebe looked down at Silas. 'I see I –' She tightened her hold. She is afraid I may hurt Silas, Jim thought. I must stop her being frightened. She makes no attempt to deny my fatherhood.

Hebe said, 'If you are –' defensively.

'I am sure I am.' Idiot, there is still time to back out.

'Yes.' She was not in doubt.

'Look,' said Jim, 'when I met Silas yesterday he was pretty upset. Perhaps we could start from there. Perhaps I could help if he is in trouble. How would that be?'

'Put the cart before the horse *again*?'

She's intelligent. Thank God. 'Put Silas first and possibly we will get to know each other.'

'I don't mind you getting to know Silas,' said Hebe, keeping herself out of it, reminding herself not to be possessive.

Jim, who had been sitting grim and strained, smiled for the first time. 'You don't know me,' he said. 'You can keep yourself as private as you like.' I don't mean that, he thought. I want to know her but it may take the rest of our lives to break down this privacy.

Hebe reached for her glasses and put them on to see Jim clearly. He is already assuming possession, she thought. He thinks he can barge into my life, Silas' father. I can't deny it, they are alike, he even talks like Silas. What about my Syndicate? My cooking? How does he think he will fit in with Mungo, Rory, Louisa, Lucy, with Silas who I live and work for, and Hippolyte? Does he think he can just appear like this? Do I want this man barging in? Thoughtfully she regarded Jim through her glasses.

She is not a bit my dream girl, thought Jim. She looks a fighter. The dream girl was so vulnerable. What is this woman holding my son in her arms going to do with my life? How will she fit in with my coffee trade, my antiques. And the boy, my son, what of him? Oh God, he thought, do I want all this? Resentfully he regarded Hebe, blaming her.

'If we were writing a book,' Jim said, 'this would be a joyful occasion.'

'In real life it's a positive quicksand,' said Hebe.

They succumbed to laughter and Silas woke.

32

Silas, looking from his mother to Jim, remembered where he was. The humiliations of his visit to the Reeves came crowding blackly back.

'What am I to do about my bag? I left it behind.' His duffle bag seemed of paramount importance.

'Mrs Reeves is bringing it tomorrow. We can collect it at the heliport,' said Hebe.

'And have to talk to her?' Silas was aghast. 'Meet them all?'

'We'll be with you.' Jim stood up and stretched. 'It's rather claustrophobic in this small room,' he said. 'What about a cream tea somewhere?'

'Brilliant. There's a farm which does teas over the hill. We could walk along the cliff.' Silas was delighted at the prospect. 'I'm starving.'

'Come on, then,' said Jim. 'It stopped raining long ago.'

'All right.' Hebe felt violently hungry, tried to remember when she had last eaten. Breakfast in Louisa's house in the early hours. Was it the same day? 'I'm quite hungry, too,' she said carefully.

Feathers ran ahead across the fields, carrying his tail high, signalling them to follow as might a tourist guide in St Mark's Square. They crossed the road to the cliff path winding above the sea. We look like any ordinary family, thought Jim, as they walked in single file. Family dog, child, mother, father, but the dog is not our dog, the father has not spoken to the mother for thirteen years, he only met his child for the first time yesterday. Bringing up the rear of the procession he studied Hebe's back, observing her long stride, the dark hair falling against her shoulders. She walked ahead above the sea which, calm now in the afternoon sun, was cobalt blue, the rocks shading lighter and paler over sandy patches. What is she thinking, Jim wondered. If we were what we appear to be, an ordinary family, would I know?

Silas led the way up a valley which clove the cliffs running down to a sheltered cove. Half way up there was a farm with tables on the grass, chairs and benches. They sat at an empty table. Jim ordered tea, Hebe sat slumped, white faced. She put her glasses on the table, a curiously secretive act. She doesn't want to see too clearly. Jim observed her surreptitiously. 'When did you last eat?' he asked.

'Louisa made me eat breakfast.'

'Fool.' Jim got up and went into the farm. 'Would it be possible,' he asked the woman serving teas, 'to give the lady a boiled egg? She hasn't eaten since breakfast.'

'Poor thing. She had better have two and bread and butter.'

'Thank you.' Jim went back to the table and sat in silence until the tea was brought.

Silas watched teapot, milk, sugar, scones, cream and jam placed on the table. Two brown eggs arrived next.

'Salt,' said the waitress. 'Okay?' She caught Jim's eye.

'Most okay,' he thanked her.

'Who are the eggs for?' Silas asked.

'Your mother. Eat them,' he said to Hebe, pushing the eggs towards her.

'Oh.' She looked at him quickly. 'Thank you.'

'You will need your spectacles.'

'Yes.' She put them on obediently.

They ate in silence. Jim watched colour return to her cheeks. Silas ate and drank, feeding snippets to Feathers. If I bought a house in the country we could live like an ordinary family, thought Jim, watching Hebe and Silas. We could have a dog of our own. I don't somehow see her in Fulham. I could run my business just as well in a country town. I can't believe she likes living in that hideous street. That cat of hers would like the country. We could find a house in Dorset, perhaps. He visualised Hebe against a backdrop of downland within reach of the sea. Other families who had been having tea left, wandering up a path which led to the road and their cars. From the farmhouse came sounds of washing up, an occasional laugh or burst of music from the radio.

'Did you see Amy?' Hebe turned to look at Jim. 'I have been too afraid to ask.'

'Much better,' said Jim. 'Last seen flirting with Bernard. Almost as though they were having an affair.' He failed to keep surprise out of his voice.

'Old people still have feelings,' said Hebe.

'Bernard seems to have distributed his feelings rather widely,' said Jim.

Hebe smiled, thinking, What about my feelings distributed among the Syndicate? What about them?

'Will they marry?' Silas was curious. 'They could. Amy could look after Mr Quigley.'

'I don't somehow think a sunset home for Bernard fits into Amy's calculations,' Hebe murmured.

'He is too independent to marry,' said Jim, defending the male sex.

'But he likes romance,' said Hebe, amused.

'Even so, he will go on living alone in that isolated house. And some day the postman will arrive with his letters and find him dead,' Jim suggested.

'That is what he would like,' agreed Hebe.

'Amy accused him of being in love with a lot of women.'

'Probably true.' Hebe did not wish to pursue the subject. 'Did you see Hannah?' she asked. 'Isn't she looking after Amy?'

'She did appear. Brought with her a handsome black chap.'

'Ah yes, Terry.' Hebe was thoughtful. 'M'm yes.'

'They seemed bursting with the joys of life, a romance there, would you say?'

'Hannah would call it a conjunction of vibes.'

'What about George?' enquired Silas. 'He's her dentist,' he explained for Jim's benefit.

'Too dull. Hannah wants marriage and romance.'

'Will she get it with Terry?' asked Jim.

'I think she will.'

'Where does he come from?' Jim was interested. If I can find out about her friends I may discover Hebe, he thought.

'He comes from London. He is self-employed, he makes

quite a lot of money. He loves poetry, fantasy –'

'Ah –' What was that in her voice? Affection?

'He has lots of interests: music, antiques, poetry – yes, he will make Hannah happy. Gorgeous contrast, don't you think? Very fair Hannah with bitter chocolate Terry?' Hebe was enthusiastic for Hannah's future.

'Milk chocolate babies,' said Silas, munching.

'Great,' said Hebe. 'All those in favour –'

'In favour.' Jim and Silas agreed light-heartedly.

'And those against?' asked Jim seriously.

'Hannah will enjoy the challenge. You see, with Terry,' said Hebe seriously, 'she will never be bored.'

'Mr Quigley said Giles' father was boring,' volunteered Silas. 'It hurt his feelings.'

'There you are, then.' Hebe took off her glasses and looked myopically out to sea.

Watching her Jim thought, she cannot have seen me clearly when we met in Lucca, no wonder she had nightmares. Jim was not without vanity. We are no nearer what matters, he thought, disgruntled. Discussing Amy's, Bernard's, and Hannah's affairs does not help me.

'Shall we go down to the sea?' Silas suggested.

Jim paid for the tea and they walked back to the cliff path and scrambled down towards the cove. This time Jim led and Hebe brought up the rear. On a ledge of grass Hebe sat. 'You go on,' she said. 'I'll wait here.' She watched the man and boy climb down the cliff, heard their feet crunch when they reached the pebbles at the bottom. Feathers sat beside her, mouth open, panting. Hebe lay back. She could hear Silas' voice call and Jim answer. Giving way to exhaustion, she was grateful for the lulling warmth of the sun and the sound of the sea grinding the pebbles.

On the beach Jim and Silas played ducks and drakes then undressed and swam, letting the sea welcome them. They raced to the ledge of rock which flanked the cove, pulled themselves out of the water and lay on rocks warm from the afternoon sun. Silas shaded his eyes and looked up at his mother. 'Is my mother the girl you met in Italy, the girl you told us you were looking for?'

'Yes.' Jim looked at the sea, furious that he could not look Silas in the eye. This is all wrong, he told himself, the boy should not be involved until we have sorted ourselves out. This is putting the cart before the horse again.

'I thought so.' Silas lay back and closed his eyes.

My God, thought Jim, why doesn't he say something? Is he glad, is he sorry, is he even interested? Lying there so calmly he's exactly like his mother.

Silas felt the blood drumming in his ears. So I've got a father, this man, this Jim. What do I do now? What does Ma do? What did they do in Italy? Silas kept his eyes tightly shut, sparks from the sun on his eyelids. Did they kiss as people do on TV, as though they were eating a banana? What happens now? Do I go back to school as usual? What will Ma do, will she go on being a cook, a prostitute, will she be there to meet me when I get off the train? 'I'm cold,' he cried out in fear, and dived off the rock into the sea. Jim watched the boy swim back to the beach, scramble out of the water to his pile of clothes. When, twenty minutes later, he rejoined them Silas sat on guard by his sleeping mother and eyed Jim watchfully as he climbed up to them. Feathers barked and Hebe woke.

'Time to go home,' she said. 'We have a tough day tomorrow meeting Mr Reeves, Mrs Reeves, Master Reeves and the duffle bag.' She set off up the cliff. The man and the boy followed. When they reached the cars Hebe said, 'Thank you for the lovely cream tea and the eggs. I am quite restored.' She held out her hand as to an acquaintance.

'Perhaps,' began Jim, taking it, 'perhaps we can talk –'

Hebe let go his hand. 'There is altogether too much to talk about,' she said despairingly, 'or nothing.' She got into her car. 'What seems to matter most at the moment is the bloody duffle bag.' She drove off with Silas beside her. Jim followed Feathers through the fields to Bernard's house. He had never before felt so lonely.

33

It had been an interminable day. Crawling into bed after reassuring herself that Amy was on the mend and Hannah and Terry as happy as it was possible for lovers to be, Hebe prayed for sleep, but she was too tired. Her head buzzed with sounds. Traffic on the motorway, dogs barking, a jumble of voices from which she could pick Louisa's or Bernard's, the stranger in the traffic jam, the waitress at the farm, Jennifer Reeves' offensive intonation, Amy. Resolutely she excluded Jim, muttering to herself, 'I'm in no fit state', repeating, 'No fit state'. She tried to relax her fingers and toes, tried not to flinch when a late motorcycle roared up the street, tried to recover the murmur of the sea on the cobbles of the cove as she heard it that afternoon when all too briefly she had slept.

Trip nudged the duvet and crawled in beside her to settle, her gentle heaving flank pressed into the small of Hebe's back.

'Now I can't turn over.' It was ridiculous to consider the cat's comfort before her own, yet she did. Two motorcycles in rapid succession raced up the street, drunken voices shouting harshly.

'I can't sleep, Ma.' Silas, standing by the bed in his pyjamas. 'Can we talk?'

'Of course.' She sat up.

'Have you got Trip? She left me.'

'Yes.'

'I think I'll just get my duvet to wrap round me.'

'Do.'

She heard his bare feet on the landing, the rustle as he came back trailing the duvet. She resisted the impulse to switch on the light.

'I suppose it would be cowardly not to meet my duffle bag. Not to meet the Reeves tomorrow.' He settled himself at the end of her bed, a hunched figure wrapped in the duvet.

'I'm afraid so.'

'Thought you would say that.' Silas said no more for a while. She could not see his face in the dark. Another motorcycle roared up the street.

'They do make a filthy noise, don't they?'

'Terrible,' she agreed.

'What are you going to do about Jim?'

'I –'

'He's my father, isn't he?'

'I think so. Yes.'

'Funny, isn't it? He's been looking for you for years. He told Mr Quigley and me about it yesterday evening.'

Yesterday evening she had walked by the river with Rufus and the other dogs, been happy, gone in to find Mungo and Rory with Louisa. Another life. 'How did that come about?' she asked.

'Mr Quigley wanted to cheer me up, he was joking. He asked Jim whether he had ever been in love. Jim told us about this girl he had met at a fiesta in Italy. There was a procession, people, crowds, incense and a band played tumpity-tump. He was really there, Ma, at the fiesta. Bought you a nut necklace. Then he lost you. He said he'd been looking for you ever since. What happened to the necklace, Ma?'

'I left it behind when I ran away from home.' Surprised, she remembered the necklace. A lone motorcycle sputtered up the street, not as fast as its predecessors. 'They take the baffles off the silencers to make more noise. It's "machismo".'

'Yes. I don't want a motorbike.'

'I'm glad.'

'Shall you marry Jim, Ma?'

'I don't know.'

'Oh.'

'I don't know much about marriage. What do you think?' she asked.

Silas sat thinking. Then, 'I don't know much, either.' He laughed.

'You should hear Giles about Hannah and his father and you should see Mr and Mrs Reeves. Oh, God, you will tomorrow.' He stopped laughing.

'Yes, I shall.'

The town clock struck one, the sound reverberating in the exhausted afterstorm atmosphere.

'Married people *can* be happy.' He was speaking again. 'I think Terry and Hannah will be a riot. Super for Giles.' He sounded envious.

'Yes.'

'What do you know about marriage, Ma?'

'My sisters –'

'Sisters? Do I have *aunts*?' Silas jerked upright in surprise.

'Yes.'

'Could you tell me, or are they a big secret? It's embarrassing at school not to have relations. The boys boast about theirs. Are they tarts or what?'

'I'm the only tart in the family.'

'Oh, Ma.' Silas moved up the bed to crouch beside her. 'I nearly sat on Trip. What happened to them?'

'They married.' Hebe thought of Ann, Beata and Cara. 'Ann married a man called Robert. They had a Jaguar. Beata married Delian. They had an Alfa Romeo. And Cara married Marcus and they had a Range Rover.'

'Rich.' He was surprised.

'That was it.'

'What do you mean?' Silas was made anxious by her tone. There was a tightness in her throat.

'Well.' She found herself speaking more freely. 'They were a lot older than me. I used to watch and listen to them. They talked a lot about men and marriage. Whenever one of them met a new man they discussed him. They'd say, "I've met a new man," and the others always asked, "Is he rich?" It didn't seem to matter whether he was talented or good looking. It was always, "Is he rich?" '

'Rich?' Silas repeated the word. 'Rich?'

'Of course they were all suitable,' said Hebe.

'What's suitable?'

'Suitable meant – oh, suitable meant public school, related

to nice people, the right sort. They'd ask, "Is he rich?" Then they'd ask, "Are his people nice, are they our sort?" '

Christ, just like school, thought Silas.

'Then they would telephone copiously, giggle and shriek down the telephone. They never minded being overheard. It was a sort of ritual.'

'Charming.'

'I never felt I fitted.'

'I don't want to be suitable,' said Silas, who had been mulling the word.

'I don't think there is any danger of that.'

'I'm awfully hungry, Ma, shall we raid the larder?'

Wrapped in their duvets they trailed downstairs. Robbed of her warm covering Trip furiously burrowed under the pillows. Hebe made bacon sandwiches and they returned to her bed carrying plates and glasses of milk. Trip went out of the window into the night.

'What were your father and mother like?' Silas asked with his mouth full, munching.

'I never knew them. They were killed in an air crash when I was a baby. My grandparents brought us up.'

'Were they "suitable"?' He adopted the word.

'I saw them this morning.'

'*What?*' Silas put his glass down with a thump. 'Where?'

'On my way home. I met them in a lane, a short cut I was taking, they'd had a collision with a Land Rover.' Hebe described the scene as she remembered it. 'They had a sweet dog. He called it away when I was going to stroke it and I said, "I'll find a long-haired yobbo, a black layabout to mend your car." What are you laughing at? I didn't really say that.'

'It's so funny. What does it mean? Why should you say that?' Silas went off into a fit of laughter.

Hebe found herself describing the inquisition, the family meeting, the planned abortion, the grandparents, the sisters, the brothers-in-law, the running away, the journey down to Cornwall hitching lifts, the final arrival on Amy's doorstep, her recurrent nightmares. She did not mind that at moments Silas bubbled off into near hysteria. She guessed his laughter was as necessary for him as her tale-telling was for her. Now that she had begun she could not stop. She poured out the life that she had kept secret from him. The town clock struck twice and at last three times. Far away in the country a cock crowed, and on the town roofs the seagulls started screaming. Hebe trailed to a stop. Silas rolled into a ball in his duvet, managed to reach up and kiss her and say: 'I don't think Jim is suitable,' before falling asleep, and Hebe pulling her duvet to her ears relaxed at last, feeling as close to her child as she had been when he was still in her womb.

While Silas slept she reviewed the day ahead.

First the duffle bag must be collected from the Reeves, an ordeal for Silas, who dreaded the embarrassment. Was it only the duffle bag and the Reeves, she mused, or something else? Her mind clear now after the disgorgement to Silas, she reviewed Silas' situation. Did not the Reeves represent the sort of people, the nice sort of friends he was meant to be happy with at school?

'But he isn't happy,' she whispered to the cat coming in from her patrol, creeping up on to the bed. 'He isn't happy at all.' With the clarity that extreme fatigue occasionally engenders she reviewed her plans for Silas, the opportunities he was to have of friends and education. It began all right, she thought. Before boarding school she had left him for short periods with Amy while she cooked for Lucy, Maggie Cook-Popham or Louisa. And once the Syndicate got going she again left him with Amy, latterly only working in term time so that holidays would be free for Silas.

'And now?' she whispered to the cat, lying warm against her neck. 'Now Amy is not well enough to help, Silas is not happy and I,' she whispered, 'must decide what to do.' Listening to the gulls' angry shrieking she faced the question, Did she send Silas away for his good, so that he would get the best education, or did she send him away so that she could enjoy her Syndicate? 'Is he at school for his sake or mine?' she whispered to the purring cat. But she was not really in doubt. She thought of the weekends in Paris with Hippolyte, the high spirits and delicious food, of the weeks with Mungo whom she was fond of. 'He has improved so,' she whispered to the cat, 'we've been on such lovely trips,' and of Rory not yet tried, Rory of whom she felt she could grow very fond. Oh God, she thought in tense alarm, there's this Jim, Silas' father. What of him? She felt threatened.

We have no memories in common, she thought, feeling recalcitrant. I do not even know whether he likes cats. 'It's altogether too much,' she said aloud. 'First things first. Concentrate on the duffle bag.'

34

Mungo drove with verve and dash. They had spent the night in an hotel by the Helford river. He had feared, when Alison insisted on stopping at a chemist in Truro, that she was planning one of her fucking headaches (to be exact a non-fucking headache) but this fear had been groundless. After dinner with Rory, who entertained them during the meal with a description of his life as a milliner, he had, elevated by circumspect consumption of wine, gone up to their room to find that she had bought not, as he supposed, soluble aspirin, but a choice of contraceptives.

'Which do you prefer?' Alison presented her offerings. 'Arousal? Elite? Fiesta?'

Mungo cried, 'Fiesta every time. Or should we,' he suggested, recollecting the night in Louisa's house, 'rename it, "Stable Door"?'

'Face that fence when we come to it.' Alison had drawn him into bed. '*I* wouldn't say no to another baby.'

'There's a lot to be said for you girls from the Shires,' said Mungo, hugging her.

Driving towards Penzance, Mungo considered Alison's trip to Santa Barbara had done her a power of good. I am a fair man, he thought, as he drove. I owe that bastard Eli a vote of thanks. That there had been times when Alison should have been similarly grateful to Hebe did not occur to him.

Rory, silent as they drove through Cornwall, listened to Mungo and Alison talk. They seemed to look forward to the reunion with their children, the horrible little boys. Had not Mungo cursed them as positive millstones when in his cups?

'We should have Michael to stay next holidays,' said Mungo. 'We owe it to the Reeves.'

'Why not the family Reeves for Christmas?' suggested Alison. 'Invite the lot.'

'A tallish order, Jennifer's heavy going, bit of a drag.'

'I'll take care of her. You can take Julian out shooting or play golf.'

'Okay,' said Mungo good-humouredly.

'I believe they have a boy from Michael's school with them. If Ian and Alistair have taken to him we could invite him too. They can't have enough friends. He's bound to be all right if Jennifer has passed him.'

'Is this Jennifer – a – er – an –' asked Rory.

'Expert,' said Mungo. 'A powerful sort of lady, knows who's who, goes in for influence and the right sort of chums for her boy. Any boy she has to stay must be er – um – you know what I mean.'

'The right sort,' Alison suggested.

'Socially oke – oke?' Rory teased. 'Okay? One of us?'

'Yes, of course.'

Rory thoughtfully compared Mungo reunited with Alison, doing his loving husband, father-of-the-family bit with the Mungo wailing for his mistress who had shared his bed three nights before. Leaves the field a bit clearer for me, he thought, as he plotted a tour of garages who might know Hebe's car. Possibly, he thought hopefully, the AA might help or even, if really stuck, the police.

'Car park's bloody full,' said Mungo, swinging off the road into the heliport entrance. 'Where can I fucking park?'

Alison compressed her lips.

Mungo cast her an affectionate glance. 'Not allowed that word. Won't happen again except in the right place.'

How does Hebe put up with him, for crying out loud? Rory asked himself.

'I think that must be their helicopter.' Alison craned her neck as Mungo squeezed the car into a gap. 'Jennifer said they'd be on the twelve-thirty.'

Standing beside Hebe in the heliport lounge Silas, already nervous at the prospect of meeting the Reeves, was seized by a fresh horror. 'Oh, God, Ma, Mr Reeves will have to pay excess on my bag. It says here,' he pointed to a notice, 'that "excess baggage costs thirty pence a kilogram".'

'If it's excess I'll pay. Don't worry so.' He is working himself into a stew and it's making me jumpy, thought Hebe, feeling sorrow and sympathy for her child. 'Here comes a helicopter. It's probably theirs.'

'Oh, God,' muttered Silas, 'what am I to say?'

'Just be normal.'

'What's normal?' cried Silas, anguished.

They watched the helicopter clattering down, standing close together, braced for the confrontation.

Jim, arriving late, having been delayed by Bernard's obsessive need to buy flowers for Amy (I am making up for fifty years of gross neglect), approached the heliport as the helicopter shut off its engine. He ran to the arrival lounge, pushing in behind two men and a woman who were apparently also meeting friends. A party from the helicopter came surging into the heliport hall. A trickle of confident vowels, swelling to a stream as their voices bounced off the formica tables, tinkled round the fruit machines, rose high in greeting as they sighted the people ahead of Jim.

'Alison, darling!'

'Jennifer, love, Julian!'

'Dear Mungo, how are you, how well you look.'

'This is my cousin Rory Grant, Jennifer Reeves.'

'How do you do and you know Alistair, Ian and Michael, of course. Do look round, dear, that tiresome woman is supposed to be here to collect her wretched boy's bag.'

Jim watched Hebe and Silas as they faced the crowd of people, sunburned, healthy, laden with baggage, overladen with self-confidence. Silas had drawn himself up to stand by his mother, hair ruffled, brown eyes so like Hebe's glaring down his nose. He experienced a thrill of pride. Hebe, recognising Alison, Mungo and Rory, struggled to keep her heart from her boots. This was the appalling sort of coincidence she had blithely felt could never happen.

Passengers from the helicopter milled through to the car park to stow their luggage, pack themselves into their cars, fasten seat belts, drive away to London, Bristol, Birmingham, Stevenage and Harlow new town.

Jennifer Reeves cried again in her carrying voice, 'Look

round, Julian, and see whether you can see that woman.'

'No need to look far,' said Hebe stepping forward.

The group of the confident vowels was stilled, frozen into what Silas in later years described as social glue.

'Thank you very much.' Hebe took the duffle bag from Michael. 'Do I owe you for excess weight? Silas has been worrying.' She turned towards Julian. 'Oh, hullo.'

With his back to the light Julian resembled momentarily the man with whom there had been the fiasco long ago in Rome. Hebe's heart took another lurch downwards. Julian, recognising in Hebe the sort of woman for whom one could almost risk alienating Jennifer for ever, responded with a hearty 'Hullo', and a delighted grin. Jennifer, sniffing danger and fast off the mark in defence of her own, brushed aside Julian's hand extended towards Hebe as he said, 'It's been super having Silas.' He was about to add that he hoped Silas would come again and Hebe must come too. This must be stopped.

But Hebe was smiling with relief, which had nothing to do with Jennifer, at the realisation that what she had recognised in Julian was a potential applicant to joint the Syndicate. She had taken off her glasses and while staring at them with her myopic gaze was fully occupied choking back unsuitable mirth. This charge of feeling between Hebe and the Reeves by its very variety created a spark which was near tangible. Watching them Jim felt a sensation of mad elation.

Alison, coming up to Hebe, taking the hand which Julian had hoped to shake, said, 'How *nice*. It's you who saves my mother-in-law's life with your wonderful cooking, isn't it? All that exquisite food.' She kept hold of Hebe's hand.

'That's right.' Hebe fought to recapture her cool. 'I love working for her, she's so appreciative.'

'And so is Mungo,' said Alison, smiling up at Hebe, almost a head taller.

'And are these your boys, the little millstones?' asked Hebe, laughing affectedly to hide incipient hysteria.

'Yes,' said Alison, squeezing Hebe's hand before letting it go. 'He doesn't hate them all the time. We may even have another.' She lowered her voice confidentially, distancing herself from Jennifer as she stood beside Hebe, smiling up as friendly as you please.

'Women!' gasped Mungo admiringly to Rory. 'Old Julian damn near put his great foot in it there, nearly made a bid.'

'How dare he?' whispered Rory, disgusted.

But Julian, undeterred by his wife, was persevering. 'Why don't we make a date? We could – perhaps next holidays –'

Jennifer, interrupting again, said, 'We never see you at the School Sports or on Founder's Day.' She struggled to regain the superiority she considered her right.

'I fear now it's unlikely that you shall,' Hebe replied coolly. 'There's a good comprehensive school here full of nice people of the right sort.' Beside her Silas flushed and glowed with joy. 'Ah, there you are,' she said to Jim who had ranged up beside her.

'Shall I take the bag?' asked Jim. 'You can't keep this up much longer,' he said in an aside.

'I don't think you have met Silas' father,' said Hebe, raising her voice, looking round at the ring of faces blurred as much by her emotion as her nearsightedness. 'Yes, do take the bag, darling.' She surrendered the bag to Jim.

Rory came up to Hebe. 'I had hoped, I was going to look for – to look –'

'Me?'

'Yes. Your – er – car number is – er – is –'

'Cornish?'

'Oh, Hebe.' He stood before her.

Whereas Hannah had decided between a hop and a skip to remarry and almost immediately found Terry, Hebe was faced by temptation. How easy to take Rory, unhesitatingly loving. How tempting to settle in his Georgian house with the fanlight and the dolphin knocker. How agreeable to spend weekends in his Great-aunt Calypso's bluebell wood. There would be no hassle. There would be peace. Perhaps too much peace. It would be unfair. Short-sightedly she met his anxious eyes.

'Goodbye, Rory, dear. Give my love to your Aunt Louisa.' She did not touch him. 'I have liked working for her more than anybody. One of these days I will come and buy one of your hats.'

'Will that be all?' Rory's usually swivelling eyes looked directly at Hebe.

'I'm afraid so,' she said sadly.

'I will design – a – er – an especially marvellous one.' Rory was valiant.

'I shall wear it on celebration days,' she said.

'I wish – er – oh, I wish *I* could celebrate.'

Reluctantly Rory followed the others, who were now drifting awkwardly away, saying, 'Well, I suppose we'd better be going.'

'See you soon, I hope.'

'Have we got everything?'

'What about lunch one day?' and things of that sort.

Alison did not, Mungo took note, invite Jennifer to bring her lot to stay for Christmas.

Michael, Ian and Alistair did not speak but exchanged looks, raised eyebrows and tried to catch Silas' eye to seal a non-existent friendship.

Julian, striving to regain ground grown slippery, was speaking to Jennifer.

'I promise you I never clapped eyes on the girl before.' His intonation guilty.

'I don't believe you for one moment. She recognised you, she said "Hullo".'

'She said hullo to us all.' Desperately Julian tried to distract his wife. 'She's a perfectly ordinary girl.'

'I think she's a perfectly ordinary tart. You *shall* tell me how and where you –' Striding towards their car Jennifer began the inquisition. If anything united the group which had been so confident it was a general feeling of commiseration for Julian who, it was felt, was in for a tough time, undeserved for once.

'I always suspected old Jennifer of a mean streak, of being a bit bogus.' Mungo headed the car towards home.

'Of course she is bogus.' Alison assimilated the fresh view of the family friend. 'And it's silly to be publicly jealous.' A few miles on she said: 'I've always thought we should consider state education as an alternative to Eton.'

Mungo drove in surprised silence for several miles before responding, 'We shall have to consider it if we are adding to the family.'

'My goodness, what a bill and coo.' Rory began what was to be a long process of cheering up.

Ian and Alistair had exchanged sly looks, reassessing their parents, as Mungo manoeuvred the car out into the holiday traffic. They had seen Silas running and jumping across the heliport garden, his every movement as he threw up his arms and leapt the flower beds an expression of unadulterated delight as he ran to find Giles. Ian later suggested to Alistair that Silas had been shouting 'I'm not out of a bottle,' which Alistair said was nonsense.

Slumped on the back seat behind his warring parents, Michael continued the sulky drift into adolescent revolt which had started at the supper table during Silas' visit.

35

The people in the helicopter office were indifferent to Hebe and Jim. They had telephones to answer, bookings to make, cups of coffee to consume. The next helicopter would leave in an hour and a half. Until then they could exchange pleasantries, flirt, catch up on gossip.

'I must apologise for calling you darling,' said Hebe stiffly.

'That's quite all right,' said Jim.

'It was a temptation,' said Hebe.

'I quite understand,' he said.

'Thank you.'

'There's a seat outside, shall we sit on it?'

Has he noticed my knees are knocking together? I must not give way now. I wish Silas had not rushed off and left us. I wish I felt something. I wish I knew what I feel.

'There, sit there,' he said. 'It's nice in the sun. No need to say anything.'

How does he know? she asked herself, sitting on the seat. There's a hell of a lot to say. How ghastly this is. Why doesn't he say something?

Jim said nothing.

Hebe said, 'Did you hear me? I told that woman Silas wouldn't be going to that school any more.'

'Yes, I did.'

'He isn't happy there,' Hebe cried. 'He's miserable.'

'You are doing the right thing, then.'

'Do you think so? Do you really think so?'

'Yes, I do.'

'I do so want him to be happy,' she exclaimed.

'Yes.'

'Oh,' Hebe cried, '*Bang* goes my Syndicate!'

Jim did not know what she was talking about.

What can I say without putting my foot in it, he thought. I don't know this woman. What the hell does she mean – Syndicate? If I ask she may bite my head off. I wish I was home in Fulham with my coffee shop and antiques, without all this bloody bother. 'Oh, Christ!' he exclaimed. 'You are crying.' She was racked by sobs. He fished out a handkerchief. What a messy crier. He gave her the handkerchief. (What have I let myself in for?) She blew her nose. (If she were a man I'd say she trumpeted.) She stopped crying. She looked a mess. He waited for her to say, 'I look a mess.' She did not. She gave her nose a final blow, crushed up the handkerchief and put it in her bag.

'Thanks,' she said.

The handkerchief was one of my best, he thought, admiring her action. I doubt whether I'll see it again.

'You'll get it back when it's clean,' she said.

It must be her knowledge of men which enables her to read my thoughts. He felt rather pleased with his percipience.

'You got the duffle bag back all right,' he said, to get the conversation flowing.

'Yes.'

'And decided Silas' future.'

'Yes.'

'Are you always so impulsive?'

'I've been thinking about it for quite a while.' Several days, she thought.

'He looked awfully pleased, radiant.'

'Did he? I had taken off my glasses.'

'That chap Julian Reeves –'

Hebe began to laugh. I may tell him, she thought, if I ever get to know him, about that fiasco in Rome.

'I felt rather sorry for the one who looks like a rabbit.'

'Hare. He's a hatter.'

'But the one with the wife who allied herself with you found it all rather funny. Is she a friend of yours?'

'She may become so.'

'But he seemed to know you very well, her husband.'

Hebe, eyes and nose puffed by crying, looked at him pityingly.

'Oh, I see,' said Jim, latching on, 'he's one of –'

'Yes.'

'I get it. They were all –'

Hebe nodded. 'Nearly all.' She looked away.

He tried to guess what she was thinking, watching her face, trying to read her thoughts.

They sat on in the sun.

Jim thought, We ought to be talking. She should tell me what the hell she's been up to all these years. She should tell me about her lovers. She should explain her life, tell me how she manages. She could tell me about her cooking jobs and then we could get on to the men. She obviously can't carry on with that lot, but are there others? She should tell me about her friends, about our child.

Hebe sat beside him apparently relaxed, sleepy.

I should tell her how I've chased after every girl who looked remotely like her. I should tell her that I've never got her out of my system, that I've always hoped to find her, that I'm in love with her. But am I? He watched her as she sat, face held up to the sun, eyes closed, her glasses held loosely in her lap. He shivered. I am a coward, he thought.

'In Lucca.' He cleared his throat. 'I –'

Hebe turned towards him, put on her spectacles, measured her words.

'It is just an idea,' she said, 'an idea you had. I am not that girl you remember. I am not silly and naive any more. You remember her, I remember a smell. I didn't know the smell was you until yesterday. I am grateful for your help with Silas. I am grateful for your help today, I –'

'Oh, shut up,' said Jim, furious.

'That's what my grandfather always said to my grandmother.'

'He was probably right,' Jim snapped.

'No, he wasn't,' Hebe shouted in fury.

'How old are you?' Jim asked.

'Thirty. Why?'

'I wanted to calculate how many years we have to talk and fight.'

'Oh.'

'Shall we start with a row? Then you can tell me about your

bloody grandfather,' cried Jim, his patience gone. 'I can tell you about myself. You can tell me what you know of Silas, our son. We have years and years. Come on –' He no longer wished himself back in Fulham, he wondered what would happen if he hit her, she would probably hit him back. 'Come on, he said, 'let's begin. Talk.'

'All right,' she said, and wondered whether the half of it would get said and knew it did not matter. 'Where shall we start?'

'Was that the lot?' Jim asked.

'What lot?' she prevaricated.

'The entire Syndicate.' He tried to be patient.

'M'm.' She took off her glasses. 'No.'

'Don't take them off. You must see me clearly.'

Hebe pushed the glasses up her nose defiantly, turning towards him, meeting his eyes.

'How many more?' asked Jim bravely.

'One.'

What will she do about that one, he asked himself, and found his heart was beginning to beat rather fast.

'I had better telephone. Have you got any change? It's long distance,' she said.

Jim emptied his pockets, gave her change, watched her walk to the telephone booth, dial, insert coins, push the button, begin to talk. He felt horror. What a fool I am, he thought. Why did I let her telephone? The bloody man will tell her to look sharp and come at once. No, he will say. Stay where you are. I am coming to fetch you. How can I have been so idiotic, so moronic, I've positively handed her over. He watched her talking, trying to read her lips, shuddered when she laughed, winced when she said something so sweetly, so confidingly he could have killed whoever she was talking to. At last she came back and sat beside him.

'So,' she said. 'So.' She was weary.

Jim said, 'What did he say?'

'He said, "*Quel garce*".'

'Oh?'

'That was Hippolyte,' said Hebe, 'the founder of –'

'Your Syndicate?' Jim felt a rush of fury.

'I told him what has happened,' she said gently. 'I – um – explained. He now has a restaurant in London. He has offered us free meals in perpetuity.' Her mouth twitched into a smile. She did not look at him. Just as he had admired her over the handkerchief he respected her for not saying 'You will like him.' Like hell he would. She had again taken off her glasses.

They sat on in the sun while Jim's heart resumed its usual tempo. Presently revived, he said, 'All peacocks gone.'

'Peacocks?'

'Surely you know the story of your namesake, Hebe, or must I tell you?'

'I do know it,' she admitted.

'Suppose I volunteer to be harnessed. What would you say to that? I must stipulate that I run solo.' He took her hands. It was the first time he had touched her since Lucca.

Letting her hands rest in his, Hebe watched his face. She longed to say something witty and original which they could remember in years to come, but all she said was, 'You're on.'

George Scoop, who had been alerted by his receptionist Jean of rumours of happenings in Wilson Street, thought he would drive past the heliport in his lunch hour. Having a horror of scenes and a great fear of getting involved in matters which might turn nasty, he was yet sufficiently curious, keeping a safe distance, to drive that way. He was disgusted to observe Hannah, wearing an outrageous purple dress strolling with her black beau who sauntered, dressed entirely in white so that his damson coloured skin vividly contrasted with Hannah's fairness. They laughed their heads off at some joke shared with the boys Giles and Silas as they walked along the prom eating ice creams. Blackamoor, Coon, thought George with rage. What perfect teeth. To hell with Giles. He had thought, when he had it in mind to marry Hannah, that he would accept the challenge of Giles' teeth, straighten them as a wedding present to his bride. I am well out of that, he congratulated himself. I was right to get shot of her. (Already he persuaded himself that he had denied Hannah, not she him.) Let her boy go through life with his teeth as they are, he thought sourly, refusing to acknowledge Hannah's merry wave or Terry's cheerful shout. There are other fish, he told himself.

Driving past the heliport he espied Hebe sitting on a bench with a strange man. He peered through his windscreen, trying to get a better view. Was she laughing or crying? He slowed the car, thinking, I could offer her a lift home. It's time I got to know her better, find out what she's all about. But from the way Hebe and the stranger sat sideways on the bench, turning towards each other, there did not seem room for a third party. A car behind George tooted its horn. George accelerated and drove on.

A Dubious Legacy

Mary Wesley

'Mary Wesley holds you by the hand and you follow wherever she takes you'
KATE KELLAWAY, OBSERVER

Henry brought his new bride, Margaret, to Cotteshaw in 1944. On the threshold she gave him a black eye and went straight to bed where she remained, apart from the occasional malevolent outburst, for the rest of her life.

The two young couples, who encountered her first in 1954, became regular if uneasy house guests over many years, listening, speculating, keeping a watchful eye on Margaret's door until finally, piecing together the gossip, the rumours, the mystery, they found themselves tangled in the web of Henry's life.

'Mary Wesley does it again, only more so; this year's is a vintage *cru* . . . an excellent story-teller and surer-footed than before. She marches straight into her tale, intriguing from the beginning, keeping up a pace that rarely slackens'
LITERARY REVIEW

'Wesley's books are a delight . . . a beautifully crafted tale, very sexy, very funny, I just didn't want it to end'
SUNDAY TIMES, PERTH

'Wesley breezes along with customary grace and nonchalance, sniping maliciously at her characters while giving them a more or less good time'
FINANCIAL TIMES

0 552 99495 2

BLACK SWAN

Jumping the Queue

Mary Wesley

'A virtuoso performance of guileful plotting, deft characterization and malicious wit'
THE TIMES

Matilda Poliport, recently widowed, has decided to End It All. But her meticulously planned bid for graceful oblivion is foiled, and when later she foils the suicide attempt of another lost soul – Hugh Warner, on the run from the police – life begins again for both.

But life also begins to throw up nasty secrets and awkward questions: just what was Matilda's husband Tom doing in Paris? How is the soon-to-be-knighted John (or Piers as he likes to be called) involved? Was Louise more than just a lovely daughter? And why did Hugh choose Matilda as his saviour?

Jumping the Queue is a brilliantly written first novel brimming over with confidence and black humour, reminiscent of Muriel Spark at her magnificent best.

'Great verve and inventiveness . . . (Matilda is) a convincing original'
TIMES LITERARY SUPPLEMENT

0 552 99082 5

BLACK SWAN

The Camomile Lawn
Mary Wesley

'A very good book indeed . . . has the texture and smell of real life, rich in detail, careful and subtle in observation, mature in judgement'
SUSAN HILL

'It is hard to overpraise Mary Wesley's novel . . . exceptional grace and understanding . . . so tingly and spry with life that put a mirror to the book and I'll almost swear it will mist over with the breath of the five young cousins'
THE TIMES

Behind the large house, the fragrant camomile lawn stretches down to the Cornish cliffs. Here, in the dizzying heat of August 1939, five cousins have gathered at their aunt's house for their annual ritual of a holiday. For most of them, it is the last summer of their youth, with the heady exhilarations and freedoms of lost innocence, as well as the fears of the coming war around the corner.

The Camomile Lawn moves from Cornwall to London and back again, over the years, telling the stories of the cousins, their family and their friends, united by shared losses and lovers, by family ties and the absurd conditions imposed by war as their paths cross and recross over the years. Mary Wesley presents an extraordinarily vivid and lively picture of wartime London: the rationing, imaginatively circumvented; the fallen houses; the parties, the new-found comforts of sex, the desperate humour of survival – all of it evoked with warmth, clarity and stunning wit. And through it all, the cousins and their friends try to hold on to the part of themselves that laughed and played dangerous games on that camomile lawn.

'Extraordinarily accomplished and fast-moving . . . plotted with great deftness and intelligence'
MARTIN SEYMOUR-SMITH, FINANCIAL TIMES

'Nothing old-fashioned or even ladylike about it. With the verve and jollity of youth . . . a book as scatty and chatty as a gossip column'
MAIL ON SUNDAY

'Delightful . . . wholly believable and exact. I like the mixture of warmth and wit . . . More, please'
DAILY TELEGRAPH

0 552 99126 0

BLACK SWAN

The Vacillations of Poppy Carew

Mary Wesley

'Once again she deploys her admirably comic skill to good effect; puncturing the pompous, exposing humbug, nudging our perceptions in the directions of the absurd'
FINANCIAL TIMES

'In Mary Wesley's book the dark sides of life are there all right, but never more weightily than is proper in light fiction. There are death (but what a marvellous funeral), desertion, but where would the plot be without them — and a potentially lethal road accident where Poppy is rescued by just the right free-range pig farmer in the nick of time. All the detail in this book is either cleverly and recognisably horrible, like the half-finished, cockroach-ridden North African hotel, or perfectly delightful, like the Italian dress in which Poppy goes to the funeral of her once-milkman father, with a genius for ladies and for racecourses, who so surprisingly left her so much money. Miss Wesley's book is persistently light, ingenious, cheerful. I recommend'
MARGHANITA LASKI

'Mary Wesley is high-spirited and inventive, and keeps her wayward plot moving forward at a spanking pace'
DAILY TELEGRAPH

'Wesley's narration is as fast and surprising as ever; her sub-plots are well worked out and rich in detail; she has a sharp ear for the idiocies uttered by nurses in hospitals, publishers at parties and people in fish-shops. Her observations on old age are admirably forthright'
TIMES LITERARY SUPPLEMENT

0 552 99258 5

BLACK SWAN

Second Fiddle

Mary Wesley

'She writes like an avenging angel, with a freshness, vigour and zest for sex (but never for sleaze) that belie her years. The lovely Miss Wesley has a steel-tipped talent. Long may she hone it'
SUNDAY TELEGRAPH

Laura Thornby, independent, individual, and slightly exotic manages her life with exquisite control. Her affairs are brief but delightful, her career fulfilling, and she copes with her two rather peculiar elderly relatives with wryness and humour.

But when she meets twenty-three-year-old Claude Bannister, struggling to be a writer, she is swept by an irresistible desire to interfere, manipulate, experiment with him – for his own good of course.

What she does not foresee, however, are the possibilities that he, one day, may write well, and that she might fall in love.

'*Second Fiddle* will delight the healthily growing number of Mary Wesley enthusiasts and offer a delicious treat to those who have yet to discover this unique author'
PUNCH

0 552 99355 7

BLACK SWAN

Not That Sort of Girl

Mary Wesley

'Rose, don't leave me. Promise never to leave me,' said Ned on their wedding night, revealing an unexpected chink in his perfect armour of wealth, good looks, and country estate. Rose promised.

Before the wedding, Mylo had said, 'In bed, with Ned, you will wonder whether this curious act of sex would not, with Mylo, turn into something sublime – When I send for you urgently to come and meet me – just come.'

For the whole of Rose's respectable married life, she had kept faith with both men. To Ned she was a perfect wife, mother of his son and elegant hostess of Slepe. To Mylo, Rose was an impetuous and unconventional mistress, answering his erratic and impassionate calls throughout fifty years of tactful duplicity.

After Ned's funeral Rose looks back on a life of dual constancy, passion, humour, and the ambiguities of love – and chooses her future.

'A witty and charming love story among the middle classes with surprising twists. One of the things that I love about Mary Wesley is that she has reached an age when she can say dangerous or naughty things without shocking'

PHILIP HOWARD, THE TIMES

0 552 99304 2

BLACK SWAN

A Sensible Life

Mary Wesley

'I loved every word of it'
CHRISTOPHER WORDSWORTH, THE GUARDIAN

She was a thin, lonely child with huge eyes and an extensive vocabulary of French foul language. Amongst the elegant middle-class British families holidaying in Dinard in 1926 – leading their privileged lives of secure routine pleasures – Flora was a ten-year-old misfit. Ignored by her self-absorbed parents, unloved, and pitied by the pleasant, stylish people in Brittany that summer, Flora was – peripherally – included in their gracious circles. And there, meeting kindly civilised people for the first time, she fell in love – with Cosmo – with Hubert – with Felix. It took forty years for the love affairs to be explored, consummated, and finally resolved.

'It is delicious . . . she writes with the knowledge and wisdom of serene old age and the emotional exuberance of glowing young womanhood'
PATRICK SKENE CATLING, THE DAILY TELEGRAPH

'Such good company that in more than one sense it's hard to put down'
DAVID HUGHES, THE MAIL ON SUNDAY

'This is a splendid novel; it is a delight to see Wesley in glorious form'
MIRANDA SEYMOUR, EVENING STANDARD

0 552 99393 X

BLACK SWAN

Out of the Shadows

Titia Sutherland

The house was one of the most enduring influences in Rachel Playfair's life. It was really too large for one woman, but she liked the memories it held, the graceful garden, and even the amiable resident spirit who lived on the top floor. When Rachel's authoritative and somewhat pompous sons tried to persuade her out of her house, she decided to make changes in her solitary life. With three children who needed her only spasmodically, and a small lonely granddaughter who needed her quite a lot, she made plans, first of all to take in a lodger and then, with the help of the unhappy Flora, to research the past of her house. Both decisions were to shatter the structure of Rachel's tranquil life.

The lodger proved to be a beguiling but disturbed man who was instantly fascinated by his cool landlady, and the delving in the past reopened a moving and poignant wartime tragedy that held curious overtones of events in Rachel's own life.

0 552 99529 0